# HELEN MARIA WILLIAMS, JULIA (1790)

# Chawton House Library Series: Women's Novels

*Series Editors:* *Stephen Bending*
*Stephen Bygrave*

## Titles in this Series

1 *The Histories of Some of the Penitents in the Magdalen-House*
edited by Jennie Batchelor and Megan Hiatt

2 Stéphanie-Félicité de Genlis, *Adelaide and Theodore, or Letters on Education*
edited by Gillian Dow

3 E. M. Foster, *The Corinna of England*
edited by Sylvia Bordoni

4 Sarah Harriet Burney, *The Romance of Private Life*
edited by Lorna J. Clark

5 Alicia LeFanu, *Strathallan*
edited by Anna M. Fitzer

6 Elizabeth Sophia Tomlins, *The Victim of Fancy*
edited by Daniel Cook

## Forthcoming Titles

Elizabeth Hervey, *The History of Ned Evans*
edited by Helena Kelly

Sarah Green, *Romance Readers and Romance Writers*
edited by Christopher Goulding

Sarah Green, *The Private History of the Court of England* edited by Fiona Price

Marie-Jeanne Riccoboni and Frances Brooke, Françoise de Graffigny and Rose Roberts, *Translations and Continuations* edited by Marijn S. Kaplan

# Helen Maria Williams, *Julia* (1790)

Edited by

Natasha Duquette

LONDON AND NEW YORK

First published 2010 by Pickering & Chatto (Publishers) Limited

Published 2016 by Routledge
2 Park Square, Milton Park, Abingdon, Oxfordshire OX14 4RN
711 Third Avenue, New York, NY 10017, USA

First issued in paperback 2016

*Routledge is an imprint of the Taylor & Francis Group, an informa business*



BRITISH LIBRARY CATALOGUING IN PUBLICATION DATA

Williams, Helen Maria, 1762–1827.
Julia. – (Chawton House library series. Women's novels)
1. France – History – 1789 – Fiction.
I. Title II. Series III. Duquette, Natasha.
823.6-dc22

ISBN 13: 978-1-138-23591-5 (pbk)
ISBN 13: 978-1-8519-6662-2 (hbk)

Typeset by Pickering & Chatto (Publishers) Limited

# CONTENTS

# ACKNOWLEDGMENTS

Many people and institutions have helped me along the way towards envisioning and completing this new edition of Helen Maria Williams's *Julia, a Novel Interspersed with Poetical Pieces*. I first encountered the novel as a graduate student during a short time of research at the British Library and immediately ordered a microfilm copy. I would therefore like to thank the staff in the reproductions department of the British Library for facilitating my access to the novel while completing my doctoral work. While writing two chapters on sublimity in the work of Helen Maria Williams for my dissertation, I was encouraged to persevere in the project by the community in the English Department at Queen's University in Kingston, Ontario, Canada. I would like to thank especially John Pierce, Shelley King, Leslie Ritchie and Susan Bauman for responding to my early work on Williams. A huge acknowledgement of heartfelt gratitude must also go to Deborah Kennedy; her pioneering critical biography *Helen Maria Williams in the Age of Revolution* (2002) has inspired and informed my own work from graduate school up to the creation of this edition.

Two modes of formal aid from which this particular project has benefited are the Chawton House Library Fellowship that I held during the summer of 2008 and a Biola University Research Grant for 2009, which allowed me to return to Chawton House and to conduct research at the Bibliothèque Nationale. Through their ties to Chawton House via the University of Southampton, Gillian Dow and Stephen Bygrave have bolstered this project from its beginning, and the Chawton House librarian Jacqui Grainger actually first planted the idea in my mind. Susan Carlile, the other Chawton House Fellowship holder in 2008 and thus my roommate in the Chawton Stables, and Isobel Grundy, as a senior member of the Chawton House board, have both been very supportive as well.

In Southern California, my colleagues at Biola University have shown understanding as I have taken time to work on this project, and I would like especially to thank Sandy Smith and Aaron Kleist for helping me trace Williams's various Miltonic and Shakespearean allusions. Anita Helmbold also aided me in that endeavour. In the last stage of this project the librarians at the Huntington Library were invaluable. Librarians Claire Kennedy and Catherine Wehrey were gracious and thorough while facilitating my work in the Huntington rare books room. David Worrall and Georgina Lock of Nottingham Trent University were amiable and informative colleagues to work alongside at the Huntington. Elisabeth Lenckos and Emily Hollingshead kindly read over the final draft of this edition. The two people who supported me most as I saw this edition to completion were my research assistant Jessica Danger and my husband Fred Duquette.

# INTRODUCTION

> There is such feminine sweetness in her style and observations – such modesty and indulgence in her satire – such genuine unaffected piety in her effusions and remarks, that we warmly recommend her novel to our young female readers, who will here meet with refinement of sentiment, without a very great alloy of romantic notions.
> –from Mary Wollstonecraft's 1790 review of *Julia*

In her early review of *Julia, a Novel Interspersed with Some Poetical Pieces*, Mary Wollstonecraft succinctly summarizes key strengths of Helen Maria Williams's first and only novel: its radically feminine sensibility, its gracious social satire, and its moments of elevating spiritual sublimity. She also admires Williams for refining the dross of romantic clichés out of the novel of sentiment through her fine balance of rational, detached sense with emotional, particular sensibility. However, Wollstonecraft does not touch on the novel's decidedly democratic and revolutionary thrust, despite the date of her review and of Williams's novel, both published within a year of the beginning of the French Revolution in 1789. The social satire of aristocratic cruelty within *Julia*'s prose and the alternative vision presented by its 'poetical pieces', ranging in topic from moonlight contemplations in natural landscapes to the terrors of imprisonment in the Bastille, together form a trenchant political critique. This introduction will explore the interconnections between Williams's rhetoric of poetic sensibility, her construction of contemplative sublimity, and her attraction to revolutionary freedom.

Helen Maria Williams is today best known as the writer of political correspondence detailing the events of the French Revolution. Her *Letters Written in France in the Summer of 1790, To a Friend in England* (1790) and *Letters from France* in eight volumes (1790–6) share her early passion for the revolution and her sorrow over the loss of Girondist friends at the Guillotine. Williams wrote in multiple genres, however, and like her heroine Julia, was very much a poet of sensibility, especially early on in her publishing career. Williams was born in London on 17 June 1761 to a Scottish mother, Helen Hay, and a Welsh father, Charles Williams. Her father was an army officer who died in 1762, when his daughter was only an infant. After his death her family moved to Berwick-Upon-

Tweed. As Helen Maria Williams's literary mentor, Rev. Dr Andrew Kippis would later explain, she was 'a native of London, but was removed, with her family, in very early life, to a remote part of the kingdom, where her sole instruction was derived from a virtuous, amiable, and sensible mother'.[1] Williams herself believed that her early writing revealed 'the disadvantages of a confined education',[2] limited to the teaching of her mother in the North East corner of England, far from adequate libraries or schools. Williams's penchant for Psalm paraphrase in her early verse and multiple scriptural references in *Julia*, however, do reveal the lasting influence of her mother's dissenting Presbyterian biblical knowledge. Deborah Kennedy observes, 'Mrs. Williams's piety was legendary', and the family 'regarded the Bible as the most important book in the house'.[3]

In 1781 Helen Maria Williams moved, along with her mother and two sisters, back to London and met the individual who was to have a significant impact on her aesthetic, theological and political views, as well as her publishing career: Rev. Dr Andrew Kippis. At Kippis's prompting she published her first work – a long, pacifist poem – anonymously, as *Edwin and Eltruda, a Legendary Tale, by a young lady* (1782). Kippis was a minister who preached at the Princes Street Presbyterian Church in Westminster and also spoke in dissenting 'meeting houses' for public events such as ordinations. He facilitated Williams's introduction into the literary, religious, and political circles of London. While living in London, Williams continued publishing pacifist poems, producing first 'Ode on the Peace' (1783), celebrating the Treaty of Paris that concluded the American Revolution, and then *Peru: A Poem in Six Cantos* (1784), a long, narrative poem which unabashedly denounces the violence of colonization. Her next publication was a collection entitled *Poems in Two Volumes* (1786), which included psalm paraphrases, hymns and more narrative verse, as well as reprintings of 'Ode on the Peace' and *Peru*. The subscribers to this collection included fellow poets Joanna Baillie, Elizabeth Carter, and Anna Seward, bluestocking Elizabeth Montagu, painter Joshua Reynolds, dissenting preacher Richard Price, and the Archbishops of Canterbury and York. The diversity of these supporters testifies to the wide appeal of her poetic sensibility across boundaries of gender difference, political commitment, and denominational affiliation. For Williams, sensibility, defined as the ability to experience compassion for the oppressed, had the capacity to lessen suffering in the world. This active sensibility motivated her anti-slavery stance in her next publication, 'A Poem on the Bill Lately Passed for Regulating the Slave Trade' (1788), as well as her honest portrayal of the daily socioeconomic realities faced by late eighteenth-century women, from all classes, in her novel *Julia*.

## *Julia*'s Early Reception

*Julia*'s third-person narrator tells the story of two women, cousins Charlotte and Julia Clifford, who are in love with the same man, Frederick Seymour. After he has already become betrothed to Charlotte, Frederick meets the intelligent young poet Julia, and falls madly in love with her. Frederick dutifully marries Charlotte yet still remains passionately attracted to Julia, and the plot of the novel follows Julia's efforts to maintain her virtue, and her close friendship with Charlotte, in resistance to Frederick's flattery and, eventually, professions of love. Along with its title, the novel's love triangle affirms its stance as a reworking of Jean-Jacques Rousseau's *Julie, ou la Nouvelle Héloïse* (1761); however, Williams envisions one man between two women, rather than one woman between two men.[4] This same distinction exists between the psychological structuring of *Julia* and another eighteenth-century fictional love triangle, that between Werther, Charlotte, and Albert in Johann Wolfgang von Goethe's *The Sorrows of Young Werther* (1774). Towards the end of *Julia* Frederick Seymour and Julia Clifford debate the merit of Goethe's novel, with Frederick defending it as a moving tale of powerful pathos, and Julia questioning its morality, stating simply, 'everyone must acknowledge that it is well written, but few will justify its principles' (see p. 144). Julia's own moral philosophy is reflected not only in her maintenance of individual virtue, through passive resistance to Frederick's advances, but also in her social consciousness, as she actively supports poor, widowed, orphaned and oppressed characters throughout the narrative.

Early reviewers accepted Williams's framing of her narrative as a cautionary tale and praised *Julia* for its pedagogical rhetoric, realistic characterization, and poetic style. All of the reviewers were charmed by what they perceived as the narrator's refreshing innocence. The *English Review* contrasted *Julia* with other novels of the time, writing, 'Here, as is often the case in modern *novels*, we are shocked by no gross pictures of immorality ... the whole relates to an affair of love, which is managed throughout with simplicity.'[5] The *European Magazine* recommended *Julia* 'to those whose uncorrupted hearts are capable of tasting with delight the simplicity of nature, the modesty of virtue.'[6] The 'useful moral' of the narrative impressed the *Monthly Review*.[7] Even Mary Wollstonecraft imagined that 'sound principles' must 'animate' the 'conduct' of the authoress of *Julia*.[8] A terse review in the *Edinburgh Magazine* begins by railing against the proliferation of modern novels, comparing them to a plague of 'insects on the banks of the Nile' or 'locusts', and then exempts *Julia* from this general condemnation, presenting it as 'a simple, instructive, and affecting story' with characters 'for the most part, well drawn'.[9] Wollstonecraft also admired the realistic imagery of *Julia's* landscapes 'highly finished in watercolours, and characters delineated with a degree of truth and proportion'.[10] Almost all of the reviewers admire what they variously refer to as the harmony, brilliance and elegance of the poetry that Williams has interjected throughout her prose narrative, singling out Julia's poem 'The Linnet' as the strongest piece in the novel.[11]

The negative critique of *Julia* is scant in the early reviews. However, some reviewers did object to implausible circumstances in the plot, and a lack of significant action, as well as to what they perceived as Williams's over-reliance on literary models, a fault perhaps forgivable in such a young writer (Williams was twenty-nine when her novel was published). Wollstonecraft found Julia's fixed virtue too idealistic, arguing that the best tragedies allow for more human imperfection and error in judgment. The anonymous writer in the *English Review* viewed Charlotte's ignorance of her husband's desire for Julia during the bulk of the novel as unbelievable and objected to Williams's overuse of quotations from poets such as Thomas Gray and Oliver Goldsmith. Most interesting among the critiques is the below complaint from the *European Magazine*:

> We think too great an admiration of the writings of Mrs. Smith may be discovered. Julia, the heroine of the piece, like her archetypes, Emmeline and Ethelinde, is a character of consummate perfection, who possesses prudence and courage sufficient to resist the progress of a passion which overwhelms her heart.[12]

Like Wollstonecraft, this reviewer remarks on Julia's level of moral perfection but then compares this to the heroines of Charlotte Smith's novels *Emmeline* (1788) and *Ethelinde* (1789). The idea of Smith's influence on Williams is actually an exciting probability, as it testifies to patterns of feminine sociability and intellectual correspondence in the 1780s and 90s.[13]

This artistic, literary influence between women carried forward to the novels that appeared shortly after Williams's *Julia*. The sensitive Julia shares strong parallels with Ann Radcliffe's poet-heroine Adeline in *The Romance of the Forest* (1791). Both women poets draw on the works of William Shakespeare and John Milton in their verse, within which they express emotions ranging from bitter disappointment to elegiac nocturnal wonder. The influence of *Julia*'s proto-feminist themes, such as the importance of women's friendship across socioeconomic divides, is clear in Wollstonecraft's own novel *Maria, or the Wrongs of Woman* (1798), written after she had met Williams in Paris.[14] Reflecting her own awareness of Williams's novel, Jane Austen includes a direct reference to *Julia* in the mock-gothic narrative of *Northanger Abbey*, begun in the early 1790s. In an attempt to prove his admiration of women's novels to Austen's heroine Catherine Morland, Henry Tilney states, 'I myself have read hundreds and hundreds. Do not imagine you can cope with me in a knowledge of Julia's.'[15] Austen was reading Williams's work as late as 1815,[16] and the influence of Williams's class-based satire and aesthetics of sublimity is evident in Austen's *Persuasion* (1817) as well as in the final version of *Northanger Abbey* (1817). Like Austen's wry narrators, the narrator of *Julia* reflects on cultural expressions of sensibility, both false and true.

## Social Satire and Poetic Sensibility

The narrative of *Julia* directs nuanced social satire towards a disingenuous, competitive community of sophisticated characters, 'people of *ton*' living in London, against which a supportive, affective community of sensibility is defined. Early on in the novel, the scheming Mrs Melbourne, for example, appears as an unsympathetic character, scorning anyone she perceives as below her socioeconomic status, including Julia. The narrator compares the mercenary Mrs Melbourne to Shakespeare's villain Iago in *Othello* and later, along with her daughter, to the witches in *Macbeth*. Mrs Melbourne is delighted when her daughter marries the wealthy Mr Seymour, Frederick Seymour's older brother, despite the fact that 'ambition, and long commerce with the world had entirely blunted his sensibility' (see p. 22). When Julia travels to London to visit with her cousin Charlotte who has been staying with the Melbournes and Seymours, she discovers that days in town are passed in vacuous pursuits. At first she is wryly amused by the philosophical, aesthetic contemplation with which Londoners shop for ribbons, but she moves from satirical delight to active distaste when she finds 'that understanding was of no current value at a card-assembly, except to serve the purpose of applying the rules of whist, a science for which her country education had taught her but little reverence' (see p. 23). Williams emphasizes the satirical edge of her novel through ironic uses of terms such as 'sentimental' and even 'sensibility' and through references to works of comic social commentary, such as Oliver Goldsmith's *The Vicar of Wakefield* (1766) and Richard Sheridan's *School for Scandal* (1777).

In contrast to the more cut-throat, aristocratic characters, such as Mrs Melbourne and her daughter Mrs Seymour and son-in-law Mr Seymour, Julia represents a form of active sensibility attuned to the aesthetic appeal of natural landscapes, receptive to the textual force of sublime poetry, and responsive to the extremes of human suffering. In her own verse, Julia addresses a female personification of poetry, writing:

> The idle crowd in fashion's train,
> Their trifling comment, pert reply,
> Who talk so much, yet talk in vain,
> How pleased, for thee, Oh nymph, I fly! (see p. 8)

Julia first expresses her sensibility through friendship with the 'nymph' poetry but soon shows her capacity for real, human, enduring friendship with her cousin Charlotte and later with the impoverished and abused character Mrs Meynell.

Julia acquires her capacity for social connection and her attitude of care towards the vulnerable from her grandfather, who teaches her lessons 'of humanity', encouraging her to teach the local cottagers' children to read, and 'recommending tenderness to animals' (see p. 40) by quoting Luke 12:6, 'Are not five sparrows sold for two farthings, and not one of them is forgotten before God?' Williams's construction of sensibility is very much rooted in her dissenting knowledge of scripture, which was instilled in her by her Presbyterian mother.

*Julia*'s protagonist, like her creator Helen Maria Williams, is both a poet of sensibility and an exemplar of dissenting social consciousness. As Deborah Kennedy notes, Julia's 'benevolent works'[17] distinguish her from the other characters in the novel, and 'her rural upbringing gives her a moral strength'.[18] Eleanor Ty argues that Julia's choice of friendship and loyalty to Charlotte, over competiveness in a battle to win Frederick's love, expresses a communal, charitable sensibility akin to that found in twentieth-century feminist ethics. Ty pushes her argument too far, however, when she claims, 'the aggressive, selfish deeds of the male characters are displayed against the altruistic, affective endeavours of the females'.[19] As seen above, Mrs Melbourne and her daughter Mrs Seymour are fully capable of self-seeking, divisive and cruel behaviour, and it is Julia's grandfather, a male character, who inculcates biblical values of tenderness and concern for others into Julia.

Julia's capacity for sincere friendship and social consciousness is undergirded in the novel by Williams's multiple allusions to and quotations of scripture. These references include a quotation – in Volume 1, Chapter 20 – of the widowed Ruth's cry to her bereaved mother-in-law Naomi: 'Whither thou goest I will go, and where thou lodgest I will lodge; thy people shall be my people, and thy God shall be my God; where thou diest will I die, and there will I be buried. The Lord do so to me, and more also, if aught but death part thee and me' (Ruth 1:16–17). Williams clearly admires this statement of lifelong friendship from one woman to another, and terms it a 'sentiment of stedfast [*sic*] fidelity' (see p. 84). Within *Julia*'s narrative she applies this statement to a friendship, across classes, between two men during the American Revolution. Williams advocates a Christian ethos of active, ameliorative sensibility, and she does not restrict such capacity for such caring, loyal community to one gender or one nation.

The poems of sensibility written by Julia illustrate her progress from the exuberance of her youth towards more tranquil intimations of actualized and sustainable community. Williams's narrator informs us, 'Julia discovered at a very early age a particular sensibility to poetry'. She composes her first poem when she is 'eight years old' and within it meditates 'on the departure of one of her young companions' (see p. 7). Julia's very first poem is inspired by a childhood friendship. Next, in 'An Address to Poetry' she seeks the source of poetry in dazzling brilliance, and then, after experiencing various forms of suffering, which result in the melancholy tone of 'To Hope', she finds consolation in quieter, more soothing imagery in 'To the Moon'. The forms of communion Julia experiences and then captures in her poetry include real friendships, imagined connections to characters in literature, and sympathetic affinities with natural, and at times sublime, landscapes.

## Contemplative Sublimity

Through her construction of a contemplative, feminine sublime in *Julia* Helen Maria Williams makes an important contribution to late eighteenth-century debates on the aesthetic categories of the beautiful, the sublime and the picturesque. Williams's novel was published the same year as Immanuel Kant's *Critique of Judgment* (1790), for example, and she was aware of Edmund Burke's *Philosophical Enquiry into the Origin of our Ideas of the Sublime and the Beautiful* (1759).[20] Julia's poem 'An Address to Poetry' extols a 'Wild Poesy' found 'in haunts sublime' who 'delights ... to pour' her music into the hollows of craggy cliffs and rush of sweeping torrents (see p. 11). In this poem, specifically, Julia symbolizes spiritual and affective generosity as a fluid spilling out of the self into the landscape. Feminist theorist Patricia Yaeger's recent articulation of a generous 'sublime of expenditure'[21] in women's verse can help us understand the uniqueness of Julia's 'Wild Poesy' within the discourse of late eighteenth-century aesthetics. Yaeger uses this phrase to describe the modification of what she refers to as Kant's 'sovereign sublime'[22] by twentieth-century women writers. That this ethic of generosity was already present in Williams's work is evident through Julia's deployment of words like 'lavish' and 'pour' (see pp. 9 and 11) in her verse.

Williams's poetry and prose in *Julia* supplements such images of feminine generosity with ascension to sublime heights, in the name of wonder and communion, rather than mastery. Again, as well as aligning with what recent feminist critics have termed a 'female sublime', Williams's moral sublime of communion, generosity, and hospitality also reflects her dissenting, Christian worldview. In her 'Thoughts on Devotional Taste' (1773), Williams's friend, fellow dissenter and poet Anna Barbauld argues that affective, social bonds motivate 'everything sublime'[23] in 'generous action'[24] and then presents the biblical Psalms as poems that 'carry the mind out of itself, and powerfully refine the affections from everything gross, low and selfish'.[25] James Beattie's *Dissertations Moral and Critical* (1783) likewise argue that sublime poetry elevates the affections above 'avarice'[26] to 'love of virtue'.[27] He connects sublimity and social consciousness when he argues that sublime fortitude and generosity 'discover a degree of virtue, which is not everywhere to be met with; and exert themselves in actions, that are at once difficult and beneficial to mankind'.[28] Both Barbauld and Beattie move beyond the impact of sublime poetry on the individual to suggest that experiences of sublimity should lead to social action in the real world on behalf of the oppressed.

In *Julia* Williams associates her heroine's experiences of sublimity not only with her ability to resist the temptations of Frederick but also with her constructive actions in community. In Volume 1, Chapter 8, before she has met Frederick, and while living on the Clifford family estate in the North of England, Julia walks out into the landscape with Charlotte and is suddenly struck by the sound of a waterfall and the light of the moon reflected on a lake. The narrator remarks:

> Julia gazed upon the objects which surrounded her with a transport of mind which she had never felt before. She uttered frequent exclamations of admiration and wonder; but she found it impossible to express the sensations with which her soul was overwhelmed. It is in such moments as these that the soul becomes conscious of her native dignity: we seem to be brought nearer to the Deity; we feel the sense of his sacred presence; the low-minded cares of earth vanish...and we repose with divine confidence on him, who has thus embellished his creation. In the country, the mind borrows virtue from the scene. When we tread the lofty mountain, when the ample lake spreads its broad expanse of waters to our view, when we listen to the fall of the torrent, the awed and astonished mind is raised above the temptations of guilt (see p. 32).

Williams develops her definition of the sublime through language of 'transport', and 'admiration and wonder', as Julia's soul is 'overwhelmed' with a sense of divine presence. Williams here draws on several traditions of the sublime. In the 1786 printing of his *Dictionary* Samuel Johnson defines the noun 'transport' as '3. Rapture; ecstasy'. In his *Grounds of Criticism* (1704) John Dennis associates the sublime with enthusiastic spiritual experiences of wonder and joy as well as terror. According to Edmund Burke's *Philosophical Enquiry*, an overwhelming terror that 'hurries us on' in a passionate rush is the primary indicator of the sublime, though he allows that 'admiration, reverence and respect' occur as 'inferior effects'.[29] Barbauld and Wollstonecraft more adamantly emphasize 'deepest reverence'[30] and 'profound reverence'[31] as integral to sublimity. Both women writers characterize the sublime as an experience of awed stillness rather than hurried passion. Barbauld, Williams, and Wollstonecraft all define sublimity in terms of an expansive, uplifting, and calming movement away from the temptations of narrow self-interest, towards love of God and increased social consciousness.

Later in the novel, Julia walks alone on the Clifford estate anticipating the 'solitary rambles' of Austen characters such as Marianne Dashwood and Elizabeth Bennet, but in contrast to Marianne's solipsistic experiences of sublimity, Julia's lone walks, 'gazing at the majestic scenery', lead directly into social responsibility. 'On her way home' after one such ramble, for example, 'she stopped at a cottage near the house, and, seating herself near the door, patiently listened to a good woman's anecdotes of her poultry' (see p. 39). Julia fulfils an almost pastoral role, reaching out to others in receptive silence after finding a degree of repose in the sublimity of nature. There is a similar movement in Ann Radcliffe's novel *The Romance of the Forest* (1791) where the pastor La Luc finds his 'manners more than usually benevolent'[32] after time spent amidst 'solemn and tremendous scenery.'[33] La Luc's mind is 'lifted above this world and opened to ... the sublimity of another'[34] while walking in the Alps, just as Julia 'lifts her eyes to heaven' in 'gratitude and praise' after a Northern landscape has 'soothed and elevated her mind' (see p. 48). Such fictional descriptions participate in the discourse of natural theology; Williams's dissenting belief in the human incarnation of providential care also ensures that hers is a theology of social justice.

## Revolutionary Freedom and Social Justice

Williams was integrating her aesthetic construction of sublimity with poetic expressions of dissenting, faith-based, resistance to tyranny from early on in her publishing career. In *Peru* (1784), Williams opens with the prophetic female figure 'Peruvia's Genius' lamenting the violence of Spanish colonialism before introducing the indigenous Peruvian bard Zamor who consoles the Peruvian people with poetry inspired by visions of 'Freedom' on sublime Andean heights.[35] Williams's 'Poem on the Bill Lately Passed for Regulating the Slave Trade' includes a similar visionary image of 'green hills where Freedom roves'[36] in the course of detailing the agonies of the Atlantic passage, supporting a bill created to lessen the suffering inflicted on Africans by slave traders and calling, prophetically, for the absolute abolition of slavery. Williams's use of prophetic imagery to critique tyranny and call for social justice does suggests strong links between dissenting church community, sublime verse, and the desire for social change. Her mentor Rev. Kippis spoke of 'deliverance from the most dreadful evils'[37] in 'eternal freedom,'[38] adding, 'How sublime a display of the benevolence of the Deity!'[39] In her texts, Williams suggests that it is our social duty to ameliorate dreadful suffering and bring about freedom from oppression *in this world*. In defense of events in France, she would later argue that the French Revolution inspired such 'sublime public virtue'.[40]

In itself, the implicit critique of a hierarchical 'sovereign sublime' in the poetics and aesthetics of *Julia* reflects Williams's early support of the French Revolution's egalitarian ideals. The date when *Julia* was first published – March 1790 – itself makes the novel of import to any study of British responses to the Revolution, which began with the storming of the Bastille on 14 July 1789. Julia questions the corrupt and wealthy society represented by Mr and Mrs Seymour and offers glimpses of sublime feminine communion as an option to such artificial social ties in her poems 'An Address to Poetry', 'Sonnet: To Hope', and 'Sonnet: To the Moon'. In each of these poems, she privileges sorrowful sympathy over dazzling power and force. Eleanor Ty reads *Julia* as 'politically suggestive' in opposition to the politically explicit work of Mary Wollstonecraft, but nevertheless notes that the political 'target of satire in *Julia* is the fashionable upper-class society of London with its preoccupation with wealth, social prestige, and political power'. Drawn to Williams's depiction of Julia's freedom of existence outside of predetermined, rigid societal roles, Ty uses revolutionary language to describe her feminine agency, writing, 'Julia maintains her liberty and right to decide'.[41] One of the decisions Julia makes is to befriend a woman, Mrs Meynell, who has been scorned by the Melbournes and Seymours due to her lower socioeconomic status.

The enduring power of Julia's friendship withstands trials not only in her relationship to her cousin Charlotte but also in the case of Mrs Meynell, which Williams uses to take her idea that compassion can bring about freedom and justice from the national to the domestic sphere. Through her depiction of Mrs Meynell's economic and domestic oppression within London, Williams reveals that social cruelty and injustice can exist in the heart of England as well as in far off locales such as Peru or the British West Indies. Williams presents hope for social transformation in the 'sublime public virtues' extended to Mrs Meynell through Julia's friendship. Julia maintains her compassionate friendship with Mrs Meynell in complete indifference to the judgmental opinions of the more elitist 'people of *ton*'. Mrs Meynell is a 'poor relation' (see p. 112) of the Seymour family, whom Mr and Mrs Seymour keep hidden away, but whose existence Julia discovers during a conversation with their ex-servant, Mrs Evans. Mrs Meynell was initially taken in as an orphan by the Seymour family, and later pressured to marry a near bankrupt captain on half-pay – known for his pride, brutality, and 'ferocious nature' (see p. 114) – by the elder Mr and Mrs Seymour, Frederick's parents. Mrs Evans, the current servant to Frederick Seymour's elder brother, confides to Julia, 'that monster, my master (for monster he is to be sure) persuaded her husband, who is but thick-headed, to stay in London' (see p. 109). She continues by explaining to Julia that Mr Seymour has kept Mrs Meynell in London because he plans to seduce her. Mrs Meynell is not only legally tied to a man with 'no money at all' who 'married her in hopes that her great friends would provide for him', she is also prey to the sexual harassment of one of those 'great friends', Mr Seymour. Listening to Mrs Evans's narrative causes Julia's heart to throb in anger 'with indignation at the oppressor' and melt 'with compassion for the oppressed' until she sees 'the arm of indignant Heaven tearing the veil by which iniquity was concealed, and making manifest the sufferings of innocence'(see p. 110). Julia continues to visit Mrs Meynell throughout the novel, and in the end, Mrs Meynell joins Julia and Charlotte in the home of

Charlotte's father, forming a sublime, and egalitarian, feminine community that can extend itself out to others in acts of public virtue.

*Julia*'s narrative shows more explicit support of the French Revolution's ideals in 'The Bastille: A Vision', a poem that appears towards the very end of the novel, at the conclusion of Volume 2, Chapter 33. In *Sign of Angellica*, Janet Todd observes that, to some readers, *Julia* was 'rendered more obnoxious by an inserted poem in praise of the French Revolution'.[42] The combination of claims to prophetic vision with commitment to progressive politics would have been particularly irksome to those most suspicious of the French Revolution. In his study *Elations: The Poetics of Enthusiasm in Eighteenth-Century Britain*, Sean Irlam argues that references to visionary enthusiastic passions would have alarmed some English readers after the British Civil War, when enthusiasm had become 'a labile political term liberally applied to almost all perceived enemies of Church and State, every variety of theological and political discontent (Puritan, Papist, Quaker ...etc)'.[43] The character Mr F— does situate this poem as political critique of state power and control, at least in France, when he tells Julia that it was written by a friend of his imprisoned in the Bastille 'for some *supposed* offense against the state' (see p. 148). He explains further, 'the horrors of his solitary dungeon were one night cheered by the following prophetic dream' (see p. 149). Here, Williams's engages with an interface between poetic prophecy and political justice key to eighteenth-century poetry from Thomas Gray's 'The Bard' (1757) onwards. The speaker of 'The Bastille: A Vision' has a troubling vision of past atrocities. The poem itself acts as a justification of the revolutionary events in 1789, including the storming of the Bastille, as a valid reaction to tyranny.

Reflecting the context of British responses to the French Revolution, and published just months before Edmund Burke's *Reflections on the Revolution in France* (1790), *Julia* rewards reading alongside novels such as *The Romance of the Forest* (1791) and political treatises such as Mary Wollstonecraft's *Vindication of the Rights of Woman* (1792) as a key text of the early 1790s. Within the prose narrative of *Julia* Williams foregrounds her own ideas about how the empathy of sensibility can confront tyranny and indifference to poverty, specifically women's poverty, in her own British society. The delightful and engaging narrative of *Julia* is infused with not only a poetics of sensibility, ethic of social virtue, and aesthetic of contemplative sublimity, but also with powerful political commentary on the corruptions of the upper class and the abuses perpetuated by any form of arbitrary power, whether public or domestic.

## Notes

1. A. Kippis, 'Advertisement, by the Editor', in H. M. Williams, *Edwin and Eltruda, a Legendary Tale, by a Young Lady* (London: T. Cadell, 1782), p. i.
2. H. M. Williams, 'Preface' to *Poems, in Two Volumes* (London: T. Cadell), vol. 1, p. iii.
3. D. Kennedy, *Helen Maria Williams and the Age of Revolution* (Lewisburg, PA: Bucknell University Press, 2002), p. 23.
4. For comparisons of *Julia* to *Julie* see Janet Todd's *Sign of Angellica: Women, Writing, and Fiction, 1600–1800* (New York: Columbia University Press, 1989), p. 231; Peter Garside's 'Introduction' to a 1995 facsimile reproduction of *Julia* (London: Routledge, 1995), p. xii; and Jacqueline LeBlanc's 'Politics and Commercial Sensibility in Helen Maria Williams's *Letters from France*' in *Eighteenth-Century Life*, 21:1 (1997), p. 39.
5. Anon., *English Review*, 15 (April 1790), p. 304.
6. Anon., *European Magazine*, 17 (June 1790), p. 435.
7. Anon., *Monthly Review*, 2 (July 1790), p. 334.
8. M. Wollstonecraft, *Analytical Review*, 7 (May 1790), p. 98.
9. Anon., *Edinburgh Magazine and Literary Miscellany*, 52 (July 1970), p. 338.
10. Wollstonecraft, *Analytical Review*, p. 97–8.
11. See Wollstonecraft, *Analytical Review*, p. 99; and Anon., *European Magazine*, p. 435.
12. Anon., *European Magazine*, p. 435.
13. Williams likely knew Charlotte Smith from the early 1780s (see Kennedy, *Helen Maria Williams*, p. 27). Roger Lonsdale notes that William Wordsworth visited Smith in 1791 in order to obtain a letter of introduction to Williams on his way to France (*Eighteenth-Century Women Poets* (Oxford: Oxford University Press, 1989), p. 413).
14. See Wollstonecraft's letter of 24 December 1792, to her sister Everina, where she confides, 'Miss Williams has behaved very civilly to me and I shall visit her frequently, because I *rather* like her, and I meet french [*sic*] company at her house' (*Collected Letters of Mary Wollstonecraft*, ed. J. Todd (New York: Columbia U P, 2003), p. 215).
15. J. Austen, *Northanger Abbey and Persuasion* (London: J. Murray), vol. 1, p. 252.
16. In a letter to her sister Cassandra, dated Friday 24 November 1815, Austen mentions that she has borrowed a work by 'Miss Williams' from her publisher John Murray. See 'Contexts' in *Emma: A Longman Cultural Edition*, ed. F. Ferguson (New York: Pearson Longman, 2006), p. 388.
17. Kennedy, *Helen Maria Williams*, p. 47.
18. Ibid., p. 48.
19. E. Ty, *Unsex'd Revolutionaries: Five Women Novelists of the 1790s* (Toronto: University of Toronto Press, 1993), p. 83.
20. In her non-fiction prose she claims that Paris is sublime and London beautiful 'according to Mr. Burke's definition of these qualities' (*Letters Written in France to a Friend in England* (London, T. Cadell, 1790), p. 73–4).
21. P. Yaeger, 'Toward a Female Sublime', *Gender and Theory*, ed. L. Kauffman (London: Blackwell, 1989), p. 202.
22. Yaeger, 'Toward a Female Sublime', p. 202.
23. A. Barbauld, 'Thoughts on Devotional Taste', in *Anna Letitia Barbauld: Selected Poetry and Prose*, ed. E. Kraft and W. McCarthy (Peterborough: Broadview, 2002), p. 219.
24. Ibid., p. 219.
25. Ibid., p. 220.
26. J. Beattie, *Dissertations Moral and Critical* (Stuttgart: Fromann Verlag, 1970), p. 620.
27. Ibid.

28 Ibid.
29 E. Burke, *Philosophical Enquiry* (London: R. and J. Dodsley, 1759), p. 96.
30 Barbauld, 'Thoughts on Devotional Taste', p. 232.
31 M. Wollstonecraft, *Vindication of the Rights of Men*, in *The Works of Mary Wollstonecraft*, ed. Janet Todd and Marilyn Butler (London: William Pickering, 1989), vol. 5, p. 46.
32 Radcliffe, *The Romance of the Forest*, 3 vols (London: T. Hookman & J. Carpenter , 1792), vol. 3, p. 56.
33 Ibid.
34 Ibid., p. 58.
35 For a closer reading of Williams's *Peru* see my chapter 'Horrific Suffering, Sacred Terror, and Sublime Freedom' in *Through a Glass Darkly: Suffering, the Sacred, and the Sublime in Literature and Theory* (Waterloo, ON: Wilfred Laurier University Press, forthcoming in February 2010).
36 H. M. Williams, *Poem on the Bill Lately Passed for Regulating the Slave Trade* (London: T. Cadell, 1788), l. 127.
37 A. Kippis, 'St Paul's Reasons for not being Ashamed of the Gospel, Preached at Salter's Hall, May 15, 1782' (London: J. Buckland, 1782), p. 23.
38 Ibid., p. 24
39 Ibid.
40 H. M. Williams, 'Introductory Remarks on the Present State of Science and Literature in France', to *Poems on Various Subjects* (London: Whittaker, 1823), p. xix.
41 Ty, *Unsex'd Revolutionaries*, pp. 73, 80.
42 Todd, *Sign of Angellica*, p. 231.
43 S. Irlam, *Elations: The Poetics of Enthusiasm in Eighteenth-Century Britain* (Stanford, CA: Stanford University Press, 1999), p. 23.

# SELECT BIBLIOGRAPHY

## Primary Sources

### *Reviews of Julia*


Anon., *Critical Review*, 69 (May 1790), p. 593.

Anon., *Edinburgh Magazine and Literary Miscellany*, 52 (July 1790), p. 338.

Anon., *English Review*, 15 (April 1790), pp. 304–05.

Anon., *European Magazine*, 17 (June 1790), pp. 435–8.

Anon., *Monthly Review*, 2 (July 1790), pp. 334–6.

Wollstonecraft, M., *Analytical Review*, 7 (May 1790), pp. 98–9.


### *Other Editions of Julia*


*Julia, a Novel Interspersed with Poetical Pieces*, 2 vols (Dublin: Chamberlaine and Rice, P. Wogan, P. Byrne, H. Colbert, W. McKenzie, J. Moore, J. Jones, Grueber and McAllister, W. Jones, G. Draper, R. White, J. Milliken, 1790).

*Julia, a Novel Interspersed with Poetical Pieces*, 2 vols, in facsimile, introduced by G. Luria (New York: Garland, 1974).

*Julia, a Novel Interspersed with Poetical Pieces*, 2 vols, in facsimile, introduced by P. Garside (London: Routledge, 1995).


### *Other Works by Williams*


*Poems on Various Subjects* (London: Whittaker, 1823).

*Edwin and Eltruda, a Legendary Tale, by a Young Lady* (London: T. Cadell, 1782).

*A Farewell, for Two Years, to England, a Poem* (London: T. Cadell, 1791).

*Letters Containing a Sketch of the Politics of France and of the Scenes which Have Passed in the Prisons of Paris*, 2 vols (London: G. G. & J. Robinson, 1795).

*Letters Written in France in the Summer of 1790, to a Friend in England* (London: T. Cadell, 1790).

*Letters from France*, 5 vols (London: G. G. & J. Robinson, 1792).

*An Ode on the Peace, by the author of Edwin and Eltruda* (London: T. Cadell, 1783).

*Paul and Virginia, translated from the French of Bernardin Saint-Pierre* (London: G. G. and J. Robinson, 1795).

*A Poem on the Bill Lately Passed for Regulating the Slave Trade* (London: T. Cadell, 1788).

*Peru, a Poem in Six Cantos* (London: T. Cadell, 1784).

*Poems*, 2 vols. (London: A. Rivington and J. Marshall, 1786).

*Poems on Various Subjects* (London: Whittaker, 1823).

*A Tour in Switzerland* (London: G. G. and J. Robinson, 1798).

## *Eighteenth-Century Works Referred to in* Julia

Fordyce, J., *Sermons to Young Women in Two Volumes* (London: A Millar & T. Cadell, 1766).

Goethe, J. W. von, *The Sorrows of Young Werther: a German Story*, trans. R. Graves (London: J. Dodsley, 1784).

Goldsmith, O., *The Deserted Village* (London: W. Griffin, 1770).

—, *The Traveller: A Poem*, 9th edn (London: T. Carnan and F. Newberry, 1774).

—, *Vicar of Wakefield: a Tale, Supposed to be Written by Himself*, 2 vols (Salisbury: B. Collins, 1766).

Gray, T., *Elegy Written in a Country Churchyard* (London: R. Dodsley, 1751).

—, *Odes by Mr. Gray* (Strawberry Hill: R & J Dodsley, 1757).

Gregory, J., *A Father's Legacy to His Daughters* (London: T. Cadell, 1774).

Hawkins, J., *The Life of Samuel Johnson, L.L.D.* (London: J. Buckland et al., 1787).

Home, J., *Douglas: A Tragedy* (London: John Bell, British Library, 1791).

Hume, D., *The History of England, from Julius Caesar to the Accession of Henry VII*,

6 vols (London: A. Millar, 1762).

Jenyns, S., *The Works of Soame Jenyns, in Four Volumes* (London: T. Cadell, 1790).

Kippis, A., *The Life of Captain James Cook* (Dublin: H. Chamberlaine et al., 1788).

Moore, J., *Zeluco, Various Views of Human Nature, Taken from Life and Manners, Foreign and Domestic* (London: T. Cadell, 1789).

Pope, A., *Essay on Criticism* (London: W. Lewis, 1711).

—, *The Moral Epistles* in *The Works of Alexander Pope Esq. Volume Three*, ed. W. Warburton (London: J. and P. Knapton, 1753).

—, *Rape of the Lock: an heroi-comical poem. In five cantos* (London: Bernard Lintott, 1714).

Romaine, S., 'The Knowledge of Salvation Precious in the Hour of Death; Proved in a Sermon Preached, January 4, 1759, upon the Death of the Rev. Mr. James Hervey', in *The Works of the Late Reverend James Hervey, Volume V* (Edinburgh: P. Whyte and J. Roch, 1769), pp. 123–53.

Rowe, N., *The Fair Penitent, a Tragedy* (London: Jacob Tonson, 1703).

Sheridan, R., *School for Scandal, a Comedy* (London: sold by S. Bladon, 1779).

Sterne, L., *A Sentimental Journey through France and Italy* (London: T. Becket and P. A. de Hondt, 1768).

Thomson, J., *The Seasons* (London, printed in 1730).

## Secondary Sources

Alfrey, S., *The Sublime of Intense Sociability* (Lewisburg, PA: Bucknell University Press, 2000).

Blakemore, S., *Crisis in Representation: Thomas Paine, Mary Wollstonecraft, Helen Maria Williams* (Madison, NJ: Fairleigh Dickinson Press, 1997).

Bray, M., 'Helen Maria Williams and Edmund Burke: Radical Critique and Complicity', *Eighteenth-Century Life*, 16 (1992), pp. 1–24.

Brownell, M., *Alexander Pope and the Arts of Georgian England* (Oxford: Oxford University Press, 1978).

Chaplin, S., *Law, Sensibility and the Sublime in Eighteenth-Century Women's Fiction* (Burlington, VA: Ashgate, 2004).

Duquette, N., '"Dauntless Faith": Contemplative Sublimity and Social Action in Mary Anne Schimmelpenninck's Aesthetics', *Christianity and Literature*, 55 (2006), pp. 509–33.

—, 'Horrific Suffering, Sacred Terror, and Sublime Freedom', in *Through a Glass Darkly: Suffering, the Sacred, and the Sublime in Literature and Theory* (Waterloo, ON: Wilfred Laurier University Press, forthcoming 2010).

Ellis, M., *The Politics of Sensibility: Race, Gender and Commerce in the Sentimental Novel* (Cambridge: Cambridge University Press, 1996).

Ferguson, M., *Subject to Others: British Women Writers and Colonial Slavery, 1670–1834* (New York: Routledge, 1992).

Garside, P., 'Introduction' to a facsimile edition of *Julia, a Novel Interspersed with Poetical Pieces* (London: Routledge, 1995), vi–xxi.

Fergus, J., *Provincial Readers in Eighteenth-Century England* (Oxford: Oxford University Press, 2006).

Ffrench, Y., *Mrs. Siddons: Tragic Actress* (London: Derek Verschoyle, 1936).

Fulford, T., D. Lee and P. Kitson, *Literature, Science and Exploration in the Romantic Era: Bodies of Knowledge* (Cambridge: Cambridge University Press, 2004).

Irlam, S., *Elations: The Poetics of Enthusiasm in Eighteenth-Century Britain* (Stanford, CA: Stanford University Press, 1999).

Janowitz, A., *England's Ruins: Poetic Purpose and the National Landscape* (Oxford: Oxford University Press, 1990).

Johnson, C., *Equivocal Beings: Politics, Gender and Sentimentality in the 1790s* (Chicago, IL: University of Chicago Press, 1995).

Jones, C., *Radical Sensibility: Literature and Ideas in the 1790s* (London: Routledge, 1993).

Jones, V., 'Women Writing Revolution: Narratives of History and Sexuality in Wollstonecraft and Williams', in J. Whale and S. Copley (ed.), *Beyond Romanticism: New Approaches to Texts and Contexts*, (London: Routledge, 1992), pp. 178–99.

Keane, A., *Women Writers and the English Nation in the 1790s* (Cambridge: Cambridge University Press, 2000).

Kelly, G., 'Bluestocking Feminism', in *Women, Writing and the Public Sphere, 1700–1830*, ed. E. Eger et al. (Cambridge: Cambridge University Press, 2001), pp. 163–80.

—, *Women, Writing, and Revolution 1790–1827* (Oxford: Clarendon Press, 1993).

Kennedy, D., 'Benevolent Historian: Helen Maria Williams and her British Readers', in *Rebellious Hearts: British Woman Writers and the French Revolution* (Albany, NY: SUNY Press, 2001), pp. 317–36.

—, '"Storms of Sorrow": The Poetry of Helen Maria Williams', in *Man and Nature: Proceedings of the CSECS*, vol. 10, ed. J. Boulad-Ayoub et al. (Edmonton: Academic Printing and Publishing, 1991), pp. 77–91.

—, *Helen Maria Williams and the Age of Revolution* (Lewisburg, PA: Bucknell University Press, 2002).

LeBlanc, J., 'Politics and Commercial Sensibility in Helen Maria Williams's *Letters from France*' in *Eighteenth-Century Life*, 21:1 (1997), p. 39.

Lonsdale, R. (ed.), *Eighteenth-Century Women Poets*. (Oxford: Oxford University Press, 1990).

Manvell, R., *Sarah Siddons: Portrait of an Actress* (New York: G. P. Putnam's Sons, 1971).

Mellor, A., 'The Female Poet and the Poetess', in I. Armstrong and V. Blain (eds) *Women's Poetry in the Enlightenment* (London: Macmillan, 1999), pp. 81–98.

Mitchell, R. E., '"The soul that dreams it shares the power it feels so well": The Politics of Sympathy in the Abolitionist Verse of Williams and Yearsley', *Romanticism on the Net*, 29 (2003), accessed 17 July 2004 <http://www.erudit.org/revue/ron/2003/v/n29/007719ar.html>.

Myers, P., *The Bluestocking Circle: Women, Friendship, and the Life of the Mind in Eighteenth-Century England* (Oxford: Clarendon Press, 1990).

Richardson, A., 'Epic Ambivalence: Imperial Politics and Romantic Deflection in Williams's *Peru* and Landor's *Gebir*', in *Romanticism, Race, and Imperial Culture, 1780–1834*. (Bloomington, IN: Indiana University Press, 1996), pp. 265–82.

Robinson, P., 'Traduction ou Trahison de *Paul et Virginie*? L'Exemple de Helen Maria Williams', *RHLF*, 89 (1989), pp. 843–55.

Smylitopoulos, C., 'Rewritten and Reused: Imaging the Nabob through "Upstart Iconography"', *Eighteenth-Century Life*, 32 (Spring 2008), pp. 39–59.

Todd, Janet, *The Sign of Angellica: Women, Writing and Fiction, 1660–1800* (London: Virago, 1989).

—. *Sensibility: An Introduction* (London: Methuen, 1986).

Ty, E., *Unsex'd Revolutionaries: Five Women Novelists of the 1790s* (Toronto, ON: University of Toronto Press, 1993).

Woodward, L., 'Une Anglaise Amie de la Révolution Française: Hélène-Maria Williams et ses Amis', *Bibliothèque de la Revue de Littérature Comparée*, 64 (1960), pp. 200–30.

Yaeger, P., 'Toward a Female Sublime', in L. Kauffman (ed.), *Gender and Theory*, (London: Basil Blackwell, 1989), pp. 191–212.

# NOTE ON THE TEXT

The original manuscript of Helen Maria Williams's *Julia, a Novel Interspersed with Poetical Pieces* does not survive. The first edition was printed in two volumes in March of 1790 in London by Thomas Cadell, on the Strand, before Williams's more famous work *Letters Written in France in the Summer of 1790, to a Friend in England*, also published by Thomas Cadell that same year. The first edition of *Julia* was shortly thereafter followed by an Irish edition, which appeared later in 1790, printed in Dublin by Chamberlaine and Rice, P. Wogan, P. Byrne, H. Colbert, W. Mckenzie, J. Moore, J. Jones, Grueber and McAllister, W. Jones, G. Draper, R. White, and J. Milliken. There are no significant variations between these two editions, besides the fact that the Irish edition is in smaller print, set closer together, and has page numbers that run continuously, rather than starting again at the beginning of the second volume. It is of note that Williams's name appears clearly, and boldly, on the title page of both the London and Irish editions; her early works, such as *Edwin and Eltruda* (1782) and *Ode on the Peace* (1783) were published anonymously.

The Chawton House Library copy of Thomas Cadell's first edition printing of Julia is unique due to the fact that it has been bound together with a copy of the first volume of Williams's *Poems, in Two Volumes* (London: Thomas Cadell, 1786), added after the text of the novel. This 1786 collection of Williams's poetry also bore her name clearly on its title page. Most likely an admirer of Willliams's poetry purchased the first, unbound, volume of her *Poems*, perhaps directly from Thomas Cadell, and then requested that it be bound along with both volumes of *Julia*. Reviewers did see parallels between Williams's own early poetry of sensibility and the poetry she presented as the productions of her heroine Julia, which is supported by this literal binding together of her 1786 *Poems* and her 1790 novel. A review in the August 1786 issue of *European Magazine*, for example, compares Williams's *Poems* to collections produced by other British women and then concludes: 'in true elegant simplicity of poetic expression and colouring, and in the natural easy flow of her versification, she is unrivalled by any of her sisters' (p. 89). Similar language appears in the first reviews of Julia which praise the novel for being 'elegant in style,' 'simple,' and 'finished in watercolours,' and especially for its inclusion of 'ingenuous and harmonious' poetry. Of the ten poems 'interspersed' throughout *Julia* at least five – 'The Linnet,' 'Sonnet to Hope,' 'Elegy on a Young Thrush,' 'Sonnet to Peace,' and 'Sonnet to the Moon' – bear a strong resemblance to those found in her 1786 collection. These five poems are also the most frequently commented on or reproduced in the reviews. Not one reviewer remarks on the final poem in Julia, 'The Bastille: a Vision.'

The endorsement of the French Revolution as a struggle for social justice in 'The Bastille: A Vision' may be one of the contributing factors to the lack of later, nineteenth-century, editions of *Julia*. Since the London and Dublin editions were printed in 1790 the novel has virtually been out of print, being reproduced only in facsimile copy, once in 1974 and again in 1995. The poetry from the novel was reproduced, however, in both French and English. *Recueil de Poésies extraites des Ouvrages d'Helena Maria Williams, traduites de l'anglais par M. Stanislas de Boufflers et M. Esménard* (Fr. Cocheris Fils, Libraire: Paris, 1808) includes 'ÉpÎtre a la Poésies,' 'Sonnet sur L'Espérance,' 'A un Oiseau,' 'Sonnet sur la Paix de L'Ame,' and 'Sonnet a la Lune,' but, interestingly, includes no translation of 'The Bastille: A Vision.' Williams's early nineteenth-century collection *Poems on Various Subjects* (London: Whittaker, 1823) reprints 'An Address to Poetry,' 'The Bastille: A Vision,' 'Sonnet to Hope,' 'Sonnet to Peace of Mind' (slightly revised title, perhaps following the French translation), 'Sonnet to the Moon,' 'Elegy on a Young Thrush,' and 'The Linnet and the Cat' (slightly revised title),

In creating this new edition I have made very few changes to the original text, except where obvious errors in punctuation had occurred in the printing. For example, there are places in the first edition where a small letter follows an exclamation mark, and I have capitalized those letters at the beginning of the new sentence. I have left the original eighteenth-century spellings in the text ('shew,' 'intirely,' 'tho,' etc.) as spelling had not been regulated at that point in British history. This leaves Williams's agency in choosing her spellings intact. The only spelling that I have changed is the word 'charard,' which is now 'charade' in this edition. In eighteenth-century texts the word 'charad' or 'charade' appears, but no instance of 'charard' exists, so there is a high probability that this was an actual typo. I have maintained Williams's use of spacing and indentation in all of her poems. Except for the small corrections to punctuation mentioned above and the change of one word's spelling, the text is an extremely close reflection of Thomas Cadell's original setting and printing in 1790.

# *JULIA*,

A

NOVEL;

interspersed with some

POETICAL PIECES.

by

HELEN MARIA WILLIAMS.

in two volumes.

LONDON:

printed for T. Cadell.

m.dcc.xc.

# ADVERTISEMENT

The purpose of these pages is to trace the danger arising from the uncontrouled indulgence of strong affections; not in those instances where they lead to the guilty excesses of passion in a corrupted mind – but, when disapproved by reason, and uncircumscribed by prudence, they involve even the virtuous in calamity; since, under the dominion of passion, if the horror of remorse may be avoided, misery at least is inevitable; and, though we do not become the slaves of vice, we must yield ourselves the victims of sorrow.

The materials of the following sketch are taken from nature. The perfection, however, of a picture does not depend on the colours, but on the hand by which they are blended; and, perhaps, the pen which records this narrative may, in vain, have attempted to rescue it from oblivion.

I have been encouraged, by the indulgence which my former poems have met with,[1] to intersperse some poetical pieces in these volumes; but the uncertainty of being able to engage the continuance of favour, leads me to offer these farther productions in verse, with as little confidence as this first attempt in prose.

# VOL. I.

## CHAP. I.

An officer, to whom we shall give the name of Clifford, derived from his ancestors a very honourable descent, being able to trace their possession of an estate in the northern part of England thro' several centuries. That estate, however, was dissipated by the imprudence and extravagance of his parents; and Captain Clifford, who had received a very liberal education, and was brought up with the expectation of an ample inheritance, found his only remaining possession was his commission in the army. He married a beautiful young woman, the daughter of a neighbouring family, to whom he had been long attached, and who died a few years after their marriage, leaving him one daughter. To this child he transferred the tenderness he had felt for her mother, and undertook himself the charge of her education. Dispirited by his domestic misfortune, wounded by the disappointment of his early views in life, and the mortification of seeing many raised above him in the army, because he was unable to purchase promotion, he retired in disgust, and lived upon a captain's half-pay,[2] in a small village in the neighbourhood of London, where his father, who was far advanced in years, made a part of his family.

In this retreat Captain Clifford found consolation and employment, in devoting his time to the improvement of his daughter; and his own mind being highly cultivated, she derived greater advantages from his instructions than she could have received from the most expensive education, under a less anxious as well as a less able preceptor.

Nature had liberally bestowed upon Julia Clifford the powers of the understanding, and the virtues of the heart: her sensibility was quick,[3] her disposition affectionate, and her taste was improved by the society of her father, till it attained an uncommon degree of elegance and refinement; but of her superiority to others she seemed intirely unconscious. Her manners were perfectly modest and unassuming; her conversation simple and unstudied; she spoke from the impulse of her heart, and she possessed the most amiable candor and frankness of disposition. Julia was above the middle size: her figure had not been much molded by the dancing-master; but nature had given it a gracefulness 'beyond the reach of art.'[4] She had a madona face, and an expression of intelligence and sensibility in her countenance, infinitely engaging.

Captain Clifford's younger brother, after the paternal estate was disposed of, went in pursuit of fortune to the East Indies[5] – he was a man of a plain understanding and an excellent heart. Just in his principles, and generous in his disposition, he acquired wealth slowly, but honourably. Mr. Clifford married at Bengal, and his only daughter, Charlotte, was sent when a child to England for education, and committed to the care of her aunt Mrs. Melbourne, the sister of Charlotte's mother. – At eighteen Charlotte was taken from school at Queen Square, to live with her aunt, till the return of her father from the East Indies. Charlotte was one of those sweet lively characters, whose unaffected manners and invariable good-humour strongly engage the affections, and with whom one would wish to pass thro' life. The gay powers of wit and fancy are like those brilliant phænomena which sometimes glow in the sky, and dazzle the eye of the beholder by their luminous and uncommon appearances; while sweetness of temper has a resemblance to that gentle star, whose benign influence gilds alike the morning and the evening.[6] But the distinguishing and most amiable trait of Charlotte's character, was her perfect exemption from envy. She was sensible of her inferiority to Julia, whom she tenderly loved; and whenever any preference was shewn to herself she seemed conscious of its injustice. Quite content to remain in the back-ground, she embraced with the most natural and lively pleasure every opportunity of displaying the accomplishments of her cousin. – Charlotte was little, her features were not regular, but her countenance had a very agreeable and animated expression. Her chief motive for rejoicing at her removal from school, was the hope of a more frequent intercourse with Julia, for her aunt had small hold on her affections.

Mrs. Melbourne's maiden name was Wilson – her father, who was an eminent merchant in the city, became a bankrupt when she had just attained her twenty-third year. A young man who had been her father's clerk, and was now married and engaged in a flourishing business, invited Miss Wilson, from a principle of gratitude towards her father, to take up her residence at his house, where his wife received her with great kindness. Meanwhile her younger sister, who was then eighteen years of age, was fitted out at the expence of her relations, and sent to the East Indies in pursuit of a husband; or rather in search of the golden fleece,[7] which is certainly the aim of such adventures, and the husband is merely the means of attaining it. – The God of Love in the East frames his arrows of massy gold; takes the feathers of his quiver not from the soft wing of his mother's dove, but from the gaudy plumage of the peacock; and points all his shafts with the bright edge of a diamond.[8] – Miss Charlotte Wilson was married soon after her arrival in Bengal to Mr. Clifford, and died some years before his return to England.

At the house where Miss Wilson found an asylum, Mr. Melbourne frequently visited, the mistress of the house being his near relation. – He was a man of parts, and had attained considerable eminence in the law, a profession in which above all others eminence is honourable, since it is invariably connected with distinction of mind.[9] – Miss Wilson was tolerably handsome, and Mr. Melbourne paid her some attention: she had an admirable degree of sagacity, and perceived that this young man, notwithstanding his superior understanding, was the dupe of vanity. She soon betrayed the most violent passion for him; and this display of fondness, which would probably have excited disgust and aversion in a man of delicacy, had a very different effect on Mr.

Melbourne. He was handsome, and vain of his figure, as well as of his talents – he did not think it unlikely that he should inspire a violent passion – Miss Wilson appeared desperate in her love; and he married her in good nature, and merely to prevent suicide. Mrs. Melbourne continuing with great judgment to flatter his weaknesses, he made her an excellent husband, and at his death left her a considerable jointure, and her daughter an independent fortune of twenty thousand pounds.

Mrs. Melbourne had a large acquaintance, by whom she was respected as a woman of sense, but not beloved; for her manners were stiff and disagreeable. – She gave some alms to the poor, because she thought a little charity was requisite to secure a good place in heaven; but she found no duty more difficult, and wished that any other had been enjoined in its place. 'One cannot help pitying the unfortunate,' (she would exclaim) 'and yet there is not one in a thousand who is not so in consequence of imprudence; one must therefore be sorry for the imprudent, or not sorry at all.' She penetrated with nice discernment into the characters of her acquaintances; could perceive all their follies, and descant upon them with great acuteness; – no foible escaped her accurate observation; and her friends met with none of that species of partiality which shades the weaknesses of those we love. Whenever her visitors departed, they were sure of being analysed, and of having their defects weighed in a rigorous scale, without the slightest peculiarity being omitted. She had, indeed, too strict a regard for truth to invent any slanders of her acquaintance. All Mrs. Melbourne could be charged with, was interpreting every word and action her own way, which was invariably the worst way possible; and with great perseverance refusing to assign a good motive for any thing, when a bad one could be found. She often remained silent in company, while she was storing her memory with materials for future animadversion; and Mrs. Melbourne's memory was like a bird of prey, which seizes on such food as milder natures would reject. This lady was unfortunately quick in discovering imperfection, but very liable to overlook what was worthy of regard: she left others to enjoy the flowers which are scattered over the path of life, while she employed herself in counting the weeds which grew among them. She might, indeed, have acknowledged with Iago, 'that it was her nature's plague to spy into abuses;' and might properly enough have added with him, that 'oft her jealousy shap'd faults that were not.'[10] In her family Mrs. Melbourne was morose and ill-humoured. She scolded her servants with little intermission, which she considered an indispensable part of the province of a good housewife; and her servants, whom habit had reconciled to reproach, listened to her with the most perfect indifference; as those who live near the fall of a cataract, or on the banks of the ocean, hear at length the rushing of the torrent, or the rage of the billows, without being sensible of the sounds. The only seasons memorable for Mrs. Melbourne's tenderness were, when any of her connections or family were ill. She was then the most courteous creature existing, and began to love them with all her might, as if she thought there was no time to lose, and that she must endeavour to crowd such an extraordinary degree of fondness into the short space which was left, as might counterbalance her neglect or unkindness through the whole course of their lives. The way to make her regard permanent was to die – her affection was violent when her friends came to the last gasp; and after having settled the matter with her own conscience by these parting demonstrations of sorrow, she submitted with pious resignation to her loss. The ruling passion of Mrs. Melbourne's soul was her love of her daughter; but it was carried to an excess that rendered it illiberal and selfish: her mind resembled a convex glass, and every ray of affection in her bosom was concentered in one small point. She considered every fine young woman as the rival of Miss Melbourne, and hated them in proportion as they merited regard. She could not forgive Julia for being young, beautiful, accomplished, and amiable, till her own daughter was married. After that period she pardoned these intrusive qualities; and at the request of Charlotte, upon her removal from school, invited Julia to spend a short time at her house in Hanover-square.[11]

# CHAP. II.

Julia discovered at a very early age a particular sensibility to poetry. When she was eight years old she composed a poem on the departure of one of her young companions, in which she displayed, with great diligence, her whole stock of classical knowledge; and obliged all the heathen gods and goddesses, whose names she had been taught, to pass in succession, like the shades of Banquo's line.[12] Her father did not discourage this early fondness for the muse, because he believed that a propensity for any elegant art was a source of happiness.

Perhaps more lasting reputation has been acquired by the powers of the imagination, than by any other faculty of the human mind. But even where the talents of the poet are altogether inadequate to the acquisition of fame, the cultivation of them may still confer the most soothing enjoyment. Though the soil may not be favourable to the growth of the immortal laurel, it may produce some plants of transitory verdure. Perhaps the most precious property of poetry is, that of leading the mind from the gloomy mists of care, or the black clouds of misfortune, which sometimes gather round the path of life, to scenes bright with sunshine, and blooming with beauty.

We shall venture to insert the following Address to Poetry, written by Julia a short time before her visit to town, as a proof of her fondness for that charming art.

## AN ADDRESS TO POETRY.

While envious crowds the summit view,
Where danger with ambition strays;
Or far, with anxious step, pursue
Pale av'rice, thro' his winding ways;
The selfish passions in their train,
Whose force the social ties unbind,
And chill the love of human kind,
And make fond Nature's best emotions vain;

Oh Poesy! Oh nymph most dear,
To whom I early gave my heart,
Whose voice is sweetest to my ear
Of aught in nature or in art;
Thou, who canst all my breast controul,
Come, and thy harp of various cadence bring,

And long with melting music swell the string
That suits the present temper of my soul.

Oh! ever gild my path of woe,
And I the ills of life can bear;
Let but thy lovely visions glow,
And chase the forms of real care;
Oh still, when tempted to repine
At partial fortune's frown severe,
Wipe from my eyes the anxious tear,
And whisper, that thy soothing joys are mine!

When did my fancy ever frame
A dream of joy by thee unblest?
When first my lips pronounc'd thy name,
New pleasure warm'd my infant breast.
I lov'd to form the jingling rhyme,
The measur'd sounds, tho' rude, my ear could please;
Could give the little pains of childhood ease,
And long have sooth'd the keener pains of time.

The idle crowd in fashion's train,
Their trifling comment, pert reply,
Who talk so much, yet talk in vain,
How pleas'd for thee, Oh nymph, I fly!
For thine is all the wealth of mind,
Thine the unborrow'd gems of thought,
The flash of light, by souls refin'd,
From heav'n's empyreal source exulting caught.

And ah! when destin'd to forego
The social hour with those I love,
That charm which brightens all below,
That joy all other joys above,
And dearer to this breast of mine,
Oh Muse! than aught thy magic power can give;
Then on the gloom of lonely sadness shine,
And bid thy airy forms around me live.

Thy page, Oh Shakespeare! let me view,
Thine! at whose name my bosom glows;
Proud that my earliest breath I drew
In that blest isle where Shakespeare rose! –
Where shall my dazzled glances roll?
Shall I pursue gay Ariel's flight,[13]
Or wander where those hags of night
With deeds unnam'd shall freeze my trembling soul?

Plunge me, foul sisters! in the gloom
Ye wrap around yon blasted heath,
To hear the harrowing rite I come,
That calls the angry shades from death! –
Away – my frighted bosom spare![14]
Let true Cordelia pour her filial sigh,[15]
Let Desdemona lift her pleading eye,[16]
And poor Ophelia sing in wild despair![17]

When the bright noon of summer streams
In one wide flash of lavish day,
As soon shall mortal count the beams,
As tell the powers of Shakespeare's lay;
Oh Nature's Poet! The untaught
The simple mind thy tale pursues,
And wonders by what art it views
The perfect image of each native thought.

In those still moments when the breast,
Expanded, leaves its cares behind,
Glows by some higher thought possest,
And feels the energies of mind;
Then, awful Milton, raise the veil
That hides from human eye the heav'nly throng!
Immortal sons of light! I hear your song,
I hear your high-tun'd harps creation hail![18]

Well might creation claim your care,
And well the string of rapture move,
When all was perfect, good, and fair,
When all was music, joy, and love!
Ere evil's inauspicious birth
Chang'd nature's harmony to strife;
And wild remorse, abhorring life,
And deep affliction, spread their shade on earth.[19]

Blest Poesy! Oh sent to calm
The human pains which all must feel;
Still shed on life thy precious balm,
And every wound of nature heal!
Is there a heart of human frame
Along the burning track of torrid light,
Or 'mid the fearful waste of polar night,
That never glow'd at thy inspiring name?

Ye southern isles, emerg'd so late**
Where the pacific billow rolls,
Witness, tho' rude your simple state,
How heav'n-taught verse can melt your souls:
Say, when you hear the wand'ring bard,
How thrill'd ye listen to his lay,
By what kind arts ye court his stay,
All savage life affords, his sure reward.[20]

So, when great Homer's chiefs prepare,
A while from war's rude toils releas'd,
The pious hecatomb, and share
The flowing bowl, and genial feast;
Some heav'nly minstrel sweeps the lyre,
While all applaud the poet's native art,
For him they heap the viand's choicest part,
And copious goblets crown the muses fire.

Ev'n *here,* in scenes of pride and gain,
Where faint each genuine feeling glows;
*Here,* Nature asks, in want and pain,
The dear illusions verse bestows;
The poor, from hunger, and from cold,
Spare one small coin, the ballad's price;[21]
Admire their poet's quaint device,
And marvel much at all his rhymes unsold.

Ye children, lost in forests drear,
Still o'er your wrongs each bosom grieves,
And long the red-breast shall be dear
Who strew'd each little corpse with leaves;
For you, my earliest tears were shed,

* 'The song of the bards or minstrels of Otaheite was unpremeditated, and accompanied with music. They were continually going about from place to place; and they were rewarded by the master of the house with such things as the one wanted, and the other could spare.'
Cook's Voyage. (Williams's note)

For you, the gaudy doll I pleas'd forsook,
And heard with hands up-rais'd, and eager look,
The cruel tale, and wish'd ye were not dead!

And still on Scotia's northern shore,
'At times, between the rushing blast,'
Recording mem'ry loves to pour
The mournful song of ages past;
Come, lonely bard 'of other years!'
While dim the half-seen moon of varying skies,
While sad the wind along the grey-moss sighs,
And give my pensive heart 'the joy of tears!'

The various tropes that splendour dart
Around the modern poet's line,
Where, borrow'd from the sphere of art,
Unnumber'd gay allusions shine,
Have not a charm my breast to please
Like the blue mist, the meteor's beam,
The dark-brow'd rock, the mountain stream,
And the light thistle waving in the breeze.

Wild Poesy, in haunts sublime,
Delights her lofty note to pour;
She loves the hanging rock to climb,
And hear the sweeping torrent roar:
The little scene of cultur'd grace
But faintly her expanded bosom warms;
She seeks the daring stroke, the aweful charms,
Which Nature's pencil throws on Nature's face.[22]

Oh Nature! Thou whose works divine
Such rapture in this breast inspire,
As makes me dream one spark is mine
Of Poesy's celestial fire;
When doom'd for London smoke to leave
The kindling morn's unfolding view,
Which ever wears some aspect new,
And all the shadowy forms of soothing eve;

Then, Thomson, then be ever near,
And paint whatever season reigns;
Still let me see the varying year,
And worship Nature in thy strains;

Now, when the wintry tempests roll,
Unfold their dark and desolating form,
Rush in the savage madness of the storm,
And spread those horrors that exalt my soul.[23]

And Pope, the music of thy verse
Shall winter's dreary gloom dispel,
And fond remembrance oft rehearse
The moral song she knows so well;
The sportive sylphs shall flutter here,[24]
There Eloise, in anguish pale,
'Kiss with cold lips the sacred veil,
And drop with every bead too soft a tear!'[25]

When disappointment's sick'ning pain,
With chilling sadness numbs my breast,
That feels its dearest hope was vain,
And bids its fruitless struggles rest;
When those for whom I wish to live,
With cold suspicion wrong my aching heart;
Or, doom'd from those for ever lov'd to part,
And feel a sharper pang than death can give;

Then with the mournful bard I go,
Whom 'melancholy mark'd her own,'[26]
While tolls the curfew, solemn, slow,
And wander amid' graves unknown;
With yon pale orb, lov'd poet, come!
While from those elms long shadows spread,
And where the lines of light are shed,
Read the fond record of the rustic tomb!

Or let me o'er old Conway's flood
Hang on the frowning rock, and trace
The characters, that wove in blood,
Stamp'd the dire fate of Edward's race;
Proud tyrant, tear thy laurel'd plume;
How poor thy vain pretence to deathless fame!
The injur'd muse records thy lasting shame,
And she has power to 'ratify thy doom.'[27]

Nature, when first she smiling came,
To wake within the human breast
The sacred muses hallow'd flame,

And earth, with heav'n's rich spirit blest!
 Nature in that auspicious hour,
With aweful mandate, bade the bard
 The register of glory guard,
And gave him o'er all mortal honours power.

 Can fame on painting's aid rely,
Or lean on sculpture's trophy'd bust?
 The faithless colours bloom to die,
The crumbling pillar mocks its trust;
 But thou, oh muse, immortal maid!
Canst paint the godlike deeds that praise inspire,
 Or worth that lives but in the mind's desire,
In tints that only shall with Nature fade!

 Oh tell me, partial nymph! what rite,
What incense sweet, what homage true,
 Draws from thy fount of purest light
The flame it lends a chosen few?
 Alas! these lips can never frame
The mystic vow that moves thy breast;
 Yet by thy joys my life is blest,
And my fond soul shall consecrate thy name.

# CHAP. III.

Julia, for the first time, accepted with pleasure Mrs. Melbourne's invitation; for her former visits to that lady had been productive only of weariness and disgust. She had always been treated by Miss Melbourne with great neglect, and by her most intimate companions, the Hon. Miss C—'s, with particular rudeness. Miss Melbourne had discernment enough to perceive Julia's merit, and, had she been more obliged to fortune, and less to nature, would have valued her acquaintance highly; but no honour could have been gained with people of *ton*,[28] by an intimacy with one in Julia's situation; while, at the same time, her engaging qualities would have been perpetually in the way, and obtruded themselves in a manner very troublesome to Miss Melbourne. Her bosom friends, the Hon. Miss C—'s, had an unconquerable antipathy to female beauty: they agreed with many wise men in the opinion, that beauty often proves fatal to the possessor; but, notwithstanding this conviction, these ladies had the magnanimity to wish that this dangerous property had been entirely confined to themselves.

The eldest of these sisters, who had just reached her twenty-eighth year, had also an insuperable aversion to the age of nineteen. Julia, therefore, who had the accumulated misfortune of being beautiful, and just nineteen, was the object of general dislike to these ladies. The Miss C—'s, who were of all Mrs. Melbourne's parties, usually placed themselves in a corner of the room with Miss Melbourne, and found amusement in laughing at the rest of the company as they entered. When any gentleman approached their circle, the laugh was increased; for they were of that order of young ladies who, having heard of the attractions of sprightliness, affect perpetual mirth, and fancy that vivacity consists in a titter, and wit in a pert remark: yet it was easy to discern that their gaiety was artificial, because it was always beyond what the occasion justified. It resembled those flowers which are reared in winter by the force of art, and are destitute of that delicious fragrance which nature only can bestow. Miss Melbourne and the Miss C—'s had long been on a very intimate footing, professed the most violent mutual regard, and were commonly called friends: yet this intimacy, which was dignified with the name of friendship, had no other foundation than selfishness; for, had Miss Melbourne renounced her balls and concerts, or the Miss C—'s been deprived of their rank, this sentimental[29] intercourse would instantly have terminated: mean while their affection appeared fervent, because it was untried; and durable, because it was yet unshaken by misfortune. Miss Melbourne was lately married; the visits of the Miss C—'s were therefore no longer frequent at her mother's house; and Julia looked forward to nothing but pleasure in the society of the affectionate and amiable Charlotte. She also promised herself a new kind of gratification, in mixing for awhile with the gay and elegant parties at Mr. Seymour's, the gentleman whom Miss Melbourne had married, and who indulged her in her fondness for splendor and dissipation. – Nature, who had been avaricious of the qualities of taste and sensibility to Mrs. Melbourne, had given an accumulated portion of both to her daughter, together with more than an hereditary share of beauty. She was a painter and a musician; but her vanity perverted every natural and acquired talent, 'grew with her growth, and strengthened with her strength,'[30] and kept pace with her understanding and accomplishments. Vanity made her selfish; for she was so extravagantly fond of admiration, that, in the continual pursuit of it, she could think only of herself, and forgot all the claims of others. But she felt that sentiment was amiable; she was, therefore, made up of sentiment: – she also knew, that persons of refinement were often, from the wayward circumstances of life, extremely miserable; she, therefore, deemed discontent the test of feeling, and, with scarcely a wish ungratified, she thought that to be happy, with what would make any vulgar mind happy, would be only proving that she was dull. – She spoke, therefore, in a plaintive voice, and often complained of melancholy, but left the cause of it concealed; which was such as no understanding could penetrate, and no heart could guess. Sometimes, indeed, she smiled, while she descanted, in well-chosen words, on what was weak, low, or ridiculous; but the pensive cast of countenance quickly returned, and an affected sigh explained the difficulty she felt in assuming gaiety. If she carved at table, or made tea, she did both with a sort of slow and solemn movement, to convince the company that she was in a frame of mind, from which it cost her a cruel effort to descend to the common offices of life. She seemed to think eating a coarse and vulgar toil; and her conversation frequently wandered from a roasted duck to Minerva's owl, or Jove's eagle.[31] She could not hear an Italian air without weeping; she pitied the miseries of the poor in very pathetic language; and lamented being obliged, in conformity to her situation in life, to spend much more than she wished upon dress, which put it out of her power, in the account of her annual expences, to reckon the claims of benevolence, and confined her to a negative sort of good-will towards the unfortunate. Yet she often declared, that she complied with the rules of fashion, merely because she thought such compliance fit and right. If Mrs. Seymour's notions on this subject were just, and conformity to fashion is virtue, how extensive was her merit! How upright had been the past, how perfect was the present, and how certain was the prospect of future excellence! – But she did not recollect that it is easy to discern whether the motive from which we act be duty or inclination; our obedience is so much more exact in the one case than in the other. If she had been swayed solely by the former principle, there would probably have been sometimes a little relaxation in the labours of the toilet; nor would every ribbon and feather have been placed in such unquestionable submission to the last mode.

When Mrs. Seymour received company, she advanced to meet them not with the pleasure which kindness or affection dictates. She spoke to her visitors as if she were interested in what she said, but she scarcely knew what it was. She was not thinking of the persons who had just entered: her concern was that her manner of receiving them might be thought graceful by the spectators. She was scarcely ever at home, but spent her time in lamenting, wherever she went, the fatigues of a large acquaintance. She imposed upon herself the duty of going to every ball, or card-assembly, to which she was invited; but performed the rigadoon step,[32] and dealt the cards, with sentimental pensiveness, and as if she were fully persuaded that dancing was vanity, and whist vexation of spirit.[33] Her complaints, however gracefully delivered, were often ill-timed: she would invite a social party to dinner, and then, instead of promoting chearfulness and good-humour, be languishingly mournful the whole day. The nightingale judges better than Mrs. Seymour did, for *she* never begins her elegies of woe amidst the freshness of the morning, and the lustre of a bright horizon, when we would rather listen to the rapture of the lark; but waits till the fading scenery, and the melancholy of twilight, shall dispose us for a dirge.[34] But in truth, though Mrs. Seymour affected the plaintive notes of the nightingale, she had no congenial taste with that pathetic[35] bird for the shade, but was as fond of sunshine as the lark himself.

# CHAP. IV.

On her arrival in town, Julia expressed a great desire to go to the theatre; and Mrs. Seymour engaged a box at Drury-lane[36] for the next evening, when the tragedy of Douglas[37] was performed. Julia admired with enthusiasm that charming play, which never 'oversteps the modesty of nature,'[38] and is so true to her genuine feelings; but which had not, till some years after this period, its full effect upon the heart, in having the part of Lady Randolph represented by Mrs. Siddons,[39] whose power over the human passions it is far more easy to feel than to delineate.

Julia and her cousin went to dinner at Mrs. Seymour's, and were anxious to reach the theatre before the performance began: Mrs. Seymour affected to wish so too; but, after the carriage came, she found so many pretences for delay, that the first act was almost over before they reached their box. This was what Mrs. Seymour desired: she chose to excite attention by disturbing the performance, and drawing the looks of the audience from the stage to herself. When she was seated, she began talking to Julia with great seeming earnestness, who was too much engaged by the scene before her to pay attention to Mrs. Seymour's remarks; and indeed that lady did not desire it: her whole mind was occupied in performing her own part gracefully, while she remained an object of general observation. She spoke to be *looked at*, not to be *heard*; and her lips moved, or were still, from no other impulse than as she thought speech or silence would have the best effect in perspective.

Julia and Charlotte soon became deeply absorbed in the sorrows of Lady Randolph,[40] and their tears flowed often and irresistibly. Mrs. Seymour now thought proper to display her sensibility too,[41] of which she really possessed a considerable share; but in her eagerness to discover her feelings in the most pathetic parts, to shew her admiration of the finest passages, and to weep at the precise moment when it would do her taste most honour, she lost the charm of the illusion; and her sympathy was so interrupted by her vanity, that at length she could scarcely force a tear; and all that was left in her power, was to lean in a pensive attitude on the side of the box, and assume a look of dejection.

The next day Julia went with Mrs. Melbourne and Charlotte to dine at Mrs. Seymour's, where a large company was assembled.

Mr. Seymour's was a house of show, rather than of hospitality; a house where ostentatious entertainments were occasionally given with the most lavish expence, but where no intimate guests were led by friendship, and detained by kindness; for that cordial welcome which springs from the heart, was in this family neither understood nor practised.

The company were obliged to wait dinner some time for Mr. Charles Seymour, who was always too late by rule, which he very methodically observed. Mr. Charles Seymour was the youngest brother of Mr. Seymour, and had, thro' his interest, obtained a place at court. He was a young man of weak understanding, but he made up in pliability and finesse, what he wanted in good sense. His person was genteel, he had acquired a graceful ease of manner, danced well, dressed with elegance, courted the great by all those little attentions which only little minds can pay, and was rewarded for his assiduity by frequent invitations to splendid and fashionable parties. He was a young man whose acquaintance every lady, when she gave a ball, was proud to acknowledge, and happy to embrace; for he seemed made on purpose for such an occasion, and, whenever it occurred, was found a treasure to society; for he was the leader of cotillons,[42] the example of fashion, and the oracle of etiquette.

The company who now waited for him at his brother's house, began to appear tired. The gentlemen had finished the politics of the day, and the ladies had discussed the subject of the opera; besides having descanted for a considerable time on the complexion, features, age, person, voice, and manners of a young lady, who had the week before made a great marriage, to which the Hon. Miss C—'s insisted she had not the smallest pretension. Fashionable conversation is not very extensive: it goes on rapidly for a while, in a certain routine of topics, and reminds us of our street-musicians, who, by turning a screw, produce a set of tunes on the hand-organ; but when they have gone through a limited number, the instrument will do no more, and the performer hastens to a distant street, where the same sounds may be repeated to a new set of auditors.

Mr. Seymour, with some displeasure, rang the bell for dinner, and at that moment Mr. Charles Seymour was announced. He heard with the most polite non-chalance, that he had kept the company waiting, muttering however something between his teeth of his having been particularly hurried that morning.

The conversation at dinner opened a new fund of knowledge to Julia. She found that among the fashionable world eating had become a science. The gentlemen were all skilled in the complicated art of cookery, talked in a decisive tone of the proper flavour of every dish, discriminated with the nicest accuracy the different ingredients of the sauces, devoured each other's remarks with 'greedy ear,' and seemed to take as much heart-felt satisfaction in the delineation of a ragoût,[43] as 'if to live well, meant nothing but to eat.'

The ladies left a dissertation on French wines unfinished, and returned to the drawing-room. Mrs. Seymour ordered coffee, and the gentlemen soon followed. Mr. Seymour, who was much charmed with Julia, though he had no leisure for admiration at dinner, began a conversation with her, which she found extremely agreeable, and which promised her some compensation for all she had heard of ragoûts, and French wines;[44] but which was almost immediately interrupted by the arrival of Mrs. Melbourne's carriage; who instantly hurried away to a card-assembly, followed by Charlotte and Julia, who, as she went down stairs, could not help repeating to herself, with the author of the Epistle to Spleen,

'Defend us, ye kind gods! tho' sinners,
From many days like this, or dinners.'[45]

The week following, Mrs. Seymour gave a dance. The splendor of the apartments, elegantly decorated, and illuminated; the gaiety of the company, the chearfulness of music, and the animation of dancing, were all highly delightful to Julia, to whom such scenes had the charm of novelty. She was much admired, and was asked to dance by some young men of rank, whom the Hon. Miss C—'s had in their own minds appropriated to themselves. This was at once so mortifying, and so strange, that the Miss C—'s wished there were no such entertainment as a ball; or at least, that the men had no such impertinent privilege as a choice of partners, since they were so apt to chuse ill, and make the evening disagreeable. Envy is a malignant enchanter, who, when benignant genii[46] have scattered flowers in profusion over the path of the traveller, waves his evil rod, and converts the scene of fertility into a desart.

Mr. F—, the gentleman who paid Julia the most marked attention, was a man of family and fortune, as well as of considerable talents; and was a particular favourite with Mrs. Seymour, who valued superior abilities when they were united with fortune, and could be found within that fashionable circle, beyond the limits of which no promise of intellectual enjoyment could have tempted her to stray; for she could perceive no beauty in the gems of wit or fancy, unless their light was thrown from a particular situation, and blended with the lustre of wealth. Mr. F— was intirely occupied by Julia, and perfectly insensible of Mrs. Seymour's mortification; who secretly resolved not to invite that young lady the next time she gave a dance. She came frequently to that part of the room where Julia was sitting, and spoke to her oftener than was necessary, when so large a company required her attention. She tried to catch the tone of Mr. F—'s mind, advanced with a pensive air when she saw him look serious, and dressed her face in smiles when she observed that he was conversing with gaiety. These transitions she performed with admirable skill; but, far from producing the effect she desired, they were not even observed by the person to whom they were directed. With inexpressible chagrin she perceived, that when Julia danced with any other person, Mr. F— sat down and contemplated her figure. Mrs. Seymour felt the tears of vexation fill her eyes; she had never met with any incident so provoking; there is surely, thought she, a perverse and contradictive spirit in man, which makes the whole sex odious. Any evening but this, she would have forgiven Mr. F—; but to choose her own ball-room for the theatre of her mortification, was refining on ill-nature. Any evening but this, she would have attributed his preference of Julia to some neglect of her own person; an unbecoming cap, or too pale a ribbon: but on this occasion there was no such refuge for her vanity; for she was dressed with the most studied elegance, and rouged with the most careful delicacy. She recalled the general idea of her own figure in the looking-glass after the labours of the toilet were finished, and found no room for self-reproach on account of inattention to her appearance. Her retentive memory then traced each particular part of her dress, the posture of every curl, the arrangement of every flower, and the flow of every feather, and found no subject of dissatisfaction even in this minute retrospection. She well remembered that no toil had been omitted, no time had been spared, nothing overlooked, or unfinished:

her aim had been perfection, and her efforts were proportionably arduous to attain it. She determined, however, to hide her real sensations under the appearance of particular gaiety: she danced continually, and laughed excessively whenever she came within sight or hearing of Mr. F—, though she would much rather have cried, if she had thought crying would have suited her purpose as well.

Whenever Miss C— was not asked to dance by a man of fashion, she suddenly grew tired, and chose to sit down; where she remained with inquietude in her looks, and spite in her conversation. What so wretched as a neglected beauty of the *ton*, when the gay images of coronets, titles, and equipages, which have long floated in her imagination, and seemed within her grasp, at length vanish, as the luxuriant colours of an evening sky fade by degrees into the sadness of twilight? Her feelings are more acute than those of a losing gamester, as she is compelled in secret to acknowledge some deficiency in her own powers of attraction, to cast an oblique reflection on nature, as well as fortune, and has no hope of retrieving her disappointments, since the fairies have long ago used every drop of that precious water which could renew expiring beauty.

Miss C— was seated for a short time next Julia, and began to relate anecdotes to the disadvantage of some of the company present, with whom she appeared to be on a footing of great cordiality: anecdotes of this kind she was careful to collect, and happy not merely to detail but embellish. This lady had some powers of ridicule, and could sprinkle over her discourse a little smart repartee, which many people mistook for talents. She delighted to play at quart and tierce[47] in conversation; but her weapons were very blunt, compared to the fine-edged instruments of genuine wit. Julia, however, made it an invariable rule, not only never to speak slander, but never to listen to it. She considered it as one of those poisons, which not only corrode the frame they touch, but whose subtile venom infects the purity of the surrounding air: she therefore fled from such communication with disgust, and obliged Miss C— to go in search of a more willing auditor.[48]

Mr. Charles Seymour danced with the Miss C—'s most indefatigably, went with unwearied perseverance from one sister to the other, and divided his attentions between them with most exact propriety; repeated to each of them all the fashionable cant he had acquired; laughed when they laughed, and was of the same opinion with them on every subject; muttering every syllable with his teeth almost closed, and his face as close to his fair partners as propriety would admit. When he had fulfilled his duty to the Miss C—'s, he deliberated with himself upon the next object of his choice, which required a little reflection. Mr. Charles Seymour admired beauty, but he was one of those prudent young men, who are too well trained in the school of the world, to be the dupes of any tender sensibility. He chose his partners at a dance by other rules than the proportion of their features, or the grace of their persons: the darts poured from bright eyes fell blunted on his heart, unless the fair object had the more solid recommendation of fortune. To such only he devoted his gallantry; for even when he had no particular view of engaging their regard, he considered their acquaintance as useful, and their favour as tending towards the accomplishment of his ultimate aim in life, which was to acquire distinction, and obtain interest in the fashionable world.

Charlotte had the prospect of a larger fortune than any young woman at the dance, but then it depended on certain contingencies. The other young women had their property in possession. Mr. Charles Seymour, after making a hasty calculation of the difference between a hundred thousand pounds at Bengal, and ten thousand in the bank of England-after gliding in imagination over the boundless ocean through which the gold must pass, considering the stormy Cape which must be doubled, and the 'moving accidents by flood and field'[49] which must be hazarded[50] – at length recollected how much eastern gold had happily surmounted these perils, and, without farther deliberation, decided in favour of Charlotte. He endeavoured to entertain her in the same manner he had done the Miss C—'s; but Charlotte was equally insensible to all his fashionable grimace, and indifferent to his conversation. She had, indeed, the happiest face of the whole group; pleasure and exultation sparkled in her eyes. Her manner of thinking on the subject of a ball was entirely different from that of the Hon. Miss C—'s: Charlotte loved dancing for its own sake, and without any other care about her partner than that he did not put her out in the figure. She allowed herself no interval of rest; for she was never so fully convinced of the value of time as at a ball, where she thought not one moment was given to be lost, and pursued her favourite occupation with a degree of delight, of which one must have the extreme youth, the gay spirits, and light heart of Charlotte to judge.

Julia, who frequently sat down, heard several of the gentlemen complain pathetically to each other of the hardships of dancing, and enumerate the succession of private balls, which hung over their future evenings like a cloud. Mr. Charles Seymour avoided Julia carefully the whole evening, lest he should be under the necessity of asking her to dance: but when he saw her preparing to go away, he seated himself next her, muttering between his teeth, 'Miss Clifford, you come *so* late, and go away *so* soon!' – adding, how beautiful she looked that evening, how much her head-dress became her, and how cruel she was to bury such a figure in the country. – Julia heard him with a degree of contempt, which she had too much sweetness to display; but his conversation ever appeared to her of such a barren nature, that she considered listening to it like travelling over sands, and left him almost immediately; which was no less a relief to him than to herself. Julia had that evening received much entertainment from Mr. Seymour's conversation, who paid her great attention, and was endued with the powers of pleasing in a very eminent degree.

# CHAP. V.

Mr. Seymour, who was possessed of considerable talents, and great taste for literature, was brilliant in conversation. His person was elegant, and his manners frank and agreeable. He had a perfect knowledge of the world, and great penetration into character; but his ambition was boundless; and his constant aim was his own aggrandizement: he courted people of rank and influence with admirable address; and, under an appearance of infinite candour and plainness, was no common flatterer, who sets about his business in a clumsy way, and discovers his own secret. He had judgement enough to appreciate the understanding of others with nicety, and always began his operations like a wise general, by an attack on the weak side. Mr. Seymour lived in a continual plot against the rest of his species – he regarded men and women as puppets moved by various springs, which he understood perfectly how to govern, and which he could touch so skilfully, that wisdom was over-reached as well as folly. His schemes were crowned with success, and he obtained a considerable post under government: yet his pride and selfishness were still unsatisfied. He had married Miss Melbourne, whose person he did not admire, and whose character he disliked, because she had twenty thousand pounds. No man could talk with more energy of the virtues of generosity and disinterestedness than Mr. Seymour; and this not with an appearance of ostentation, but as if friendship and universal good-will were the genuine feelings of his soul. Yet, while he thus descanted on benevolence, he concealed a mind, the sole view of which was self-interest; and sometimes reminded those who knew his real character, of a swan gracefully expanding his plumes of purest whiteness to the winds, and carefully hiding his black feet beneath another element. Mr. Seymour possessed strong feelings, and his heart was capable of tenderness; but ambition, and long commerce with the world, had almost entirely blunted his sensibility; and, to the few persons for whom he still felt some affection, he would not have rendered any service, however essential to their interest, which could in the smallest possible degree ever interfere with his own. His friendship was only to be procured by bestowing favours upon him, or at least by not requiring any at his hands: to ask for such proofs of his regard was to forfeit it altogether. Every acquaintance he made was with some interested view: he had no associates among the companions of his youth, except those who, like himself, had been prosperous in the career of life: the unfortunate he left where misfortune had placed them, and shunned all intercourse with them carefully. He treated Mrs. Seymour with decent attention; but he was a man of gallantry, and made love[51] to every woman who had the attraction of youth and beauty; and Mrs. Seymour, when she thought the heroics would become her, acted a fit of jealousy admirably; complained in pathetic terms of his indifference; lamented her hard fate in not having met with a congenial soul, and in being subject to have her exquisite sensibility so cruelly wounded. From such complaints he fled with disgust and aversion, and took refuge in company, where he contributed too much to the general entertainment not to be received with pleasure.

Julia, after spending a few days more in town, left it with little regret; for, tho' she was convinced that London furnished a more enlarged and liberal society, and more elegant amusements, than could be met with elsewhere, the manner in which she had passed her time was not at all suited to her taste. The mornings had been generally devoted to shopping and dress, and the evenings to card-assemblies. Mrs. Seymour loved to range from one milliner's to another; and at first Julia was diverted with the serious air with which a cap is recommended, the contemplative spirit with which the complexion and the ribbon are compared; while she observed the particular good-humour of the handsome, who found every thing they tried becoming, and the discontent of the ugly, who quarrelled with the head-dress instead of the face: but the good-humour, and the discontent, became at length equally tiresome to Julia. She also found that the pleasures of card-assemblies were like fairy gold, which, when touched by a vulgar hand, turns to dust, and could only be enjoyed by people of *ton*; while to her, who had acquired no knowledge of cards, and no passion for a crowd, such meetings were extremely wearisome. At these assemblies she was introduced to some persons who had the reputation of wit and talents; but of their pretensions to either she had no opportunity of judging, since their conversation, to which she listened with avidity, was continually interrupted by some movement of the crowd, or some call to the card-table. She therefore found that understanding was of no current value at a card-assembly, except to serve the purpose of applying the rules of whist,[52] a science for which her country education had taught her but little reverence.

This young lady lamented nothing so much in leaving London, as her separation from Charlotte; for she found that the joys of dissipation are like gaudy colours, which for a moment attract the sight, but soon fatigue and oppress it; while the satisfactions of home resemble the green robe of nature, on which the eye loves to rest, and to which it always returns with a sensation of delight.

# CHAP. VI.

It has been mentioned, that Captain Clifford's father made a part of his family. This old man, who was heir to an estate which had descended to him through a long line of ancestors, had received a very liberal education, was possessed of a good understanding, and a most benevolent heart. In truth, his liberality was carried to excess, and he practised that profuse hospitality which was the fashion of the last century. Every guest was received at his house with the welcome of ancient times, and both his purse and his table were open to all those whose necessities seemed to claim his assistance.

His estate was a little incumbered, when he came to the possession of it. He had engaged early in a military life, and served long abroad, while his affairs were left too much to the management of his wife, a woman of unbounded vanity, who vied in expence with families possessed of much larger estates. She died suddenly, in the absence of her husband; who, at his return from Germany, found that her debts were numerous, and that he had lost a very considerable sum, for which, in the confidence of unsuspicious friendship, he became answerable for one, whose principles he considered as no less honourable than his own. He was undeceived too late. The world will blame his imprudence, and think he deserved to suffer from it: but, while foresight and policy are so common, let us forgive those few minds of trusting simplicity, who are taught in vain the lesson of suspicion, on whom impressions are easily made, and who think better of human nature than it deserves. Such persons are for the most part sufficiently punished for their venial error, as was the case with Mr. Clifford, who was forced to extricate himself from the difficulties in which he was involved by the sale of his paternal inheritance.

With a degree of anguish which can be better felt than described, he had quitted for ever a spot endeared to him by every tie of local attachment, and every feeling of family pride. He flew for refuge to his son, and implored his forgiveness of the wrongs he had done him: he was received with all the tenderness of filial regard. Captain Clifford studied, by the most delicate attentions, to soften the gloom and despondency of his father's mind: and at length the old man became soothed into a less painful recollection of the past, though at times it wrung his heart with sorrow.

The endearments of his grand-daughter, who had then reached her seventh year, gave him a pleasure mingled with sadness; and often, when she climbed upon his knees, the old man's tears would fall upon her face; for age had not yet dried their source. Yet his temper was naturally cheerful, and in happier moments he would sing to her some of his old songs, or tell her some marvellous story; and, when she was old enough to listen to the tale of his battles in Germany, he 'shewed how fields were won.'[53] Nor was he ever so eloquent as when he gave these descriptions: his language became animated, his martial enthusiasm revived, and all the misfortunes of his past life were absorbed in the gratifying recollection of having served his king and country.

This old man had infinite benevolence and sweetness of disposition, and was one of those few aged persons who rejoice in the happiness of the young. To witness the mirth and gaiety of youth, was to him a renovation of those scenes 'where once his careless childhood strayed, a stranger yet to pain.'[54] In consequence of this disposition, he was adored by Julia, and beloved by all her companions. As she grew up, she was ever ready to sacrifice every wish, and every pleasure, to his ease and comfort. She would leave with alacrity a circle of company where she was happy, to return home, and read for an hour to her grandfather in the old family bible, with a long exposition; of which he liked to hear a portion every evening. I think I see her at this moment; her chair drawn quite close to his, and her voice raised, because he heard with difficulty. I see the old man, placed in his crimson-damask chair, dressed in his long green gown, and white night-cap, listening to her with a sort of elevation in his look, and sometimes assenting to an affecting passage by the lifting up of his hands, and a movement of his lips in a short ejaculation. When she had done reading, she always stayed to converse with him a little; and, when she saw him quite cheerful, she bid him good night, and received a kiss, and a blessing.

This old man, who had kept the best company in his youth, had much of the old-fashioned politeness. The forms of ancient ceremony must have been burdensome in the intercourse of society; yet in an old person this kind of manner still appears respectable. We are charmed with the light and graceful accompaniments with which the taste of Brown[55] has decorated our modern villas, and rejoice that each alley has no more 'a brother:' but when we visit an ancient mansion, who can wish that its long avenues of venerable trees, sanctified by age, and their connection with the days of former years, and the generations that are past, should feel the destroying axe, and give place to new improvements?[56]

The old man had a taste for flowers, which he cultivated with great assiduity, and which he planted, with all the variety he could procure, round the borders of a little lawn before the house. A green slope led from the lawn to the river Thames: one solitary willow-tree grew at the top of this bank. The old man had a seat made for himself under the shade of this tree. There he delighted to sit, and contemplate the green banks of the opposite shore – the reflected landscape in the stream – the gentle motion of the current – the sun-beams playing on the waters – the long-necked swans gliding majestically by, unless tempted towards the bank by the crumbs with which he fed them – the black-bird's sweet and various note, in some neighbouring trees, sometimes interrupted by the thrush or the linnet[57] – the boats which were passing continually, and added chearfulness and animation to the picture.

The old man was visited every Saturday morning by a set of pensioners, to each of whom he gave a small weekly allowance. He had not much to give; yet he denied himself some indulgences his age required, to bestow that little; which, however trifling, was sufficient to procure some additional comfort to the receivers. The luxuries of the poor are not expensive, and the rich can make them happy by parting with so little, that it can scarcely be termed a privation. This benevolent old man felt charity less a duty than a pleasure. He might have made the same appeal to Heaven which was made by Job, 'if I have eaten my morsel myself alone, and the fatherless hath not eaten thereof,'[58] without danger of incurring the forfeiture. He felt none of that admiration of himself which the selfish feel when they perform a kind action; for he could perceive little merit in exertions which were attended with the most sweet and exquisite satisfaction. That kindness which flows from the heart, is like a clear stream, that pours its full and rapid current cheerfully along, for ever unobstructed in its course; while those acts of beneficence, which are performed with reluctance, resemble shallow waters supplied by a muddy fountain, retarded in their noisy progress by every pebble, dried by heat, and frozen by cold. This old man's chief source of happiness was drawn from religion. His devotion was more than habitual; for his mind had attained that state in which reflection is but a kind of mental prayer; and every object around him was to him a subject of adoration, and a motive for gratitude. Praise flowed from his lips like those natural melodies, to which the ear has long been accustomed, and which the voice delights to call forth.

The contemplation of a venerable old man sinking thus gently into the arms of death, supported by filial affection, and animated by religious hope, excites a serious yet not unpleasing sensation. When the gay and busy scenes of life are past, and the years advance which 'have no pleasure in them,'[59] what is left for age to wish, but that its infirmities may be soothed by the watchful solicitude of tenderness, and its darkness cheered by a ray of that light 'which cometh from above?'[60] To such persons life, even in its last stage, is still agreeable. They do not droop like those flowers, which, when their vigour is past, lose at once their beauty and their fragrance; but have more affinity to the fading rose, which, when its enchanting colours are fled, still retains its exhilarating sweetness, and is loved and cherished even in decay.

# CHAP. VII.

Verses were sometimes composed by Julia, merely to amuse her grandfather; who used to read them with a degree of satisfaction, which may, perhaps, be pardoned from the consideration that the writer was his grand-daughter. Affection is generally supposed to blind the judgment; and if so, she probably throws one of her thickest bandages across the critical taste of a grandfather, while he is perusing the productions of one, who is the darling of his age, the joy of his eyes, and the soother of his infirmities.

Julia was walking one morning upon the lawn before the house, when she saw a black cat seize a linnet that was perched upon a neighbouring tree, and to whose song she had been listening. She made an exclamation, which brought a maid-servant to the door; Julia pointed eagerly to the black cat; upon which the maid instantly ran, and, seizing the animal with great intrepidity, rescued the linnet from its gripe. After breakfast Julia scrawled the following lines upon this incident.

## *The* LINNET

When fading Autumn's latest hours
Strip the brown wood, and chill the flowers;
When Evening, wintry, short, and pale,
Expires in many an hollow gale;
And only Morn herself looks gay,
When first she throws her quiv'ring ray
Where the light frost congeals the dew,
Flushing the turf with purple hue;
Gay bloom, whose transient glow can shed
A charm like Summer, when 'tis fled!
A Linnet, among leafless trees,
Sung, in the pauses of the breeze,
His farewell note, to fancy dear,
That ends the music of the year.
The short'ning day, the sad'ning sky,
With frost and famine low'ring nigh,
The summer's dirge he seemed to sing,
And droop'd his elegiac wing.
Poor bird! he read amiss his fate,
Nor saw the horrors of his state.

A prowling cat, with jetty skin,
Dark emblem of the mind within,
Who feels no sympathetic pain,
Who hears, unmov'd, the sweetest strain,
Quite 'fit for stratagem and spoil,'[61]
Mischief his pleasure and his toil,
Drew near – and shook the wither'd leaves –
The linnet's flutt'ring bosom heaves –
Alarm'd he hears the rustling sound,
He starts – he pauses – looks around –
Too late – more near the savage draws,
And grasps the victim in his jaws.
The linnet's muse, a tim'rous maid,
Saw, and to Molly** scream'd for aid;
A tear then fill'd her earnest eye,
Useless as dews on desarts lie:
But Molly's pity fell like showers
That feed the plants and wake the flowers:
Heroic Molly dauntless flew,
And, scorning all his claws could do,
Snatch'd from Grimalkin's teeth his prey,
And bore him in her breast away.
His beating heart, and wings, declare
How small his hope of safety there:
Still the dire foe he seem'd to see,
And scarce could fancy he was free.
A while he cowr'd on Molly's breast,
Then upward sprang and sought his nest.
Dear Molly! For thy tender speed,
Thy fearless pity's gentle deed,
My purple gown, still bright and clear,
And meant to last another year;
That purple lutestring I decree,
With yellow knots, a gift to thee;
The well-earn'd prize, at Whitsun'-fair,[62]
Shalt thou, lov'd maid, in triumph wear;
And may the graceful dress obtain
The youth thy heart desires to gain.
And thou, sweet bird, whom rapture fills,
Who feel'st no sense of future ills;
That sense which human peace destroys,
And murders all our present joys,
Still sooth with song th' autumnal hours:
And, when the wintry tempest low'rs,
When snow thy shiv'ring plumes shall fill,
And icicles shall load thy bill,

* A maid-servant. (Williams's note)

Come fearless to my friendly shed,
This careful hand the crumbs shall spread;
Then peck secure, these watchful eyes
Shall guard my linnet from surprize.

# CHAP. VIII.

Mr. Clifford returned from the East Indies, and had the satisfaction of reaching England time enough to see his father again. – The old man had almost despaired of this meeting. He threw his arms round his son's neck, and embraced him for a considerable time in silence. When he was able to speak, he said to him, in the words of Jacob, for the language of scripture was familiar to him, 'Now let me die, since I have seen thy face, because thou art yet alive!'[63] – This happy family experienced those delightful sensations in each other's society, which can only be felt after long absence. Our affections are not constantly active, they are called forth by circumstances; and what can awaken them so forcibly, as the renewal of those domestic endearments which constitute the charm of our existence?

Mr. Clifford returned with an ample fortune, and without one subject of self-reproach to embitter the enjoyment of it. He induced the person who was in possession of the old family estate to part with it, by giving him a price beyond its value. This event seemed a renovation of life to the good old man; who expressed so earnest a desire to end his days in that beloved spot, that his sons determined to remove him thither by slow and easy journies.

He was accompanied, like the patriarch of old,[64] by his children and grandchildren. When they reached the summit of a hill which gave him the first view of his paternal mansion, he ordered the postilions[65] to stop; and gazed upon the scene before him with a sort of elevation in his look, which shewed that his mind was in intercourse with heaven.

As he descended the hill, he saw his tenants coming out to meet him. – The women brought their infants in their arms to receive his blessing, and the old men crawled to the side of the chaise as well as they could, and blessed God that they had lived to see their old master again. – His heart was too full for speech; but he pointed to his two lovely grand-daughters, whose eyes were suffused in tears, and at length told the people, in a broken voice, that he had brought those treasures to make them happy. Amidst blessings and acclamations, this welcome retinue reached the family-seat. The tenants were feasted in the hall; the ale flowed liberally; nothing was heard but the voice of rejoicing: and the Vicar of Wakefield,[66] who had a taste for happy human faces, would have found this a charming spectacle.

The old mansion, which was seated on the side of a hill, was embosomed in trees; and the landscape around it exhibited the most picturesque variety.[67] The house commanded a view of the celebrated lake of –; its boundaries in some places frowning in a series of rude broken crags and rocky promontories, and in others rising into verdant hills, richly wooded to the edge of the water. The sound of a cataract, which precipitated itself into the lake, was heard, and its foam was seen at a distance. A hanging wood,[68] planted on a part of the same hill where the house stood, threw the most venerable shade from its old majestic trees. – A wild irregular path led from the mansion to a deep glen, which opened into a vale where the little village of – is built. Its small white spire rises above the straw hamlets, and a clear winding rivulet wanders through this sweet tranquil vale; which is encompassed by mountains, some of whose tops are covered with snow, and some darkened by the clouds that rest upon them. The contrast between this cultivated valley, and its savage boundaries, was so striking, that it seemed like Beauty reposing in the arms of Horror,[69] and sheltered in its safe retreat from the tempests which spent their force above.

The old furniture, which had been placed in Mr. Clifford's paternal mansion, by his ancestors, still remained; for, the gentleman who had purchased the estate dying soon after, his son, a gay and dissipated young man, had never visited the place but once, when he came to take possession of it upon the death of his father, and had made no alterations.

The walls of the larger apartments were still hung with rich tapestry, on some of which was represented Calypso's enchanted island, where the blooming Telemachus stood ardently gazing on the nymphs, regardless of the frown of the venerable Mentor.[70] Some of the hangings displayed the defeat of the Spanish armada, and the taking of Cadiz, by the Earl of Essex.[71] Many tales of other times were related on the ancient walls; but on some the colours were so faded, and the action so defaced, that all that could be perceived was a half-seen figure, or a face that dimly glared from the pale groundwork, or an arm that seemed stretched out in defiance.

The great stair-case, and the floors of the state apartments, which were of oak, and had been rubbed with careful diligence for the reception of the family, shone bright as a mirror, and occasioned many a false step to the London servants, who were unused to such slippery treading. The broad and immoveable chairs of the state-rooms, holding forth their gigantic arms, seemed calculated for beings of a larger make than the present race of mortals; and these massy chairs were covered with damask so rich and durable, that it appeared to have been made for the use of the antediluvian ages.[72]

A long gallery on the first floor was hung with the portraits of the Clifford family, in antique dresses, with bushy beards, great scymetars,[73] short whiskers, and stiff ruffs; and placed in heavy gilt frames: a collection which, at a sale of pictures, would perhaps have sold no better than aunt Deborah and her flock of sheep. But the venerable owner of the mansion felt as great a respect for his ancestors, as Sir Oliver himself.[74]

Mr. Clifford had too much pride in his family to remove any marks of its ancient magnificence. He left, therefore, the tapestry, the massy chairs, and the family pictures, undisturbed, as useless but proud monuments of antiquity, in the back-ground of his apartments, while he took care to bring forward all the comforts and conveniences of modern luxury.

On the evening of their arrival at the family seat, Julia walked out with Charlotte, and felt, with particular sensibility, the beauties of nature. She had, till now, only seen the rich cultivated landscapes of the south of England; but her ardent imagination had often wandered amidst the wild scenery of the north, and formed a high idea of pleasure in contemplating its solemn aspect; and she found that the sublime and awful graces of nature exceed even the dream of fancy.[75] The setting sun painted the glowing horizon with the most refulgent colours: immediately above its broad orb, which was dazzling in brightness, hung a black cloud that formed a striking contrast to the luxuriant tints below: some of the hills were thrown into deep shadow, others reflected the setting beams. When the sun sunk below the horizon, every object gradually changed its hue. The form of the surrounding hills, and the shape of the darkening rocks that hung over the lake, became every moment more doubtful; till at length twilight spread over the whole landscape that pensive gloom so soothing to an enthusiastic[76] fancy. Every other sound was lost in the fall of the torrent, a sound which Julia had never heard before, and which seemed to strike upon her soul, and call forth emotions congenial to its solemn cadence.[77]

The moon now arose clear and lovely above the dark hills, with a circle of unusual lustre round her orb: the beams suddenly spread their light over the whole lake, except where long deep lines of shadow were thrown from the rocks on its surface. Julia gazed upon the objects which surrounded her with a transport of mind which she had never felt before. She uttered frequent exclamations of admiration and wonder; but she found it impossible to express the sensations with which her soul was overwhelmed. It is in such moments as these that the soul becomes conscious of her native dignity: we seem to be brought nearer to the Deity; we feel the sense of his sacred presence; the low-minded cares of earth vanish; we view all nature beaming with benignity, and with beauty; and we repose with divine confidence on him, who has thus embellished his creation. In the country, the mind borrows virtue from the scene. When we tread the lofty mountain, when the ample lake spreads its broad expanse of waters to our view, when we listen to the fall of the torrent, the awed and astonished mind is raised above the temptations of guilt;[78] and when we wander amid the softer scenes of nature, the charms of the landscape, the song of the birds, the mildness of the breeze, and the murmurs of the stream, sooth the passions into peace, excite the most gentle emotions,[79] and have power to cure 'all sadness but despair.'[80] 'Can man forbear to smile with nature? Can the stormy passions in his bosom roll, while every gale is peace, and every grove is melody?'[81]

A whole summer passed delightfully to the happy inhabitants of Mr. Clifford's hospitable mansion. He employed himself in arranging his affairs, redressing the grievances of which his tenants complained, and assisting such as wanted his assistance.

His brother consented to live with him; and Mr. Clifford, without his knowledge, settled five hundred pounds a year upon him for life, by a deed so framed, that it was not in his own power to revoke it. He also bound himself to give Julia ten thousand pounds at the death of her father. When the deed was executed according to all the forms of law, Mr. Clifford presented it to his brother in a manner too delicate to wound his pride, and too tender not to gratify his affection.

The happiness of this domestic circle was interrupted by the bad health of Mr. Clifford. His constitution had suffered materially from a hot climate, and his increasing complaints obliged him to go to Bath;[82] which, however, failed to produce any salutary effects. His physicians thought him unable to bear the severity of the approaching winter in this country, and he was ordered to Nice.[83] With this advice he reluctantly complied; and, before he set out for the continent, took a journey to the north, to embrace his father once more; whom he left to the care of his brother and Julia, and took Charlotte with him abroad.

The old man, who did not long survive the departure of his son, in his dying hour expressed his satisfaction at the thoughts of being buried in the tomb of his fathers: so true it is, that, 'even from the tomb the voice of nature cries, even in our ashes live their wonted fires!'[84] He expired calmly, and without a groan; nor could those who witnessed the pious resignation of his last moments, avoid wishing 'to die the death of the righteous, and that their latter end might be like his!'[85]

His corpse was attended to the place of interment by a long procession of his tenants, who hung over his grave as if unwilling to leave it; while the old recounted to the young, all they remembered of his childhood and his youth.

Mr. Clifford received at Nice the intelligence of his father's death, and felt the most sensible regret at not having been present to perform the last duties to his venerable parent. He wrote to his brother, requesting that he and Julia would prepare for a journey to Nice early in the spring; as he himself intended to visit Italy, and wished for the gratification of their society on his tour.

Mean while Mr. Clifford, after two months residence at Nice, found his health so well established, that he went from that place to pass some time at Avignon.[86] He there met with Mr. Frederick Seymour, the second brother of Mr. Seymour, who had been sent abroad as secretary to the embassy at —, where he had remained some years. When the ambassador was recalled, Mr. Frederick Seymour was invited to make the tour of France and Italy[87] with a friend, and was on his way to Rome when he became acquainted with Mr. Clifford and Charlotte, neither of whom he had before seen; for Mr. Seymour's acquaintance and marriage with Miss Melbourne had taken place some time after Mr. Frederick Seymour's departure.

This young man was of a different character from either of his brothers, and superior to both. He possessed the elevated understanding, and the fine taste, for which his elder brother was conspicuous; and he had also that love of distinction which belongs to a man of parts and spirit; but his ambition was of that nobler kind, which pursues its ends fairly, openly, and honourably. Equally incapable of the deep-laid plots of one brother, and the little artifices of the other, Mr. Frederick Seymour disdained to tread in the serpentine paths of duplicity and cunning; and his character was strongly marked by an impatience of every thing mean, selfish, or sordid. – His early intercourse with the world had not chilled that enthusiasm which is awake to every generous impression, and that warmth of feeling which long continues to animate an ardent mind, and which, in some, the disappointment of their dearest hopes, the experience of the coldness and selfishness of mankind, and even the chilling hand of age itself, have no power to repress. The noble principles which actuated Seymour's mind, gave it additional force and vigour. It will ever be found that great talents derive new energy from the virtue of the character; as when the sun-beam plays upon gems, it calls forth all their scattered radiance. Mr. Frederick Seymour's person was tall and elegant; his eyes were dark, and his countenance was strongly expressive of intelligence and sensibility. His conversation was highly agreeable, and his manners were infinitely engaging; and his good understanding had taught him to connect the polish of fashion, with plainness and simplicity. He had acquired ease without negligence, and frankness without familiarity. Perfect good-breeding undoubtedly requires the foundation of good sense; as the oak, which is the most solid and valuable, is also the most graceful tree of the forest.

Charlotte was constantly in Mr. Seymour's society, and she soon felt its powers of fascination. In the mornings they rode out in little parties, amidst scenes the most lovely and romantic. They often visited the fountain of Vaucluse,[88] and Mr. Seymour still appeared to find inspiration in its waters. He composed sonnets,[89] which Charlotte read with pleasure; he pointed out the beauties of the scenes they visited, or traced them with his pencil; and Charlotte gazed on them with delight. He perceived her prepossession in his favour, and was solicitous to improve her partiality. The sweetness and vivacity of her disposition, the simplicity of her manners, and the purity of her heart, formed a contrast to the vanity and levity of many young women in the gay circle of Avignon, very favourable to Charlotte.

# CHAP. IX.

Captain Clifford and his daughter passed the months, previous to their intended journey, in a retirement which was cheared by books, by music, and, above all, by the pleasures of benevolence. Julia rejoiced in the possession of fortune, because she could now indulge the feelings of compassion. She was no longer subject to the pain of flying from distress, which she was unable to relieve: she remembered how often her eyes, wet with tears, had been lifted up to heaven, and implored that she might one day have the power of comforting the afflicted! Her prayer had been accepted, the days of affluence were arrived, and they were devoted to the purposes of benevolence.

Julia spread a little circle of happiness around her. She had too that soothing charm in her manner, which proceeds from the most delicate attention to the feelings of others: she bestowed her alms with that gentleness and sympathy, by which the value of her donations was increased, and her pity was almost as dear to the poor as her charity.

Meantime, Mr. Clifford, though not very quick in penetration, at length discerned his daughter's partiality for Mr. Frederick Seymour, whose talents he admired, and whose character he esteemed. This indulgent father, contrary to every established rule in such cases, determined to make his daughter happy her own way. He suffered her to listen to Seymour's addresses, and consented to her marrying the object of her choice, on her return to England the following summer.

They now only waited for the arrival of Captain Clifford and Julia, in order to set out for Rome; when Mr. Clifford received the following letter from Julia.

To William Clifford, Esq.
Avignon.

My dearest Uncle,
I write to you with a degree of anguish, which renders me almost incapable of holding my pen. Last week I was all joy and exultation, at the thoughts of our journey to Avignon – Alas, those dreams of happiness have vanished for ever! My father was, three days ago, prevailed on by Mr. B— to join a hunting party. The chace was uncommonly long, and my father returned almost overcome with fatigue. We sat down to dinner, but he had scarcely eaten a morsel before he was seized with a violent vomiting of blood. I sent instantly for the Surgeon at — He arrived in half an hour, and declared that my father had burst a blood-vessel. He was put to bed, where he lay almost insen-

sible. The next morning he was somewhat better, but in the evening he spit a great quantity of blood; and the Surgeon has this day acknowledged to me, that, though my father may linger some weeks, he has no hope of his recovery. Oh my father! My ever-dearest father! How will your wretched child survive your loss? Oh, may Heaven but enable me to perform the last sad duties, and then suffer one grave to hold us! – He is sensible of his approaching dissolution, and seems to have no wish, in this world, but to see you once more. Come then, my dearest uncle, and receive his dying embrace! Hasten to him, before he is insensible of this last mark of your tenderness. Remember me to my dear Charlotte; she will pity the sufferings of JULIA CLIFFORD.

Mr. Clifford did not hesitate a moment in obeying the mandate contained in this melancholy letter: he and Charlotte left Avignon that night, in their way to England – Mr. Frederick Seymour wished to accompany them, but this they would not allow. He, however, obtained their consent to follow them in a short time to England; and Charlotte promised to write to him, on her arrival at home, and inform him of the situation of her uncle.

Mr. Clifford had the melancholy consolation of reaching home time enough to see his beloved brother once more. He found Captain Clifford in a state of great composure of mind. He talked with resignation of his approaching dissolution, and exerted all the little strength he had left in comforting his friends: he told them he felt the most firm persuasion that they should meet again in a better region, never more to feel the pang of separation. He then made Julia unloose a ribbon from his neck, to which was fixed a locket that hung upon his breast, and which contained some of his wife's hair – He desired Julia to cut off a little of his own hair, and put it into the locket.[90] He begged that his brother would keep his watch, and Charlotte a ring for his sake. They will serve, added he, as Ophelia says, 'for thoughts, and remembrances.'[91] He then grasped Julia's hand while she knelt at his bedside, and said to her, in a faint voice, 'Compose your mind, my love! you will still have a father in my brother's protection – I leave you to his care – God Almighty bless you, my child – and reward your filial goodness! You have been the comfort of my life – and death has no pang but leaving you! – but we shall meet' – His voice became inarticulate, and in a few minutes he expired. Julia was with difficulty persuaded to forsake the breathless remains of her father: she clung to his corpse in an agony of unutterable sorrow; and in vain Charlotte endeavoured to sooth her affliction; in vain Mr. Clifford attempted to console her by the assurance, that it should be the constant aim of his life to promote her happiness. In the bitterness of her soul, Julia shrunk from these assurances: the last sigh of her father seemed to her the extinction of every earthly hope, and her aching heart refused that happiness which he could no longer participate. – Her father had always treated her as a friend, and her affection for him was unbounded. When she looked back on the past, she recollected, on his part, a constant wish to make her happy; and an uniform gentleness of disposition, which rendered that wish effectual. She could recall no expression of harshness, none of those fits of moroseness, or caprice, notwithstanding which, obedience to a parent still remains a duty, but sometimes ceases to be a pleasure.

In the reflection on her own conduct towards her father, Julia felt the soothing consciousness of having done more than even duty required. She had not only implicitly obeyed every injunction, and complied with every wish of her father; but she had lived in the constant habit of making every sacrifice to his comfort, that the quick sensibility of her own heart could suggest – sacrifices of ease, of convenience, of pleasure, which arose from the confined circumstances of her father; sacrifices, which she carefully concealed from his knowledge, and of which she found the sole reward in her own bosom.

When, at length, the all-subduing influence of time had composed her mind sufficiently to enjoy the beauties of nature, the pleasures of society, and the comforts of affluence, she still frequently lamented, with tears of bitter regret, that her father had not lived to partake longer of those blessings. She reflected, that his life had been the constant struggle of an high and honourable spirit with misfortune, poverty, and neglect: she wept at the recollection of those difficulties in which she had often seen him involved, of those anxieties he had suffered for her sake; and mourned that the hour of prosperity had scarcely arrived, before the object of her pious affection was mouldering in the dust.

The tranquillity she regained, was not like the sweet glow of a summer morning, enlivened by sunshine, and the exulting song of the birds: it had more affinity to the pensive stillness of the evening, when the mildness of the air, and the fading charms of the landscape, excite in the mind a soft and tender sensation, which has a nearer alliance to melancholy than to joy.

# CHAP. X.

A few months after the death of Captain Clifford, his brother invited Mrs. Melbourne, and Mr. and Mrs. Seymour, to spend some time at his country seat, where Mr. Frederick Seymour was soon expected.

Mrs. Melbourne brought with her a young man who was her relation, and for whom she hoped, through Mr. Clifford's interest, to obtain an appointment in the East Indies. She possessed but a very moderate share of benevolence, either in thought, word, or deed, towards the human race in general; but she eagerly embraced this opportunity of providing for her own relation, and placing him above the want of farther assistance from herself.

Lately she had increased her income by a prize of ten thousand pounds in the lottery; but she found the calculation of her own wants increase in the same proportion with her fortune; and in estimating the wants of others, she was less exact in her arithmetic. This lady could hear the complaints of misery with indifference, and see the tears of the unfortunate without stretching out a hand to their assistance; and yet she contrived to live at peace with herself. Soon after her marriage, she had provided for a cousin, who, by the death of both his parents, was thrown entirely upon her protection; and, whenever her heart reproached her with any deficiency of compassion, she instantly called to mind her cousin, and persuaded herself that society had no farther demands on her benevolence.

The young man whom she now brought to Mr. Clifford's house, had lost his father, and his mother was unable to provide for him; but, happily for Mr. Chartres, he was so nearly related to Mrs. Melbourne, that her pride came in as an auxiliary to her benevolence in the determination to promote his fortunes.

Mrs. Melbourne's occasional acts of beneficence, which generally proceeded either from ostentation or fear, resembled those scanty spots of verdure to which a sudden shower will sometimes give birth in a flinty and sterile soil; while pure genuine philanthropy flows like those unseen dews which are only marked in their benign effects, spreading new charms over creation.

Mr. Chartres had been educated by the curate of a small village in Yorkshire, who had taught him Greek, Latin, and mathematics, but had not given him the least knowledge of men and manners, that being a science of which his preceptor was entirely ignorant. At nineteen Mr. Chartres returned to his mother, who had a small house in London. She was a weak vain woman, and, being exceedingly disgusted with her son's awkwardness, and quite incapable of judging of his classical acquisitions, very thankfully resigned him to Mrs. Melbourne, who introduced him in all his native simplicity to Mr. Clifford.

Mr. Chartres was tall and thin, and so perfectly erect, that he had not the smallest tendency towards a bend in his whole figure. His coat was always buttoned quite close, and displayed his shape with great exactness; his complexion was sallow, his aspect[92] solemn, and his black hair hung lank down his shoulders. He had a good understanding, and a warm veneration for literature; but his extreme awkwardness could only be equalled by his simplicity. In the company of strangers he was entirely silent. When longer acquaintance gave him courage to speak, his opinions were found to be respectable, on account of their antiquity: his sentiments were strictly moral; and, though there was no novelty in his ideas, they were generally delivered in a manner peculiar to himself. Chartres had a tender heart, felt the influence of beauty, and wished to show the most devoted attention to the ladies: but whenever he attempted any mark of gallantry, it generally ended in his own disgrace, though he never hazarded any such attempt without mature deliberation; for he was always obliged, previously to the slightest movement he made in company, to call forth all his reasoning faculties, and convince himself that it was unmanly, as well as unphilosophical, to tremble at walking across the room, placing a chair for a lady, or handing her a tea-cup. Yet even after he had settled his plans of courtesy in his own mind, much to his satisfaction, he was apt to mar them by his mode of performance.[93] But we will leave him to struggle with his bashful terrors, and return to Julia.

One evening, when the party assembled at Mr. Clifford's preferred cards to walking, she went out alone, and wandered along the border of the lake; gazing at the majestic scenery around her, which was obscured by twilight, while imagination gave new forms to every half-seen object.[94] On her way home she stopped at a cottage near the house, and, seating herself on a straw chair at the door, patiently listened to the good woman's anecdotes of her poultry.

Julia usually spent two hours every day in teaching the children of the cottagers to read. She had a particular fondness for children, which is an affection very natural to a tender heart; for what is more interesting than the innocence, the helplessness, the endearing simplicity of childhood? – The eldest child of the good woman who loved to talk of her poultry, was a girl of seven years of age, with a ruddy complexion, and auburn ringlets, and was Julia's distinguished favourite. Little Peggy did not, however, owe this distinction to any advantages of beauty over her companions; for rosy cheeks, and curled locks, were in great plenty in the village. Julia's partiality arose from an incident we shall mention.

One morning, as she passed the cottage, she looked in at the window, and saw little Peggy standing at the table, taking some flies out of a bowl of water, and placing them in the sun, where they shook their wet wings, and were assisted in the operation of drying themselves by Peggy; who put her face very close to the table, and endeavoured to revive them with her warm breath. When Julia entered the cottage, the child, who knew her well, looked up in her face, and told her to 'come and see how glad the flies were to get out.' Peggy was endeared to Julia by her kindness to the flies; for she herself felt for every thing that had life, with a degree of sensibility which many would account a foolish weakness. She had frequently been engaged in the very same business of rescuing flies from destruction; and, when she saw a worm lying in her path, had often conveyed it to a place of safety among the untrodden grass, to prevent its being crushed by some foot less careful than her own. We do not pretend to justify these actions, which people, who have firm nerves for every pain that does not reach themselves, may probably ridicule; but we think it our duty to relate the fact.

Julia had indeed no lesson of humanity left untaught by her grandfather. She had seen the linnets and sparrows, who built their nests in the neighbourhood of that good old man, secure of a comfortable provision in winter; and the robins, who ventured to his gate, had always met with an hospitable reception. He had often, when recommending tenderness to animals, pointed out to his granddaughter that passage in scripture – 'Are not five sparrows sold for two farthings, and not one of them is forgotten before God!'[95] – Dear, and venerable old man! How congenial to thy spirit was this tender assurance! – By what heart is universal benevolence[96] cherished as it was by thine! – But this beloved old man has led us from the cottage, and little Peggy; who now repeated a hymn Julia had taught her, with her hands joined together, and her voice scorning all pause as long as her breath would hold out. Julia promised her a reward if she would mind her stops; and she went to play with her brother, a child of three years of age, before the door of the cottage. A few minutes after, Julia saw her struggling to bring her brother to the door, but the little one refused to come; upon which Peggy flew to the door, pointed to her brother, and burst into tears. Julia rose hastily from her seat, and, stepping forward, saw a gentleman and his servant riding at full speed towards them; and so near the child, that she had only time to fly, at the hazard of her own life, and snatch him away. The screams of his mother, and the appearance of Julia, first informed the stranger of the child's danger, which the approach of night, and the additional gloom cast by some trees over the road, had prevented him from seeing. He instantly dismounted, and, giving the reins to his servant, hastened to Julia, expressed his concern for the alarm he had occasioned her, and enquired with great earnestness if she had recovered her terror. – After a few minutes conversation, he told her that he was on his way to Mr. Clifford's house – 'That house is my home,' said Julia. She then discovered that she was conversing with Mr. Frederick Seymour, who asked permission to attend her home. To this she readily consented; but before they set out she wiped away the tears, which still stood in the eye of her rosy-cheeked pupil, and told her she would always love her for taking care of little Tom.

Mr. Frederick Seymour followed Julia into the drawing-room without being announced.[97] Charlotte was thrown into some confusion by his sudden appearance, but soon recovered herself: the adventure at the cottage was recounted, and the evening passed away cheerfully. Even Mrs. Melbourne, whose manners were usually formal and ungracious, caught the universal gladness. She tried to be agreeable, and succeeded as well as could be expected from one not much accustomed to make the experiment. In general Mrs. Melbourne spoke but little, and never hazarded any sentiment that arose in her heart, till she had first made it travel to her head, and examined whether it was precisely such as would do her honour; and she delivered her opinions, even among her friends, with the most laboured correctness. Her understanding was always in full dress; not like that of the present times, easy, gay, and graceful; but more resembling the stiff ruffs, and stately finery of the days of Queen Elizabeth.[98]

Mr. Seymour alone had some unpleasant reflections. He saw that his brother, without the practice of duplicity, had obtained a fortune far superior, and a woman in every view more amiable, than all his own deep-laid schemes had acquired for himself. While he made these reflections, his heart sickened at the recollection of all the plots and counterplots of his head; and he lamented, that the labour of years had ensured to him a less degree of prosperity than seemed, unsolicited, to court the acceptance of his brother.

Mr. Charles Seymour felt nothing but joy at his brother's marriage, which he knew would give the whole family additional consequence, and considerably increase its influence. He determined, however, not to be outdone by his brother, but to take the first opportunity of marrying the daughter of a nabob,[99] himself.

From the moment of his arrival at Mr. Clifford's seat, he had endeavoured to insinuate himself into the favour of Julia, by paying her the most constant distinctions. He foresaw, that, as mistress of her uncle's house, which would happen on Charlotte's marriage, her importance in the fashionable world would be considerable; and, though her fortune was not sufficient to tempt him to any matrimonial designs upon her himself, he was sensible that, with her beauty and accomplishments, she could scarcely fail to marry advantageously; since he knew that, though love was much out of fashion, there still existed some young men of rank and fortune, who were addicted to that weakness; and some person, of such a temper, might probably abate a few thousands in his matrimonial expectations, in consideration of Julia's beauty. He therefore devoted his chief attention to that young lady; for Charlotte he considered as an acquisition already made to his family. Mr. Charles Seymour's principles of action were as mechanical as those of a watch, constantly regulated by the bright noonday sun; but all machines are subject to imperfection, and Charles's movements of courtesy towards Julia, which had formerly gone too slow, now went somewhat too fast.[100] She could not avoid being put in mind of his past rude neglect, which she would otherwise have forgotten, by his present obsequious attention. When he flew to meet her at her entrance into the room, when he handed her with alacrity to the carriage, or rode by her side on horseback, she recollected how often he had formerly seen her enter, and depart, without taking the smallest notice of either.

A week after the arrival of Mr. Frederick Seymour, Mrs. Melbourne, and Mr. and Mrs. Seymour, left Mr. Clifford's house on their way to Scotland, and Mr. Charles Seymour departed for the seat of Lord —. Mr. Chartres was left at Mr. Clifford's till the return of the party, a circumstance which gave him a degree of pleasure that no one suspected; for he had not yet conquered the terrors his new acquaintances inspired; and, though he admired and loved them, he had hitherto kept both his admiration and his love a profound secret, and had never hazarded more than a monosyllable at a time to any of the family. His good sense was wrapt up as carefully as a motto within a sugar-image; and the crust of awkwardness was not easily broken.

The satisfaction derived from Mr. Frederick Seymour's arrival was not confined to Charlotte: his society was felt to be a most agreeable acquisition by the whole family. In his conversation there was originality, wit, and fancy; the strength of a superior understanding, and the warmth of a feeling heart. The conversation often turned on subjects of literature, and Charlotte, though much less devoted to books than her cousin, had a mind sufficiently cultivated to bear a part in such conversations; which she enjoyed the more on account of their giving her lover an opportunity of displaying his talents. Julia, whose understanding was far superior to Charlotte's, soon perceived that the powers of Seymour's mind were not fully discerned by her cousin; that often a stroke of wit, an emanation of fancy, which she herself admired, was not comprehended by Charlotte; and that a mind less superior to the general mass of mankind would have made her happy. Yet she entertained not the least doubt of her felicity in her marriage with Seymour. She knew that Charlotte was tenderly attached to him, and that he was fully sensible of all her claims to his affection; that he was charmed with the sweetness of her disposition; and she believed that he would do her merit the justice it deserved.

Mr. Frederick Seymour and Julia were soon the best friends possible. She already considered him as the husband of Charlotte, and he sometimes, in a sort of whisper, called her his cousin. A month passed so agreeably, that its flight was scarcely perceived by this domestic circle. In the enjoyment of the beauties of nature, the charms of friendship, and the delightful intercourse of elegant and cultivated minds, the stream of time flowed not like the turbulent torrent which rushes in unequal cadence, as impelled by the tempestuous winds, nor like the sluggish pool, whose waters rest in dull stagnation: it glided cheerfully along, like the clear rivolet of the valley, whose surface is unruffled by the blast of the mountains, and whose bosom reflects the verdant landscape through which it passes.[101]

Mr. Chartres, encouraged by the gentleness with which he was treated, conquered his bashful terrors sufficiently to enjoy the amiable society in which he was placed. He no longer sat at table with as much apparent uneasiness as if he had been stretched on the bed of Procrustus.[102] He raised his eyes when he was spoken to, found it less difficult to dispose of his hands than formerly, lost his tremulous accent, and sometimes delivered his opinions with the firm tone of a man at ease.

Mr. Clifford had some affairs to regulate previously to his daughter's marriage, which was therefore deferred two months longer: mean while Charlotte, who delighted to display the merits of Julia, and wished her beloved friend to be a favourite with her future husband, was at pains, in her frequent conversations with Seymour, to give him the most amiable picture of Julia; described her filial tenderness, her candour, her benevolence, and every amiable quality she possessed, with all the enthusiasm of affection. This was unnecessary – Frederick Seymour had, at first sight, greatly admired Julia's beauty; and, as she had conversed with him with the utmost frankness and cordiality, he found that the purity of her mind, and the goodness of her heart, were equal to the excellence of her understanding; nor could he refuse his friendship to one so dear to Charlotte. He loved to talk to Charlotte of her cousin; he loved to think of her when alone; and at length he discovered that Charlotte's society lost its charm when Julia was absent. He could deceive himself no longer: Julia had inspired him with the most violent, the most unconquerable passion.

The gradations from friendship to love are often imperceptible to the mind. Like successive shades of the same colour, they blend so finely together, that it is difficult to mark the precise point at which their distinctions commence. Love comes to the bosom under the gentle forms of esteem, of sympathy, of confidence: we listen with dangerous pleasure to the seducing accents of his voice, till he lifts the fatal veil which concealed him from our view, and reigns a tyrant in the soul. Reason is then an oracle no longer consulted; and happiness, often life itself, become his victims.

Seymour, called upon by every tie of honour to fulfil his engagements with Charlotte, resolved to stifle his unhappy passion for Julia, to treat her with reserve, and to avoid her as much as possible. That young lady had already perceived the situation of his mind. A thousand little circumstances in his behaviour had betrayed to her penetration the emotions of his heart – but indeed every woman is quick-sighted on this subject. The perturbation of an impassioned mind cannot long be concealed from the object of its inquietude. In vain it may assume the look of indifference, or wear the smile of tranquillity: the most trifling occurrences will serve to discover the agitation of its feelings – as the light breeze, that but gently waves the branches of the other trees of the forest, makes every leaf of the poplar tremble.

The knowledge of Seymour's passion gave Julia the most cruel uneasiness. Her heart was too pure to think without horror of supplanting Charlotte in the affections of her lover – that amiable Charlotte, whose sweetness and generosity of temper had led her to lavish upon Julia every distinction, every preference she could bestow; who, in every amusement, consulted Julia's taste, and forgot her own inclinations in studying to prevent Julia's wishes.

At first, in the fulness of her heart, she was on the point of flying to her cousin, of revealing her suspicions, and asking Charlotte's permission to leave the house till her marriage was accomplished; but a little reflection convinced her of the impropriety[103] of this measure. She knew that Charlotte's affections were deeply engaged, and was sensible that to awaken a suspicion of Seymour's indifference in her mind, would destroy her peace for ever. She was convinced that he meant to fulfil his engagements, and she had too much confidence in his honour and integrity, to doubt that he would treat Charlotte, when his wife, with tenderness and attention. She hoped that Charlotte's sweetness of disposition, and the separation which would then take place between Seymour and herself, would entirely conquer his unhappy prepossession in her favour; and she determined, mean while, to lock the fatal secret within her own breast, and to hasten the marriage by every means in her power.

# CHAP. XI.

Frederick Seymour and Julia now avoided each other by a sort of tacit agreement. They never met but at those seasons when the whole family were assembled; they were careful to place themselves at a distance from each other at table; and in the walks, which they frequently took along the wild and rugged boundaries of the lake, where they sometimes wandered near the edge of the cliffs, or descended the hills by steep and formidable paths,[104] Mr. Seymour, even when Charlotte was escorted by any other gentleman, never offered his arm to Julia, if there was any other lady present. Julia was no less reserved towards him; but, if she happened to walk behind him, she always observed, that when the path was dangerous, he could not resist looking back repeatedly, to see if she was safe. He appeared to be solicitous to converse with any of Charlotte's female visitors in preference to Julia: yet, notwithstanding this behaviour, it was easy for that young lady to perceive that he was acting a part which he performed with great difficulty; but she was happy, at least she believed she was happy, that he had resolution enough to observe this conduct.

Seymour, by unremitted efforts, concealed the state of his mind from Charlotte. All her unsuspecting heart perceived, was his reserve towards Julia, for which she could not account; but which gave her uneasiness; and with the frankness natural to her disposition, she sometimes complained to him of his inattention to her cousin, and reminded him of particular instances of neglect; which he generally excused, by observing that he had been wholly occupied by herself. Charlotte once mentioned to Julia something of Seymour's inattention to her. Julia coloured violently; Charlotte thought it the blush of resentment, and said no more on the subject.

Had Mr. Clifford been a man of much observation, it is probable he would have remarked the change in Seymour's behaviour to his niece. But Mr. Clifford paid little attention to the minuter traits of manners, and being at present wholly occupied in arranging his affairs, previously to his daughter's marriage, and improving the grounds round his house, the sensations of Seymour's mind were by him entirely unnoticed. Mr. Clifford was delighted to see his lawns assume a brighter verdure; his shrubbery filled with every plant that could embellish it; his woods affording the most venerable shade, or opening into vistas, that presented the most sublime landscape[105] – and was unconscious, that to the wounded spirit of Seymour, nature had lost her beauty, and the earth its pleasantness! – Mr. Clifford was in the situation of one of those sheltered trees, which grew in his own cultivated vallies, protected from the violence of the winds, and feeling only the gentlest influence of the seasons; while the unhappy Seymour, agitated by the utmost violence of conflicting passions, resembled one of those plants which are scattered on the bleak mountains, undefended, and exposed to all the fury of the elements.

Seymour was sometimes thrown into great perturbation, by the observations which Chartres, in the simplicity of his mind, made upon his conduct. One evening, when there were some company from the neighbourhood, Seymour was relating, at the tea-table,[106] a ludicrous adventure which had happened to him in France, and which he embellished with all the graces of wit and fancy. While he was proceeding with great vivacity, a servant came, and spoke to Julia; upon which she immediately left the room. Seymour fancied he saw her change colour as she went out; and occupied in conjecturing what could be the reason of it, he made a pause in his story. – 'Pray go on,' said Charlotte. – He resumed the narrative, but Chartres almost instantly interrupted him, saying, 'I beg your pardon Sir, but you have not begun at the place where you left off, and the parts of the story have lost their connection: you know Sir –' Chartres then added a Latin quotation of some length, which we believe was very apposite; but which, as we are entirely ignorant of Latin, we must leave our learned readers to guess. While Chartres was displaying his erudition,[107] Seymour recovered himself sufficiently to proceed in his narrative; but the tone of his voice was changed; the spirit of the story evaporated; and when it was finished, every body appeared disappointed: and though this is a circumstance which often happens to the retailers of stories, many people having an everlasting propensity to speak, from the want of sufficient understanding to be silent, Seymour, who possessed considerable talents for narration, was accustomed to be heard with applause. He perceived the disappointment of the company, and added, in a confused manner, 'I have done my adventure great injustice; but a disagreeable recollection came across me, and I could not for my soul get rid of it.' – Julia returned just as he had done speaking, and Chartres, who thought, that after Seymour's own confession that he had spoiled the jest, there could be no impropriety in his avowing the same opinion, told Julia, that she had not lost the most agreeable part of the story; 'for, ma'am,' added he, 'Mr. Seymour gave us no more wit after you left the room.' Julia tried to smile, and Seymour walked to the window, affecting to join in the general laugh, which was usually excited by the solemn tone in which Chartres delivered his sentiments. The company present were not remarkable for penetration, and were more occupied by the awkward formality of the young man's manner, than by the force of his remark. There was, however, one lady of the party, whose observation was more acute than that of her companions. Miss Tomkins had perceived an unaccountable degree of restraint in the behaviour of Seymour and Julia toward each other. She had remarked, that Seymour faultered in his story upon Julia's leaving the room; but the effect which Chartres's speech had had upon them both, betrayed at once to Miss Tomkins a secret, which she carefully treasured up in her own mind, and of which she made a most ungenerous use, as will be seen hereafter.

Most of the company went to cards, and Chartres followed Seymour to the window; who turned towards him with such a resentful air, that Chartres, terrified at the thoughts of having given offence to one whom he so highly respected, began in an audible voice to solicit pardon. 'I am heartily sorry, Mr. Seymour,' said he, 'if I have made any comment on the story that is offensive to you; but I thought Miss Julia Clifford would like to hear, that as it grew less agreeable just as she left the room, she had not lost much by going. I feel an innocent satisfaction in saying any thing that will please her, when I have an opportunity.' 'Pray, Mr. Chartres, talk no more of it,' Seymour replied, in an impatient and disturbed manner. After pausing a little, he added, 'I am not very well this evening; will you come and take a walk with me?' Chartres thankfully consented. Seymour burthened himself with this young man's company, because he was afraid, that if left with the ladies, Chartres might make some farther animadversions on the story; but he excused himself from conversing with his companion on pretence of indisposition; and wandering along the rocky shores of the lake, indulged his own gloomy meditations.[108]

Julia longed to take a walk; but she confined herself to the corner of the card-table, because she dreaded meeting Seymour. When he returned, she retired for a short time to her own apartment, and gave way to that sorrow which the perplexity of her situation wrung from her heart. She was indeed persuaded, that she felt no other uneasiness than what arose from the agitation with which she perceived that Seymour's mind was struggling; but perhaps there was something of self-deception in this young lady's reflections; as to a passenger, in a boat that glides rapidly down a stream, the current only appears to move, and the boat seems perfectly still, while in reality the waves bear it impetuously along.

But whatever were Julia's real sensations, her conduct was irreproachable. Her ideas of rectitude were of the most exalted kind; and no pain would have been so insufferable to her pure and feeling bosom, as the consciousness of having in the smallest degree deviated from those principles of delicacy, truth, integrity, and honour, which were not only the inviolable sentiments of her soul, but the stedfast rules of her actions. If her heart was not quite at peace, its exquisite sensibility was corrected by the influence of reason;[109] as the quivering needle, though subject to some variations, still tends to one fixed point.

# CHAP. XII.

Mr. and Mrs. Seymour, and Mrs. Melbourne, returned to Mr. Clifford's seat, where they had promised to pass a week or two on their way home. It was the time of the assizes[110] at –, and Mrs. Seymour heard with great satisfaction that Mr. Clifford's family were going to a ball at that town the following evening.

Mr. Chartres, on the first intelligence he received of the ball, instantly asked Julia to dance: 'I own,' added he, playing all the time with his fingers, and looking very foolish, for he felt that his request was a bold one; 'I own I shall appear but aukward, having never been at any ball, except my dancing-master's; but I am determined to improve myself in dancing, which I think a very pleasant device, and what reflects honour on the inventor.' Some young ladies, as secure as Julia of having their choice of many partners, would have refused Mr. Chartres without much remorse; but it was not in her nature to exert power in giving pain when it could be avoided; and though she disliked her shackles, she determined to wear them with cheerfulness. Frederick Seymour was secretly rejoiced that Julia was engaged to Chartres, being conscious that, had she been provided with a more agreeable partner, it would have given him some very unpleasant sensations.

Charlotte mentioned to Mrs. Seymour, at dinner, that she would probably meet her acquaintance, Mr. F—, at the ball, 'Miss Tomkins,' added she, 'who is on a visit at Lord —'s seat, told me that Mr. F— was expected this evening; and what will he do, Julia, when he finds you are engaged? – Mr. Chartres, I advise you not to be too happy tomorrow, for I have a strong suspicion that you will be robbed of your partner.' 'I am conscious, Madam,' said Chartres, laying down his knife and fork with great solemnity, 'I am very conscious of my unworthiness of Miss Julia Clifford, and you know, Madam,' continued he, turning to Julia 'I offered this morning to give up the honour of your hand to Mr. Frederick Seymour, for a dance or two, if he should happen to ask it.' Julia coloured violently; but it was not perceived by any one present except Mr. Seymour; for Frederick Seymour, at that moment, spilt a glass of wine as he was putting it to his lips, on Charlotte's gown, and occasioned some confusion. Charlotte again renewed the subject of the ball, and Julia, who saw that Mr. Seymour's penetrating eyes were fixed upon her, endeavoured to conquer her embarrassment. Mrs. Seymour asked her, if the ball-room at — was a good one. 'Yes,' replied Julia; 'but it seems rather strange, since the time of the assizes is chosen for particular gaiety, that the town-house should be made to contain both the assembly-room and the prison: they seem placed with little judgment so near each other.' 'I believe,' said Mr. Seymour, 'the mirth of the company in general will not be much disturbed by this reflection, though it comes very naturally from the person who made it.' 'A ball-room,' said Frederick Seymour, 'divided only by a thin partition from a prison, reminds one of a magical lanthorn, where all the gay colours are thrown on one little spot, and every thing round it is involved in complete darkness.' 'Well, pray talk no more of it,' said Charlotte.' 'Indeed,' cried Mrs. Seymour, with a sigh loud enough to be heard by all present, 'my feelings are so wounded by what has passed, that I am sure I shall be miserable the whole evening; and I must beg of you, Miss Clifford, to excuse my going.' 'O no,' replied Charlotte, 'I will not excuse you.' Mrs. Seymour acquiesced in silence, and expressed no farther desire of remaining at home.

The next morning Charlotte proposed a ride. A carriage was ordered for Mrs. Melbourne, and horses for the rest of the company, immediately after breakfast; when Charlotte observed that Julia looked pale. 'I have a slight head-ach,' said Julia, 'and as I intend to dance a great deal at the ball, I hope you will excuse my going out with you this morning,' 'Certainly,' said Charlotte, 'if you wish it; but I am sure you will be quite well in the evening; I never had a head-ach but once, when I was going to a ball, and the sound of the fiddles carried it off directly.' Julia smiled at her cousin's remedy for the head-ach, and left the room.

She retired to her own apartment for an hour, and then wandered to a wood on the side of a neighbouring hill, completely shaded from the sun by thick interwoven trees. She seated herself on a green bank, at the foot of an old oak: the lake was seen, and the sound of the torrent was heard foaming down the cliffs at a distance. The trees formed a thousand wild avenues, and the paths of the wood appeared as if they had never been trodden by any human foot-step.[111] Julia, in this solitude, found 'room for meditation even to madness.'[112]She recalled the beloved image of her father; she thought of the past with tender regret, and the present seemed involved in perplexity and sadness.

The beauties of the landscape at length soothed and elevated her mind. She lifted her eyes to heaven, for her admiration of the works of nature was ever accompanied with emotions of gratitude and praise; her heart became full – her tears flowed fast, but not painfully – when her reverie was disturbed by the rustling of the leaves near her. She looked round, and saw Frederick Seymour almost close to her, and gazing at her with earnestness. It instantly occurred to her, that some accident had happened, and occasioned the return of the party; and she enquired with eagerness and terror the reason of his coming. He told her, in a confused manner, that he had received letters, after she left the room, which required an immediate answer, and had obliged him to remain at home. The truth was, that no sooner had Julia declared her intention of staying at home, than Frederick Seymour, who disliked his sister-in-law, and abhorred Mrs. Melbourne, felt a great disgust at the thoughts of going. A few minutes after Julia quitted the room, letters were brought to him by the post, and he could not resist the temptation they offered him of pretending that they required an immediate answer, and of desiring, on that account, to be excused joining the party on horseback. He was sensible that he was acting in direct opposition to every rule he had prescribed for his conduct; he felt that it was madness to court that dangerous society, which had already proved so fatal to his peace; but the sensations which impelled him to remain behind, were too powerful to be combated by any effort of his reason. Alas! There *are* moments when the exertions of reason are ineffectually opposed to the violence of passion! – There *are* moments in which passion, like the ocean-flood, overthrows the mounds which were opposed to its progress! – Charlotte, with her usual sweetness, accepted Seymour's apology for not attending her in her ride, and went with the rest of the company.

When Julia discovered that Seymour had not joined the party, a consciousness of his motive for declining it took instant possession of her mind. Surprise gave place to embarrassment, and a deep blush, which overspread her face, betrayed what was passing in her breast. She remained silent. – 'Are you angry with me,' said he, in a faultering voice, 'for intruding upon your solitude? – My letters were finished; I was going to walk; and was it possible for me to turn my steps another way, when I knew you were here?' – Julia had by this time recovered from her painful confusion. Without taking notice of what he had been saying, she expressed her regret at having lost the morning's ride. 'The day,' added she, 'is so favourable, that the prospect from the hills will be seen to particular advantage.' 'I am sorry you regret it,' he replied; 'I have no such sensation – but may the interest which all who know Miss Clifford must feel in her happiness, give me a right to enquire into the cause of those tears which only ceased upon my intrusion, and which I would sacrifice my life to wipe away?' 'Indeed,' said Julia, quickening her pace towards the house, 'my tears were nothing more than a movement of admiration at the view of nature: the solitude and grandeur of the scene affected me, and my tears flowed, because I felt pleasure in shedding them.' 'Oh,' exclaimed he, with passionate vehemence, 'may your tears never proceed from any other source than that of pleasure! May you, most amiable of women, be happy, and I can never be quite miserable!' – 'What strange language is this! Mr. Seymour,' She answered, in a tone of resentment. 'I suspect, Sir,' she added, 'that your letters this morning have conveyed some disagreeable intelligence; you appear disordered. If you will return to the spot I have just quitted, you will find its stillness more favourable to composure of mind than any company whatever.' 'Ah, Miss Clifford,' resumed he, 'if I may never hope for composure of mind, but in a spot which *you* have just quitted, how poor is my chance of attaining tranquillity!' They reached at that moment a little cottage which stood between two hills: a clear rivulet ran along the narrow valley, and a plank was thrown across it. A young man was resting himself on the grass before the door of the cottage; his eldest child stood behind him, peeping over his shoulder at a younger infant, who was placed upon his knees; his wife, a pretty clean young woman, sat at work on the root of an old elm. Joy sparkled in the looks of the whole family at the approach of Julia. She had spent the past winter in relieving the distresses of the neighbouring poor, and, 'when the eye saw her it blessed her!' – She stopped a few minutes to speak to the cottagers, and then hastened towards home. 'What a charming picture of domestic enjoyment we have just seen!' exclaimed Seymour, with enthusiasm. 'If in the higher ranks of life we were not the slaves of the world, what other scheme of happiness could be so precious to a heart endued with sensibility, as that which this family groupe displays?'[113] – Julia was silent. – 'But then,' he continued, with increased eagerness, 'the world can only be renounced with pleasure for the object of all others most dear to the affections. It must be a connection not formed from interest, from a combination of circumstances, which entangle the mind, and warp its inclinations; it must be the free election of the soul![114] What felicity to live for one beloved object, to prevent every wish, to study every look, to anticipate every desire! – And in that beloved object, to discern fidelity never to be shaken, even in the greatest conflicts and convulsions of fortune; to meet with everlasting support and sympathy, with the charm of unbounded confidence, the –' 'No more Sir,' said Julia, interrupting him, 'I have no pleasure in being led into the regions of romance.' 'By the happy,' he replied, 'the dream of imagination may be discarded; but it is the refuge of misery, and –' 'To me,' said Julia, again interrupting him, 'the language of discontent never appears more unreasonable than amidst such beautiful scenes as these, which seem formed to inspire tranquillity.' 'Complaint,' resumed he, vehemently, 'has indeed no language which can convey an adequate idea of my peculiar wretchedness.' Julia made no reply, but walked as fast as she was able. Seymour preserved a gloomy silence till they came to the lawn before the house. While they were crossing the lawn, he said, in a low voice, 'I fear I have offended you, from your evident anxiety to get rid of me: Ah! I acknowledge the infatuation, the madness of this intrusion! – could I dare to expect, could I even hope for your sympathy! – Oh no! I am not such a wretch as to wish that your peace should be a moment disturbed by any pity for the wretchedness, the extreme – I know not what I am saying. – Forgive me, Madam; forgive the incoherent expressions of a distracted mind – I will not offend again! – Never shall your ear again be wounded by my complaints; I will suffer in silence.' – He opened the door of the saloon. Julia entered without speaking, made him a slight curtesy as she passed him, and hastened to her own apartment. He looked after her till she was out of sight, and then wandered to a distant scene, unconscious where he was going, and absorbed in profound melancholy.

Julia for some time gave way to tears; but she wiped the traces of sorrow from her eyes before the return of Charlotte, and determined to decline no parties in future, however disagreeable to her, that she might not again be exposed to an interview so painful to her feelings, as that which had just past.

# CHAP. XIII.

When Charlotte returned from her ride, her first care was to hasten to Julia's apartment, and enquire if her head-ach had ceased. At that moment Julia felt Charlotte's kindness like a reproach; her heart was full, and tears started into her eyes. 'What is the matter, my dearest friend?' said Charlotte: she then enquired if it was the thoughts of going for the first time into public since the death of her father that affected her. Julia now wept without restraint. 'If you are so much hurt at going, my dearest girl,' resumed Charlotte, 'I will not insist upon it.' – Fearing, however, that if she remained at home, Frederick Seymour would attribute it to the effects of their meeting, Julia told Charlotte that she was determined to go, and begged that she would take no notice to any one of the depression of her spirits. Charlotte threw her arms round her friend's neck, and embraced her tenderly, with the most soothing expressions of affection. They then parted, in order to dress for the ball.

When Charlotte left the room, Julia threw herself on her knees, and implored the assistance of that Being, to whom she had been ever accustomed to fly, as to the refuge of calamity. Her heart was formed for devotion, and the consolation it afforded her will be only disbelieved by those who have never tried its influence. – These young ladies appeared at dinner dressed alike, and with the most graceful simplicity. Julia's complexion was a little flushed by the agitation she had suffered, which served to heighten her beauty; and Charlotte gazed at her with as sincere delight as if she had not been handsomer than herself.

Mrs. Seymour was very fantastically arrayed, and her sensations at the appearance of Julia were of a very opposite nature from those which glowed in the generous bosom of Charlotte. Mrs. Melbourne also discovered by her looks, and by more than usual peevishness of manner, her entire disapprobation of the increased bloom of Julia's complexion, who was placed at dinner between Mr. Seymour and Chartres. 'Did you take a long walk this morning, Ma'am?' said Chartres. 'No, a very short one,' replied Julia. 'Why, walking *alone* is dull enough,' said Mr. Seymour, looking at her earnestly. 'I do not think so,' answered Julia; 'but I was not alone, I met Mr. Frederick Seymour.' 'Oh, so he found you out, Ma'am,' exclaimed Chartres: 'well, I really thought you would have hid yourself; for, although woman, as well as man, is certainly a social being, yet there are seasons when solitude is more valuable than society.' 'What does Mr. Chartres say about hiding yourself, Julia?' said Charlotte, who was sitting at some distance. 'He says,' replied Mr. Seymour, 'that your fair cousin is very cruel, and stays at home to hide herself most maliciously from us, who live only in her sight.' Julia smiled faintly, and Mr. Seymour immediately changed the subject.

While they were at tea, Mr. Seymour described with rapture the falls of the river Clyde,[115] which he had visited in his tour through Scotland. Mrs. Seymour said, she had been particularly pleased with the romantic beauties of the river Evan, as it runs through Hamilton Wood, passing by Chat'lherault, to join the Clyde, at a bridge in sight of Hamilton House.[116] 'But what', added she, 'perhaps, impressed the beauties of that spot upon my mind more strongly than those of any other, was some verses which were given to me by a lady in that neighbourhood, and which, she told me, were written by two intimate friends of her own, in their days of courtship. I took a copy of the verses, together with a little account of the writers, which their friend had scrawled on a blank leaf of the paper.' Charlotte begged Mrs. Seymour would produce the verses; which she did immediately, and desired Mr. Frederick Seymour to read them. He took the paper, and read as follows:

A young gentleman, born on the banks of the Evan in Scotland, had formed a strong attachment to a young lady in that neighbourhood; but fortune refusing even that competency, which would have satisfied two minds equally divested of ambition and avarice, he accepted of an offer of going to the East Indies. Time and distance had no power to obliterate the traces of a sacred and serious passion, such as may perhaps still be found in the bosom of retirement. On the banks of the Ganges his imagination often wandered to that humbler, but, in his mind, far more beautiful stream, which winds in delightful mazes through the wood of Hamilton, and whose banks, of a romantic height, are covered with the freshest verdure, and crowned with trees of the most venerable antiquity. This had been the scene of his early passion. Under the shade of those majestic trees, by the brink of that beloved stream, he had often wandered with his mistress; and in his mind, every impression of beauty, and every idea of happiness, was connected with the borders of the Evan.

With such feelings, it is not surprising that, having acquired a fortune far greater than would have been sufficient to have fixed him in the arms of love and happiness in his native country, he immediately determined to return. A short time before his departure, he composed the following song; and some years after his return, he accidentally found a little ballad, which his mistress had written during their separation; an unequivocal proof, among many he daily experienced, that their love was reciprocal.

## SONG.

### *I.*

Slow spreads the gloom my soul desires –
The sun from India's shore retires –
To Evan's banks, with temp'rate ray,
Home of my youth! He leads the day.

Oh banks to me for ever dear!
Oh stream whose murmurs still I hear!
All, all my hopes of bliss reside
Where Evan mingles with the Clyde.

*II.*

And she, in simple beauty drest,
Whose image lives within my breast,
Who trembling heard my parting sigh,
And long pursu'd me with her eye!
Does she, with heart unchang'd as mine,
Oft in the vocal bowers recline?
Or, where yon grot o'erhangs the tide,
Muse while the Evan seeks the Clyde?

*III.*

Ye lofty banks, that Evan bound,
Ye lavish woods that wave around,
And o'er the stream your shadows throw,
Which sweetly winds so far below –
What secret charm to mem'ry brings
All that on Evan's border springs!
Sweet banks! – Ye bloom by Mary's side;
Blest stream! – She views thee haste to Clyde.

*IV.*

Can all the wealth of India's coast
Atone for years in absence lost?
Return, ye moments of delight,
With richer treasures bless my sight!
Swift from this desart let me part,
And fly to meet a kindred heart!
Nor more may aught my steps divide
From that dear stream which flows to Clyde.

## BALLAD.

Ah Evan, by thy winding stream
 How once I lov'd to stray,
And view the morning's redd'ning beam,
 Or charm of closing day!

To yon dear grot, by Evan's side,
 How oft my steps were led;
Where far beneath the waters glide,
 And thick the woods are spread.

But I no more a charm can see;
 In Evan's lovely glades;
And drear and desolate to me
 Are those enchanting shades.

While far – how far from Evan's bowers,
 My wand'ring lover flies;
Where dark the angry tempest lowers,
 And high the billows rise!

And oh, where'er the wand'rer goes,
 Is that poor mourner dear,
Who gives, while soft the Evan flows,
 Each passing wave a tear?

And does he now that grotto view?
 On these steep banks still gaze?
In fancy does he still pursue
 The Evan's lovely maze?

And can he still with rapture think,
 On every wounded tree?
The secret path, by Evan's brink,
 So often trod with me?

Oh come, repass the stormy wave,
 Oh, toil for gold no more!
Our love a dearer pleasure gave,
 On Evan's peaceful shore.

Leave not my breaking heart to mourn
 The joys so long deny'd;
Oh soon to those green banks return,
 Where Evan meets the Clyde.

When the songs were finished, Mrs. Seymour mentioned that her Scotch acquaintance, who had a sweet voice, sung these words to some of the old simple tunes of her own country – 'Which was the very circumstance that made them interesting,' replied Mr. Seymour. 'The tricks of execution,' he added, 'may surprize, but are too remote from nature to touch the passions: they are more easily moved by striking one tender string, than by flying through all the notes of the gamut.'[117] 'I like Scotch music,' said Chartres, 'because the tunes are easily comprehended; whereas, in complicated pieces, I never can understand what the composer means to express; and the whole appears to me a contrivance, to show how much may be done in a short time.' Chartres had just finished his speech, when the carriages came to the door, and the party set off for the ball.

# CHAP. XIV.

Mr. F—, who came to pay his compliments to Mrs. Seymour, on her entering the assembly-room, soon directed his principal attention to Julia, and obtained her permission to ask Mr. Chartres to resign her hand for one dance. Mrs. Seymour had no time to be out of humour at Mr. F—'s attention to Julia, being immediately asked to dance by Lord —, and after that she felt no inclination; for, if the female brow is ever clouded by ill-temper, it is certainly not in those moments when vanity is gratified.

Frederick Seymour danced with Charlotte, and Julia with Chartres; who wore a look of great solicitude, while by the most serious and unremitting attention he made himself master of the figure of each country dance, before he began to practise it. His performance of his lesson was, however, somewhat ludicrous. He flung out his arms and legs in a very singular manner, and, by his indefatigable efforts to dance with spirit, afforded infinite diversion to the whole company. This young man, whom nature had formed more on the plan of the yew than the osier,[118] had, while dancing, rather the appearance of a puppet than of a human form; for his figure seemed to be framed of wood, and his movements directed by wires: but he believed that extended arms denoted ease, and that a high spring demonstrated spirit; while, in truth, his performance was as remote from either, as the stiff ringlets of our learned counsellors wigs,[119] (those stupendous symbols of knowledge,) from the graceful flow of natural curls. Julia alone appeared insensible to the awkward motions of her partner, because she was not willing to give him pain. She saw that he observed, with mortification, the tittering of the young ladies whenever he approached; and she determined to appear perfectly satisfied with his abilities for dancing; though sometimes, when he sprang unusually high, with out-stretch'd arms, she found it difficult to suppress a smile.

Mr. Chartres, after the labour of two dances, which, by his mode of performance, had been rendered no trifling fatigue, consented to a suspension of his toils, and resigned his partner to Mr. F—, for one dance; telling her, 'That he would sit in the mean time, and meditate on the pastime before him, which he thought was very delightful to behold.' Frederick Seymour knew nothing of this arrangement till he saw them standing up together. He had persuaded Charlotte to sit down during that dance, and, as the ball-room was very hot, she proposed going to the card-room, where Seymour was leading her when he first perceived Julia and Mr. F—. He felt a pang of jealous anguish at the sight, and an irresistible desire to observe their behaviour to each other. Suppressing his emotion, he turned to Charlotte, with as much carelessness in his manner as he could assume, and said, 'This is a very lively tune, and, if I thought you could forgive me for being so whimsical, I should confess that I feel a great inclination to go down this dance.' 'And so do I too,' replied Charlotte, hastening to her place, 'it's a pleasure to oblige you, when you chuse to dance; but one really finds it difficult to sit down; so pray don't take that humour again.'

After Julia and Mr. F— had passed them in the dance, Frederick Seymour said to Charlotte, in a tone of indifference, 'How has your fair cousin contrived to get rid of her first partner?' 'She has only got rid of him for one dance,' replied Charlotte. 'Mr. F— was miserable when he heard she was engaged, and was determined to dance one dance with her at least: I can see,' added Charlotte, 'that Mr. F— is in love with Julia.' Seymour felt that Mr. F—'s love was a subject on which he was not likely to speak with much success, and therefore prudently forbore to make any reply. When the dance was finished, he could not resist leading Charlotte to the same bench where Julia and Mr. F— were sitting; walking himself about the room, almost unconscious where he was, or what he was doing.

Mrs. Melbourne sat and contemplated Mrs. Seymour, while she was dancing, with the fondest admiration. Her whole stock of applause she lavished upon her daughter; and at length, dazzled with the graces and attractions which she perceived in this favourite object, she turned her eyes for relief upon the rest of the company, where she easily discovered some shades of imperfection; distributing the whole number of female defects among the young ladies present, and, with laudable impartiality, giving to each of them an equal share. Julia, whose beauty eclipsed that of all others, she regarded with as much malignity as if she had herself been her rival; held Mr. Clifford's understanding in the highest contempt, on account of his having received into his family one, whose superior attractions must ever bear away the palm from his own daughter; and was ready to exclaim to Charlotte, in the words of Shakespeare,

> 'Thou art a fool, she robs thee of thy name,
> And thou wilt show more bright when she is gone.'[120]

Mrs. Melbourne then reflected how much more sagaciously she would have acted in the same circumstances; at what a prudent distance she would have separated a beautiful niece from her own daughter, by leaving her in that safe obscurity, where she would have been secure from danger herself, and could neither have excited admiration or envy in others.

Mr. Chartres, after the interval of repose he had enjoyed, felt himself prepared for fresh exertions, and claimed his partner the next dance. Charlotte could not be perfectly happy, even in dancing with her beloved Seymour, while she saw Julia devoting the evening to such a partner as Chartres. The affectionate Charlotte had long made Julia's happiness necessary to her own. Her heart was attuned to joy; but when she fancied Julia's was not in unison, the strings of pleasure in her own bosom refused to vibrate.

She proposed to Frederick Seymour, that he should ask Chartres to allow him to dance one dance with Julia, and added, that she herself would dance with Chartres 'It will really divert me,' said Charlotte, 'to go down one dance with him; and we shall do vastly well, for I'll make him get the figure by heart before we set off.' Seymour, however, appeared but little diverted with Charlotte's plan, which threw him into such perturbation, that he scarcely knew what he said. 'Yes – certainly – if you wish it' – he replied, in a stammering manner. 'Surely it cannot be disagreeable to you,' rejoined Charlotte, with some surprize at his hesitation. No – I did not mean – I – shall I go and ask Miss Julia Clifford's permission?' 'Certainly,' answered Charlotte. He went up to Julia, asked her to dance, and added, in a low voice, that he should not have presumed to solicit that honor, if Miss Charlotte Clifford had not commanded him. Julia could alledge no pretence to Charlotte for refusing: she therefore gave her consent, and he led her to the dance. He was two or three times out in the figure, and Julia's countenance wore an expression of gravity and reserve. When the dance was finished, Julia, followed by Frederick Seymour, went in search of Charlotte, who was at that moment surrounded by a number of her acquaintances; and Julia could find no vacant place except at a little distance, where she sat down, and Frederick Seymour placed himself next her. He endeavoured to converse with her, but his powers of entertainment failed him, and her manner towards him was cold and distant. Julia's usual manners had the most engaging frankness: her heart seemed to hover on her lips, and every emotion of her soul was clearly seen in her expressive countenance. Frederick Seymour had observed that she conversed with Mr. F— with the utmost sweetness and vivacity; and the contrast in her behaviour towards himself, struck his mind so forcibly, that, after a silence of some minutes, during which he had wrought up his feelings to a degree of agony, he said to her, 'Miss Clifford, I am conscious that I deserve your resentment, yet I find the pang it inflicts is insupportable: from my very soul, I implore you, Madam, to forgive the frenzy of this morning. If you could look into my mind, if you could know what passes within this bosom, you would perhaps think that I am punished enough.' 'I will endeavour, Sir,' replied Julia, 'to forget what it is so disagreeable to me to remember.' She then rose hastily from her seat, and joined some ladies of her acquaintance.

The company went to tea; and Mr. Chartres, who was conscious that dancing was not his forte, determined at least to distinguish himself by his services to the ladies during tea. He arose with great alacrity to hand some bread and butter; but no sooner did he find himself standing upright, a public spectacle to the whole circle, than all the excellent arguments, by which he had spurred his courage to this enterprize, suddenly failed him, and his confusion was so great, that it seemed to bereave him of his faculties: he hastily placed his tea-cup upon the chair on which he had been sitting, and, while undergoing the pains of presenting the cake, let the plate slip out of his trembling hand, which fell in pieces on the floor. Overcome with horror at this accident, he immediately retreated to his chair, unmindful of the tea-cup which he had placed upon it, the contents of which now flowed upon the ground. Mrs. Seymour fell into convulsions of laughter, nor could Charlotte resist joining with her heartily. Julia checked her inclination to laugh, in compassion to poor Chartres, whose whole face became scarlet, and who suffered such torments of mind, that though his legs were a good deal scalded, he was for some time insensible to his bodily pains; and when he did feel them, had not courage either to complain or move from his seat, till Frederick Seymour perceived his situation, and offered to accompany him to another apartment. When he had changed his stockings, and felt his sufferings assuaged, he

**BIN TRAVERLER FORM**

**Cut By:** Rosa Castillo #32 **Qty** 26 **Date** 07/23/26

**Scanned By:** Rosa **Qty** ______ **Date** ______

**Scanned Batch ID's**

______ ______ ______

**Notes / Exceptions**

______

complained bitterly, that Mrs. Seymour made no more conscience of laughing at him, than if he was not related to her by the ties of blood; and lamented that a man's zeal to serve the most amiable part of the creation should expose him to such disgrace.

Mr. Seymour was not unemployed at the ball, though he did not dance, and forbore to play at whist, of which he was exceedingly fond. But lady — did not chuse to play, which was Mr. Seymour's reason for declining it: he seated himself next her, and exerted all his brilliant talents for her entertainment. She had been acquainted with him in London, and was so dazzled by his wit, and so charmed with the warmth and frankness of his manner, that he had gained a high place in her admiration and esteem: and he now contrived to blend some very delicate and agreeable flattery to herself in his remarks on the company. Lady — was handsome, amiable, and not insensible to praise, which was particularly grateful to her from Mr. Seymour, because she respected his abilities, and had a firm persuasion of his candour and sincerity. She believed, that had she been in the most obscure situation of life, he would have admired her as much, and loved her as fervently. She fancied that she had made a powerful impression on his heart; and, notwithstanding Lady —'s disposition was virtuous, and she was determined never to deviate in essential points from the duty she owed to her husband, her early intercourse with the fashionable world had given her mind a laxity in its opinions on the subject of gallantry, though it had not power intirely to pervert her principles. She thought there was no harm in a fine woman's inspiring passion in other men as well as her husband; and in listening to the language of love, or even in feeling the sentiment in her own bosom, so long as her conduct was without reproach. Having hitherto walked safely in a dangerous path, though it led along the edge of a precipice,[121] she had now lost the apprehension of falling. Perhaps she would have been in more danger from Mr. Seymour than any of her other admirers, because he pursued the gratification of his passions with indefatigable perseverance, and with consummate powers of insinuation. But another object, with whom the reader will shortly be acquainted, at present occupied his heart; and his sole aim, in this tender attention to lady —, was to obtain the exertion of her influence with her lord, which was very considerable, to procure Mr. Seymour some additional emoluments[122] to the office he held under government. 'Well,' said she, after they had conversed together a considerable time, 'I must leave you now – our *tête-à-tête* has been quite long enough.' 'Perhaps for *you*,' he replied, with a sigh. 'No, indeed,' interrupted lady –, 'I'm not at all tired of you; but, if I stay any longer, these good country-folks will be making some obliging comments upon it.' 'What! on your chatting with an old married man.' I think a *tête-à-tête* with so harmless a creature as I am, can scarcely furnish the gossips with a subject, notwithstanding the dearth of conversation in these parts.' 'If I thought you *were* harmless,' answered lady —, 'I should like your friendship of all things.' This confession was followed by the most profuse, tender, ardent professions of regard on the part of Mr. Seymour. Their plan of friendship was immediately fixed, and he took a future opportunity of disclosing his political scheme, at the moment when he saw it would succeed; alledging such plausible reasons for the application, that she had not the least suspicion that it originated in the most sordid avarice. Lady —, who scarcely knew the value of money herself, was not aware that Mr. Seymour could never be convinced that he possessed enough, while there was any means left untried of obtaining more. Avarice is a passion as despicable as it is hateful. It chuses the most insidious means for the attainment of its ends: it dares not pursue its object with the bold impetuosity of the soaring eagle, but skims the ground in narrow circles like the swallow.

Mr. F— danced with Miss Tomkins; who, however, perceived that his whole thoughts were bent upon Julia; a discovery which produced sensations of a very painful nature in the mind of Miss Tomkins, who had for some time formed a serious matrimonial plot upon this gentleman, which she now perceived would very probably be defeated. It is necessary to give a short sketch of the character of this young lady.

Miss Tomkins was of low birth. Her father had a plodding head, and raised himself by unwearied diligence, and a constant and watchful attention to the main chance, from which nothing diverted his thoughts a single moment. He was one of those persons whom Sterne describes as walking straight forward through the path of this world; turning neither to the right hand, nor the left;[123] and his application to business was at length rewarded by his obtaining the office of steward[124] to a nobleman possessed of a very considerable estate. His daughter, who was at that time in her twenty third year, was a young woman of superior understanding, and quick penetration into character. She had received an excellent education; and her mind was highly cultivated. Her talents had introduced her into a respectable society of the middle rank, perhaps the society of all others from which the greatest improvement may be derived; for the middle station of life appears to be that temperate region, in which the mind, neither enervated by too full a ray from prosperity, nor chilled and debased by the freezing blast of penury, is in the situation most favourable for every great and generous exertion.

No sooner was her father appointed steward to the earl of —, than Miss Tomkins perceived that a new and splendid career was opened to her ambition. The countess of — invited her to spend a short time at their country seat. Miss Tomkins availed herself of this invitation with eagerness, and soon made herself well acquainted with the character of lady —, managed her foibles skilfully, and in a short time became a great favourite, and a constant visitor at her house. This acquaintance led to others of the same consequence. Miss Tomkins's friendships were formed upon the calculations of interest: she was aware that all her prospects of fortune depended upon her father's life, and was anxious to provide farther securities of future affluence, in case this should fail. But she concealed the utmost subtlety of worldly policy, under the appearance of the greatest disinterestedness, and the most tender and genuine sensibility.[125] Among her friends, she could number many people of talents, as well as rank; for her real character was only known to a few, to whom long acquaintance had developed it; but those few had too much honour to betray her, and felt more contempt than indignation at her total neglect of them, now she was introduced into an higher circle.

Mr. F— was a frequent visitor at the house of her patroness. Miss Tomkins found that he possessed accomplishments sufficient to gratify her pride, and a fortune ample enough to satisfy her ambition. He had appeared pleased with her conversation, and she hoped, in the course of a few weeks passed with him at lord —'s seat, to confirm her empire over his heart; when the superior attractions of Julia at once defeated all her projects. How often do we build a gay palace in the air, decorate it with gold and purple, and almost fancy the foundation is a substantial one; till a passing breeze shakes the fair fabric, and scarcely leaves even a broken pillar on which the imagination may rest!

# CHAP. XV.

A few days after the ball, lord and lady —, Miss Tomkins, and Mr. F—, were invited to dinner at Mr. Clifford's. Mr. F— devoted his whole attention to Julia, which Mrs. Seymour was in no disposition to witness with the same complacency she had done at the ball; for lord — was placed next another lady, and the other gentlemen at table were plain country squires.

Miss Tomkins affected to distinguish Julia with particular fondness, in order to conceal the envy and aversion which rankled in her heart.[126] The pain she felt in making this effort, was perhaps a sufficient punishment for her malignity; and it would have cost her less trouble to conquer those bad passions, than it did to hide them from observation.

Charlotte entertained her guests in the most engaging manner. Her sweet countenance beamed with good-humour and vivacity; nor had she a suspicion that any of her company were strangers to that conscious serenity which filled her own gentle bosom. The pure and delicate sensations of a first passion, which is opposed by no duty, and embittered by no obstacle, shed over the mind a sweet enchantment, that renders every object agreeable, and every moment delightful: it is like that first fresh and vivid green which the early spring awakens; that lovely and tender verdure which is not found amidst the glow of summer, and is as transitory as it is charming.

Julia felt nothing but indifference for Mr. F—; but she saw that her behaviour was watched by Mr. Seymour, and was glad to avoid his scrutinizing looks, by engaging in conversation with that gentleman; which she did with an appearance of pleasure that threw Frederick Seymour into the utmost perturbation. This did not pass unnoticed by his brother, who had discovered, from many little circumstances since his arrival, that unhappy secret which Frederick Seymour thought was concealed from all observation. Mr. Seymour, however, determined to make no other use of his discovery than that of hastening, as far as was in his power, his brother's marriage with Charlotte, which he considered as a connection too advantageous to be lost for any reason whatever; nor did Mr. Seymour think that a passion for one woman was the smallest obstacle to a marriage with another. He was himself a libertine, both in principle and practice: he had conversed chiefly with the most worthless part of the female sex, and had conceived a very contemptible opinion of the principles of the female mind. He thought it was probable that Julia would soon marry: he saw, or fancied he saw, that his brother was not perfectly indifferent to her, and believed, that if he could not conquer his passion, he might at length find it returned. – Mr. Seymour's opinion was founded on his observation of Julia's extreme sensibility; but the conclusions of this reasoner were drawn from false premises: he did not know that in a mind where the principles of religion and integrity are firmly established, sensibility is not merely the ally of weakness, or the slave of guilt, but serves to give a stronger impulse to virtue;[127] nor could his own mind, which was hardened and debased by the freedom of a licentious life, form a conjecture of that horror which the idea of vice excites in a pure and ingenuous bosom. He did not know, that to a heart framed like that of Julia's, self-reproach would be the most insupportable of all evils; that she had sufficient fortitude to sustain any misery that was not connected with guilt, and sufficient rectitude never to separate the idea of pleasure from that of virtue. Virtue is indeed the only true support of pleasure; which, when disjoined from it, is like a plant when its fibres are cut, which may still look gay and lovely for a while, but soon decays and perishes.

Mr. Seymour, who had a curiosity to know if Chartres had any suspicion of his brother's partiality for Julia, proposed a walk to him, and, after a little conversation on other subjects, said to him, 'Well, Mr. Chartres, is your heart in no danger among these fine young women? I suppose you feel no small envy of my happy brother.' 'Why really, Sir,' said Chartres, 'if I did not guess from my own feelings that it must be a pleasant thing to be on the point of marriage with Miss Charlotte Clifford, I should never find it out from Mr. Frederick Seymour; for, to tell you the truth, I think if he disliked the marriage, he would behave precisely as he does now.' 'Did you ever make this remark to any one before?' 'Yes, Sir; Miss Julia Clifford and I were walking together, a few days ago, as we generally do; for I believe Mr. Frederick Seymour would see her fall down a rock before he would offer to assist her, so I have that honour; and perhaps I acquit myself but awkwardly, yet she always seems better satisfied when I attend her, than when your brother offers his help. I really do not know how it has happened, Sir, but she and Mr. Frederick Seymour seem to have taken a great aversion to each other; Is it not very strange?' 'Very strange indeed, Mr. Chartres,' said Mr. Seymour drily, 'that they should feel so *great* an aversion as you mention: but let me hear what passed in your walk with Miss Julia Clifford.' Why, Sir, as we walked under the shade of that woody hill near the house, I heard Miss Julia sigh very deeply. 'Pray, Ma'am,' said I, 'don't sigh so heavily, *you* are not going to be married.' 'What do you mean, Mr. Chartres?' said she. 'Why, Ma'am,' I replied, 'what I meant was this, that Mr. Frederick Seymour, who *is* going to be married, does nothing but sigh all day long; that is, when he and I are alone together; for, when any of you appear, he starts up, rubs his eyes, and puts on quite another sort of countenance. Now this behaviour seems to me quite inconsistent with reason, if he is happy; and by no means consonant to philosophy, if he is otherwise.' 'Well Sir,' said Mr. Seymour, 'and what answer did the young lady make to these observations?' 'Why, Sir, she was silent so long, that I thought she was not going to answer at all; but at last, she said, 'that the seriousness which I had remarked was probably natural to Mr. Frederick Seymour's disposition, since he had certainly great reason to be happy at present;' she then begged I would not mention his fits of gravity to Charlotte, because such intelligence would give her no pleasure.' 'I entirely approve of Julia's advice,' 'said Mr. Seymour, 'and therefore we will keep the secret to ourselves.' 'With all my heart, Sir,' said Chartres; 'I own this is the first secret with which I was ever entrusted, but I have no doubt I shall be able to keep it.'

Though some circumstances had betrayed Frederick Seymour's passion to his brother, it escaped the vigilant observation of Mrs. Melbourne, who indeed seldom saw him but at meals. She however perceived that he was sometimes absent and thoughtful, which occasionally happened in spite of all his efforts, and she never failed to mention what she had remarked to Charlotte, only giving to absence and thoughtfulness, the epithets of sullenness and caprice; immediately after, asserting how much such qualities were to be dreaded in a husband; assuring her, at the same time, that the heart of man was composed of such slippery materials, that it could not long be retained by any plan of conduct, and that, upon the whole marriage was but another name for misfortune. Charlotte listened in submissive silence to these comfortable assertions, but felt no inclination to bewail her own fate; and, notwithstanding the gloomy forebodings of her aunt, thought that the evil, if such it was, of a union with the man she loved, might be submitted to with resignation. She could not be persuaded, in conformity to her aunt's doctrine, that happiness was as rare as the flower of the aloe, and that life was too short for its cultivation; but believed that the blossoms of joy were scattered as liberally as the primrose, or the violet, and that every traveller through the path of life might enjoy a share of their sweetness.

Meanwhile Frederick Seymour grew more and more wretched. Sometimes, with a degree of sophistry which passion dictated, he reasoned himself into a persuasion that it would be more generous to undeceive Charlotte, by making known to her the real state of his mind, than to impose on her credulity, by receiving her hand, when his heart was devoted to another. But a high sense of honor soon overturned this wretched casuistry. To inflict anguish on a heart which reposed on him with unsuspicious confidence, was an idea he could not long support; and he knew Julia's rectitude of mind too well, not to be convinced that such a conduct would banish him from her sight for ever. He felt that every principle of justice, and generosity, demanded the absolute sacrifice of his own feelings; and he determined to marry Charlotte, to make her happiness his chief object, and to confine his wretchedness within his own bosom.

Yet, while he formed these laudable resolutions, he contrived, with strange infatuation, to cherish his unhappy passion. One evening Charlotte, while she was making tea, requested Julia to try some new music, which she had received from London, on the piano forte. Julia pulled off her gloves, and placed them hastily on her lap: one of them dropped on the floor while she was playing. Frederick Seymour, who was walking up and down the room, seized a moment when Charlotte was talking to Mrs. Seymour, and pretending to be looking over some songs which lay on the piano forte, dropped one of them on the spot where the glove lay, which he contrived to pick up, at the same time putting it hastily into his bosom. When Julia had finished the piece of music, she rose from the piano forte, and missed one of her gloves: she stooped to look for it, and Frederick Seymour affected to be busy in looking for it too; but in a few moments left the room with precipitation. Julia continued a little longer her vain search, and then hastened to join the company, disturbed and uneasy from a suspicion of what had really happened, which arose in her mind upon Seymour's leaving the room.

Seymour, when he reached his own apartment, locked the door, pulled the precious prize from his bosom, pressed it to his heart and lips ten thousand times, and was guilty of the most passionate extravagancies.

Affection, like genius, can build its structures 'on the baseless fabric of a vision;'[128] and the estimation which things hold in a lover's fancy, can be tried by no calculations of reason. The lover, like the poor Indian, who prefers glass beads and red feathers to more useful commodities, sets his affections upon a trifle, which some illusion of fancy has endeared, and which is to him more valuable than the gems of the eastern world, or the mines of the west; while reason, like the sage European, who scorns beads and feathers, in vain condemns his folly.

When Seymour returned to the drawing-room, he was more gay, more animated, more agreeable than usual; while Julia marked her resentment of his conduct in the only way in her power, by behaving to him with the utmost reserve and coldness.

Mr. F—, after finding some pretence every day for a visit to Mr. Clifford's, at length ventured to declare to Julia her power over his heart, and to make proposals of marriage to her. Julia was sensible that by accepting Mr. F—, she would put a final end to her present perplexities, and perhaps banish for ever, from the mind of Seymour, that unhappy passion which her presence nourished. She felt too that Charlotte's friendship claimed every sacrifice in her power; and, perhaps, many will think the sacrifice it now required, might have been very easily made; and that, independently of all considerations respecting Charlotte, nothing could be more absurd than to hesitate in accepting so advantageous an offer. It must be acknowledged, that the young people of the present age have in general the wisdom to repress those romantic feelings which used to triumph over ambition and avarice, and have adopted the prudent maxims of maturer life. Marriage is now founded on the solid basis of convenience, and love is an article commonly omitted in the treaty. But Julia, who had passed her life in retirement, was not so far advanced in the lessons of the world. Her heart, delicate, yet fervent in its affections, capable of the purest attachment, revolted at the idea of marrying where she did not love; and, though she was now unhappy, she determined not to fly from her present evils to a species of wretchedness, of all others the most intolerable to a mind of her disposition.

She refused Mr. F— in such a manner as convinced him that he possessed much of her esteem. He was a man of sense and spirit: he did not, therefore, degrade himself by abject solicitation, or disgust the object of his affection, by reiterating those expressions of passion, which he knew were more likely to change indifference into aversion, than love; as the pale evening flower shrinks from the warmth of those beams by which other flowers are cherished. Mr. F— accepted with gratitude the friendship Julia offered him, and was, perhaps, not without hopes of inspiring her in time with more tender sentiments.

Miss Tomkins, mean while, left lord —'s seat, and Mr. F—, with infinite reluctance. But she saw that he was an object of perfect indifference to Julia, and believed, that when rejected by that young lady, he would renew his attentions to herself.

## CHAP. XVI.

One morning, when Mr. Clifford and Mr. Seymour were gone on a fishing party, and Mrs. Seymour was engaged in writing letters, Julia, at the request of Charlotte, went out with her on horseback, accompanied by Frederick Seymour, and Chartres. Charlotte proposed that they should take a path they had not yet explored, near the borders of the lake, which led to the ruins of an old abbey,[129] about six miles distant.

The country afforded a wild variety of landscape, but the view was sometimes obstructed by hills, and the path sometimes winded under hanging rocks, piled rudely together.[130] At length they came to a narrow road, which led for two miles along the edge of a precipice. A ridge of horrid cliffs frowned above, and at the bottom of this dangerous path was a deep chasm, through which a noisy, rapid stream, rolling over a stony channel, forced its way into the lake. Seymour trembled at every step, not for himself for no life was more indifferent to him than his own; but Julia was mounted on a very sprightly horse, who, if startled by any object, would inevitably throw his fair rider into the gloomy abyss beneath. Seymour's imagination was so possessed by this frightful image, that he was sometime before he could recover his composure, after they had reached the end of this formidable road, which opened to a wooded hill, near whose broad base, on a gentle declivity, the ancient abbey was seated; commanding a view of the lake, with its sublime scenery,[131] and shaded by large groups of venerable trees.

Before he approached the abbey, Seymour insisted that the ladies should not repass that formidable road on horseback; and they agreed to send the servants and horses forward, and walk those two miles. Chartres expatiated on the prudence of this plan, after having made a declamation of some length, on the disagreeable sensations of fear.

The party now came to the remains of an old wall, of considerable extent, that appeared to have surrounded the building. A mouldering gothic gate[132] led to a spacious area overgrown with tall grass: huge fragments of stone, which had fallen from the decayed towers, were scattered upon the ground, and rendered the access difficult to the inner part of the abbey, which was on this side entirely dismantled; there being only the remains of the ruined walls, and towards the east a large gothic window, which shook at every blast, and appeared to be entirely supported by the branches of tall elms that had grown in the inside of the building, among its scattered fragments.

On the other side of the abbey, a narrow stone staircase of one of the towers still remained; which Chartres having ascended, hastened to assure the ladies that the ascent was extremely easy, and that when they reached the top they would find themselves amply rewarded for their trouble. Charlotte, however, had not sufficient courage for this expedition; but Julia was eager to explore every part of the ruins, and ascended the staircase with Chartres, notwithstanding the remonstrances of Seymour, who was persuaded she would meet with some accident, and cast an indignant look at Chartres for making the proposition. Julia found the staircase much decayed: many of the steps were broken; the roof was so low that one could not stand upright; and the light was only admitted through narrow clefts in the thick stone wall. This ascent opened on a turret which commanded a noble prospect, and connected the shattered towers together; leading also to a narrow footway round the top of the chapel, the walls of which were still entire, though the whole roof had fallen in, except one arch, carved with the most exquisite fret-work, and which, when surveyed from below, seemed suspended in air, and threatened with every breeze to crush the prying mortal who trod those hallowed precincts. Seymour was obliged to remain below with Charlotte; and, when he looked up and saw Julia on that dangerous height, felt all his enthusiasm for ruined abbies vanish, and wished this tottering pile had long ago been levelled to its foundations. Meantime, Julia gazed from the turret on the sublime landscape which surrounded her, and the venerable ruins, with that solemn emotion so grateful to a contemplative mind.[133] 'Surely,' thought she, (in the fervor of an elevated spirit,) 'surely the inhabitants of this retreat were happy! – Ah, could it be difficult to renounce a world, where an ardent heart so often finds its hopes disappointed, its joys embittered, and seek for 'Peace, the sacred sister of the cell!' This vast expanse of water, the distant sound of that falling torrent, and those lofty mountains that arrest the clouds in their progress, must have inspired a frame of mind, in which the concerns of the world are considered in all their littleness, and have no power to affect our tranquillity.' – Such were the reflections which passed in Julia's mind, but which only lasted till she was out of sight of the abbey.

When she descended from the turret, they walked over the floor of the chapel, which was now covered with loose stones, half overgrown with nettles. Under the towers were a number of gloomy subterraneous apartments with vaulted roofs, the use of which imagination was left to guess, and could only appropriate to punishment and horror.

Charlotte, who had in vain reminded Julia several times of going home, now told her, 'That she hoped she was not determined to take up her abode at the abbey; because,' added Charlotte, 'though our own house is less sublime, it has the advantage of being roofed.' Julia consented to go; and, as they passed through the area of the building, they heard the shrill cry of the daws and rooks,[134] and the twittering note of the swallows and martins,[135] which now occupied this habitation, deserted by man.

When the party had passed through the old gateway, they stopped to look at the thick moss, and rich folds of ivy, whose mantling branches overspread, with the wildest luxuriance, this haunt of desolation. The wind had risen, and the lake was violently agitated: Julia turned her eyes from the abbey, to contemplate the surges of the lake, while Charlotte, who was at a little distance behind, leaning on Seymour, stopped to look at a cavity in the wall, in which the snail had made his nest. At that moment a gust of wind shook the building, and some loose stones fell from the top of the wall and rolled with velocity down the hill, in the direction where Julia was walking; whom they would inevitably have crushed in their passage, if Seymour had not flown with impetuosity and snatched her from the impending destruction. She received no other injury than a blow from a small stone, that struck her ancle, which was bruised by the stroke, and became swelled and painful from the swiftness with which he had hurried her over the rough and hilly grounds. Supported by Charlotte and Seymour, who, in his present agitation, forgot his usual scruples, and felt no disposition to resign his charge to Chartres, Julia walked on slowly. Chartres was sent forward to the place where the servants and horses were waiting, with orders that one of the men should hasten home, and send the carriage to that spot. In the mean time, Julia walked with great difficulty along that narrow and dangerous road which has been before described, and which was two miles in length; but she had not gone far before her ancle swelled so much, that it could support her weight no longer, and she was unable to proceed. 'I will go,' said Seymour, 'and bring the servants to assist me, in conveying Miss Clifford to the carriage.' 'No, no,' replied Charlotte, 'here is no place for Julia to rest on: you can support her better than me, and I will run to the top of this rising ground, and look for the carriage.' 'Mr. Seymour will go faster than you,' said Julia. 'I shall be back instantly,' replied Charlotte; and she flew with a light step up the hill, before Julia had time to frame any farther objection to her going. Julia felt uneasy at being left alone with Seymour: she was obliged to lean on his arm, and he hung over her in silence, but with a look that spoke his feelings more forcibly than any words he could have uttered. – She wished to speak, but had no power to make the effort; and appeared to feel considerable pain. 'Oh, why was I not a moment sooner,' said Seymour, with much emotion, 'that I might have saved you those sufferings!' 'They are very trifling,' said Julia, 'and you have surely no cause of self-reproach on that score, since you preserved my life at the risk of your own.' 'Oh,' cried he with vehemence, 'if you knew in how little estimation I hold my life, you would not think I had any merit in having hazarded it: – but the reflection that I have been the instrument of your preservation, I shall ever cherish as the most delightful that can occupy my mind!' He spoke, but Julia could no longer listen: overcome with pain of body, and agitation of mind; she grew faint; and Charlotte, at that moment, returned with Chartres: and the servants, who assisted Seymour in conveying Julia to the carriage. She had walked a considerable way after the accident: her ancle was violently swelled; and bruised by the blow, and the pain she suffered, joined to more than common fatigue that morning, occasioned some degree of fever; and she was confined a few days to her room.

Frederick Seymour now found, that, however painful were his sensations in her presence, the pang which her absence awakened was more insupportable than any other. Although she constantly treated him with a degree of reserve, which wrung his heart with anguish, it was still a consolation to be near her. It was soothing to hear her voice, though her lips to him had lost their utterance. It was a pleasure to hang upon her looks, though from him her eyes were averted. He was so restless and uneasy, that he did little else but wander from one apartment to another, seizing with avidity the most trivial information he could procure respecting her, from any of the family.

Mr. Seymour was almost as anxious as his brother for Julia's recovery; for he saw, that if her illness lasted much longer, there was some reason to fear that his behaviour would betray the secrets of his heart, and that Charlotte's great fortune would be lost to the family. When Julia was well enough to leave her room, she was led to the drawing-room by Charlotte, who placed her on the sofa, and then left her to dress for dinner. A short time after, Frederick Seymour entered the room, without knowing she was there. His delight at seeing her was too great to be suppressed: he flew to the sofa, seized her hand, which she in vain endeavoured to withdraw, pressed it to his lips, and poured forth expressions of the most unbounded rapture at her recovery. 'You seem determined, Sir,' said Julia, snatching her hand from him, 'to make me wish I was still confined to my room.' 'How cruel, how inhuman,' cried he, 'after so many days of distraction, to forbid the momentary expression of joy, which rushes from my soul to my lips at the sight of you! What have I done? How have I deserved?' – 'Oh heaven!' said Julia, leaning back on the sofa, and turning very pale, 'how have *I* deserved this persecution? – Leave me, Sir, instantly; I am too weak at present' – She stopt, unable to proceed. Seymour, with a frantic look, passionately exclaimed, 'Oh, wretch that I am! – you are ill – look up, angelic excellence! – What have I said? Have I dared to utter a complaint? a complaint of you! – Oh, say but you forgive me! Men stretched upon the rack; in the extremity of their misery; are sometimes wicked enough to impeach the guiltless.' – Mr. Chartres at this moment entered the room, and made Julia a low bow, accompanied with all the positions, which were very familiar to him at present; for he had practised a little dancing privately in his own room every day since the ball, with a laudable wish to make himself more agreeable to the ladies. He congratulated Julia upon her recovery, informing her, at the same time, 'that the whole human race were subject to accident, and infirmity; that such was the law of our nature, from which neither the vigor of youth nor the bloom of beauty were exempt; and recommending to her earnestly the study of mathematics, which, if she felt any disposition to repine, would fortify her mind against the casualties of life.'

Julia, though she was unable to listen to his harangue, found a relief in his presence, and in a few minutes grew better; while Frederick Seymour walked up and down the room in a distracted manner, frequently putting his hand to his forehead with the action of a man in despair, and enquiring of Julia, a thousand times over, if she found herself better; till the appearance of the rest of the family obliged him to rouse his faculties, and assume a look of calmness to which his heart was a stranger.

Charlotte, during Julia's confinement to her room, had found her one morning looking over some papers; and spied among them a Sonnet to Hope, written by Julia, of which Charlotte took a copy.

## SONNET to HOPE.[136]

Oh, ever skill'd to wear the form we love!
To bid the shapes of fear and grief depart,
Come, gentle Hope! With one gay smile remove
The lasting sadness of an aching heart.
Thy voice, benign enchantress! Let me hear;
Say that for me some pleasures yet shall bloom!
That fancy's radiance, friendship's precious tear,

Shall soften, or shall chase, misfortune's gloom. –
But come not glowing in the dazzling ray
Which once with dear illusions charm'd my eye!
Oh strew no more, sweet flatterer! On my way
The flowers I fondly thought too bright to die.
Visions less fair will sooth my pensive breast,
That asks not happiness, but longs for rest!

## CHAP. XVII.

Mr. Seymour now fixed the day for his departure from Mr. Clifford's seat, where the uniform mode of living began to grow extremely irksome to him, who required variety of amusements, who was accustomed to a wide range of dissipation and gaiety, and could not long be confined, without disgust, to the circle of domestic enjoyments. Besides, every purpose of his visit was now fully answered, having staid a sufficient time to ingratiate himself completely into Mr. Clifford's favor, who conceived the highest opinion of his worth, and offered to assist him with all his influence, (which his large fortune rendered very considerable in the county where he lived,) in some electioneering business. Independently, however, of this particular consideration, Mr. Seymour had foreseen that Mr. Clifford's interest might on many occasions be of use, and had therefore determined to secure it himself, trusting but little to the mediation of Frederick Seymour, who he knew was a novice in the arts of solicitation, and was not likely to make any improvement in a science which he disdained.

Mr. Seymour had secured Julia's esteem by his apparent candour and benevolence, and had obtained her admiration by the brilliancy of his conversation, and his fine taste for those elegant arts which she loved with the fondest enthusiasm. She saw that he had long discovered his brother's passion for her, and felt grateful to him for the kindness and delicacy with which, on many occasions, he had relieved her embarrassments, without appearing to observe them, and had often saved Frederick Seymour from betraying his emotions, by giving a playful turn to the conversation. Julia was not aware, that Mr. Seymour's motive for this conduct was neither kind nor delicate; and arose merely from his apprehension of his brother's losing an advantageous marriage, in which the interest of the whole family was concerned. But the real motives which influence men of the world, can be as little known from their actions, as the original hue of some muddy substance, which, by chemical operations, has been made to assume a tint of the purest colour.

The task of obtaining Julia's friendship was by no means unpleasant to Mr. Seymour, who was charmed with her beauty, and sometimes extolled it with a freedom of admiration, which he found was extremely disgusting to a mind so delicate, and from which he had therefore at length the prudence to desist.

It was agreed that Frederick Seymour should accompany Mr. and Mrs. Seymour, and Mrs. Melbourne, to London, to settle some affairs, and to hire a villa which Mr. Seymour recommended to him, about thirty miles from town; where he might bring

Charlotte immediately upon her marriage, which was to take place within a fortnight.

Mrs. Melbourne looked forward with secret satisfaction to the period of her departure from Mr. Clifford's for she began to grow exceedingly tired for want of her usual occupations; having no servants to scold when alone, and to complain of when in company; and, though in Mr. Clifford's numerous train of domestics she saw a fine field for action, yet she was not at liberty to display her talents for command, and could take no part in the management of the household, except that of warning Charlotte against the impositions of servants, whom she always mentioned as the most degenerate of the human race. But, unhappily for the success of these doctrines, Charlotte had already found by experience, that kindness awakened gratitude, and that confidence ensured affection. The human heart revolts against oppression, and is soothed by gentleness, as the wave of the ocean rises in proportion to the violence of the winds, and sinks with the breeze into mildness and serenity. Mrs. Melbourne met with as little encouragement in the comments which she occasionally made upon the visitors at Mr. Clifford's house; where she could find no person to whom sarcasm and severity were agreeable, except Mrs. Seymour, and began to pine for more auditors.

In this mansion, which was the abode of benevolence and universal good-will, Mrs. Melbourne was in the situation of an unfortunate wasp who has lost his sting, and, though he still feels a great inclination for mischief, has no power to gratify it. The frequent reading parties at Mr. Clifford's afforded that lady as little amusement as the stile of conversation in this family; where the best new publications were sent from town, and perused with a degree of candour, which gave her no small offence. She felt that, next to bestowing money, nothing was so disagreeable as bestowing praise; and was almost as avaricious of commendation as of gold, to all except her daughter, to whom she was ever ready to give an accumulated heap of both. Mrs. Melbourne was, however, too prudent to dispute the merit of those literary performances, whose claims to applause had been long appreciated by the voice of the public; but, where genius was not clad in the strong armour of mature reputation, she crept like the snake to the cradle of Hercules,[137] and with better success, for she could dart upon an infant author with great skill and ingenuity –

> 'Damn with faint praise, assent with civil leer,
> And, without sneering, teach the rest to sneer.'[138]

But what, more than either her desire of power, or her fondness of satire, impelled Mrs. Melbourne to hasten her departure, was, that she had caught a cold, and began to apprehend that the air of the north was too sharp for her constitution. She had a more than common horror at the thoughts of dying, and, whenever that terrific idea obtruded itself, hastened to banish it from her affrighted mind by every effort in her power; and, when she failed of success, endeavoured to find comfort in recollecting all the instances of longevity she had ever heard, and which were carefully treasured in her memory. She found some refuge for her fears in such of her acquaintances as were older, and more infirm than herself; and hoped, by an unremitting care of her own person, to extend life to its utmost limits: but, when attacked by the slightest malady, she instantly fancied that she perceived the approaches of the grisly phantom, couched under the head-ach, or advancing in the rear of a cold, and armed herself for defence with a formidable force of medicine. Nor was there a disorder to which the human frame is liable, of which she had not felt, at some period or other, the most indubitable symptoms. Her physician, who was a man of a very liberal mind, sometimes reasoned, and sometimes laughed at her weakness; but pleasantry and reason were both administered in vain to her distempered imagination, which preferred a prescription to argument, and a cordial drug to the gayest effusions of wit.

The day of Mr. Seymour's departure arrived, and Mr. Clifford proposed, with his daughter and niece, to accompany the travellers twenty miles on their journey. The whole family accordingly set out together. Julia was at some pains to avoid going in the same carriage with Frederick Seymour; and, at the inn where the party stopped to breakfast before they separated, she was careful to place herself at a distance from him. He did not venture to approach her, but appeared thoughtful and melancholy.

When the carriages were ready, Charlotte took hold of Mrs. Seymour's arm, and they went out together. Frederick Seymour was near the door, and Julia kept back, pretending to look at something from the window, till she thought he was gone: but he suffered the other gentlemen to pass him, and then, after desiring aloud to have the honour of handing her down stairs, he stopt her for a moment, and said, in the greatest agitation, 'Must I, then, leave you under the cruel impression of having entirely forfeited your esteem.' 'If *that*, Sir, was of any value to you –' '*If*,' interrupted he, with vehemence, 'it was of any value to me! What a cruel surmise! – Ah, when that esteem is altogether lost, the link by which I hold my existence will be broken. In pity to the wretchedness of my heart, say that you will forgive the past.' 'I will remember it no more.'

They now reached the door of the inn, and Frederick Seymour, in the perturbation of his mind, almost forgot to bid Charlotte farewel; who, however, attributed his apparent chagrin to the thoughts of his separation from herself.

Mr. Chartres had displayed so much unaffected sorrow at the prospect of leaving Mr. Clifford's, that he received an invitation from that gentleman to remain with him till his return to town. This young man had one peculiarity in which he resembled Mr. Nathaniel Transfer*;[139] (a personage whose acquaintance every reader of taste is, no doubt, proud to acknowledge). Mr. Chartres only liked those things to which he had been long *accustomed*. He had looked forward to his introduction at Mr. Clifford's with a degree of apprehension which sometimes deprived him of appetite, and sometimes of rest; but, being now *accustomed* to the family, he desired no happiness beyond its society, and was in transports of joy when he found that happiness would be prolonged;[140] remarking, in their way home, 'That pleasure, after uneasiness, was particularly grateful to the heart of man; and, in my opinion,' added he, 'the country, to those who have a competent knowledge of Greek, Latin, and experimental philosophy, is far preferable to a town.' 'Well, Mr. Chartres,' said Charlotte, 'I can entertain myself in the country without being obliged to any of your auxiliaries.' But a man who has leisure,' rejoined Chartres, 'should

* Vide Zeluco. (Williams's note)

not live merely for his own entertainment, but have recourse to science, for the benefit of posterity.' Charlotte asked him, 'if he intended, in kindness to posterity, to adopt those studies when he came back from the East?' 'Certainly,' answered Chartres; 'and although I consider riches as an ignoble pursuit, my love of experimental philosophy will prompt me to acquire wealth, in the hopes of adding something to the stock of useful learning at my return to my native country.'

Mr. Clifford and his party, in their way home, came to the foot of a very steep hill, and Charlotte proposed that they should alight, and walk up the hill. In their way, they passed a small cottage, or rather hut, where they saw a lovely young woman, who appeared about eighteen years of age, sitting at the door, and crying bitterly: two little girls were crying with her. 'What is the matter?' said Charlotte: one of the children answered, 'that *she* cried because Hannah cried.' 'Have you met with any misfortune?' said Charlotte. 'My poor dog, Madam,' answered the young woman, sobbing, 'I have lost him.' 'Is that all?' rejoined Charlotte, 'you can get another dog.' 'But he will not have been Harry's dog,' replied the young woman; who then, in a voice often choaked by tears, told Charlotte her story. She had been courted by a young peasant, and the day was fixed for their wedding. Her father and mother were both dead; but her brother, with whom she lived, had bought her a new gown, and a set of red ribbands for her marriage; when her lover returning home from his work one stormy night, across a rapid stream, the boat overset, and the young man was drowned. His dog, Rover, had jumped into the water, dragged his master on shore, and then lay down near the dead body moaning most piteously. Hannah, and her brother, who began to fear, from Harry's long stay, that some evil had befallen him, went out to look for him, and found his corpse on the bank of the stream, and Rover stretched beside it. Poor Hannah, at the sight of her dead lover, wished to die too; but her brother intreated her to be comforted, and live for the sake of her young brothers and sisters. It was with difficulty that Hannah could be torn from her lover's corpse, and Rover seemed as unwilling to leave it as herself. 'Rover,' she said, 'if he had been a christian, could not have loved his master better, or took his loss more to heart; and ever since that time, it had been a sort of comfort to her to have the poor dog always with her. Many a time,' she said, 'she had talked to him of his master, and often, when they had not victuals enough for themselves and Rover too, she had gone without a morsel, to give it to him; for Rover eat as much as any of the children; and now he had gone and lost himself in the wood.' Julia asked her 'if it was not a pleasure to take care of those pretty children, and see them thrive.' She said 'Yes, she would try and live as long as she could, for their sakes, but she knew her heart would break at last.' A countryman now appeared at a distance, calling out, 'Hannah, Hannah!' He was her brother, with Rover in his arms. Hannah flew to the dog, kissed him a thousand times, and asked him, how he could leave her? Rover wagged his tail heartily, and seemed to partake in the joy of their meeting. There were many marks of extreme poverty discernible in these poor people, and their habitation, although they made no complaint. But it would seem that the precious essence of content can be more easily extracted from the simple materials of the poor, than from the various preparations of the rich. Its pure and fine spirit rises from a few plain ingredients, brighter and clearer than from that magical cup of dissipation, where the powerful, and the wealthy, with lengthened incantations, pour their costly infusions – 'double, double, toil and trouble!'[141]

Mr. Clifford asked Peter, 'How he could get enough by his work to maintain so large a family?' Peter said, 'To be sure it was not easy, but they were good children, and moreover, he had promised his father, when he lay a dying, to take care of them; but sometimes he could get no work, and then it went a little hard with them to be sure.' Mr. Clifford, touched by the simple goodness of this young peasant, generously offered to give him a cottage in his own neighbourhood and to employ him in working in his grounds. The proposal was accepted with transport; and, the very next day, Peter, accompanied by Hannah, the children, and Rover, set out for his new habitation.

Julia and Charlotte employed themselves in making camlet-gowns and round caps for the children, who were delighted with their new finery; while poor Hannah cried, and said, 'she never thought to be so happy again; and she wished Harry had but lived to see the little ones in their new gowns, for he always loved the children.' The happiness of this poor family was amply shared by their kind benefactors. Charlotte was so busy in furnishing their cottage, and providing for their wants, that she almost forgot the absence of her lover; and Julia assisted, with delighted assiduity, in these offices of charity.

# CHAP. XVIII.

Frederick Seymour, in his letters to Charlotte, informed her that business would detain him in town longer than he expected; and the day he fixed for his return was only that preceding the day of his marriage. Afraid of trusting his feelings in so critical a situation, he determined to delay his return as long as it was possible.

The day before that on which Seymour was expected, Mr. Clifford was invited to a gentleman's house in the neighbourhood, where an old friend of his was just arrived from the East Indies, and was to pass one night in his way to the habitation of his parents. Mr. Clifford could not deny himself the satisfaction of presenting his daughter to his friend; and Charlotte, though her mind was too much occupied by the approaching change in her situation, to leave her any inclination for company, determined to go, because her father wished it.

Julia, agitated and oppressed, desired nothing so much as a day of solitude, in which she might fortify her mind by reflection, form plans for her future conduct, settle every account with her own heart, and prepare to meet Frederick Seymour with composure, and even chearfulness. She therefore complained of being slightly indisposed, and requested permission to remain at home, which was reluctantly granted. Mr. Chartres accompanied Mr. Clifford and Charlotte, and Julia saw them depart with pleasure, soothed with the prospect of one day of tranquillity. She walked to her favourite nook, that over-hung the lake, and contemplated the majesty of nature; passed some hours in meditation, and returned home with a mind elevated above the sadness and depression with which she had set out.

After dinner she visited some of the cottagers.[142] It was a bright afternoon in October, and she loitered in her way home to admire the rich variety of tints which were cast on the surrounding scenery; she then saw the setting sun sinking slowly behind a hill at some distance, from which a vapour ascended that was tinged, as it arose, by the glowing rays, and gave the broad summit of the hill the appearance of a stream of floating flame.

Julia had never before observed this effect of the setting sun, which she gazed at till the bright vision gradually dissolved, and 'Twilight grey, had in her sober liv'ry all things clad.'[143] To a lover of nature, the last days of autumn are peculiarly interesting. We take leave of the fading beauties of the season with a melancholy emotion, somewhat similar to that which we feel in bidding farewell to a lively and agreeable companion, whose presence has diffused gladness, whose smile has been the signal of pleasure, and whom we are uncertain of beholding again: for, though the period of his return is fixed, *who*, amidst the casualties of life, can be secure, that, in the interval of absence, *his* eye shall not be closed in darkness, and *his* heart have lost the sensation of delight?

When Julia returned to the house, she found one of the servants was sent back by Charlotte with a note, informing her, that her father had been prevailed on to remain that night. Julia was thankful for this reprieve. She congratulated herself on the comfort of one evening of undisturbed calmness, brought a volume of each of her favourite poets, Pope and Thomson,[144] from the library, and ordered tea, to which she thought that stillness and poetry gave a more agreeable flavor than usual, when the door was suddenly opened by Frederick Seymour. At his appearance, she started from her seat; but, immediately recollecting herself, spoke to him with all the composure she could assume. 'Mr. Seymour,' said she, 'you were so little expected to-night, that my uncle and Charlotte are gone to pay a visit.' 'I thought,' he answered, with great emotion, 'that it would not have been in my power to return to-night, but, as my business was finished, I had little inclination to remain absent till to-morrow.' He appeared in much agitation. Julia, on her part, determined to support the trial of the evening with firmness and dignity, talked on subjects of indifference. Afraid of any interval of silence, she made an effort, the most painful, to keep up a conversation, almost intirely unsupported on the part of Seymour; and, without seeming to observe his confusion, continued speaking, till at length he recovered some degree of composure.

When other topics were exhausted, Julia, disturbed and unhappy, almost unable to speak, and yet terrified to remain silent, had recourse, in her perplexities, to the setting sun, whose uncommon appearance that evening she described; though, in the present perturbation of her thoughts, it had lost all power of affecting her imagination: she painted the scene with little energy, and the picture seemed to interest Seymour still less than herself. She then talked of the country, which was, at present, as indifferent to her as the setting sun; and obliged Seymour to repeat descriptions of the sublime scenes of Switzerland,[145] which he had often given her before with animation and spirit, and which he now gave with the utmost coldness and difficulty. Thence she took refuge in Italy, and made him lead her through half Europe, glad to be transported, as far as possible from herself.

Tea was protracted as long as she could – it was having something to do. When that resource failed, she took up her work, affected to be very busy, and asked him to read some of Pope's moral epistles,[146] which lay upon the table. He read very ill, and with such absence of mind, that, when Julia, at the end of an epistle, mentioned the passages which particularly pleased her, he answered in such a manner as shewed that he scarcely recollected the subject. At length the description of Timon's villa[147] put him in mind of the contrast between that and the beautiful villa he had just taken; and he laid down the book, to give Julia an account of the disposition of the grounds, with which she appeared extremely pleased. 'And when will you visit it?' said Seymour, in a tone of emotion. 'Probably next summer,' she answered. 'Not till next summer!' rejoined Seymour. 'You will, I believe, be settled in town,' said Julia, 'before my uncle leaves this place; if not, we shall certainly come in search of Charlotte.' 'Charlotte!' he repeated – 'she is very amiable.' 'She is indeed,' said Julia, with earnestness, 'every thing the heart can wish in a domestic companion.' She then gave Seymour the history of the poor peasant's family, and described, with enthusiasm, Charlotte's active benevolence. 'Oh! why,' said Seymour, with an emotion he seemed wholly unable to control, 'why, when Charlotte possesses so many virtues, should there exist *one*, to whom Charlotte – Oh Julia! Your penetration has discovered' – She immediately rose to leave the room. 'Oh stay but one moment,' he eagerly cried, 'in compassion, Madam, stay but while I solemnly assure you, that you have nothing more to fear from my complaints – that they shall never again be uttered in your presence, that they shall never again disturb your felicity. – Oh may every felicity attend you! – May *you* be happy, when the grave shall have covered my despair, and my heart shall retain no longer those sensations, which are interwoven with my existence.' Julia walking towards the door as fast as she could, he came up to her: 'Say but you forgive me – Oh go not, Madam, if you wish me to preserve life or reason, go not from me in displeasure!' She turned back: her eyes were filled with tears. 'I return, Sir,' she said, in a faltering voice, 'only to tell you, that another scene like this, will force me to forsake the asylum I have found beneath my uncle's roof, and conceal myself where I may never more be heard of.' 'Oh do not terrify me with such images; in compassion forgive the ravings of madness, and never shall they again offend you.' The anguish of his looks, and the extreme perturbation of his voice and manner affected her. 'I will forget what is past,' she faintly pronounced. He seized her hand, and pressed it to his heart. She hastened out of the room: he held the door open, and looked after her, till she had crossed the saloon, and was out of sight.

When she had sufficiently recovered herself, she rung the bell for her maid, told her she was not very well, and desired, that one of the servants would beg of Mr. Seymour to order supper for himself at what hour he chose. Seymour passed the evening in an agitation of mind, which gave him reason to repent of the weakness that had led him to change his resolution not to return till the next day.

Julia, for a short time, indulged that sadness excited by the painful scene which had past. She then tried to read, but could not command her attention, and walked to a window, where she saw, above some dark rocks, that overhung the lake in the shape of ruins, the sky tinged with a variety of colours, which were reflected on the surface of the water. The northern lights flashed over the hemisphere, and their motion was stronger than usual. Julia gazed a considerable time on those beautiful appearances of nature, and in such contemplation, which had ever a most powerful effect on her mind, regained some composure before she retired to rest.

# CHAP. XIX.

The following morning Julia breakfasted in her own apartment, and Mr. Clifford and Charlotte returned soon after. Through the course of this day, Julia avoided, as much as was in her power, the sight of Seymour, for she trembled lest any discovery of his feelings should yet prevent the marriage, and earnestly wished for the arrival of the succeeding day, which would for ever unite him to another, and, by banishing all suspence and doubt, lead him to exert the constancy and resolution of his spirit. And she hoped, that when his situation was irrevocable, the certainty of its being so would prove a great and powerful antidote against the indulgence of unavailing regrets.

Mr. Clifford was in high spirits, and Chartres displayed, though somewhat in a bungling manner, his sympathy in the felicity of his friends. The whole house was a scene of general chearfulness; the servants were busy in adjusting their silver favours, and making preparations for the marriage day; and, as Charlotte was beloved by every individual in the family, all were solicitous and proud to display their joy and exultation.

Mean while, Seymour passed the day in the most violent struggles of passion, the most cruel conflict between honour and inclination. But, when we attempt to describe the struggles of passion, how inadequate is language to its purpose! – Where are the words that shall convey a just idea of the pangs of wounded affection? – Alas! the heart can feel more strongly than the imagination can paint; and, even while we heave the sigh of commiseration for the sufferer, we do not reflect on the full force of his sufferings. We cannot exactly judge of the bitterness of those moments when the overwhelmed spirit flies to solitude to give vent to its stifled agonies; when sorrow absorbs every faculty of the soul; when it rejects every thought of consolation, and finds a gloomy indulgence in nourishing its own wretchedness! Yet Seymour was obliged to appear not merely contented, but animated and happy. Oh, surely the moment in which misery is most intolerable to the human mind, is, when we are condemned to conceal its despondency under the mask of joy! To wear a look of gladness, while our souls are bleeding with that wound which gives a mortal stab to all our future peace! It is then that the anguish, which has been for a moment repulsed to make room for other ideas, rushes with redoubled force upon the sickening heart, and oppresses it with a species of torment little short of madness. The effusions of gaiety, which are so exhilarating to a mind at ease, come to an aching breast as a ray of the sun falls upon ice, too deep to be penetrated by its influence.

Charlotte and Julia, the next morning, went in one carriage, and Mr. Clifford, Seymour, and Chartres, in another, to the church of —, where the marriage ceremony was performed. They returned, accompanied by the clergyman, to breakfast, after which, the new-married pair were to set out for the country seat that was prepared for their reception and where they were to pass some weeks. When the carriages which were to convey the married couple, and their attendants, were ready, Charlotte, after embracing Julia, and taking leave of Chartres, felt her heart too full at this awful separation from her father, to bid him farewell before a number of witnesses: she could not trust her voice, but, taking his hand, led him to another room. The clergyman and Chartres sauntered, mean time, to the door of the saloon, to examine the equipage in waiting; and Seymour and Julia were left together. 'Will you suffer me,' he said, 'Miss Clifford, before I go, to express the regret – the contrition I feel, for all the uneasiness my conduct must have given you? May I implore you to banish from your remembrance, that persecution for which I feel the truest penitence; and to believe that my respect, my admiration of your virtues –' 'Talk no more, Sir, of the past,' she replied: then, rising from her seat, she added, 'I must go in search of Charlotte.' 'Will you not,' rejoined Seymour, 'greatly as I have offended, bestow one generous wish for my peace at parting?' 'I sincerely wish, Sir, your felicity, and surely no mortal has a fairer prospect of happiness than yourself.' 'Of happiness!' he exclaimed, and, after a moment's pause, added, 'May *you*, Madam, be happy as your virtues deserve, happy as *I* wish you! – To hear of your felicity will be the only' – then checking himself, he said, 'but I will not presume to detain you.' Julia was hastening out of the room, when Mr. Clifford and Charlotte returned: the two friends again embraced each other in silence. Mr. Clifford led his daughter to the carriage, Seymour followed, and in a few minutes Charlotte was out of sight of her paternal dwelling.

Mr. Clifford feasted his tenants liberally; who drank with much vociferation to the happiness of their fair mistress; and the day was passed in festivity. Chartres joined heartily in the general mirth, and, when his spirits were elevated by repeated toasts to Charlotte's felicity, sung his best songs for the entertainment of the company. He had a very powerful voice, and sung as he danced, with all his strength and might, and as if he thought the first excellence of singing was to be loud.

Julia, in an adjoining apartment, thankfully listened to this noisy merriment, which, by engaging Mr. Clifford's attention, spared her the task of struggling with a conscious sadness that weighed upon her heart, and which, though she determined to subdue it, refused to be instantly repulsed by any effort of her reason. Chartres alarmed her not a little, by enquiring of Mr. Clifford, 'what could be the reason that Mr. Seymour turned as pale as death when he presented his bride with the wedding-ring?' Mr. Clifford replied, 'That it was not uncommon to be agitated on so solemn an occasion.' To this Chartres rejoined, 'That Mr. Seymour's countenance that morning, had convinced him, that matrimony was a very solemn affair indeed.'

# CHAP. XX.

Julia's perplexities were now over. She felt that she ought to be happy, and endeavoured to persuade herself that she was so. Nevertheless, the scenes which had passed with Seymour, had left her mind in a state of disturbance and depression, which she could not immediately conquer, but which she determined not to indulge.

By her affectionate attention, she tried to supply to Mr. Clifford the loss of his daughter; made every effort to be cheerful; and when, in spite of her efforts, her cheerfulness forsook her, she imputed it to an anxious solicitude which hung upon her mind respecting Charlotte's happiness.

It was fortunate that Julia had at this time but little leisure for solitude, or reflection, Mr. Clifford's house being crouded with a succession of visitors, who came to congratulate him on his daughter's marriage. We must add, much to the honour of Charlotte, that their congratulations were not made in opposition to their feelings: and what higher eulogium can we bestow on Charlotte's merit, than to declare that her prosperity excited no envy? Her uniform sweetness of disposition, her kind and unassuming manners, and constant attention to promote the satisfaction of others, had endeared her to all by whom she was known; and even those who had the greatest insensibility of temper, agreed, that if some one in the world must be more fortunate, more happy than themselves, Charlotte was the very person who best deserved that distinguished lot.

Among Mr. Clifford's visitors was Mr. F—, who was dressed in deep mourning, and appeared in great dejection of spirits. In the course of a walk, which Mr. Clifford proposed, Mr. F— took an opportunity of telling Julia, that he had lately lost his only brother. 'The circumstances of his death,' said he, 'are such as I am unable to relate, but they were particularly affecting, and, if you will give me permission, I will send you a packet which contains the account, and which, I believe, will interest you.' The next morning Julia received the following letters:

To G— F—, Esq.  
Long Island, August, 1776. [148]

My dear Sir,

To communicate afflicting intelligence is so painful a task, that I am only prompted to undertake it by the consideration that it is a duty which friendship on this occasion demands. I must not leave you to be informed by public report of our mutual misfortune. Your gallant brother, my dear friend, fell in the action of yesterday.

As we marched to the attack, he was uncommonly gay. Having received a severe wound in the arm, he refused to leave the ranks, and continued to encourage the soldiers, till a second shot brought him to the ground; and even then he would not permit any of the men to leave the action to carry him off. The surgeon dressed his wounds on the spot where he fell. After we had driven the enemy from the intrenchments, he was borne to a hut by four grenadiers.[149] 'Albeit unused to the melting mood,' their cheeks were bathed in tears. As they passed one soldier who lay wounded on the ground, the poor fellow, seeing his officer, raised his languid head, and said, 'God Almighty recover, and bless your honour!' My friend insisted on their stopping: he took the soldier by the hand, saying, 'I thank you, my brave lad; be of good cheer, I'll send your friends for you directly.' The soldier repeated, 'God Almighty bless you!' and expired.

I passed the night with your brother; and it was a most affecting night. He talked with much emotion of the anguish you would feel. He desired his effects might be given to certain officers whom he named: his ring to one; watch to another, &c. hoping they would keep them as remembrances of a departed comrade and friend. He then took from his bosom the profile of a young lady, whom I had often heard him mention with rapture. 'Send this profile,' said he, 'by the first proper opportunity, to my beloved Sophia: let her know that I parted with this dear remembrance but in death! – Alas! how will she sustain this affliction? – Heaven support and comfort her! – Oh my Sophia! Shall we meet no more?

His ruling passion, a thirst for military fame, did not forsake him even in these last moments; and I am convinced that he regretted his approaching dissolution most on account of its cutting him short in the career of glory. To me he made a present of his sword. 'May it be your protector in the hour of danger,' said he, laying his cold hand on mine – 'and lead you to a degree of distinction, to which I once hoped it would have conducted me. I regret not the loss of life; but, my dear Edward, I do regret, like Douglas, 'to be cut off glory's course'[150] – 'which,' added he, with a dying voice, 'never mortal was so fond to run!' Judge, my dear friend, how I was affected – how I am affected! – I cannot continue.

Julia found, inclosed in the foregoing letter, a packet which Mr. F— had received from the same gentleman, some weeks after the former.

My dear Sir,
We are preparing to march, and I have only time to transmit to you the enclosed packet, which I received a few days ago. Adieu – God bless you.

E. C.

Sir,

The intelligence you received by the messenger who brought your letter to me, conveying the tidings of Captain F—'s death, and enclosing my friend Sophia Herbert's profile, was, alas, too true. When your messenger left this place, she lay in the delirium of a fever. You tell me, in your second letter, that a better principle than curiosity leads you to enquire into the history of this unfortunate attachment. To gratify this request will be a relief to my afflicted mind.

Mr. Herbert had an estate in the neighbourhood of Norfolk, in Virginia, and his house was within half a mile of the town. This gentleman had two sons and a daughter. The eldest son, who was personally known to General Washington,[151] had been appointed one of his aid-du-camps, and was with the main army: the younger son remained with his father, and was walking with him, and his sister, on the lawn before their house, when the cry of arms was heard. The young man hastily tore himself from his sister, flew to his arms, and rushed towards the town: his father prepared to follow. Surprise and horror had, for a few moments, deprived Sophia of the power of speech or motion; but she now clung round her father's neck, and implored him not to desert her. He disengaged himself from her hold, intreated her to be calm, and go instantly to the house; told her he would soon return, and recommended her to the care of Heaven.

Sophia looked after him in silent agony, and, when he was out of sight, still continued standing in the same attitude, unable to shed a tear. At length she saw a soldier running past the end of the lawn, and called to him to stop. The soldier paused a moment – he was one of her father's tenants. 'Ah, Madam,' he exclaimed, 'all is over; our troops have given way, and the English have set fire to the town; I have no time' – 'Stop,' she eagerly cried, with horror in her looks, 'Have you seen my father, and brother?' 'Ah, Madam, you will never see your brother more; I served in his company, and saw him fall, and I fear –.' Sophia waited not for more, she gave a piercing shriek, and flew with precipitation towards the town; but, as she approached, the sight of the spreading flames, the tumultuous cries of the women, and the clash of arms, made her shrink back involuntarily. She had, however, gone too far to retreat, and was mingled with a crowd of helpless women and children, who were flying in desperation, they knew not whither; some hastening from the scene of desolation, others returning, with distracted countenances, to save an aged parent – or a helpless infant from the fury of the flames. Careless of danger, and almost insensible of her situation, Sophia still pressed forward, till she was stopped by a bleeding corpse which opposed her passage; when casting her eyes down, she perceived the features of her brother, disfigured by death, and covered with blood. She clasped her hands – her lips moved, but they had lost the power of utterance: her whole frame trembled, and she fell senseless on her brother's corpse. When she recovered, she found herself supported by an English officer, who gazed on her with a look of earnest solicitude. She appeared for some minutes unconscious of all that had passed; but, when her recollection returned, and she perceived the dead body of her beloved brother, her sufferings were renewed in all their bitterness. Disengaging herself from the arm that supported her, she pressed the remains of her brother to her bosom, and bathed them with her tears. The officer intreated she would permit him to lead her from that spot, telling her the flames would soon reach it, and that her life was in danger. 'My brother!' she cried, 'my beloved brother!' Then, starting with sudden horror, she exclaimed, 'Oh merciful Heaven, my father! Where's my father?'

She attempted to spring forward, but the officer seized her arm, assured her that the town was nearly consumed, and entirely deserted, and begged she would suffer him to conduct her to some place of shelter.

Without daring to cast her eyes again on the fatal object at her feet, she walked slowly away, leaning on her protector's arm. They turned from the town, and reached the lawn, which led by a gentle ascent to her father's house. 'At the end of this lawn,' said she, 'is the dwelling where –' 'Ah, I fear,' answered the stranger; but, before he could proceed, Sophia lifted her eyes and perceived the whole mansion was in flames.

A person, wringing his hands in all the anguish of despair, approached: he was her father. She threw herself on his bosom; 'Have I still my dear father left me?' said she, in a voice half choaked with sobs. 'My son!' exclaimed the wretched parent, 'my dear boy!'

After a scene which can be better imagined than described, Mr. Herbert and his daughter retired to a hamlet in the neighbourhood, where the English officer, Capt. F—, when he went to visit them the next day, found Sophia sitting by her father's bedside, whom fatigue of body, joined to the most vehement emotions of mind, had thrown into a fever. His pulse throbbed violently, and his soul seemed bursting with indignation and despair. Sophia's countenance was pale, and her looks spoke the complaints to which her lips refused utterance. Soon after Capt. F— reached the cottage, a peasant led into the room an old man near eighty years of age; who was an Englishman, that had gone to America in his youth, as the servant of Mr. Herbert's father, and now passed his declining years under the protection of the son. This old man had crawled to the town the preceding night, in search of his master, and had been seen sitting under the shelter of a barn, by an American countryman who knew him, and led him to the cottage. Sophia flew with eagerness to meet him: she had been taught to reverence him in infancy, and more advanced years had confirmed the habit of childhood into a sentiment of the soul. Robert had served her grandfather with a simplicity of affection, and a pride of integrity, which claimed the warmest returns of gratitude. This valuable domestic had felt towards his master that sentiment of stedfast fidelity which Naomi expresses to Ruth, in the beautiful language of Scripture, 'Whither thou goest I will go, and where thou lodgest I will lodge; thy people shall be my people, and thy God shall be my God; where thou diest will I die, and there will I be buried. The Lord do so to me, and more also, if aught but death part thee and me.'[152]

Sophia took the old man's arm from the countryman: 'Robert,' said she, 'I hope you are not much hurt.' 'Ah, Miss Sophy,' said he, shaking his head, 'no matter, since you are safe, and my master.' 'Robert!' said Mr. Herbert; but his voice seemed choaked, and he did not attempt to proceed. 'I see you are ill, Sir,' replied the old man, 'and no wonder. Poor Mr. Charles – I loved him like my own child, and he was pleased to let me call him so; but the dear youth is now' – A flood of tears bedewed the old man's cheeks; he wiped them away with his white locks. 'Ah, Robert,' said Sophia, 'you will kill us if you talk so.' 'I'll say no more,' answered he, 'though, if it had pleased Heaven to take a poor old man, and spare him' – 'Sit down, and compose yourself,' said Sophia. The officer assisted in placing him at the foot of his master's bed. Mr. Herbert fixed his eyes upon him, with a gloomy look, in which despair was painted.

'I am a good deal bruised,' said the old man. 'How were you bruised, Robert?' said Mr. Herbert. 'Last night, Sir, when I found you were all three gone, what, thought I, should I stay for here? If any harm happens to them, thought I, I shall have nothing more to live for; so I crawled on, and reached the place where poor Mr. Charles –' Here the old man paused a moment. 'I kissed his poor corpse, Sir, and spoke to it, as if it could answer me, and then when the flames came near, I dragged it away as well as I could; but my strength failed me, and I fell against some stones, that bruised me a good deal. So I lay all night by my poor young master's side; and when it grew light, and they came to bury the dead, I kissed his cold hand, and went a little way off: but I saw where they laid him; I shall know the spot if the grass should grow over it.'

Capt. F— went up to Robert, and begged he would say no more: Robert answered, 'I have done, Sir; he's in his grave; but if you had known him, Sir, so kind-hearted and so humble he was –: He has often made me lay hold of his arm, and led me to my wicker seat at the end of the garden. 'Sit down, Robert,' he would say, 'and bask a little in the sun, it will do you good: but it's all over now. Yes, Sir,' turning to his master, 'they have destroyed every thing – the shrubbery is all cut down, and torn to pieces, except a branch here and there, that is blown by the wind; it would have broke your heart to see it.'

Mr. Herbert's fever increased, and, for some days, his life was in danger. Captain F— brought the surgeon of his regiment to visit him, and witnessed, in his own frequent visits to the cottage, the filial piety of Sophia, who watched day and night by the bed-side of her father, attended him with unremitting tenderness, and at length had the consolation of seeing his health restored.

You will not wonder, Sir, that those distresses which rendered Sophia's beauty more touching, and served to display the virtues of her heart, soon converted Captain F—'s pity into the enthusiasm of passion. Nor was Sophia insensible to the merit of her generous lover. Although Mr. Herbert lamented that Captain F— was an Englishman, he did not suffer political prejudice to subdue those sentiments of esteem and gratitude which the conduct of that young man had nobly merited, and consented that his daughter should marry Captain F— at the end of the summer compaign. Mean time he conducted her to this distant village, which he knew our early friendship would render an agreeable situation to her, while she waited the events of the summer. Before Mr. Herbert set out for this place, he went, attended by Sophia, to take a last look of his ruined possessions. When Sophia had described to me the melancholy picture they presented, she added these words – 'I could bear to gaze upon the ruins of that once happy dwelling, did I consider them merely as the relics of lost splendor: but it was the scene of all my pleasures! This is what affects me. Had the same ties, the same soothing recollections, endeared the shelter of a cottage, the straw that thatched its roof would have been sacred, and called forth my affections as forcibly as the mansion which is laid in dust. Passing by the side of that small stream which runs near the bottom of the lawn, I saw some of the sticks with which my father had himself formed my laurel bower, taken away by the current. They floated on the surface of the water; I looked after them with a vehement sensation, which I almost tremble to recall. When I turned, I spied some scattered branches of the laurel, which he had twisted round those very sticks, withering on the ground: I snatched them up instantly, bathed them with my tears, and have preserved them till their last leaf is withered.'

Mr. Herbert placed his daughter under my mother's protection, and soon after joined the army. Their separation was final; he fell in the first engagement; and Sophia, in the midst of her affliction at this event, received a most angry letter from her brother in Pensylvania, who had heard with the utmost indignation of her engagements to Captain F—, and seemed to feel less concern for his father's death, than regret at the weakness which had led him to bestow his daughter on a man who had drawn his sword against America.

Sophia lamented the prejudices of her brother, but determined to adhere inviolably to those engagements on which all her hopes of happiness depended, and which had received the sanction of parental authority. In the mean time she counted the hours of separation, which she believed, though long and melancholy, would at length pass away, and restore the object of her affection.

While she indulged this fond illusion, your letter, conveying the fatal tidings of Captain F—'s death, arrived. Sophia received this intelligence without complaint. She shed no tear, but her blood seemed chilled in her veins: she started frequently, and there was a wildness and disorder in her countenance, that alarmed us for her reason. She was put to bed, her pulse beat high, the struggles which for some time past she had undergone, had weakened a frame naturally delicate. This last stroke she was unable to sustain, her fever increased every moment, and the following night her reason entirely forsook her. I perceived a sudden change in her manner that shocked me. 'Do not be uneasy,' said she, 'I am better – much better – that bloody engagement at Long Island! – and yet he's safe – it was foolish to be so uneasy – I cried for whole nights together – my head still burns.'

The physician, who now entered the room, she mistook for her brother, and shrieked at the sight of him. 'Oh my God!' cried the unhappy Sophia, 'he's dead – and that's his murderer.' – Then falling on her knees, 'Save him – save him yet,' said she, 'have you the cruelty to kill him? – He loves you – indeed he does – I'm your sister – don't break my heart – spare him – spare him – Oh it's too late! – You've murdered him already: – fly – fly, my beloved – all that's dearest to my heart! – All that's left me on earth! Fly for my sake – here – here – I'm ready to die – why look so at me? – I can't save you! – How he groans! – He's covered with blood – I can bear it no longer.' She sprang up in her bed, but, overcome by these violent emotions, sunk back in a kind of stupor: I knelt by her bed-side, and she again revived a little. 'Is that Captain F—?' cried she, putting out her hand, 'Heaven – Heaven preserve! – Write whenever the battle's over – I shall have no rest till a letter comes.' 'Do you not know me, my dear friend,' said I, taking her hand. 'Yes, yes, there's no occasion to kneel – tell my brother I consent to our parting – but I can never love again – I never lov'd but one! – Who stands there? – Mercy! – Mercy! My brother! – Bury yourself deep in earth – he's dead – quite dead – would you kill him in the grave? – Have you no pity? – Oh, he feasts on my tears! – He scorns me!'

Again exhausted by these efforts, she sunk into almost total insensibility; in which state she remained some hours: her pulse grew weaker every moment, and, as death approached, her reason was in some measure restored. She again opened her eyes, and asked for me; I flew to her. 'My dear Frances,' said she, in a faint voice, 'I feel myself dying: to you, my dear friend, I leave the care of our poor old servant; comfort, comfort the good old man for our loss.' Then, lifting up her hands and eyes, 'Oh, my Creator and my judge,' cried she, 'Thou, whom I have sought in the sincerity of my soul; thou, whose bounties in the days of my happiness I loved to acknowledge, forgive me if I have suffered affliction to prey too much upon my heart, and have shortened my life! Thou canst witness, that amidst my sorrows, never has one murmuring thought arisen against thee! Oh, best of beings! Object nearest to my heart! Of thy benevolence and goodness it has never doubted for a moment. When thy dispensations appeared dark and mysterious, I have looked round on nature, and seen it beaming with benignity and beauty. I have searched my own breast, and found it formed for happiness and virtue; and thou hast not formed it thus in vain. Thou wilt justify thy ways: thou hast afflicted me on earth, but my sufferings are past, and thou wilt make me for ever happy in thy presence.' Her voice now faltered – she looked on me – and expired. Oh, my friend! My sweet, my amiable companion! You, whose heart, far from being wrapped in selfish woe, could forget its own sufferings to comfort the unhappy; you, whose soothing pity could heal the wounds of the afflicted; who seemed born, in this period of general distress, to lighten the burden of human wretchedness; to be the ministering angel of sorrow! – Where shall the desolate mourner now look round for aid? He asks thy sympathy, but thou canst not hear his complaint: it is only poured to the cold earth that covers thee! Oh, when I think of all thy perfections, the tenderness of thy disposition, the virtues of thy heart, How can I live without thee? How can I drag on a wretched existence which thy friendship endears no longer? But thou art happy. Yes, she is united to that amiable and unfortunate lover, whom she could not survive.

I have been visiting the grave where the remains of my friend repose. I have poured out my complaints; but the sorrow I feel is not for her, but for myself. She is at rest, and this cruel war had made her happiness impossible. Alas, how dreadful are the effects of war! Every form of evil and misery is in its train: the groans of despair are mingled with the song of triumph, and the laurels of victory are nourished with the tears of humanity.

I am, Sir,
Your obedient Servant,
FRANCES LAWRENCE.

# VOL. II.

## CHAP. XXI.

Mr. Clifford, accompanied by Julia, and Chartres, arrived in London soon after Christmas, where a spacious and elegant house, at the west end of the town, was prepared for their reception.

Frederick Seymour had taken a house for himself in the neighbourhood, and he and Charlotte were settled in town a few days before Mr. Clifford arrived. Julia, since the period of Seymour's marriage, had endeavoured, by every effort in her power, to banish his idea from her mind. She carefully avoided thinking of him, because she now felt herself inclined to pity, while she blamed his unfortunate passion; since he had fulfilled his engagements, at the price of peace, and had renounced all chance of happiness, to comply with the demands of honor. But Julia was conscious, that though this conduct gave him some claim to her esteem, esteem was a sentiment which it was dangerous to cherish, and that, on this subject, reflection was at cruel variance with repose; since, whenever the idea of Seymour recurred to her mind, she was imperceptibly led into a comparison between him and others; and the decision which her heart involuntarily made, was by no means conducive to its tranquility. But, though she had not the merit of insensibility, the purity of her mind corrected the softness of her heart. Rectitude stood in the place of indifference; and, since she could not entirely controul her feelings, she disregarded them altogether, and only studied, with a fervent desire of acting right, to regulate her conduct by the strictest propriety.

It was at her solicitation that Mr. Clifford remained in the country till after Christmas. He was impatient to see his daughter, but Julia always found some reason for delay, and procrastinated the journey to town, till no farther pretence could be urged, without incurring suspicion. She attended him to town, prepared to act a part which she felt would be difficult, but which she stedfastly resolved should be free from self-reproach.

The day before her departure from the country, she visited alone the ancient chapel, where the remains of her father, and grandfather, were deposited. Here she continued kneeling a considerable time at the tomb, wrapt in meditation, and finding it every moment more difficult to tear herself from the spot. At length she arose, and, clasping her hands together, while she continued gazing on the tomb, 'Oh my father,' she cried, 'thou canst no longer guide and direct thy child, but may she never forget thy precepts! And thou ever beloved and venerable old man, whose honored image still lives in my heart; oh, may thy sacred remembrance be the surest guard of my conduct! If I am ever tempted to deviate from the path of rectitude, may I but think of thee, and surely my heart will return to its duty: oh, never, never can I meditate on *thee* and persevere in what is wrong! – Dearest old man! Though the grave hides thee from my view, the recollection of thy goodness, thy sanctity, shall be as a shield to thy offspring; and may thy exemplary piety have entailed a blessing on thy descendants! Oh, may I live – and may I die, like thee!'

Mr. Clifford, when near London, sent a servant forward to inform his daughter of his coming. Frederick Seymour was not at home, but Charlotte hastened to her father's house, where she had soon the pleasure of receiving him. When their first emotions at meeting had subsided, Charlotte intreated her father and Julia to go home with her, and spend the day at her house. They were preparing to set out, in Charlotte's carriage, when Julia's maid came into the room and begged to speak to her. Julia went out, and the maid said to her, 'Indeed Ma'am, I could not help calling you out, for I went into the hall just now to look after some of the boxes, and there's a poor old man standing at the foot of the steps, that says, Ma'am, he knows you, and begged me, for the love of God, to supplicate you to see him; and indeed, Ma'am, I had not the heart to refuse the poor old creature, he looked so pitiful.'

Julia desired she would tell him to come into the hall. The old man ascended the steps with great difficulty, leaning on a stick with one hand, and holding by the palisades[1] with the other. His face was pale, and deeply furrowed with wrinkles, and his features, which were strong, had a marked expression of settled sorrow. A considerable quantity of white hair, which was parted in the middle of his forehead, hung down his cheeks: his coat, which frequent patching had rendered of many colours, did not appear dirty; and his linen was perfectly clean. His figure, though much bent by age and infirmity, still retained something of a military air; and, though he tottered as he walked, his step was not that of a clown.

Julia recollected him instantly: he was an old soldier, who had served in her grandfather's company, had sought the same battles, and shared the same dangers. After nineteen years service, he obtained his discharge on account of ill health, but was not entitled to the benefit of Chelsea-hospital.[2] His son, however, who was a carpenter, maintained him by his labour. Julia remembered, from her infancy, this old man, who used to make frequent visits to her father's house, where he was always received with kindness. She had often flown with eagerness, when a child, to announce his arrival to her grandfather, by whom she had been early taught,

> 'To press the bashful stranger to his food,
> And learn the luxury of doing good!'[3]

Julia was shocked at seeing the old man so much altered, and emaciated. He told her, that his son had died four months ago, of a fever, and that, since that period, he had suffered extreme distress. 'I have been forced, Madam,' said the old man, 'to part with every bit of furniture that was in our room, to pay the rent, and keep body and soul together. I have nothing left but the bed I lie on – but all won't do, Madam, and I must go to the parish at last! Oh, wherefore,' said the old man, bursting into tears, 'wherefore is light given to him that is in misery, and life unto the bitter in soul; which look for death, but it cometh not, and seek for it more than for hid treasures? But I heard, Madam, two days ago, that you would be here, so I thought I would see you once more before I die. I knew you would have compassion for me.'

'Yes, indeed,' said Julia, with eagerness, 'my good old friend, you shall never want while I can relieve you: think no more of going to the parish, we will provide for you.'

The poor old man could not speak, but he wept bitterly. Julia led him herself into a parlour. A porter, who had been assisting to carry in the baggage, and passed through the hall while she was carefully leading the old man, with the tears standing in her eyes, said to one of the servants, 'Aye, she may die when she likes, for (swearing a terrible oath) she's sure enough of going to heaven.' Julia ordered wine for the old man; and, when he was revived by it, left him, to tell her uncle what had passed. She returned with Mr. Clifford and Charlotte, who listened with the utmost compassion to the old man, while he repeated his tale of sorrow, and dwelt on the virtues of his son. When he had eased his heart by this recital, he talked of his old master, and of Captain Clifford, fought over his past battles, and lamented Captain Clifford's untimely death with a simplicity of honest sorrow, which drew tears from all his auditors. Julia was so much affected, that her uncle and Charlotte hurried her away; but not till the old man had received a liberal donation, together with the assurance of a comfortable provision for the remainder of his life. While he, putting his feeble hands together, implored that the 'blessing of him who was ready to perish, might be upon them.'

In the way to Frederick Seymour's house, Julia dried her tears, and endeavoured to compose her mind, that she might meet him with the calmness she wished; but the figure of the old soldier presented itself to her imagination, and the words he had uttered concerning her father rested upon her heart. She felt the deepest depression of spirits; but when the carriage stopt at Seymour's door, and she saw him hastening through the hall to receive them, she summoned all her spirit, and assumed an appearance of serenity. Seymour was far from being so collected: his embarrassment was but too evident to Julia. He used, again and again, the same expressions of pleasure, and repeated the same enquiries, till he was at length checked by Chartres, who gravely declared, that the question which Mr. Seymour then asked him, he had answered three times already. Had Charlotte been less unsuspecting, or Mr. Clifford more penetrating, they could not have failed to observe the strange and distracted manner in which Seymour performed the honours of his table. When the servants had withdrawn, 'Come,' said Mr. Clifford, 'my dear children, let us drink a bumper[4] to the happiness of our new married pair. Julia, my love, come, fill your glass to the brim, and pledge me to your cousin's happiness!' Julia filled her glass, wished Charlotte all happiness, bowed to Seymour, and, after swallowing a few drops, put down her glass. 'Fie, Julia,' said Mr. Clifford, 'you ought to have emptied your glass to this toast.' Julia changed colour, and again took up her glass. 'Why, really, Julia,' resumed Mr. Clifford, 'you drink *my* toast, as if it were a very serious business.' 'Indeed, my dear,' said Charlotte, 'you've performed your part with as much sad solemnity as if you had a presage that we were *not* to be happy.' This remark, in Julia's present state of agitation, was more than she could bear: her emotion was too great to be controuled, and she burst into tears. 'My dearest Charlotte,' said she, taking her cousin's hand, 'be but as happy as *I* wish you, and you will be blest indeed.' 'My dear friend,' said Charlotte, 'I know all your affection; but why indulge this sadness? I assure you, I shall find happiness a very dismal thing, unless you will consent to be happy too.' 'This old soldier has affected you,' said Mr. Clifford; 'but you must not indulge low spirits, my love; you must be chearful for my sake: you know you are my only child, now Charlotte has forsaken me, and I can't live without you.' 'I am grateful,' said Julia, in a broken voice, 'indeed I am.' Seymour, during this scene, sat fixed like a statue: his eyes were riveted on Julia, his lips sometimes moved, but he did not utter a word. Julia, recovering herself a little, cast a glance at Seymour, perceived his situation, and feared that Charlotte would observe it. 'Will you give me a glass of water, Mr. Seymour?' said she, in order to rouze him from his stupor. He started as from a dream, and poured some water into a glass. 'I am quite ashamed of myself,' said Julia: 'few have so much reason to be happy as I have; but the old soldier has sunk my spirits. However,' added she, with a smile, 'I promise never to behave so ill again, and this once you must all forgive me.' Charlotte and Julia, soon after, left the room.

When they were gone, Mr. Clifford filled his glass; 'Come,' said he, 'Seymour, let us drink your cousin's health.' 'With all my heart,' said Seymour, filling his glass hastily. 'Really,' said Chartres, 'Miss Clifford seems vastly ill: I never saw her look so pale,' added he, turning to Seymour, 'except the day *you* were married.' 'Yes – I recollect – I mean I remember –' replied Seymour speaking with difficulty, 'she was affected at parting with her friend.' 'I do not wonder she is ill,' said Mr. Clifford 'the old soldier talked of my poor father and brother, till I could scarcely bear it myself.' 'But,' rejoined Chartres, 'Miss Clifford was certainly ill before the old soldier arrived. I fancy the air of London disagrees with her, and she seemed to feel it at some miles distance; for I observed that, during the last stage, her colour went and came every minute.' Seymour listened in agony to these observations, which, however, made no impression on Mr. Clifford; who, when Chartres had finished his speech, said, with warmth, that Julia was a charming creature, and that he loved her like his own child. 'Indeed,' added he, 'she is one of those women whom it is impossible not to love.' Impossible indeed! thought Seymour. 'Her disposition is very amiable,' he replied. 'So amiable,' said Mr. Clifford, 'and her person so lovely, that I wonder any young man can see her with indifference.' Ah, thought Seymour, who *can* see her with indifference! 'She is a charming young woman,' he rejoined. 'I hope,' said Mr. Clifford, 'to have the pleasure of seeing her happily settled this winter. Her countenance and figure, tacked to ten thousand pounds, I think, bid fair for a good marriage; and, when she is settled, I shall have nothing to do but to die.' Seymour listened to this matrimonial project with the feelings of a criminal who hears his own condemnation. His soul recoiled at this plan of felicity; and he longed to persuade Mr. Clifford that happiness and matrimony had formed no inseparable alliance, but, on the contrary, were often quite estranged from each other. He had, however, the prudence not to trust his feelings on this subject, and remained silent; while his uneasiness was entirely unobserved by Mr. Clifford.

When Seymour reflected on what had past, he was not much displeased at the recollection of the cause of Julia's emotion at dinner; nor was he concerned at the information that she looked pale on the day of his marriage, and that her colour went and came during the last stage. Such is the selfishness, the inconsistency of passion, that Seymour, though he would chearfully have sacrificed his life to save Julia the slightest uneasiness, would yet willingly have excited in her mind those sensations which overwhelmed his own with anguish, and have been soothed by acquiring an influence over her heart, which, he well knew, would never, in the smallest degree, affect her conduct; and which, indeed, his own principles of honor, and a respect for her character, which amounted almost to idolatry, prevented him even from wishing it should. He might, therefore, have reflected, that any sensibility to his passion, could only serve to involve her in a degree of misery, which was almost insupportable to himself. But, the region of passion is a land of despotism, where reason exercises but a mock jurisdiction; and is continually forced to submit to an arbitrary tyrant, who, rejecting her fixed and temperate laws, is guided only by the dangerous impulse of his own violent and, uncontroulable wishes.

# CHAP XXII.

Mr. Charles Seymour lost not a moment in paying his respects to Julia, upon her arrival in town; expressed the most lively pleasure at seeing her; expatiated on the encreased bloom of her complexion; spoke in his lowest tone, and assumed his most finished mode of address. Julia, at length, quite fatigued with softness, and oppressed with panegyric,[5] told him, 'that she was obliged to go out;' finding that, like most other dull people, he was subject to the error of making long visits; and was, at present, too much engrossed by the care of acting his part gracefully, to remark her extreme weariness of his performance. He intreated to have the honor of attending her where she was going; and they walked to her milliner's,[6] where caps and ribbons seemed to sharpen his wit, and furnish him with new modes of compliment; and where he waited with great resignation, while she purchased several articles of dress. No set of people are so patient as the interested. They drudge on indefatigably in the same circle, and with one uniform pace, as quietly as a horse in a mill, contentedly expecting the end of their labours. Julia could at last only get rid of Mr. Charles Seymour's attendance, by calling on Charlotte, at whose door he took his leave; filled with self-complacency at the progress he was convinced he had that morning made in her favor; but at the same time recollecting, that the extraordinary trouble he was now obliged to take, was owing to his former entire neglect of the lady; and marking it, as one of his future maxims, that a young woman, who has a rich uncle in the East Indies, although she has no fortune herself, is to be treated with gallantry. In the mean time, he reconciled himself to his past conduct, by reflecting, that there are some events, which no prudence can foresee; and some errors, which experience only can correct.

Charlotte was going to call on Mr. Chartres's mother, where Julia accompanied her. They were received with infinite delight by Chartres, who had returned to his mother's house, where he found nothing that could atone for the loss of their society: and Mrs. Chartres was also glad to see them, not solely on account of their kindness to her son, but likewise because she thought so splendid an equipage as Charlotte's, did honor to her door, and reflected some of the lustre of its silver trappings on herself. It is necessary to give a sketch of this Lady's character.

Mrs. Chartres was one of those persons to whom time is a burden, which, without the assistance of cards, would be insupportable. She considered whist as the first end of existence, and the sole pleasure of society; for she thought conversation the dullest occupation in the world; and, although she knew there was such a term as friendship, her feelings did not convey much force to its meaning. Yet, she was not insensible of some preference towards those who gave her the best dinners. A present of a brace of woodcocks, of which she was remarkably fond, would also secure her partial regard, and a young hare never failed to win her heart. With too little sensibility to feel her own deficiencies, and too little discernment to perceive when she was treated with contempt, Mrs. Chartres could bear neglect without mortification, and derision without resentment. She was perfectly satisfied with being admitted into company, as one who helped to make up the necessary number at a whist table, and to act a part, which an automaton, with a very little farther improvement in mechanism,[7] could have performed as well. It was fortunate for Mrs. Chartres, that she was not difficult in her choice of society, or rigorous in her demands of attention and respect; for she found solitude the most insupportable of all evils. Her mind resembled an empty mirror, which has no character, no images of its own, borrows every impression from some passing object, and, if left to itself, would for ever remain vacant.

Mrs. Chartres delighted in new acquaintances; for, in proportion as she was known, she generally found people's civilities decline. But this never gave her any uneasiness, because she contrived, with great ease, to provide herself with a succession of new visitors. She kept a pack of visiting tickets[8] in her pocket-book, and, wherever she went, distributed them liberally to any strangers who were near her, or with whom she happened to play at cards. By these means her acquaintance was numerous, though not very select; but she comprehended so little the difference between one person and another, if they were equally well dressed, that she would only have been puzzled and perplexed by a greater power of choice.

Whenever Mrs. Chartres was disengaged, she was sick, and passed the day in bed; but, when she was fashionably dressed, quite secure of a good dinner, and an evening party at cards, she felt the charm of existence, could think of the evils of her own lot with resignation, and of the evils of others with the most perfect equanimity.

Mrs. Chartres had a habit of laughing whenever she spoke. Having therefore laughed at a storm of snow, been no less merry at the bad roads, and found her son's awkwardness an equally good joke, she told Charlotte and Julia, with a titter, that she would send them cards of invitation the next morning, to meet a party at her house that day fortnight; adding, that she was sure they could yet have no engagements, as they were but just come to town, and that they would for ever oblige her by coming. In vain these ladies assured her, that they should prefer coming when she had no other visitors; and, that they liked conversation better than cards. Mrs. Chartres would no more *bear* a reason, than she would have *given* one, 'on compulsion;' and, without paying the smallest attention to what they said, continued to urge her request with such vehemence of entreaty, that, at length, they yielded to her importunity, and promised to come.

As the morning was fine, Julia got out of the carriage at Charlotte's door, and walked home. In her way, she saw a young bird that was unable to fly, hopping on the pavement. A boy seized it, whom she bribed with a shilling to relinquish his prize, which she was taking home, when it escaped from her hand, and fell down the area of a house. She desired the servant, who attended her, to knock at the door; and a search was made for the little fugitive, but it could no where be found. Julia wrote the following lines on this incident.

## ELEGY

On finding a young THRUSH in the Street, who escaped from the Writer's Hand, as she was bringing him home, and, falling down the Area of a House, could not be found.

Mistaken bird, ah, whither hast thou stray'd?
My friendly grasp, why eager to elude?
This hand was on thy pinion lightly laid,
And fear'd to hurt thee by a touch too rude.

Is there no foresight in a Thrush's breast,
That thou down yonder gulph from me would'st go?
That gloomy area lurking cats infest,
And there the dog may rove, alike thy foe.

I would with lavish crumbs my Bird have fed,
And bought a crystal cup to wet thy bill;
I would have made of down and moss thy bed,
Soft, though not fashion'd with a Thrush's skill.

Soon as thy strengthen'd wing could mount the sky,
My willing hand had set my captive free:
Ah, not for her, who loves the muse, to buy
A selfish pleasure, bought with pain to thee!

The vital air, and liberty, and light,
Had all been thine: and love, and rapt'rous song,
And sweet parental joys, in rapid flight,
Had led the circle of thy life along.

Securely to my window hadst thou flown,
And ever thy accustom'd morsel found;
Nor should thy trusting breast the wants have known,
Which other Thrushes knew, when winter frown'd.

Fram'd with the wisdom Nature lent to thee,
Thy house of straw had brav'd the tempest's rage;
And thou, thro' many a spring, hadst liv'd to see
The utmost limit of a Thrush's age.

Ill-fated Bird! And does the Thrush's race,
Like Man's, mistake the path that leads to bliss;
Or, when his eye that tranquil path can trace,
The good he well discerns, thro' folly miss?

# CHAP. XXIII.

The Honourable Miss C—'s waited on Julia a few days after her arrival in town; profuse in professions of regard, and eager to know if she meant to give many concerts and balls, in the course of the winter. Julia felt as much contempt for their present civilities, as for their former neglect; and received them with a degree of coldness, by which they found that a plan of tender and romantic friendship, intended to commence that very morning, was not likely to succeed.

These ladies talked much to Julia of the fashionable amusements, mingling, with great address, instruction with entertainment;[9] and, while they informed her what every body of a certain fortune *did*, obliquely hinted what she ought to *do*. Julia forced herself to hearken to their remarks; but, the moment the Miss C—'s left the room, she forgot their existence; nor did she recollect that there was any such thing as gaiety in the world – her whole thoughts being absorbed by the observations she had made on Frederick Seymour's behaviour since her arrival in town. She saw him struggling with ill-concealed wretchedness: she bitterly reproached herself for her weakness on the first day of their meeting; and endeavoured to atone for it, to her own mind, by avoiding all particular conversation with him most carefully. She perceived that he now no longer exerted that resolution which had formerly led him to shun her society; but that, on the contrary, he always attended his wife when she visited her father; and was always at home when Julia was expected. He seemed unable to refuse himself the indulgence of seeing her; and when they parted, he was only occupied by the consideration when they should meet again; for he found that the charms of her conversation soothed his unhappiness, and that the tumult of his feelings was often calmed in her presence. His disturbed mind resembled a tempestuous flood, whose waves arise dark and turbulent, except where the sun-beam throws a line of trembling radiance across their agitated surface.

When the evening arrived, on which Mrs. Chartres's card-assembly was to take place, Charlotte called upon Julia, and the two ladies went together. Mrs. Chartres's room could not hold four card-tables without some inconvenience to the company; but, unluckily, the point of her ambition was *five*. Her aspiring mind preferred grandeur to ease. She felt a noble contempt of difficulties, when her aim was glory; and, as she thought that five card-tables, filled with well-dressed persons, was a very sublime *coup d'ceil*,[10] she contrived to place them with such masterly arrangement, that not one inch of ground was lost. There was also a loo-table,[11] in an adjoining room, or rather closet, round which the company had just sufficient space to fit, with their chairs close to the wainscot. One of the card-tables in the large room was so near the door, that the candle placed next to it blew out every time the door was shut or opened. Mrs. Chartres regretted that the wind was high: but then her five card-tables had a fine effect; 'and it is so easy,' thought she, 'to light a candle, and besides, who knows but the wind may fall?'

Charlotte and Julia arrived before Mrs. Chartres had adjusted all her card-tables, and gained admittance with some difficulty. Mrs. Chartres pushed through the crowd to receive them; and, having a very small space to move in, by a swing of her arms, which she thought fashionable, she overturned a candlestick which stood on a card-table in her way, and set fire to her gauze apron. Many screams, and much confusion, ensued: but the flame was soon happily extinguished; and, after lamenting for some time the depredations of fire on gauze aprons, she left that fierce element to itself, and returned to the duties of the evening. She told Charlotte and Julia, 'That she would not ask them to sit down till the card-tables were fixed, when they would obtain a good seat.' They stood for a considerable time; but at length, (perceiving there was little chance of the ceremonies being adjusted, and finding themselves much incommoded by the sudden and frequent movements of Mrs. Chartres, and her son, whom she repeatedly ordered to be alert, and who often met her in mid-way, and ran against her in all directions,) Charlotte and Julia procured a seat for themselves; and had leisure to contemplate the scene before them. It seemed as if the art of receiving company consisted in perpetual motion. Mrs. Chartres flew from one part of the room to the other, without intermission; enquired, in the hurry of her task, if those guests were cold, whose faces were scorched by being placed too close to a large fire; and hoped Julia found the room warm, who was seated with her back against a door, which was perpetually opening, while she was almost frozen by a blast which issued from it. Neither enquiry on the part of Mrs. Chartres, or complaint on that of Julia, could serve any purpose. The company were packed for the evening, and no person could move without causing a general disturbance.

One card-table was still vacant, and the task of making up another whist party remained yet unperformed. The attack was begun on a Mrs. Sanford, who at first absolutely refused to play; but at length, overcome by the steady perseverance of Mrs. Chartres, she gave her reluctant consent.

After lavishing much eloquence, Mrs. Chartres prevailed on three other persons to make up the party, who had before refused to play. Some time was spent in settling the price; and when this was done, Mrs. Sanford, who had retired to a corner of the room, was told the party waited for her. But Mrs. Sanford, who had by this time gained sufficient fortitude to sustain another siege, resolutely refused to play. The attack, however, was renewed with fresh vigour, and poor Mrs. Sanford at last yielded to its violence. The party was settled, and Mrs. Chartres, relieved from this load of anxiety, found leisure for a little conversation with such of the company as would not be enlisted in the service of the card-table; though she felt much indignation at their refractory conduct. She now rejoiced that one lady had escaped cold – hoped her neighbour on the right had escaped too – and regretted that her on the left was still hoarse. Then she enumerated all her own complaints – expatiated on her weak nerves – and afterwards, by a very easy transition, passed from bodily to mental evils; lamenting that she had had nothing but ill-luck the whole winter, and that she had lost three crowns a night; and declaring that her best fortune was never more than five small trumps, without one king or queen. Mrs. Chartres expected to awaken general sympathy in her losses; but she forgot that there is more distress in the world than pity, and that the world cannot afford to waste any of its little stock upon five small trumps. She then complained how much company had disappointed her, and told Charlotte she had received twenty apologies that morning. A little while after, she related to another lady the same circumstance, with the addition of ten more excuses; and, when Frederick Seymour arrived, complained to him how ill her acquaintances had behaved; 'For no less than forty cards of apology,'[12] said she, 'have I received this morning.' 'The men in buckram[13] will soon be here,' said Charlotte. 'I cannot help thinking,' rejoined Seymour, in a low voice, 'that these forty excuses were well-timed; unless Mrs. Chartres could adopt Milton's plan with the evil spirits, and, by some commodious transformation, suit the dimensions of her company to those of her apartment.'[14]

Mrs. Chartres soon after told Julia, in the confidence of friendship, that her old uncle was dead. 'But I only received the account last night,' said she, 'and it would have been so much trouble to forbid all the company, that I thought I would let them come, and keep it a secret; – don't tell!'

Tea was brought by Thomas, a young countryman, who had enlisted in one of the new-raised regiments; but having been in a short time discharged, because his size was below the military standard, he had entered into the service of Mrs. Chartres. His figure was squat; his shoulders broad and high; and his livery somewhat old-fashioned, with a profusion of buttons, and long waistcoat pockets; and, upon the whole, he bore a very striking resemblance to Mr. Parsons, in the entertainment of High Life above Stairs.[15] It was easy to perceive that Thomas had been accustomed to march by beat of drum; and though, in the exercise of his present peaceable profession, he wore no defiance in his aspect, but, on the contrary, hung down his head, and looked meek as a lamb, yet his military step still rendered him formidable. He presented the tea-cups in the same abrupt manner in which he had been taught to present his firelock;[16] and, Julia being unprepared for these martial movements, a cup of tea was spilt on her gown. Thomas's face became like scarlet at this accident. Mrs. Chartres scolded loudly, and declared she believed it would be impossible to cure him of his awkward ways. 'Then,' said she, 'he blunders forever; I never knew him once do right; he brings me into such scrapes! – I ordered him, a month ago, to leave two tickets at Mrs. C—'s, and Mrs. N—'s, which he thought proper to forget; and now Mrs. C— is gone to the East-Indies, and Mrs. N— is dead: – how provoking! Mrs. Chartres's discourse did not proceed without interruption; for, whenever a knock was heard at the street-door, she instantly started from her seat, obliged the company to make way, and stationed herself at the door of the apartment, where she paid her compliments to her visitors, before she suffered them to pass the threshold; and where, for the most part, she stood a considerable time in expectation; Thomas being so unwilling to leave the company above, to admit those who were waiting in their carriages below, that his mistress was, more than once, compelled to remind him of his duty by a push on the shoulder.

The rubber[17] being now finished, at the table where Mrs. Sanford had been compelled to sit down, she came to Mrs. Chartres, to know who was to cut in. 'I know of nobody,' said Mrs. Chartres, with great composure, 'you must play on.' At this moment, Frederick Seymour, who had been called away, returned, fortunately for Mrs. Sanford, who instantly quitted the table. Seymour had little inclination to play. He however came prepared to do penance; and, being convinced, like other votaries of mortification, that his merit would be great, in proportion as his sensations were disagreeable, he quietly seated himself at whist.

A young man now entered the room foppishly[18] dressed; and, casting a look of self-importance around the company, he advanced with a sauntering step to Mrs. Chartres, and apologized for his sister's not coming, who, he said, was detained by two friends, that had just arrived from the country. 'La,' said Mrs. Chartres, 'I wish she had come, and brought her two friends with her, they would have helped to fill up the room.' 'You are very good Ma'am,' replied Mr. Burton; 'upon my word we never thought of that.' He then turned to speak to an acquaintance, and Mrs. Chartres took that opportunity of informing Julia, that she had asked Mr. Burton on purpose to meet her; for, 'I know,' said she, 'you are a great reader; so I thought you would like him; for, I do assure you, he's vastly clever, and knows all about Cicero,[19] and Hume's History of England.'[20] By this time the connoisseur in Cicero, having finished his compliments, returned to Mrs. Chartres's circle, and, placing himself next to Julia, asked her if she had seen the new play?' She said she had not. 'I'm surprized at that Ma'am,' rejoined Mr. Burton, 'I assure you every body likes it.' 'Well, I really long to go,' said Mrs. Chartres, with her usual laugh;' 'but Mrs. Smith has been so much engaged, that she could not take me, and I have no notion of going to the play in a hack, and coming into the boxes with the straw about one's petticoats, as if one had just escaped from Bedlam.[21] To be sure, I might have gone a fortnight ago to the new play, but they would only give us a second row, and, at the other house, they gave us a first; so I thought the difference of the play didn't signify much.' 'And pray what was the play you saw, Ma'am?' enquired Mr. Burton. 'Macbeth,'[22] replied Mrs. Chartres: 'I declare I was quite disappointed, for I had never seen it before, and I had a notion Lady Macbeth was a good sort of woman; and there is such wickedness going on, and so many extravagant fancies!' Mrs. Chartres concluded, as she had begun, with a laugh, and then made her way to another part of the room.

Meantime Mr. Burton intreated Julia to join the party at loo, declaring that he was sure she would win, and he would bet any sum upon her cards. When he found she was inflexible in her determination not to play, he endeavoured to entertain her, while he displayed his own knowledge of fashionable life, by talking of the public places, particularly the theatre; and by discussing at large the merits of the different actors and actresses; only interrupting his criticism to give her a significant wink at the manner in which Thomas presented the lemonade. Julia, quite disgusted with his vulgar and impertinent familiarity, rose to change her seat, which was a matter of some difficulty. Placing herself near three young ladies, who were dressed in the utmost extreme of the fashion, she endeavoured to avoid Mr. Burton's assiduity, who followed her with officious gallantry, by entering into conversation with these ladies; but she found herself wholly unqualified for the task. Their conversation consisted entirely of anecdotes of the nobility, and minute details of all that had lately past in the great world. In vain, however, did these ladies attempt to dazzle and awe each other, by the rank and importance of their respective friends; for, if one mentioned an incident, which had happened to her friend, Lady such a one, the other young ladies immediately recollected some circumstance, as well worth relating, of a friend of equal rank.

Frederick Seymour now left the card-table, where he had been scolded, the whole time he played, by his partner, a little fat woman, above forty, with a pert countenance, and a manner still more pert than her physiognomy, who kept herself in pocket-money by cards, and was eagle-eyed to the smallest deviation from what she thought the rules of the game. She and Seymour gained the first rubber. One of their opponents happened to have no silver, and, while she was trying to get change, the other laid down a crown to Seymour, which his partner instantly snatched up, saying that the other lady should pay Mr. Seymour, for she herself was so apt to forget! After cutting for partners,[23] she was again Seymour's lot; and they soon lost double the sum they had gained. When Seymour left the table, Mrs. Chartres enquiring if he had won, he said, 'he had no subject of satisfaction, but the success of others.' His disagreeable partner now joined their circle, affected to talk of her ill-luck with indifference, and began sympathizing with Mrs. Chartres, who again brought forward her own bad fortune. 'I observe,' said Seymour to Julia, 'that people are at as much pains to display their feelings, on occasions when they feel nothing, as to hide them at cards, when they are losing their money, and really feel a great deal.' Mrs. Chartres watched her opportunity, and, while she fancied herself unobserved, could not resist moving towards the card-table which Seymour had quitted, and gently lifting the candlestick, to see if the card-money had been duly remembered. Being satisfied of this, she came up to Julia, and complained of her not calling upon her in a morning. 'I seldom pay morning visits,' said Julia. 'Oh, I know you're always reading,' said Mrs. Chartres; 'I suppose you shut yourself up at home: aren't you charm'd with the Pangs of Sensibility?'[24] 'Is that the title of a book?' said Julia. 'La, why, is it possible you haven't read the new novel, the Pangs of Sensibility?' 'No indeed I have not,' answered Julia, 'Well, I'm so surprized! Nor you, Mrs. Seymour, not read the Pangs of Sensibility?' 'No.' 'Nor have you never heard of it, Mr. Seymour?' 'I must acknowledge my ignorance of the book,' said Seymour, 'whatever imputation it may be upon my taste.' 'Oh, pray do buy it,' resumed Mrs. Chartres; 'it will only cost you six shillings, and its so excessively pretty; but the end's very dismal.' 'Well,' said Seymour, 'I shall be prepared for the worst; and you may depend upon it we will have six shillings-worth of sensibility to-morow morning.'

Thomas now announced Mrs. Seymour's carriage, not by coming forward, and telling her the agreeable tidings in a low voice, as is usual; but, having collected all his courage in coming up stairs, he opened the door, and, with a firm countenance, called out, as loud as he could, Mrs. Seymour's carriage *ready!* which last word he pronounced so short and quick, and in such an elevated tone, that it had the effect of an electrical shock, and no person of weak nerves could hear it without starting. Charlotte rose instantly, and was hastening away with great alacrity; but she found this a more difficult enterprize than she imagined. Mrs. Chartres seized both her hands, declared she must not go so soon, assured her it was very early a hundred times in a breath, and, gathering fresh courage as she proceeded, at length, in a most authoritative tone, insisted upon her staying. Although unprepared for so violent an attack, Charlotte, when she had recovered her surprize, assigned a reason for going, which she thought unanswerable: she told Mrs. Chartres, 'that she made it a rule not to keep her servants and horses in waiting in bad weather.' 'La,' said Mrs. Chartres, 'why, your servants can come into the house, and as for the horses, you told me two of your's were sick, and you had job horses; so why need you care about their waiting, since they are not your own?' Charlotte answered, 'that, indeed, *that* reason had never occurred to her; but though the horses are *not* my own,' said she, with some emphasis, 'I must be gone this moment:' and she was again hastening away, when Mrs. Chartres suddenly placed herself between her and the door; declared that she had prepared a supper below for a small select party; expatiated on the cruelty of refusing to stay this once, when her supper was prepared; and then petitioned, implored, and persecuted, till she wrung from the distressed Charlotte her slow consent to send away the carriage for an hour.

The chosen party which Mrs. Chartres distinguished by an invitation to supper, waited a considerable time after the rest of the company were dispersed, before the repast was announced. Mrs. Chartres had not proportioned the number of her guests to the size of her table, which was so crouded, that the company were obliged to sit sideways, and, whenever a plate was changed, or a dish removed, to give way by general consent. But these inconveniences Mrs. Chartres perceived with perfect indifference, and only lamented, that she could not prevail on more of her friends to stay. She heard, with equal composure, the vain applications which were made to Thomas for plates, knives, and forks. Thomas, when called upon, answered, 'Yes,' with great alertness; but, as nothing can come of nothing, it was entirely out of his power to supply the demands of the company. All that wisdom could suggest, or promptitude achieve, Thomas performed. When desired to bring desert spoons, of which there were none in the house, he presented tea-spoons; and when called upon for oil (an article which, in the hurry of preparation, had been forgotten) he produced vinegar, by way of substitute.

Mr. Burton had taken care to place himself next Julia, to whom he devoted his whole attention, and begged to have the honour of helping her to some chicken, enquiring what part she chose. She desired a wing. 'Well, I declare,' said Mr. Burton, 'that surprizes me; I think a leg so much better. I believe I have a strange taste; but I like the legs of all fowls better than the wings; I even prefer the drumstick of a turkey.' Julia made him no answer, as it was a point she felt not the least inclination to discuss. After supper there was much loud merriment; for the company in general seemed to be of opinion, that mirth and noise were synonymous terms, and gaiety merely a counterfeit, unless it was powerful enough to disturb the neighbourhood. When the party became a little fatigued with this vociferous conviviality, Mr. Burton, in order, as he declared, 'to keep it up,' volunteered a song in the Italian manner; but in a voice that scorned all tune, and with so many strange cadences, that Charlotte, who was in good spirits, found it extremely difficult to avoid laughing. Mr. Burton, however, was so perfectly satisfied with his own performance, that, when the song was finished, he looked round to collect the applause of his audience. He then proposed sentimental toasts, which, he said, he liked of all things, among clever people: but Charlotte's carriage was now announced, who, impatient to be gone, hastened away with too quick a pace to be again stopped. Julia followed as fast as she could, happy to leave the ladies who were in friendship with the nobility, and escorted to the carriage by the gentleman, who knew so much about Cicero, and had such a taste for the drumsticks of turkies. Frederick Seymour hastened after the ladies; but they could scarcely be convinced they had escaped, till they were out of the house; for Mrs. Chartres pursued them along the passage, with repeated wishes that they might not get cold, repeated thanks for their company, and a thousand 'good-nights,' till they were quite out of hearing.

In their way home, Charlotte laughed heartily at the recollection of all that had passed; while Julia declared, she thought the evening the longest she had ever spent. Seymour expressed his indignation at the horrible penance he had undergone; and all of them agreed never to make such a sacrifice of time again.

Mrs. Chartres, on the contrary, dismissed her guests with much self-complacency. She had given a card-assembly, and a *petit-souper*;[25] and had not sufficient penetration to discern that her sketch of elegance was a wretched daub; and, though it was copied from what she had heard of high-life, had as little resemblance to its model, as the picture of King William on a sign-post, to the real features of the hero it represents. When the company departed, Mrs. Chartres told her son, with an air of triumph, that the evening had *gone off* remarkably well. Chartres was by no means of opinion that the evening had gone off *well*: but that it was gone at last, was to him a most comfortable reflection; to whom it had produced nothing but confusion, perspiration, and distress.

# CHAP. XXIV.

Mrs. Melbourne, and Mr. and Mrs. Seymour, who had been some weeks at Bath, arrived in town; and soon after Mrs. Melbourne took an opportunity to repeat, what she had already more than once insinuated to Mr. Clifford, that Julia was incapable of the management of his family, and that he ought to watch her narrowly, and limit her expences. It may seem strange, that Mrs. Melbourne took the trouble to interest herself in Mr. Clifford's family affairs: but she had no less than two motives for this conduct. Since Julia was the age of seventeen, this lady had had a standing quarrel with her, on account of her beauty; and, though she had patched up a reconciliation on Mrs. Seymour's marriage, her former animosity revived, when she saw Julia mistress of her uncle's house, and living in greater splendor than her own daughter. But, independently of this parental jealousy, Mrs. Melbourne was a person who often intermeddled in the concerns of other people, merely as an exercise for the activity of her own mind. She had the highest opinion of her own penetration, was fond of command, wished to be the directing star of all her acquaintances, and distributed counsel, admonition, and reproof, with infinite liberality. There is, however, a remarkable difference in the value placed upon advice, by those who give, and those who receive it; and Mrs. Melbourne's tutelar care of Mr. Clifford's household, met with so cold a reception from that gentleman, that she determined to deprive him of the benefit of her instructions in future.

Mrs. Seymour soon invited Julia to a party at her house, where her chief amusement arose from the observations she made on Charles Seymour's behaviour. She could guess the rank or fortune of the persons with whom he conversed, with as much precision as if she had read their names in the Court Calendar,[26] or had learnt from their broker the state of their funds: for, had the title, or wealth, of each of his acquaintances been weighed in one scale, and the degree of his attention in another, the counterpoise would have been found exactly even, without one grain of courtesy, one atom of kindness being wasted, or misplaced. If the rule of his conduct had been somewhat more noble, nothing could have been more praise-worthy than his diligent adherence to it; which was uniform, and undeviating; neither relaxed by tenderness, or moved by admiration. Politeness, in him, was the offspring, not of benevolence, but of selfishness; and though he laboured to conceal its hereditary likeness, under the mask of ostentatious urbanity, and studied candor, yet some lurking meanness, or insolent neglect, occasionally betrayed, to persons of penetration, its ignoble origin.

He devoted half an hour, in the course of the evening, to Julia; which was certainly half an hour lost, both to her and to himself; though he was gay and tender, witty and pathetic, by turns; muttered, sighed, and smiled, and repeated those flattering things, to which he was well convinced no woman could listen with indifference, when they proceeded from his lips. When he thought Julia had heard enough to be almost seriously in love with the speaker, to prevent that mischief, he sauntered to the youngest Miss C—, who was sitting at some distance with a very grave countenance; but, when she saw him approaching, her features became more gay every step he advanced, and she was so sprightly by the time he drew near, that she received him with an encouraging titter, which she honoured his wit by renewing at proper intervals.

Meantime, Frederick Seymour, wholly absorbed by Julia, played at whist without knowing a card in his hand, and followed her with his eye wherever she moved. He saw her conversing with Mr. F—; observed that she seemed to have pleasure in the conversation; and that she smiled upon him with great sweetness: and, while he meditated with horror on the satisfaction expressed in her countenance, he finished the rubber very expeditiously, by making some capital mistakes. He paid his losses with great alacrity, and hastened to Mr. F—, whom he engaged in conversation; but he had no power to detain Julia, and she left her seat in a few minutes. Seymour did not dare to follow; and, while he was employed in watching her movements, entirely forgot that he was conversing with Mr. F—, till that gentleman left him and hastened to the party of ladies whom Julia had joined. Frederick Seymour now perceived, that in quitting the whist-table, he had only procured for himself a change of misery: again Mr. F— spoke, and again Julia listened. In vain Seymour endeavoured to witness this second conversation-scene with composure; – in vain he struggled to suppress his sensations; – it was a thing impossible! 'Ah! Who can hold a fire in his hand, by thinking of the frosty Caucasus?'[27] Seymour, in a fit of despair, went to Charlotte, told her he was going to pay a visit, and hastened away. But, by the time he reached the street door, he heartily repented having left the room. He fancied he saw Julia rejoicing in his absence; and Mr. F— happy in her smiles. He wished to find some excuse for returning: but the present agitation of his mind was not favourable to invention; and he was at last reduced to hope, that his horses feet might slip, his carriage break down, and that some kind disaster might furnish him with a pretence to go back. But while these things were passing in his mind, his coachman conducted him in perfect safety to his own door. He hastened to his study, but with no intention to read; walked up and down the room, then flung himself into a chair; then walked again; listened to every carriage that passed; thought Charlotte would never return; reflected how much time Mr. F— had had for conversation; and was little comforted when Charlotte appeared, and told him she had left her father and Julia behind, as his carriage was not come. Seymour was surprised Mr. Clifford chose to stay so late, wondered Charlotte did not offer to set him down, and desired to know what company she left behind. Charlotte mentioned several names, but omitted Mr. F—, and Seymour was obliged to ask if he was gone when she came away? 'Oh, no,' said Charlotte, 'I beg Mr. F—'s pardon, I declare I quite forgot him, and I wonder at that, for I left him talking to Julia.' Seymour rose hastily from his seat, and walked two or three times across the room. He then enquired at what hour Mrs. Seymour's parties generally broke up; and gained no information. Meantime Charlotte grew somewhat tired of her husband's interrogatories: 'Yet,' thought she, 'it is easy to repeat a few names, and answer a few questions; and though I find them a little dull, because I am sleepy, I am glad he is amused.'

At length, however, when Seymour again renewed the subject of Mr. F—, 'Do, my dear Mr. Seymour,' said Charlotte, 'let me bid that worthy gentleman good night; and we'll have him served up at breakfast to-morrow morning.' Charlotte went to sleep, as unconscious of the pain she had inflicted, by her intelligence respecting Mr. F—, as a child who sports with images of death, and prattles about the tall feathers of the hearse, to the afflicted mourner, who feels every syllable a wound.

Julia, though she had conversed with Mr. F— with apparent cheerfulness, felt no such sensation at her heart. She had perceived Frederick Seymour's jealousy and perturbation, and trembled lest his unhappy passion should be discovered, and spread a wider circle of misery. She found some relief, after he was gone, in conversing with Mr. Seymour, who saw she was in bad spirits, and exerted his brilliant talents for her entertainment. He had a high place in her esteem. She respected his abilities, was charmed with his conversation, and sometimes secretly lamented, that he was not united to a woman more capable of conferring domestic happiness. But an incident happened, which totally altered her opinion of his character.

Mr. Clifford hired a housekeeper, on the recommendation of an old friend of his, to whom she had been long known. This person had only been a few days in Mr. Clifford's family, when she acknowledged to Julia, that she had lived many years with Mr. Seymour's mother, and that she had only left Mr. Seymour's service one year. Julia enquired into the reason of her quitting it. 'Ah, Ma'am,' said she, 'it was because I was too honest, and loved that poor dear young lady, Mrs. Meynell, too well.' 'Who is Mrs. Meynell?' enquired Julia. 'Have you never heard of her, Ma'am?' 'No, never.' She then related to Julia, that Mrs. Meynell's mother, who was the daughter of a Scotch Lord, married her father's chaplain, a Mr. Forbes. Her family renounced her; and her brother, who soon after succeeded to the title, would never hear her name. Her husband died some years after their marriage, and Mrs. Forbes was so much afflicted at his death, that she fell into a consumption, and soon followed him to the grave; leaving one daughter. Several years before Mrs. Forbes's marriage, her eldest sister had married Mr. Seymour, an English gentleman, who was the father of the present Mr. Seymour. Upon the death of Mrs. Forbes, Mrs. Seymour, who was then a widow, took her orphan child under her own protection. 'She was just seven years old, Ma'am,' said the housekeeper to Julia, 'when she came to my mistress, and she had so many engaging ways, Ma'am, that she soon won all our hearts. Pretty creature! She would sit and talk of her poor mama, by the hour together. 'To be sure, (she would say) my aunt is very good to me, but I suppose, Mrs. Evans, an aunt never loves one like a mama.' 'My dear,' says I, 'your aunt will be a mama to you now.' 'Yes,' says she, 'my aunt said so yesterday, and told me I might call her mama, if I pleased, and so I shall: but for all that, she's not my own true mama that was put into the coffin.' 'Poor little soul! I remember very well going into the room one day, and the child was standing at the window, crying: so, says I, What are you crying for, my dear? says I.' 'Nothing, Mrs. Evans, only,' (and she sobbed,) 'only that black coach, that went by, put me in mind of my mama; I was thinking how she kissed me, the last time, before she died; and I remember every word mama said. She took me in her arms, and held me *so* fast, and said, "My poor child! – My sweet darling! – Must I leave you? – God Almighty bless you, my poor orphan!" And then she said something more about the fatherless[28] – and then my mama *cried* so, Mrs. Evans! – and I cried very much indeed. – Pray, Mrs. Evans, what made my mama call me poor child? I'm not *poor*, you know; I have frocks enough, and a new black sash; and yet every body that comes to see my aunt kisses me, and says, Poor little thing! But *I* can guess why they call *me poor*; it's because I have no mama, and other little girls have a papa and mama too.' 'I could not bear to hear her innocent prattle, Ma'am, it went to my very heart. 'Heavens bless you, my love,' said I, 'and keep you from all evil!' 'And pray, Mrs. Evans,' said she, 'what is evil?' 'I wish you may never know,' said I. 'But come, my dear,' says I, 'come into my room, and I'll give you a great peach.' 'No, I thank you, Mrs. Evans,' says she, 'keep it for me till to-morrow, if you please; I shall like the peach best when I'm not thinking of my mama.'

'Well, Ma'am, she grew up, as one may say, like a fine plant, tall, and straight, and a very lovely creature she is: she has something, Ma'am, of your mild look. And so, Ma'am, as I was saying, my mistress could not help being fond of her, and gave her fine cloaths, and took her every where a visiting with her.'

Mrs. Evans then informed Julia, that at the death of Mrs. Seymour, which happened when Miss Forbes was two and twenty, she was left entirely destitute; as Mrs. Seymour had nothing but her jointure,[29] and it was not in her power to provide for her niece. The young lady, upon her aunt's death, determined to go out in the world, however unfit she felt herself to struggle with its difficulties. But this measure Mr. Seymour strenuously opposed, informing her, that he was going to be married, in a few months, to Miss Melbourne, and intreating that she would still consider his house as her home. He assured her of his utmost endeavours to make her situation happy; and proposed that, till his marriage took place, she should board with a family of which he had some knowledge.

'So, Ma'am,' continued Mrs. Evans, 'she hardly knew what to do. So, Ma'am, I advised her to go, till she could look about her: so she went, and, as soon as ever Mr. Seymour was married, he invited her to his house; but she said to me, the night she came, 'says she, Mrs. Evans,' says she, 'I am come here for a few weeks, because Mr. Seymour urged it with so much kindness that I could not well refuse. But I am determined not to live in a state of dependance, and shall only stay till I can provide myself with a proper situation.' 'Well, Ma'am, Mrs. Seymour was prodigious civil to her at first; but she soon behaved so disrespectful, and so spiteful, you can't think. I believe in my conscience it was all *pure* envy, because Miss Forbes was handsomer than herself; for, Ma'am, Miss Forbes looks like a queen when she's dressed: Mrs. Seymour isn't fit to hold the candle to her. So, poor thing, she used to complain, Ma'am, of ill health, and never would appear when there was company, or go out with Mrs. Seymour; so Mrs. Seymour kept it a secret she was in the house.' 'And where is she now?' said Julia, with eagerness. 'Why you shall hear, Ma'am. She was resolved to go out in the world, but she couldn't hear of a situation directly; so Mr. Seymour told her she would make him miserable if she thought of it; but, if she disliked his family, she should go and board where she was before; so, Ma'am, she went, till she could hear of a place. Well,

Ma'am, then he came every day to visit her, on pretence, to be sure, that she was his cousin; but at last, Ma'am, he had the assurance to make downright love to her. So she sent for me, all of a hurry, and cried bitterly, and told me of it; for, Ma'am, though I should not say it myself, I had always done my duty by her, and she knew how I loved her, and so she treated me like a friend. So, Ma'am, there was a captain on half-pay,[30] a Captain Meynell, that visited where she was, and had made proposals of marriage to her; and, it was said, he had a good deal of money in the stocks; and so the best advice I could give her was, to take him for better for worse, though, to be sure, he was a little rough, and ugly enough, God knows. Well, Ma'am, she was half distracted, and at last she consented to marry the Captain, in despair, as one may say. So, Ma'am, Mr. Seymour gave me leave to go and dress her wedding dinner, and be with her; and plague enough I had with their awkward servants, to be sure. There was a pretty dish of green pease overboiled, that cost Mr. Seymour a guinea; for he sent them, though she wou'dn't see him, and a very handsome dish it was, to give the devil his due. There was a very good dinner to be sure, for the matter of that; I remember to all the dishes. I'm sure I had vexation enough: the ducklings were over-roasted, and that sweet creature cried so; many a salt tear I shed with her. I was so vexed about the ducklings, I never met with such an accident before; and many a pair have I sent up in my time, roasted to a turn; but then I had all my things proper about me. Moreover, Ma'am,' says I, 'what does it argufy,'[31] says I, 'taking on so now, when the deed's done; but poor soul! she only cried the more for that. She was dressed all in white, Ma'am, and as plain as could be, but she looked charmingly for all that. Well, Ma'am, she wanted to go directly and live in the country, to hide herself from the world, as she called it; but do you know, Ma'am, that monster my master (for a monster he is to be sure) persuaded her husband, who is but thick-headed, to stay in London, and he would get him some place or another; but all he wanted was to keep her here for his own vile ends. And now, Ma'am, he's always going there, on pretence of seeing Captain Meynell; but she takes on so, I believe she'll fret herself to death soon.' 'Where does she live?' said Julia; 'Why, Ma'am, in a little miserable sort of a lodging in Charles-street, West-minster. I'm sure I little thought for to see her come to that; and, I believe, she often goes without her dinner: for it turned out, that Captain Meynell had no money at all, and, only married her in hopes that her great friends would provide for him; and, I believe, Ma'am, Mr. Seymour knew well enough he was poor when she married him; but he wanted to get her more into his own clutches. Well, Ma'am, and Mrs. Seymour goes sometimes to see her, but it's only to vaunt over her. Oh, Ma'am, it sets my blood up so when I think of it. So one day I gave it to Mr. Seymour pretty roundly, for all his doings; and told him a piece of my mind. And 'Sir,' says I, 'I should expect a curse, Sir,' says I, 'would come upon me, if I eat your bread any longer; and I desired to be paid my wages, and went off that very night.' Julia was now called away, but Mrs. Evans's narrative had made a deep impression on her mind. She determined to get acquainted with Mrs. Meynell, and felt a generous impatience to soften her misfortunes, by administering all the comfort which her unhappy situation would admit. With respect to Mr. Seymour, she felt that severe disappointment which is experienced by an ardent and ingenuous mind, when it is forced to exchange the fervent glow of esteem and confidence, for disgust and aversion; and when, finding itself grossly deceived in its opinions of another, it is led with painful regret to lower its general standard of human excellence. She lamented that Mr. Seymour's character, which appeared open, liberal, and elevated, should so ill bear a close inspection; and that his mind resembled one of those pictures which must be viewed by the dim light of a taper; since their coarse and glaring colours, which attract the eye in the deceitful medium, shrink from the full and clear sunshine of truth.

But, while Julia's heart throbbed with indignation at the oppressor, and melted with compassion for the oppressed, she fancied she saw the arm of indignant Heaven tearing the veil by which iniquity was concealed, and making manifest the sufferings of innocence.[32] And, while she hoped to act as the agent of Providence,[33] in protecting afflicted virtue, she exulted in the strengthened conviction, that evil, like a baleful meteor, has its appointed course, and then must set in darkness.

# CHAP. XXV.

Julia felt all the eagerness of ardent benevolence to become acquainted with Mrs. Meynell, and to endeavour, by every effort in her power, to alleviate her misfortunes. She determined to wait upon her immediately, but had too much respect for her unhappy situation to visit her without the customary forms of introduction.

She hastened to Charlotte, impatient to be informed if she had any knowledge of Mrs. Meynell, and anxious to solve a most painful doubt which arose in her mind, lest Frederick Seymour should be capable of deserting his amiable relation because she was unfortunate. A doubt of those in whose integrity we have confided, in whose virtue we are interested, is a situation of mind the most gloomy and comfortless. Suspicion is like a mist, which renders the object it shades so uncertain, that the figure must be finished by imagination; and, when distrust takes the pencil, the strokes are generally so dark, that the disappointed heart sickens at the picture.

Julia related to Charlotte the circumstances which Mrs. Evans had told her concerning Mrs. Meynell, concealing, however, her account of Mr. Seymour's criminal designs, which she thought it was improper to communicate to any one. Charlotte told her, that she had frequently heard Frederick Seymour speak of Mrs. Meynell with the most affectionate concern. 'We have scarcely had a moment's *tête-à-tête*,' said Charlotte, 'since you came to town, or I should certainly have mentioned to you what I had heard of her. Mr. Seymour has often told me how much he was shocked, at his return from the continent, to find her married to such a man as Captain Meynell; and he has visited her three or four times since we came to town, but she will not allow him to bring me to wait upon her. He says, he is sure that Mrs. Seymour has been insolent to her, and, I suppose, she apprehends the same treatment from me: I cannot intrude upon her against her consent, but I hope she will be persuaded to see me in time.' 'But, my dear Charlotte,' rejoined Julia, 'we will not wait these slow determinations. She has not forbidden *me* to come, and I will go directly to Mrs. Seymour, oblige her to introduce me to Mrs. Meynell, and then bring you together at my uncle's.' Julia, earnest in her project, without farther deliberation, called upon Mrs. Seymour, and enquired if she had an hour of leisure that morning. Mrs. Seymour assured her, that she was quite disengaged, and vastly happy to see her.

Since the period of Mr. Clifford's return from the East, Mrs. Seymour had behaved to Julia with the utmost cordiality, as she now thought her acquaintance eligible; though she could feel no friendship for a woman so handsome: for Mrs. Seymour was not like the world in general, attracted by 'a set of features, or the tincture of a skin;'[34] but, on the contrary, felt a generous affection for deformity. She was sensible, however, that her taste was singular, and she therefore concealed it carefully. After many expressions of kindness on the part of Mrs. Seymour, and some general conversation, Julia led to the subject of her visit, by mentioning that Mrs. Evans was now Mr. Clifford's housekeeper. Mrs. Seymour changed colour at this intelligence: 'That's strange enough,' said she; 'pray, who recommended her?' – 'An old friend of Mr. Clifford's.' – 'Well, I am sure,' added Mrs. Seymour, with affected carelessness, 'you will not keep her long. She is a most forward impertinent creature, and had been so spoilt by Mr. Seymour's mother, that I found myself obliged to part with her.' 'There is *one* circumstance, however,' said Julia, looking stedfastly at Mrs. Seymour, 'which gives me a favourable opinion of her; her strong attachment to Mrs. Meynell.' 'O yes,' replied Mrs. Seymour, in manifest confusion, 'she's a poor relation of Mr. Seymour's.' 'I wonder I never heard you mention her name,' rejoined Julia. 'Why, really,' said Mrs. Seymour, 'I thought it very unnecessary to teaze you with a long history of Mr. Seymour's relations.' 'But I think Mrs. Meynell's story so interesting, and the accounts I have heard of her from Evans have prepossessed me so strongly in her favour, that I feel a great desire for her acquaintance; and the purpose of my visit, this morning, is to ask you to come with me, and introduce me to her.' 'Bless me, my dear Miss Clifford,' said Mrs. Seymour, with apparent chagrin, 'what a strange whim! – what in the world can you have to do with Mrs. Meynell?' 'I have no other reason,' said Julia, calmly, 'for desiring her acquaintance, than that her character and situation interest me. But come, why should we waste time in talking of our visit? Mr. Clifford's carriage is at the door: I suppose you often call on Mrs. Meynell, and there will be nothing very singular in taking me with you.' 'Oh, my dear,' said Mrs. Seymour, 'you don't know what confusion the sight of a new carriage will create. It will shake Mrs. Meynell's nerves for a fortnight; she'll be flying into her bed-room to tie on a clean apron, and come to us in such a tremble!' '*That* will give me pain indeed,' said Julia. 'I assure you,' rejoined Mrs. Seymour, 'going there is the most distressing thing in the world. I was made so ill last time I went, by an unlucky circumstance. – You must know she lodges at a taylor's and the men work in the garret: so the last time I called, her little girl of a servant was out of the way, and a sour ill-looking fellow opened the door, and, when my servant enquired if Mrs. Meynell was at home, answered 'Yes,' and walked away. So I got out of the carriage and was going up stairs, for I knew it was in vain to wait for any body to announce me; and just as I reached the first landing-place, I met five or six men coming with a shocking noise down stairs. It really struck me that they were a gang of thieves, who had plundered the house, and were making off. I believe I gave a sort of scream, but they stopped, and made way for me very respectfully; and, who should these people be but the men who work in the garret, coming down to dinner. However, when I reached Mrs. Meynell, I was so ill with the fright, that I was forced to call for a glass of water. I waited a great while for it, for she was obliged to get it herself, and when I told her the reason of my being indisposed, she was so sullen that she would scarcely speak while I stayed. I suppose she very good-naturedly thought there was something of affectation in my fright. Because she is used to this formidable troop herself, she fancied that there was nothing in it to alarm *me*.'

'Well,' said Julia, 'I am not at all deterred, by your rencounter, from wishing to visit Mrs. Meynell; and feel more disposed to pity than blame her sullenness on the occasion you mention.' 'If you *will* go,' said Mrs. Seymour, with some asperity, 'you *must*; and if you find the acquaintance troublesome, remember its your own fault.' She then rung the bell for her maid, ordered, with much ill-humour, her cloak and gloves, and set off with Julia in Mr. Clifford's carriage. Mrs. Seymour was extremely sullen the whole way; and, when Julia spoke to her, only answered by monosyllables, till they drew near the door; when she advised Julia to take care to hold up her gown while she went up stairs, or she would probably have her train tolerably dirtied from the feet of the workmen.

Julia found, that though Mrs. Meynell's lodgings were mean, and such as bespoke extreme penury, the dirt and confusion, of which Mrs. Seymour complained, were violently exaggerated; but, notwithstanding this, the habitation appeared utterly unfit for the inhabitant. She seemed like a finely proportioned statue; the exquisite workmanship of Grecian hands, which those masters of art would have deemed worthy to inhabit a temple, and decorate a shrine; but which Gothic barbarity had placed in a rude and sordid hut, where it lay neglected, by those who were ignorant of its value.[35] Mrs. Meynell was about twenty-four years of age; her figure was tall, graceful, and elegant; her countenance, with a considerable degree of beauty, had a strong expression of melancholy; and there was a dignity in her manner which commanded respect, even from those who were unfeeling enough to refuse it to her situation. She had heard much of Julia's goodness from the old housekeeper, who had been to visit her since her residence in Mr. Clifford's house; and, though Mrs. Meynell was unable to account for Julia's visit, she was charmed with the sweetness of her manner, and conversed with her with evident pleasure. When Mrs. Seymour rose to take leave, Julia gave Mrs. Meynell a card with her direction, and requested to see her, in a manner which shewed how much she wished it. Mrs. Meynell promised to wait upon her, and the ladies departed.

Captain Meynell did not appear during their visit; but we will give a short sketch of his character. He was about the middle size, thin, and rather genteel in his figure; but his manners were disgusting, and his person usually dirty. His mind was a strange compound of pride and meanness. He was continually boasting of his wife's family, and was not a little proud of his own, which was also respectable, but which he himself disgraced. He behaved with the most abject meanness, to all those who he thought could serve him; yet, at times, when he fancied himself neglected or ill used, his brutality suddenly burst forth, and by a reproof, which had more of rudeness than satire, he defeated the servile practices of years, and was generally dismissed with disgrace. His sullenness, which was extreme, nothing could conquer, but his insatiable curiosity, which led him to make the most minute enquiries into the private history of his acquaintances. Such anecdotes he retailed with the greatest avidity, and often occasioned much mischief by so doing. He had as strong an affection for Mrs. Meynell as he was capable of feeling. He had married her merely with a view to secure Mr. Seymour's good offices, who had been lavish in his promises of service, being earnest, from the worst motives, to promote this ill-assorted union. But though Captain Meynell had no views in marrying, but those of interest, his wife's sweetness of temper, exemplary resignation, and uniform submission to his will, had awakened every spark of tenderness in his bosom, and led him to feel a sincere wish to make her happy: yet, his sordid meanness, vulgarity, and ill-humour, continually frustrated that desire. His ferocious nature was softened, but not subdued; and his varying humours only produced, to his unhappy wife, 'variety of wretchedness.'[36] She was either wearied with his mirth, disgusted by his fondness, shocked by his meanness, or wounded by his brutality.

In her way from Mrs. Meynell's, Julia expressed, in the warmest terms, her admiration of that lady; to whose praises Mrs. Seymour reluctantly assented. Julia returned home, exulting in plans of future benevolence. She found Mr. Clifford at home, and Frederick Seymour with him. She told them, that Mrs. Seymour had introduced her to Mrs. Meynell, and declared how much she was pleased with that lady's conversation and manners. While they were conversing on this subject, Mr. Clifford was called out of the room; and Frederick Seymour, who had listened to the history of her visit, with delighted attention, exclaimed with warmth, 'I am not ignorant, Miss Clifford, of the generous motives which have prompted you to make this visit; for I have just had a conference with my old friend Mrs. Evans, who told me she had made you acquainted with Mrs. Meynell's misfortunes.' 'She is infinitely to be pitied,' replied Julia. 'But she will henceforth be less unhappy,' rejoined Seymour, 'for she will possess *your* sympathy, she will be blessed with *your* friendship, and the evils, which are soothed by such consolation, are more to be envied than deplored.' 'It is later than I imagined,' said Julia, looking at her watch, 'I must go and dress for dinner.' 'Ah Miss Clifford,' resumed he passionately, 'must then the indulgence of conversing with you for a moment, be for ever denied me? What have I said, of what have I been guilty, to merit this severity? – Alas, Madam, far from daring to utter a sentiment unfit for you to hear, I have been lamenting the miseries of another, at the very moment when the acute sensation of my own wretchedness almost deadens every feeling of sympathy: in vain I have struggled to subdue that obstinate wretchedness' – 'Why, Sir,' said Julia, interrupting him, 'will you force me to fly from you, by using a language, which I cannot hear without indignation?' While she was hastening out of the room, he exclaimed, 'But one moment!' 'No Sir, not a moment.' She then left him, and when she reached her own apartment, forgot her intention to dress, and only thought of that look of despondency, with which Seymour saw her depart. Soon, however, rouzing herself from this dangerous meditation, she dressed, and hastened into company, determined to allow herself not a moment more for the indulgence of reflection, which she was conscious, in her present state of mind, was but another name for the indulgence of sorrow.

Seymour remained, for some time after Julia had left the room, in a state of misery not to be described. Passionately as he loved her, he had no desire but that of seeing, of conversing with her, of possessing a place in her esteem and friendship. He had the highest respect for her character, nor ever suffered himself to harbour a wish inconsistent with the purity of her heart, and the rectitude of her principles. He was, therefore, filled with remorse and anguish, when he reflected that, by the weak indulgence of complaints in her presence, he had justly incurred her resentment; and, perhaps, by wounding her delicacy, robbed himself of that share of her pity and regard, which was the sole alleviation of his misery. He left Mr. Clifford's house in the utmost perturbation of mind, and returned home disconsolate and wretched. Seymour, in vain, possessed distinguished talents, and was placed in a situation which opened a splendid and honourable career for his abilities. Absorbed by his unfortunate feelings, those talents were useless, and those advantages were lost. His mind resembled a fine-toned instrument, whose extensive compass was capable of producing the most sublime and elevating sounds;[37] but a fatal pressure relaxed the strings, and sunk its powerful harmony.

The ardent, enthusiastic spirit of this young man was susceptible of the strongest and most lasting impressions. How carefully, therefore, should he have guarded against the weak indulgence of that imperious passion, which, on such a temper, produces the most fatal effects, and subdues all energy of soul! In vain would that spark of divinity within us, pursue the course of ambition, the ardor of enterprize, the researches of knowledge, or the contemplations of philosophy. Those noble, those exalted privileges of our nature, become a painful exercise to faculties which are chained to one idea, and to a heart which flutters round one object, and can as little change that object as the magnetic needle its direction; which, while every star in the glowing firmament sheds its brightness, points only, and unalterably, to *one*.

# CHAP. XXVI.

Mrs. Meynell wished much to return Julia's visit, but was for several days prevented by the badness of the weather; and her finances did not admit of the expence of a hackney-coach.[38] For Captain Meynell, who was to the last degree mean and parsimonious in his disposition, denied her even the little indulgences his narrow income could afford; seldom allowed her to have a shilling in her pocket; and when he did, it was on the same condition upon which the Vicar of Wakefield bestowed a guinea upon his daughters; viz. with a strict injunction not to change it.[39]

The first fair day, however, Mrs. Meynell, in spite of dirty streets, set out for Mr. Clifford's house, which was in Berkley-square. She picked her way, with difficulty, through the dirt, apprehensive lest her cloaths should be splashed, which, she knew, would prevent her gaining admittance; the servants in wealthy families being, in general, very nice observes of etiquette, and proportioning their civilities, with great precision, to the dress and appearance of the visitor. In crossing over Piccadilly, Mrs. Meynell was stopped by a carriage, and, looking up, saw Mrs. Seymour, with her mother and Miss C—, in the carriage. The ladies bowed to her somewhat superciliously as they passed, and Miss C— looked after her till she could see her no longer. Mrs. Meynell conjectured that they were going to Mr. Clifford's, and, mortified at the thoughts of meeting them, and fatigued and dispirited by her toilsome walk, she felt a strong inclination to return home immediately: but, recollecting that she might, very probably, have the same disagreeable circumstances to encounter another time, she determined to proceed.

Mrs. Seymour and her party were, as Mrs. Meynell apprehended, going to Mr. Clifford's, where they were admitted. After the usual compliments, Mrs. Seymour enquired of Julia, if Mrs. Meynell had returned her visit? Julia answered that she had not. 'Oh, then she will be here presently,' rejoined Mrs. Seymour, 'for we have just passed her in Piccadilly.' 'I'm sure,' said Miss C—, 'Mrs. Meynell takes a great deal of trouble to wait on you, Miss Clifford, for we met her wading through the dirt, poor woman.' 'I shall place a particular value on her visit,' replied Julia, 'if that will be any compensation for her disagreeable walk.' 'She is certainly very much to be pitied,' said Mrs. Seymour, in a pathetic tone; 'I'm sure my feelings have been deeply wounded by her situation. I must own I'm very sorry she's coming here this morning, and I almost wish you would be denied to her; my spirits are already so low, about my poor little dog. I'm afraid I shall lose him, after all my nursing: he seemed quite well yesterday, but this morning he has had a relapse.' Julia, without once lamenting that Bijoux[40] was subject to relapses, coolly said, that 'she could not think of refusing admittance to Mrs. Meynell, as she was very desirous to have the pleasure of seeing her.' 'I believe she's a deserving young woman,' said Mrs. Melbourne, and I should ask her oftener than I do to dine with me, (for I suppose, saving a dinner at home is some object in her circumstances,) but her melancholy looks are as disagreeable as the face of a creditor to a man in debt; a sort of demand upon one's pity, that's very troublesome. Her clothes too are grown so shabby, that I can only ask her when I'm alone, and really my spirits are too weak to bear such a *tête-à-tête* frequently.' 'One cannot much wonder,' replied Julia, 'that a woman of Mrs. Meynell's sensibility is unhappy, in such a situation as her's.' 'For my part,' rejoined Mrs. Melbourne, 'I cannot understand what right people have to the indulgence of so much sensibility, who are in poverty. People in affluence may indulge the delicacy of their feelings; and mine, I own, are so affected by the company of unfortunate persons, that I am obliged, in regard to my health, to avoid them carefully. And I really blame Mrs. Meynell quite as much as I pity her. She has enough to eat and drink, and clothes sufficient to keep her warm and comfortable; but she must be hurt, forsooth, because her appearance is shabby. I suppose she wants to be dressed like Mrs. Seymour, which is absurd enough.' 'Then,' said Miss C—, 'one's obliged to be so upon one's guard in her company, for the least hint about her situation brings a fit of tears directly. I recollect, last time I met her at your house, you happened to say that you wondered, when people were poor, they didn't prefer some honest employment to living in poverty: I very innocently answered, that I supposed they found idleness easy enough; upon which she burst into tears, and left the room in heroics, saying, 'If such a situation *were* easy, Madam, I should not be affected as I now am.' 'Really these airs are intolerable.' 'I own,' said Julia, 'what strikes *me* as *intolerable*, was your hint about idleness; for I see nothing, but what is natural, in a woman of family and education resenting disrespect.' 'Family!' interrupted Mrs. Melbourne, 'the best thing, Miss Clifford, that people in poverty can do, is to forget their pretensions to family, if any such they have; and this only requires the effort of a good understanding. Poverty, and high birth, are such an inconvenient alliance, that, if Mrs. Meynell cannot get rid of the first, I would advise her by all means to banish the recollection of the latter. When she comes into my drawing-room in an old gown, with the dignity of a Countess in her own right, and expects distinction on account of her family, she really strikes me as a very ridiculous figure.' 'Ridiculous indeed!' exclaimed Miss C—, with a laugh: 'it puts me in mind of my green parrot, when his feathers have moulted. He retains only a little yellow trust on his head; but he opens his wings with all the exultation possible, though they are as bare as a picked fowl.' 'I must suppose,' said Julia, colouring with indignation, 'Mrs. Meynell as deficient in understanding as your green parrot, Miss C—, before I can believe she would expect attention from *you,* when she was not in *full* feather: I am sure she must long ago have discovered your partiality for fine plumage.' Miss C— was a little abashed by this speech, and before she had recovered herself sufficiently for the 'reproof valiant,' Mrs. Meynell was announced; whom Julia received with distinguished politeness, while Miss C— bit her lips, and was ready to exclaim, 'Why should the poor be flattered?' Miss C—, who had but a very small stock of urbanity and good-nature, always laid out her little fund upon usury; and demanded exorbitant gratifications of vanity or pleasure in return.

She therefore considered Julia's civilities to Mrs. Meynell as an extravagant profusion of an article, which, if properly applied, might be turned to some account.

When Mrs. Seymour and her party rose to take leave, after wishing Julia good morning, she turned to Mrs. Meynell, and said, 'Shall I set you down? – but I must explain that it's not in my power to take you to your own door; your lodging is so out of the world, and I have a great circuit to make to my mother's, and Miss C—'s, and very little time this morning.' 'It's quite unnecessary to make any apology to me,' replied Mrs. Meynell, coldly. 'Well, but do give me leave to take you *part* of the way,' rejoined Mrs. Seymour: 'I'll set you down at the top of the Haymarket, wherever the street looks tolerably clean; and then at least you'll be within a shilling fare of home.'

'I shall certainly put you to no inconvenience on my account,' said Mrs. Meynell: 'besides, I mean to stay a little longer with Miss Clifford.' Upon this, Mrs. Seymour made her a slight curtesy, and departed.

When these ladies were gone, Mrs. Meynell and Julia enjoyed a conversation which rendered them more and more pleased with each other; and, after consenting to dine at Mr. Clifford's, the following day, and Julia having appointed an hour at which she would call for her in the carriage, Mrs. Meynell departed, soothed and gratified by her visit. Julia's attentive kindness seemed to her desolate heart like a solitary flower, that dispenses its reviving sweetness amidst surrounding thorns. But the pleasure she derived from her visit, was embittered by some farther circumstances of mortification: for, when she reached Mr. Clifford's street-door, the servant who opened it informed her that it rained a little; and asked if she chose to have a coach. Mrs. Meynell, who was conscious that she had but a single shilling in her pocket, which was insufficient to pay her coach-hire home, and which if spent, would expose her to much brutality from her husband, told the servant that the rain was so trifling, it was of no consequence; and went away, walking very fast till she got out of sight of the house. When she reached Piccadilly, she met Capt. Meynell, and the shower increasing, they were obliged to take shelter under the porch of a door. In a few minutes, Mrs. Seymour, who had set down her mother in Hanover-square, and had since been at some shops in Bond-street, passed in her carriage, with Miss C—. The rain was now so violent, that Mrs. Seymour felt it was impossible not to offer to take Mrs. Meynell home. She therefore stopped the carriage, and begged they would come in. Mrs. Meynell, much mortified at being obliged to accept this offer, entered the carriage with regret, and her husband followed.

'My dear Mrs. Meynell,' said Mrs. Seymour, as the carriage drove on, 'I wonder you venture out such days as these: what would you have done if we had not happened to pass?' 'Why,' replied Mrs. Meynell, 'waited quietly till the shower was over.' 'But,' rejoined Mrs. Seymour, in a tone of affected sympathy, 'I'm really surprised you don't catch your death of cold, walking in such weather as this.' 'Why, you know, Mrs. Seymour,' said Miss C—, 'there's a great deal in habit: I suppose it would kill either you or me, but Mrs. Meynell is used to it.' 'Ah,' thought Mrs. Meynell, 'Is it the fault of poverty, Miss C—, if its path is rugged, and beset with thorns, that you find satisfaction in pointing their edge, and making the feet of the weary traveller bleed on his pilgrimage? Is it a crime in penury, if its bosom is defenceless, that you love to poison the arrows which pierce it?' Capt. Meynell, who had sense enough to comprehend the insolence of Miss C—'s observation on the force of habit, answered, in his usual blunt tone, 'Why, faith, Ma'am, Mrs. Meynell, till lately, was as little *used* to walk in wet weather as yourself; and if we go to her ancestors, I believe, we shall find they have been used to a coach longer than any of the forefathers of this present company: – for instance, Miss C—, I read in the newspapers, that your family was made noble about five years ago, and Mrs. Meynell's has been noble about five hundred.' Miss C— frowned, and coloured, and, afraid of another reproof of equal plainness, observed a sullen silence the rest of the way.

Mrs. Meynell returned home, scarcely finding, in the recollection of Julia's sweetness, a compensation for the mortifications which had attended her visit. Capt. Meynell was in ill-humour at seeing his wife treated with disrespect. But, though he saw the tears of vexation fill her eyes, he comforted himself with the reflection, that her regret would pass away, and that, in the mean time, he had saved coach-hire to the amount of eighteen-pence. He had no conception of the keenness of his wife's sensations, and was entirely ignorant, that though, when a blow is levelled at the *body*, the degree of its force is known, it is impossible to guess what pain may be inflicted by a blow which is aimed at the *mind*. But Capt. Meynell was of opinion, that a little indignity might be submitted to, when it saved money; and was determined never to be guilty of such a waste of pity, as to prevent a few tears, which cost nothing, at the price of eighteen-pence.

# CHAP. XXVII.

Julia, offended at the expressions which Frederick Seymour had used at their late interview, carefully shunned all particular conversation with him; though this was accomplished with great difficulty, for scarcely a day passed without their meeting. Mr. Clifford was never happy but in his daughter's society. Their parties were generally the same, their visits were often made together, and Frederick Seymour usually placed himself next Julia, except when by some contrivance she put it out of his power. Charlotte, who had not the smallest suspicion of the real state of her husband's mind, was pleased to see him renew his former attention to her friend; till some circumstances, which we must now relate, brought the fatal secret of his passion to the knowledge of the unhappy Charlotte.

Mr. Seymour's plan for the accomplishment of his base designs on Mrs. Meynell, was such as suited a mind hardened in the practice of vice. He meant to reduce her to extreme distress; and persuaded Captain Meynell, over whom he had acquired great influence, by promises of a place, or pension, to remain in London. These promises, Mr. Seymour never meant to fulfil, till Mrs. Meynell, reduced to absolute want, and sinking in despair, might be driven to accept his assistance upon the only terms on which he was determined to bestow it.

It has before been mentioned, that Mr. Seymour entertained but a contemptible opinion of the strength of female virtue: he had, therefore, formed his machinations, as he imagined, with the most artful skill, and entertained no doubt of his final success. Meanwhile, he persecuted this unhappy lady with his visits; expressed the most tender sympathy in her situation, and endeavoured to sooth her with offers of service. But he was not a little alarmed, when he heard that Mrs. Evans was housekeeper at Mr. Clifford's; being convinced, from what he knew of her character, that she would betray his designs to Julia. He also fancied he perceived a change in her manner towards him: but what gave him far greater vexation was, the progress of that young lady's friendship for Mrs. Meynell; for he saw that at the very moment when he was ready to seize upon his prey, Julia's friendship would rescue her from his grasp. He was now frequently deprived of seeing Mrs. Meynell, who spent much of her time at Mr. Clifford's; and when she was at home, he was often debarred any particular conversation with her, by finding Julia of the party. Two months were passed by him in this uneasy state of mind, when he accidentally heard, that Mr. Clifford was making interest to obtain a very profitable appointment for Capt. Meynell, in the East Indies. Mr. Seymour well knew, that Mr. Clifford's influence would render the success of his application certain. Enraged beyond all bounds at this discovery, which at once frustrated all his deep-laid schemes, and would place the object of his pursuit entirely out of his power, he returned to his own house with his whole soul boiling with indignation against Julia, whom he justly considered as the chief mover in this application of Mr. Clifford's.

Mr. Seymour was hastening to conceal his emotion in his library, when, meeting Mrs. Seymour on the stairs, she asked him to come into her dressing-room, saying she had something to tell him. When they reached the dressing-room, 'O, Mr. Seymour,' said she, 'I have such a strange piece of intelligence for you; and I want to know your opinion of it. I have this moment heard, from a person whose penetration may be well trusted, that your brother Frederick is desperately in love with Julia Clifford, and she with him, and that they were so before his marriage.' Mr. Seymour, whose prudence would have led him, in a calmer moment, to contradict a report which might produce the most mischievous consequences, being now entirely thrown off his guard by passion, disappointment, and indignation, hastily answered, that 'if Mrs. Seymour had had much penetration, she might have found out that circumstance herself.' 'Is it really true?' said Mrs. Seymour. 'I can't talk of it at present,' he replied, impatiently, 'for I have an appointment, and must be gone.' He then went hastily out of the house; for he found himself unable to support either Mrs. Seymour's company, or the solitude of his library. His impetuous passions had met with the rudest shock: the machinations of years were in a moment defeated. Stung almost to madness by the failure of his designs, he found no relief in those projects of ambition, which usually occupied his aspiring mind. Every object on earth appeared indifferent to him but that which was lost, and he gave way to uncontrouled rage, frenzy and despair. If the guilty, even in success, are unhappy, how complete is their misery in disappointment! It is the natural tendency of vice to depress the mind, which, when loaded with the additional weight of sorrow, sinks into a deep abyss of despondency; while the buoyant spirit of virtue resists the pressure of calamity, and floats upon the stormy ocean of life, unsubdued by the tempest.

When the violent agitation of Mr. Seymour's mind had a little subsided, he reflected on the imprudence into which resentment had led him, in assenting to a report which might involve his brother in so much misery. He therefore hastened home, in order to enquire from whom his wife had received her intelligence, and to charge her never to repeat it to any person whatever. But he reached home too late. Mrs. Seymour was gone out; and, as he had long perceived her envy of Julia's beauty, and was well acquainted with her disposition, he suspected she would be sufficiently ready to repeat any thing to her disadvantage. As soon as Mrs. Seymour returned, he desired to know from whom she had received the information she had given him, respecting Frederick and Julia. Mrs. Seymour, after some hesitation, being again urged by her husband to declare the author of this intelligence, at length mentioned Miss Tomkins. Mr. Seymour flew into a violent passion; swore that the circumstance gave him a diabolical idea of Miss Tomkins; and that he was convinced, she had mentioned her suspicions from some secret malignity towards Julia, who, he added, was too beautiful to escape the persecution of the women. He then enquired if Mrs. Seymour had repeated to any person what she had heard? She acknowledged that she had called upon Mrs. Chartres; that they had talked of Frederick Seymour; and that her son, who was at home, had mentioned so many strange circumstances in Seymour's behaviour, both before and since his marriage, that she was convinced he had discovered the secret: she had therefore ventured to remark, that it was a little unfortunate for poor Frederick, that his wife's cousin was handsomer than herself. 'But,' added Mrs. Seymour, 'I really repented exceedingly what I had said, when I found, that though Chartres repeated a thousand circumstances which would have brought conviction to any person of less simplicity than himself, he had remarked the effects, without ever conjecturing the cause. I am really vastly sorry for what is past, but I am certain that neither Chartres or his mother will ever mention this affair.' Mr. Seymour, however, was much disturbed at this recital, and appeared far less certain than his wife, of Mrs. Chartres's capacity for keeping a secret.

But it is necessary to explain the motives which influenced Miss Tomkins, in communicating the above-mentioned intelligence to Mrs. Seymour. Miss Tomkins had, in the course of the winter, frequently been of the same parties with Julia, at Lord–'s, at Mr. Seymour's, Mr. Clifford's, and other places. Mr. F— was always of these parties, and his attention was uniformly devoted to Julia. In vain Miss Tomkins hoped that Julia's indifference would at length conquer his passion; since farther acquaintance with that young lady did but add to his admiration of her beauty the most confirmed esteem for her character. Mr. F— had penetration enough to perceive that Miss Tomkins resented his preference of Julia; but he was not of a temper to be compelled to pay any attention, to which he was not prompted by inclination. He possessed not that finished politeness, which levels all the distinctions of the heart, and casts an impenetrable veil over its feelings. Mr. F—, on the contrary, acted from the impulses of his own mind, and possessed that independent frankness of spirit which openly avows its preferences, and is at no pains to conceal dislike.

Miss Tomkins, who had flattered herself, during the space of some months, with delusive expectations of detaching Mr. F— from Julia, returned home one evening from a party, where she had suffered so much mortification from that gentleman's neglect of herself, and attention to her rival, that, stung by envy, resentment, and despair, she determined to go the next morning, and relate what she had observed, of Frederick Seymour and Julia's mutual attachment, to Mrs. Seymour; through whom she hoped the report would spread wide enough at least to reach Mr. F—'s ear; and Miss Tomkins believed, that if the high opinion which he entertained of Julia's character was lessened, his admiration of her beauty would prove a transient sentiment, and might soon change its object. Miss Tomkins accordingly went to Mrs. Seymour the next morning, related her suspicions, and had just left the house when Mr. Seymour returned home.

His apprehensions, with respect to Mrs. Chartres, were too well founded. The moment Mrs. Seymour departed, big with the secret, full of anger against Julia and pity for Charlotte, (who was her favourite on account of a present of potted hare,[41] and a long Indian shawl)[42] Mrs. Chartres hastened to Frederick Seymour's house, found Charlotte alone, and, without much circumlocution, began by lamenting the caprice and inconstancy of men; and, after some general abuse of the sex, finished her harangue by informing Charlotte of the report she had heard. – Charlotte was too much struck by the intelligence to have the power of making any reply. She only, after a pause of some moments, told Mrs. Chartres, in a faint voice, that she felt herself not very well, that she wished to go to her own room, and begged she would excuse her. – Mrs. Chartres, after some very common-place expressions of condolence, took her leave, quite unconscious of the degree of misery she had occasioned.

Charlotte immediately retired to her room, in a situation of which no words can convey an adequate idea. Every faculty of her soul seemed suspended; she felt a sensation as if a heavy weight had been laid upon her heart; she could not shed a tear; her memory retained every image confusedly; her brain was a chaos of perplexity and disorder; and she found that to think, was distraction. When she had recovered the first numbing stroke of surprize, and horror, which seemed almost to annihilate her mind,[43] the recollection of her past happiness called forth her tears, and she wept for a considerable time with great violence. Her reflections now threw a gleam of fatal light on the past. A thousand circumstances, which had hitherto appeared whimsical or capricious in Seymour, were now too plainly accounted for, and the horrible suspicion became every moment more confirmed to her distracted mind.

Alas! In the sad catalogue of human evils, what calamity is so difficult to bear, as the discovery of indifference in that object to whom we have given our affections, and intrusted our happiness! – when we find that heart alienated, whose tenderness seems necessary to our existence; when we read coldness in that eye, on whose look our peace depends! – How severe are those pangs, for which we must not ask for sympathy, that anguish, which must be nourished in secret, and endured without complaint! – while memory recalls the images of the past, traces with cruel exactness the scenes which some passionate mark of fondness, some proof of former attachment have endeared for ever! – repeats those expressions of tenderness which are recorded in the heart; reminds us even of the tone in which they were uttered, and gives additional bitterness to our pains! – In vain we summon fortitude to our aid. The efforts of reason are insufficient to stifle the agonies of passion, and silence the voice of despair! – Time may at length bid these violent emotions subside: misery will become habitual, and the mind may, in some degree, accommodate itself to its situation: but it must pass through many a severe extreme, it must sustain many a terrible conflict before it is thus made familiar with sorrow, or finds a refuge from it in the grave!

Sometimes, in the bitterness of her grief, Charlotte felt an impulse to fly to Julia, and repose her anguish on the bosom of her friend. But she suddenly recollected, with increased affliction, that this consolation was denied to her sorrows. Friendship, and love, seemed lost together, and her whole system of happiness was wrecked at once. – Thus the affrighted shepherd on the plains of Sicily, when the desolating fires of the volcano[44] have destroyed his beloved cottage, and consumed his little treasure, longs to fly to the shelter of some holy temple, where his tutelar saints may protect him from farther calamity; but perceiving with horror the sacred fabric totter, the sainted shrines tremble: every ray of hope at once forsakes his distracted spirit.

# CHAP. XXVIII.

The unhappy Charlotte wiped away her tears before the return of her husband; for her good sense taught her, that repining, or complaint, would only serve to tear asunder the last weak cords of affection, and altogether detach a heart, which she was now sensible she held only by the ties of pity. Love is a plant of delicate texture, and, when it droops, will never be revived by the tears of reproach; which, like petrifying drops, harden, instead of cherishing, the spot where they fall.

Charlotte did not see Julia till two days after this fatal discovery, when they met at a concert at Mrs. Seymour's. Though but little disposed for music or company, Charlotte felt that it would be an easier task to go out, than to evade the anxious enquiries her father would make into the cause of her remaining at home. And, what perhaps weighed more with her than this consideration, was a conscious dread which hung upon her mind of betraying her feelings to Julia, whom she therefore wished first to meet in the bustle of a croud.

Mr. Clifford chose to go early, and he and Julia came before any other company. They found Mrs. Seymour with Bijoux in her lap; when she rung the bell for her maid to come and take charge of him, before any more company arrived. The maid advanced submissively towards him, patted his head very gently, and told her mistress how happy she was to see him in such good spirits; and she was sure his chicken had done him good. After more comments of the same kind, repeated in the tone and manner in which she would have addressed a young son and heir, and accompanied with many respectful endearments, Bijoux, who was more remarkable for beauty than good temper, snarling at being disturbed, was tenderly caressed by his mistress, and at length dismissed.

Charlotte came alone. Her father and Julia hastened to speak to her, and Mr. Clifford took notice that she looked pale. But Charlotte declared she was perfectly well, and forced herself to chat in her usual gay and easy manner, till her heart sunk at the exertion, and she contrived to place herself between two ladies who were strangers to her, and with whom no conversation was necessary. However, she soon repented of this measure; for, in the beginning of the first act of the concert, Frederick Seymour entered the room, spoke for a few moments to his wife as he passed, then hastened to the other end of the room, on pretence of paying his compliments to Mrs. Seymour, and, after a very short conversation with that lady, placed himself on a seat behind Julia, and talked to her earnestly. She answered but seldom, and seemed to wish to listen to the music; but Charlotte saw that Seymour constantly renewed the conversation. The heart of Charlotte was stung by sensations, which she had never felt before: jealousy had now taken possession of her bosom; its sharp-edged 'iron had entered into her soul!'[45] The ladies, who were seated next her, had endeavoured to engage her in discourse, and her natural disposition to oblige so far conquered her reluctance to speak, that she answered them with her usual sweetness. But, upon Seymour's placing himself by Julia, Charlotte's eyes wandered after him, her voice changed, and, though her companions still continued to talk, she no longer knew what they said, or what she herself replied. Her mind was in a state of uncontroulable agitation; and, though music has power to sooth a gentle, or even a deep and settled melancholy, the torments of jealousy, the agonies of suspence, raise a tempest in the soul, which no harmony can lull to repose.

She thought *that* act of the concert would never finish, and, the moment it was over, moved her seat, on pretence of speaking to Julia about an engagement the following day. She had scarcely seated herself by Julia, when Frederick Seymour rose, and went to speak to some gentlemen at another part of the room. Charlotte was so much hurt at his changing his place the moment she approached, which in a calmer state of mind she would not even have observed, that she could scarcely restrain her tears. But her agitation was concealed by the approach of Miss C—, who came with great eagerness, to declare how much the company had been mistaken in their admiration of a song, which had been just sung by a young lady; and which, it was the general opinion, had been executed with the most pathetic sweetness and simplicity. Other performances of the evening had been applauded, with the usual exclamations of 'Very fine! Charming! Wonderful execution! &c.;' but, when this song was finished, the cant terms of admiration were forgotten, while every eye glistened with pleasure, and every heart seemed affected. Miss C— alone was quite astonished that the song was so liked. 'For her part,' she said, 'she thought it extremely insipid; and she knew that Mrs. Seymour, who was so good a judge of music, admired that lady's style of singing quite as little as herself.' 'Ah,' thought Julia, 'when will Miss C— or Mrs. Seymour admire excellence?' Julia's reflection was founded on a just knowledge of the character of these ladies. The lustre of excellence is as painful to envy, as the rays of the sun to the bird of night, who loves to pour his shrill cry when the birds of sweetest note are absent, and to flap his sable wings when they cannot be contrasted with the majestic plumage of the swan, or the beautiful feathers of the peacock.

The youngest Miss C— did not encroach on her sister's department of criticising the song, but undertook herself to criticise the singer, whom Charles Seymour having pronounced to be beautiful, she instantly exclaimed, 'Well, I wonder you can think her handsome; her skin's so coarse, and her colour so much too high! Besides she has such a remarkable long chin, and such very short eye-lashes! – Yet she's tolerably *showy* upon the whole; but I'm surprized any body should call her beautiful.'

Before the second act of the concert began, Charlotte, who was standing near the harpsichord, with a little circle of acquaintances, with whom she had no inclination to converse, turned over some leaves of a music-book, which lay upon the instrument, and found the song, the simple melody of which had been applauded. She read the words, which were as follows.

## song.

Broad in the west the sun descends,
I love his parting ray;
The robe of purple light he lends
To dress the fading day.

For then, in yon grey mist array'd,
Soon twilight hastens near;
And softly throws the deep'ning shade
That hides my frequent tear!

From *me*, capricious Beauty, take
The fruitless boon you gave;
Those useless graces, that can make
Each youth, but *One*, my slave.

All praise but *his*, I careless hear:
*His* words, alone, impart
The charm that ever sooths my ear,
And melts my partial heart!

False youth! tho' fair Louisa's face,
Tho' bright her tresses shine,
Canst thou in her light glances trace
The tenderness of mine?

Thy form, which from my heart I tear,
No more that heart shall move;
Alas! – the indignation there,
Is but the pang of love!

Charlotte, who could not, in her present state of mind, read the sentiment expressed in this song without emotion, in much agitation shut the book, and went to a seat at some distance. Julia had gone, a short time before, to the card-room with some ladies. Charlotte, when she reached the seat, looked round for her husband, but he was not in the concert-room, and she concluded he had followed Julia. The performers were now preparing to begin the second act; and Charlotte, who knew that the sound of the music would immediately draw Julia to the concert-room, longed as impatiently for the beginning of the second act, as she had wished for the conclusion of the first; thought she had never known people so tedious in tuning instruments, and began to fear those obstinate violins would never be in unison. Alas, Charlotte! It was thy heart that was out of tune, and no longer beat in unison to pleasure or tranquillity. In a few minutes the music began, and the company returned to the concert-room. Charlotte looked wistfully towards the door, and at length Julia appeared, and Seymour soon followed. Charlotte beckoned to Julia to come and sit next her; 'for then,' thought she, 'if he follows her, I shall at least hear what passes, and that will be some small comfort.' Small, indeed, was the comfort reserved for Charlotte, who was now but too clear-sighted to the actions of her husband. He did not venture again to place himself next Julia, but contrived to engage in conversation with those who were near her; and though, in the intervals of the music, he occasionally left that part of the room for a few minutes, he was always sure to come back, and place himself where she was perfectly in his view. As a bird, that is frighted from her nest, still flutters round the spot, and continually returns by a circling flight to the dear scene of her treasure.

In this act of the concert, Mrs. Seymour and Miss C— sung a duet; so tricked out with ornament, and performed with such affected distortions of the lips, and apparent labour, that the only person who seemed touched with enthusiastic admiration was Mrs. Melbourne; who sat with her eyes rivetted on her daughter, her mouth a little open, as if to draw in the angelic sounds; and, when the song was finished, was far louder in her applause than any one else; though, the company in general considered it as their duty to have recourse to the established routine, of 'Delightful! Astonishing! and Divine!'

When the concert was over, Mr. Clifford begged Seymour and Charlotte to go home with him to supper. Charlotte consented, notwithstanding she longed to give vent to her tears; 'For,' thought she, 'though I am so wretched myself, it must always become pleasure to make my father happy: yes, yes, my father, at least, shall be happy! I will go to supper – with what appetite I may!'

# CHAP. XXIX.

Charlotte did not long succeed in concealing her affliction from Julia, who soon observed that her gaiety was assumed, and that some secret cause of sorrow hung upon her spirits. The source of her misery she could not discover; for, though she had often wondered that Charlotte had never discerned any traces of Seymour's unfortunate attachment, yet, since it had remained so long concealed, and since no particular circumstance had lately arisen to awaken suspicion, Julia concluded that his wife was still as ignorant of it as ever. In spite of all her efforts, Charlotte sometimes appeared absent and thoughtful; but, when accused of gravity by Julia, she would start, as from a dream, and endeavour to smile at being suspected of low spirits; yet Julia's penetration discerned, that the smile was artificial, and the seriousness real. She went in vain the round of conjecture on this subject. Sometimes a suspicion came across her mind, that Seymour's attachment to herself was betrayed; but she felt such horror at the idea, that she instantly endeavoured to banish it from her imagination.

The time drew near when Mr. Chartres was to embark for the East Indies. He was convinced that his going to India was a thing fit and right, and an expedition he owed his country, on account of his projected improvements in philosophy, at his return; but, notwithstanding he had the welfare of philosophy much at heart, when the hour of his departure approached, he felt that the thoughts of separation from those he loved, excited a sensation of uneasiness, which the prospect of future advantage to science had no power to remove; and that there was a chilling principle in sorrow, which damped the ardor of philosophical research,[46] to a degree he had till now thought impossible. Chartres, who possessed an affectionate and grateful heart, felt himself bound by the strongest ties of obligation to Mr. Clifford, and would have sacrificed his life to render him the smallest service. He had the most sincere esteem for Charlotte, but Julia's softness had won his soul. She was his friend, his confidant, his counsellor; and he would certainly have been in love with her, if he had not foreseen how inconvenient he should find such a turbulent sensation at the distance of Bengal. He determined therefore to confine his tenderness within the peaceful limits of friendship; for he had heard, and gave some credit, to the information, that when the heart ventured to stray beyond that tranquil boundary, the path, if sometimes covered with roses, was oftener tangled with briars; and the sky, if occasionally gilded by the rainbow, was more frequently obscured by the tempest.

Chartres came the day before his departure to bid Julia farewel. The tear stood in his eye, his heart seemed deeply depressed, and he repeatedly declared, that he looked forward to no other happiness at his return than that of enjoying her society; for in these moments his philosophical improvements were forgotten. He told her he had just taken leave of Charlotte, whom he found alone, and in great dejection; her eyes were red, and she appeared to have been crying over some papers which were lying on the table. 'I saw marked upon the back of one of them,' added Chartres, 'Sonnet to Peace, written by Julia.' 'When, at parting,' resumed he, 'I wished her every happiness, she burst into a violent fit of tears, shook her head, and desired me not to talk of happiness. I suppose she thought I was acquainted with that false report which my mother was so imprudent as to repeat to her. I see it has made her unhappy, and she has never been in good spirits since.' 'What report?' said Julia, in a faint voice. Chartres then repeated the intelligence which Mrs. Seymour had given his mother. Julia leaned back on her chair, and in a few moments burst into an agony of tears. 'I wish I had not mentioned this affair,' said Chartres, 'if it makes you uneasy; but you have philosophy enough to despise it. I convinced Mrs. Seymour of its falsehood, not merely by vague assertion, but by facts which had come under my own observation. I told her, that, far from having any liking to you, I had remarked that he was never less agreeable than in your company; and was at so little pains to entertain you, that I had frequently known him, while speaking to you, forget what he was going to say; that whenever any body mentioned you, he seemed to find the subject disagreeable, and always assented to your praise as coldly as if he thought you did not deserve it.'

Chartres was proceeding to relate the farther proofs he had given of Seymour's indifference, for his auditor had no power to interrupt him; but at this moment Mr. Clifford knocked at the door, and Julia, with a great effort, summoned sufficient strength to implore Chartres not to repeat to her uncle a report which would give him so much unhappiness. Before Mr. Clifford reached the room, Chartres promised, not only that he never would repeat it himself, but that he would also bind his mother in the most solemn manner never to mention it again.

When Mr. Clifford appeared, Julia took leave of Chartres, and with some difficulty reached her own apartment, shut the door, and flung herself on a chair, covering her face with her hands, in an agony of mind almost insupportable. 'At length,' thought she, 'the storm which has so long threatened me bursts upon my head: – Charlotte! Oh, Charlotte! Must I be the wretched cause of your misery? Must I embitter all the fair prospects of your life, and overwhelm that affectionate heart with intolerable anguish? Why do I live to fill with despair that bosom which has supported and cherished me? – Oh, my father, my ever beloved father! Would that the same grave which holds thee, had covered thy unfortunate child! – Why did my uncle receive me beneath his roof? Oh, far happier had it been for me to have been cast out a deserted orphan, than thus to spread desolation and horror in his family; to reward his benevolence by inflicting the sharpest calamity, by wounding him in the person of his child – Yes, wretch that I am! by planting a dagger in the heart of Charlotte, I shall bring her father with sorrow to the grave. Perhaps his last breath will curse me! – no, he will pity and forgive me! – but will not his pity, his forgiveness, be more piercing than reproach, more terrible than his curse?'

Julia's mind was long absorbed by these desponding reflections. She gave way to uncontrouled affliction; sent Mr. Clifford word, that she was not well; and kept her room the remainder of the day. When her thoughts had recovered their first confusion and terror, she deliberated on her future conduct; but knew not on what to determine. At one moment she thought of flying to Charlotte, of unbosoming her distress, and then forsaking her uncle's house for ever: at another moment she wished to find a refuge with Mrs. Meynell. But farther reflection convinced her that any of these measures would accelerate the mischiefs she so much dreaded, by revealing the fatal secret to her uncle, without mitigating, in the least degree, the wretchedness of Charlotte. Julia, therefore, resolved to bear her sufferings in silence, to devote herself to her uncle's happiness, and to shun Frederick Seymour more carefully than ever.

Mean time Mrs. Seymour, somewhat ashamed of her conduct to Mrs. Meynell on the rainy morning, determined to pay her a visit in her way to a party at no great distance; and, about eight o'clock in the evening, drove, with Mrs. Melbourne, to Charles-street. Mrs. Meynell had already drank tea, and, having devoted the day to mantua-making,[47] had given orders not to be at home. But her servant had gone out, unknown to her mistress, and the woman of the house came up, almost out of breath, saying, 'There were some ladies waiting in a carriage to know if she would see them.' 'Where is my servant?' said Mrs. Meynell, in great distress, 'Have you said I was at home?' 'Yes, Ma'am; but I told them I did not know whether you would chuse to see company.' 'Then I *must* see them,' said Mrs. Meynell; who, though mortified at their intrusion, threw off her embarrassment, and received them with that ease and dignity which commanded respect. Mrs. Seymour said, she was come to wait upon her to tea; but on this hint, Mrs. Meynell remained quite passive, being sensible that it was needless to ring the bell, since there was no person to answer it. The children in the room above were crying in a most terrible manner, and the mother, in order to quiet the youngest, having put it into the cradle, began rocking with a degree of violence that shook Mrs. Seymour's nerves exceedingly; who expressed great surprize at Mrs. Meynell's remaining in such a lodging. At length the servant returned, and at length tea was procured; the cradle ceased to be rocked; and Mrs. Seymour's nerves ceased to be shaken.

Mrs. Meynell's conversation was that of an elegant and cultivated mind; and Mrs. Seymour, who happened to be in good-humour, and who possessed taste and understanding, though she strangely perverted both, grew insensibly pleased with Mrs. Meynell's discourse, in spite of her lodgings. As there were no gentlemen present, she threw aside the graces of affectation; and, without having the smallest intention to be agreeable, was really much more so than usual: for she was too apt to dispose the flowers of fancy with the formality of a trim parterre,[48] when she wished to please; and it was only in a careless moment that she suffered them to bloom with the graceful negligence of nature.

Charlotte and Julia now felt a mutual consciousness which embittered all their interviews; those feelings of tender confidence which formerly made every moment of separation painful, being lost for ever. Julia saw Charlotte pining with secret grief, into which she durst not enquire, and for which she knew there was no remedy; and Charlotte felt a degree of restraint in Julia's presence, and often a pang of jealousy, which made her avoid the society of her cousin, whenever she could find a pretext for so doing without exciting suspicion in her father. But though she skilfully concealed her feelings from him, she did not succeed in eluding penetration of her husband. Frederick Seymour perceived, with inquietude and disappointment, that Julia was less frequently at his house than formerly; and, though accidental circumstances seemed to prevent it, he was convinced, from some observations he had made on his wife's behaviour, that Julia's absence was nothing less than accidental. The idea that his wife was unhappy, and unhappy from the discovery of his attachment to another, filled him with the deepest concern; and he endeavoured, by every mark of attention and kindness, to chase from her mind those gloomy suspicions which he feared she harboured. But this conduct could no longer confer happiness on Charlotte: she no longer mistook attention for tenderness, and kindness for love. Seymour was a bad dissembler, and often strove in vain to suppress his feelings. When Charlotte chose to stay at home, he frequently gave up his engagements to remain with her; but still it appeared to Charlotte a matter of duty, and not of inclination. His talents were no longer exerted for her entertainment, no longer made the hours pass almost imperceptibly away. Charlotte sometimes talked to him on subjects of taste and literature, of which he was fond, and on which he used to give her his opinions with eagerness and animation; but he now answered her enquiries in a cold indifferent manner, which shewed that he considered it as a task.

Sometimes she endeavoured to forget her wretchedness, and tried to divert him by those sprightly sallies with which he used to be amused; or indulged the fondness of her heart by an expression of tenderness; but she saw, or fancied she saw, that her gaiety, or her tenderness, were alike troublesome, and received with a degree of coldness and gravity that petrified her soul. On these occasions she concealed her emotion till he left the room, and then gave way to the tears which she had with difficulty suppressed. Yet Seymour meant to give every proof of attachment, and earnestly wished to make her happy. But when those attentions which belong to affection are prompted only by a sense of duty, there is often some failure in the execution, even with the greatest rectitude of intention. Such services, when weighed in the scale of reason, may prove rigorously just, but, in the balance of love, they will be found wanting. The head may understand the general theory of kindness, but the heart only can practise the detail; as the sculptor can give to marble an expression of human feeling, but cannot animate the image with a soul.

We have obtained a copy of the Sonnet mentioned by Chartres, in the former part of this chapter:

## SONNET to PEACE.

Oh visit, soothing Peace! The thorny dale,
Where, sad and slow, my early steps are led,
Far from the sunny paths which others tread,
While youth enlivens, and while joys prevail.
Then I no more shall vanish'd hopes bewail!
No more the fruitless tear shall love to shed,
When pensive eve her cherish'd gloom has spread,
And day's bright tints, like my short pleasures, fail!

But ah, lost Peace! On thee I call in vain.
When loud the angry winds of winter roll,
Can he who 'bides the pelting storm,'[49] repose?
The bitter storms of life have pierc'd my soul!
Yet earth one lonely spot of refuge shows,
The sheltering grave, where Peace returns again!

# CHAP. XXX.

It was about the middle of June, and Mrs. Melbourne invited a party to dine at her villa, near town. Charlotte was not well enough for this excursion. She expected in a short time to become a mother; and with delight had anticipated that period, when Seymour would have an additional reason for loving her; when the smiles of her infant would endear its mother, and convey, to the breast of both its parents, an emotion, which, though she had not yet felt, her heart told her would be exquisite. But these dreams of happiness were no more: she now only thought of the consolation she should find in bathing her unconscious infant with tears shed in secret. When Charlotte declined joining the party, Frederick Seymour declared he would remain at home; but she insisted on his going. Julia took an opportunity of intreating Charlotte to allow her to stay with her on the day of the party; but the offer was rejected with a degree of coldness, which shocked Julia so much, that she pressed the matter no farther.

The party, on their arrival at the villa, proposed to take a walk on the banks of the Thames. The villa was situated at a small distance from the village where Julia had formerly lived; and near Mrs. Melbourne's gate she met with a poor woman, whose husband, a labourer, used to work in Captain Clifford's garden. Julia stopped, and begged the company would walk on, while she spoke to her old acquaintance. They gave the woman some money, and went towards the river. At the sight of Julia, the poor woman burst into tears. 'Oh Madam,' said she, 'I've been in a power of troubles since you left the country. I've lost my husband, Madam, and a good soul he was to be sure, as ever broke bread. He never hit me a stroke in his life: we would have a *word* or *two* now and then, to be sure, but that was nothing to nobody.' She then related the hardships she had undergone since her husband's death, which were confirmed by her meagre looks and thread-bare garment. Julia, who knew she was a deserving object, gave her some present relief, and promised to allow her a weekly donation, which she should receive from the person who took care of Mrs. Melbourne's country house.

Without stopping, to hear the thanks and blessings of her pensioner, Julia then hastened to join the party, which she saw walking at some distance on the banks of the river; but at this moment, passing a little copse, she perceived Frederick Seymour coming through it to meet her. He came up to her in a few minutes. 'Why did you leave the company, Mr. Seymour?' said Julia, in a tone of displeasure –' Because I could not bear to remain with them, when you were absent, and told them I would wait for you: you know my abhorrence of the whole group of females I have left behind.' Julia made no reply, for she was so much vexed and agitated at his having left the party, for the declared purpose of waiting for her, that she had no power to rally her oppressed spirits. 'How,' continued Seymour,' can any man who has the smallest taste for simplicity and nature, have pleasure in the society of such women as Mrs. Seymour and the Miss C—'s? – but *this* day, above all others, I find their company detestable; and determined to shake off the restraint, at least for a few blessed moments.' 'I do not perfectly understand,' said Julia coldly, 'why their society should be so much more oppressive on this day, than any other.' 'Need I name the reason?' cried he passionately: 'Oh it is a day to me the most decisive of my life! It was on this very day I first saw you! – Yes, Julia, dearest, most perfect of women, since *that* hour' – 'Is it generous, Mr. Seymour,' interrupted Julia, 'thus to persecute me? to reduce me to the cruel alternative of forsaking my uncle's house, or being subject to discourse which it shocks, which it degrades me to hear.' 'Her voice faltered, and tears fell down her cheeks – 'Oh,' exclaimed Seymour, 'what have I done? if you could see the contrition of my soul; if you could form an idea of my misery –' 'Speak to me no more, Sir,' said Julia, 'for Heaven's sake let me endeavour to compose my thoughts.' 'Try then to forgive me, or, if I am unworthy of pardon, think at least of my wretchedness with some compassion!' Julia was silent, and Seymour, who saw her turn very pale, feared to increase her agitation; and durst not trust himself to speak. He bitterly lamented his indiscretion, only because he saw it had occasioned such disturbance to the mind of Julia; for, with respect to himself, he was careless what comments might be made on his conduct. The heart of this unfortunate young man had reached that fatal paroxysm of passion, when the opinions of the world become wholly indifferent; when the mind cherishes its unhappy feelings; when it lives not to itself, but to another; when every object, but one, sinks into insignificance; when all amusement becomes painful; all society irksome; and the diseased heart can only endure the gloom of solitude, in the absence of that object to whom it was devoted; while every essential good, every important consideration, all that should be dear and valuable, is sacrificed to a passion, the remorseless tyranny of which has blasted in youth every blossom of hope, subdued every principle of fortitude, and conquered every effort of reason.

When Frederick Seymour and Julia joined the company, Miss C— exclaimed, 'You look very grave, Miss Clifford, I suppose your poor woman has told you a most dismal story.' 'Why yes,' answered Julia, 'it was a melancholy narrative of feebleness and want.' 'That's the worst part of attending to these poor creatures,' said Miss C—; 'they always insist upon telling one a story of hardships of a mile long. Its no great trouble to take a few shillings out of one's purse, but a true and faithful account of their whole history, is a monstrous *bore* to be sure.' Seymour gave her a look of indignation, and Julia made no reply.

The day passed at Mrs. Melbourne's villa somewhat heavily; which generally happens, when people set out on what is called a party of pleasure. There seems to be such a perverse spirit in pleasure, that, whenever we send that capricious nymph a particular invitation, she refuses to sit down at the banquet. The form of preparation frightens her from the vacant seat, and she fancies 'the table's full.'

As it rained violently the greatest part of the afternoon, the company looked at the country from the windows, walked from one room to another, and seemed at a great loss how to get rid of the hours which remained before the carriages were ordered. Mr. Seymour, who performed the honours of the house, saw that he was expected to be gay and agreeable; but he was in no humour for either gaiety or agreeableness. He had not yet conquered the disappointment of his hopes; and, though he pursued his schemes of avarice and ambition as indefatigably as ever, Mrs. Meynell's image still floated in his imagination, and the certainty, that on the departure of her husband she would immediately banish him from her sight, disturbed his repose. Incapable of real tenderness, his passion, which had only impelled him to the destruction of its object, made him now sicken at the prospect of her happiness; nor could his mind furnish him with any soothing reflections to repel the force of disappointment. He could recall no acts of benevolence or generosity; no feelings of philanthropy or friendship; none of those kind and gentle offices, which, to a liberal and open heart are the dearest occupations of life. Mr. Seymour was conscious that his talents had never been employed for the benefit of any human creature, exclusively of his nearest relations; and that his fortune had promoted no man's enjoyments but his own. He was conscious of having intirely reversed that passage of scripture, which declares 'that no man liveth to himself,'[50] for he had lived to himself only. But it seems to be the just punishment of selfishness, that, when its crafty wisdom has over-reached the unsuspicious part of mankind, and its schemes are successful, it does but enjoy a triumph, which an honest and ingenuous mind would think far too dearly purchased at the price of those exquisite sensations which arise from the benevolent affections. And, when the views of the selfish are disappointed, they cannot fly for refuge to the bosom of friendship. They have been too much occupied by every other interest, to cultivate an interest in any human heart; and are condemned to brood over solitary sorrow. Mr. Seymour had indeed an affection for his brothers, which had led him to promote their advancement in life to the utmost of his ability: but even this sentiment was, in his breast, strongly tinctured with ambition, with the idea of aggrandizing his own family, and had something extremely selfish in its composition. When an enlarged, and comprehensive mind, such as Mr. Seymour possessed, capable of every noble exertion, and every liberal sentiment, employs its talents only to the narrow purposes of selfishness, how inadequate, how unworthy is the end to the means used for its attainment! – It seems as absurd and monstrous, as that system of philosophy, which imagined the sun, the moon, and all those innumerable worlds which fill the immensity of nature, were formed only to revolve round this little speck in creation.[51]

Mr. Seymour, discontented with himself, disgusted with others, angry at being obliged to appear pleased when he was in ill-humour, and to talk when he chose to remain silent, felt as if this everlasting evening would never close. His impatience was perceived by Mrs. Seymour, who, being in very good humour herself, Mr. F— having said some agreeable things to her during dinner, kindly saved her husband the task of supporting conversation any longer, by taking out her pocket-book, which was stored with enigmas and charades.[52] When the faculties of the company had been sufficiently exercised, Mrs. Seymour produced a sonnet, which she said she found on the carpet of her drawing-room, one evening the week before, when she had had a great deal of company. 'It was so scrawled,' added she, 'that I could not discover the hand-writing, and I can find no owner for it.' The sonnet was as follows.

## SONNET to the MOON[53]

The glitt'ring colours of the day are fled –
Come, melancholy orb! That dwell'st with night,
Come! And o'er earth thy wand'ring lustre shed,
Thy deepest shadow and thy softest light.
To me congenial is the gloomy grove,
When with faint rays the sloping uplands shine;
That gloom, those pensive rays, alike I love,
Whose sadness seems in sympathy with mine!
But most for this, pale orb! Thy light is dear,
For this, benignant orb! I hail thee most,
That while I pour the unavailing tear,
And mourn that hope to me, in youth is lost!
Thy light can visionary thoughts impart,
And lead the Muse to sooth a suff'ring heart.

Charlotte spent the day in solitude, which her unhappy reflections rendered miserable. She fancied she heard Seymour talking to Julia that soothing language which he so well knew how to use: she fancied she saw Julia listening to it with sensibility: she recalled a thousand circumstances which convinced her that Julia was not perfectly indifferent to his attention: she sighed, she wept at the recollection, and then thought of the happy moments which she had spent the preceding summer, in the society of her lover and her friend; when, favoured far above the common lot of humanity, she had no care but that of dispensing good to others, and no wish but that of deserving her own felicity. Oh Memory! Why wilt thou for ever strengthen the dark shadows of present affliction, by contrasting them with the bright rays of past happiness?

At length Seymour returned, accompanied by his brother Charles, who told Charlotte that he had never passed a more tiresome day; that they had been persecuted by wind and rain, and *bored* with charades and enigmas.

In the course of conversation, Charlotte enquired about a curious shrub which her father had given to Mrs. Melbourne. Charles Seymour said 'it was very flourishing.' 'I did not observe it,' said Seymour. 'No,' rejoined his brother, 'while we stopped to look at it, you were at a distance with Miss Clifford.' Charlotte changed colour: Seymour cast an angry look at his brother, and told, in some confusion, the story of the old woman. 'Miss Clifford seemed very little pleased with your attendance,' said Charles Seymour, 'for I never saw her look so grave: Miss C— whispered to me that she was in love.' 'I think Miss C—'s remarks,' answered Seymour, sternly, 'are seldom worth the trouble of repeating.' Charles Seymour perceived that his brother was in bad temper, and, after repeating that he thought a rainy day in the country a great *bore*, took his leave, being engaged to supper at Miss C—'s.

When Frederick Seymour and Charlotte were left together, she made some efforts to be chearful, and had the good sense to forbear from all complaints. Alas! when an impassioned mind, wounded by indifference, attempts recrimination, it is like a naked and bleeding Indian attacking a man arrayed in complete armour, whose fortified bosom no stroke can penetrate, while every blow which indignant anguish rashly aims, recoils on the unguarded heart.

# CHAP. XXXI.

Frederick Seymour, Charlotte, and Julia, seemed by mutual consent to assume the appearance of cheerfulness in Mr. Clifford's presence. They all trembled at the idea of disturbing his peace, and extending the misery which preyed upon their own minds, to the bosom of their generous benefactor. Mr. Clifford was not apt to discern what others wished to conceal: he therefore mistook this imitation of happiness for the reality, and exulted in having been the instrument of dispensing felicity to the objects of his dearest affection, feeling it the most precious use of fortune. He passed his time in the exercise of piety and benevolence, and in the society of his friends; enjoyed a rubber at whist every evening; and had no subject of anxiety except the affairs of the state. He felt, indeed, the most watchful solicitude to preserve the balance of power in Europe, and was sometimes in low spirits on account of the national debt.[54]

The youngest Miss C— had lately been left the addition of ten thousand pounds to her fortune, by the death of a rich old aunt, with whom she was a favourite; and, a few weeks after she came into possession of her legacy, was married to Mr. Charles Seymour. This young man had begun the winter campaign by paying his addresses, in very rapid succession, to the daughters of a certain lord, a rich baronet,[55] a nabob, and two bankers in the city; but was repulsed by the parents of those young women, on account of not being able to make settlements adequate to their fortunes. Upon receiving the intelligence of Miss C—'s legacy, he determined, though a little tired of acting the part of a lover, to perform that character once more. Accordingly he paid his addresses to Miss C—, was favourably received, and in a short time married. This union was formed on the wisest motives, considering the characters of both parties, notwithstanding he disliked his wife at the time of their marriage; and the feelings of the lady towads her husband, though they did not amount to dislike, calmly rested in indifference. But he knew that her fortune would be useful, and that her connections were honorable; and she, with no less penetration, discerned that his income, joined to her own, would support her with elegance. She saw that his conversation, and his shoe-buckles, his manners, and his toupee, were all perfectly *tonish*;[56] gems of the first water, in the regalia of fashion; and thought that, upon the whole, he was a husband that would do her credit. Besides, she was now twenty-seven years of age, and had, in the course of the last ten years of her life, suffered many disappointments from being very apt to construe the slightest attention from any of the other sex, into an oblique declaration of love. If a gentleman was gay in her company, it was with a wicked design to win her heart; if he was grave, it was owning to the embarrassment of passion. Miss

C— fancied herself skilled in all the symptoms of love, and often entrusted the secret of her conquests to her confidential friends, somewhat prematurely; till at length, tired of misinterpretation, she determined to prevent such disagreeable mistakes in future, by marrying Mr. Charles Seymour, without farther loss of time.

With these sentiments of mutual convenience, encumbered with no feelings of reciprocal affection, confidence, or esteem, Mr. Charles Seymour and Miss C— were united. Nor were their expectations deceived. They certainly enjoyed no domestic satisfaction, but thought *that* might well be dispensed with, as, in the crowd of successive engagements, it would have been impossible to find any time to be happy at home, even if they had felt the inclination; and when so many amusements courted their acceptance abroad, they had the moderation to think, that one small article of enjoyment ought not to be regretted. This congenial pair lived much apart; were very civil when they met; crouded a number of visits into each day; and partook of all the pleasure which dissipation can confer upon its votaries. It certainly was not a species of pleasure which an enlarged mind would pursue, or a feeling heart would relish; and occasionally it became so very tiresome, that, from the languor of their countenances, an uninformed spectator might have mistaken gaiety for penance. They sought for happiness as laboriously as an alchymist for the philosopher's stone;[57] but found, that, like that undiscovered treasure, happiness was a hidden property, which mocked all the researches of the dissipated.

Julia's perplexities and sorrows did not make her negligent of Mrs. Meynell's affairs; and, though some of the evils under which she laboured were such as admitted of no remedy, Julia determined at least to remove the miseries of penury: a situation which exposes a delicate mind to those mortifications, of which, however galling, it were abject to complain, and unavailing to demand sympathy; since, though the world is liberal of its alms to poverty, wealth has monopolized its respect.

Mr. Clifford had, at Julia's solicitation, procured for Capt. Meynell a profitable appointment in India; and, the moment the affair was settled, she flew to Mrs. Meynell, and informed her of the success of the application. Mrs. Meynell attempted to speak, but her voice faltered, and she was unable to proceed. As the eye is oppressed by sudden light after darkness, so her heart was overpowered by sensations to which it had long been a stranger, and she burst into a violent fit of tears: but, how delicious are such feelings! Alas, the sources of misery, that give rise to tears, are many and various; but how seldom do they proceed from the overflowing tide of happiness!

Julia acquainted Mrs. Meynell, that it would be necessary for Capt. Meynell to go to India in a few months, and invited her, in Mr. Clifford's name, to take up her residence in his family during the absence of her husband. Mrs. Meynell received the invitation with rapture. 'To find an asylum,' cried she, in a voice frequently interrupted by tears, 'to find an asylum beneath your roof, to enjoy your society, is to me, of all plans, the most soothing. Oh, after having so long contended with the world, after being shocked by neglect, or obliged to combat with insolence; how will your gentleness heal every wound of my heart! – Is there indeed such happiness reserved for me? Can the period be near when my days shall pass in tranquillity? – Alas, I never hoped to be at peace again! – I expected to bear the load of misery till I could no longer support its weight, and death came to my relief.' – 'Perhaps,' added she, 'I have been criminal in the indulgence of despondency: but I own to you, that I have long felt life a burden. I have been tempted to say to myself, in the morning, "Would to God it were evening!" And in the evening, "Would to God it were morning!" – But I shall be happy again, and, what will endear that happiness, I shall owe it to you!'

After an effusion of gratitude, which Julia in vain endeavoured to interrupt, Mrs. Meynell, in the fulness of her heart, mentioned the treatment she had received from Mrs. Seymour. 'While Mr. Seymour,' said she, 'was paying his addresses to Miss Melbourne, she courted my acquaintance, because her intimacy with me brought them more frequently together. Yes, Miss Clifford, when I stood in no need of her friendship, she and Mrs. Melbourne were both profuse of kindness, and lavish in profession. But as soon as the period arrived, in which their friendship would have been useful; as soon as they discovered that I was left without support, and in a manner thrown upon their mercy for protection, they instantly changed the tone of their behaviour. To their friends my destitute situation was recounted with an ostentatious parade of pity; and when left alone with them, I met with those slight indignities, those petty insults, which are perhaps more difficult to bear than any other species of misery. They do not indeed rend the heart so deeply as severe misfortunes, but tear and gnaw its surface. Perhaps those, who can thus heap wrongs on the unhappy, deserve nothing but contempt: yet, even while we despise the hand which inflicts the wound, we cannot avoid feeling pain from its smart. Had Frederick Seymour been in England,' added Mrs. Meynell, 'I should have been spared half the wretchedness I have suffered. He has a mind the most noble, and elevated; he has a heart the most generous, and affectionate!' – 'I believe so,' said Julia, faintly. 'You answer but coldly,' rejoined Mrs. Meynell; 'surely you know him well enough to have discovered his merit. But I will hazard a reflection to you, which I can scarcely bear to indulge. He appears to me not perfectly happy: there is some secret cause of depression, some lurking sorrow, that seems to hang upon his mind, and affect his spirits – Ah, Miss Clifford, you change colour! What do you know of this? Is he not happy with your cousin?' 'Indeed you mistake,' said Julia; 'you – I believe – I mean, I am sure Charlotte makes the best of wives. 'I have no doubt of it,' replied Mrs. Meynell, much astonished at Julia's embarrassment. 'Her sweetness of disposition –' said Julia, endeavouring to speak with composure; but her voice faltered, and Mrs. Meynell, after waiting some time for the conclusion of the sentence, finding she was unable to proceed, answered, without seeming to observe her confusion, 'Yes, indeed, her disposition seems formed to constitute domestic happiness, and perhaps my anxiety for him has led me into an error.'

At this moment Frederick Seymour entered the room. 'I am come,' said he, with eagerness, 'from Mr. Clifford, to give you joy of Captain Meynell's appointment.' 'You are very good,' answered Mrs. Meynell, 'Miss Clifford has just brought me those happy tidings.' 'It was an office,' rejoined Seymour, with warmth, 'which suits her perfectly.' 'Yes,' replied Mrs. Meynell, 'and I owe, not only the communication, but the event itself, to her goodness.' 'My dear Mrs. Meynell,' said Julia, rising, 'how very small must be the merit of any services, which are attended with the pleasure I feel at this moment!' She then departed, leaving Mrs. Meynell a subject of conjecture and alarm, in the confusion she had betrayed in their conversation respecting Seymour, which greatly disturbed her mind, even amidst the agreeable prospects which were just opened to herself. Julia, however, soon recovered the agitation she felt from Seymour's sudden appearance, and left Mrs. Meynell's, exulting in the felicity she had been enabled to confer. Benevolence was the ruling passion of Julia's soul. To sacrifice her own gratifications to those of others, to alleviate distress, and to diffuse happiness, were the most delightful occupations of her mind: and she had felt the same ardor of beneficence in her former confined circumstances, though it could not produce the same effects as in her present state of affluence. Charity resembles the Spring, whose benign influence, in a scanty soil, can only wake a few scattered blossoms; but in a more favourable situation, spreads a profusion of beauty, and rejoices the heart of nature.

# CHAP. XXXII.

That unhappy passion which Frederick Seymour cherished, gained every day a more fatal ascendancy over his mind. To him every hour seemed lost that was not spent in Julia's society; for life, in his estimation, had no other value. The only ideas of pleasure and pain in his mind, were her presence, or her absence: for when he saw and conversed with her, he desired nothing more on earth; and when she was absent, he no longer felt any distinction or choice of amusement or society. All other objects were to him alike indifferent; and the most agreeable company had as little power to give him entertainment, as the most insipid.

Mean time, Charlotte had too high an opinion of Julia's graces and accomplishments, and thought too meanly of her own, to believe she could ever regain the heart of Seymour. Every gleam of hope forsook her bosom: but she had sufficient command over her feelings to appear tranquil. She shuddered at the thoughts of betraying, by her looks, that acute anguish which had sunk into her soul; nor did her countenance discover those marks of agitation which a lighter affliction would naturally have impressed upon it. When a storm first arises, it throws deep lines of darkness amidst the struggling sun-beams; but when the gathered tempest has blotted out every ray, there is no longer any appearance of shadow.

Charlotte had sufficient fortitude to bear her misery without complaint; but she could not conquer her feelings, though she endeavoured to suppress them. She sometimes received Julia with great coldness, and sometimes, from an impulse of jealousy, was at pains to prevent her from being placed near Seymour. This he perceived with resentment; and Julia, though she thankfully seconded Charlotte's intentions, discerned them with anguish.

One evening, when Charlotte had company, Julia, whose spirits were deeply depressed, appeared uncommonly grave. Seymour thought she looked ill, and wanted to place himself next her; but she was surrounded by ladies, and he could not accomplish his design; upon which he became impatient and tired, and when tea was over, went up to a young lady who was sitting next Julia, and, after much solicitation, prevailed on her to play a lesson on the piano forte. Charlotte well knew that Seymour had no fondness for any but simple music; and that, when young ladies were called upon to exhibit their power of performing what was difficult, he was ever ready to exclaim, with Doctor Johnson 'Would it had been impossible!'[58] Charlotte, therefore, could give little credit to this sudden change of taste; for her heart told her, that he only wanted a pretence to place himself next Julia, and her jealousy prompted her, while he was attending the lady to the piano forte, to go and fill her vacant seat. Alas, it is the peculiar curse of jealousy, that its watchful spirit is never lulled to repose! And the reason why 'trifles, light as air, are, to the jealous, confirmation strong as proofs of Holy Writ,'[59] is, that love instructs the heart to discern those minute shades of conduct which pass intirely unnoticed by others. It is often wounded by indifference. It is often stung by unkindness, while they lurk under the usual forms of behaviour, and are altogether hidden from common observation.

Seymour, in a few moments, looked round, and saw that the young lady's chair was occupied by Charlotte; who asked Julia some indifferent questions, in which she clearly perceived that Charlotte's mind was not at all concerned, and discovered that the movement she had made was merely the effect of jealousy. When the lesson was finished, the young lady sat down in another part of the room; and, Charlotte being obliged to move on the entrance of more company, Seymour placed himself by Julia, who determined to leave him the moment she could do it without the appearance of rudeness. In the mean time, a gentleman was explaining to a circle at a little distance, a curious piece of mechanism he had just seen; in doing which he addressed himself particularly to Charlotte, who seemed attentive to what he said, but, in reality, knew not one syllable of what was passing. She was listening attentively to Seymour, and heard a few indistinct words, which heightened her chagrin, as she saw that Seymour's soul was absorbed in the conversation, and fancied that Julia heard him with pleasure. A gentleman who was placed next to Charlotte, afterwards tried to engage her in conversation; but though she was obliged to listen, she commanded her attention with infinite difficulty, her eyes often wandering involuntarily to that part of the room where Seymour and Julia were sitting. She tried indeed to smile at such parts of the conversation in which she was engaged, as seemed to require it, while her heart was over-whelmed with despair. Her absence of mind, however, was not remarked by this gentleman, who was a solemn sort of person, that studied his phrases; came into company prepared to say what were called, by courtesy, *good things*, which he always accompanied with some action that displayed his large diamond ring; and had no conception that human attention could be diverted to any other object while he was speaking.

The subject of Seymour's conversation with Julia was, the description of a scene he had been contemplating in his ride that morning. This he described strongly; and Julia, who delighted in every view of nature, could not hear him on such a subject with displeasure; seeing, however, Charlotte's eyes wandering towards them, the moment he ceased speaking, she rose and joined her party. Charlotte spoke to her very drily; and Julia was so much hurt by this coldness, that tears started into her eyes; and, as soon as the carriage was announced, she hurried out of the house, ready to exclaim, in the words of Shakespeare,

> 'Is all the counsel that we two have shar'd,
> The sisters' vows, the hours that we have spent,
> When we have chid the hasty-footed time
> For parting us – O, and is all forgot!'[60]

More than usually depressed and wretched, it was some hours that night, after Julia went to bed, before she could compose herself to rest; and, when at length she fell asleep, her imagination was disturbed by dreams of horror. Sometimes she fancied herself wandering among fearful precipices, that overhung a deep abyss of waters, which rolled black and turbulent beneath; while on the edge of the highest cliff stood Charlotte, with her bosom uncovered, and her hair dishevelled by the winds! Her face had lost all its sweetness; her eyes had a look of frenzy; and darting a furious glance on Julia, she accused her of having brought her to distraction! Julia was going to reply, but she sobbed violently, and the agitation of her mind awaked her. She fell asleep again; and fancied she saw Seymour stretched upon the floor; his eyes closed, and his features distorted by death. She called to Charlotte for help. – Charlotte appeared – her face was pale, her eyes were languid, and she tottered as she walked. When she came near she gazed on the lifeless figure at her feet, with her hands clasped. In an agony of grief, she knelt by the dead body, and kissed it a thousand times: then turning mournfully to Julia, she cried, 'This is your doing, but I forgive you!' Julia sprang forward to embrace her, and awoke. She determined to avoid a repetition of these gloomy visions, and arose earlier than usual.

Mr. Clifford went out as soon as breakfast was over, and Julia, who was much indisposed, gave orders to admit no company; but when her uncle returned, Frederick Seymour, whom he had met in the street, was with him. 'I have bought some drawings for you, Julia,' said Mr. Clifford, as he entered; 'do, Seymour, shew them to her, while I speak to the person who is waiting in the hall; I shall be back immediately.' He then left the room. Julia turned pale at being left alone with Seymour. She was overwhelmed with the sensations of the past evening, and the impression which the gloomy visions of the night had left on her imagination: but she endeavoured to assume, though not with much success, an appearance of tranquillity; and forced herself to talk of the drawings. Her remarks, however, were not very acute; and Seymour, though a connoisseur in drawing, displayed but a small share of critical judgment on this occasion. One of the drawings was Thomson's Lavinia.[61] Julia made some observations on the picture; but Seymour now preserved a gloomy silence, which she dreaded would end in some passionate exclamation, and therefore continued speaking, though she found it no easy task either to collect her ideas, or to articulate her words. 'Thomson,' said she, 'is, of all poets, to me the most soothing; and when I feel any vexation, a few pages of the Seasons serve to calm my mind immediately.'[62] 'Poetry has no such effect on me,' replied Seymour: 'it only renders me more susceptible of misery. Happy is the man who can imitate the wisdom of Chartres, who seeks for solace in mathematics instead of belles letters, and employs his understanding, while his feelings are at rest.'

One of the engravings was the picture of Charlotte at Werter's tomb.[63] Julia, on seeing it, laid it hastily aside, and was going to examine another print: 'Do let me look at the tomb of Werter,' said Seymour. 'I think it is ill executed,' replied Julia. 'You will at least allow that the subject is interesting,' he rejoined. Julia was silent. 'Are you of a different opinion?' said Seymour. 'I think there can be but one opinion of that book,' replied Julia: 'every one must acknowledge that it is well written, but few will justify its principles.' 'I am one of those few,' replied Seymour. 'I am sorry for it,' answered

Julia; 'but we will talk no more about it, for I do not wish to like it better.' 'But *one* word,' said Seymour, 'and I have done. People talk of the bad tendency of this book, and blame the author for blending virtue and vice in the same character, because the example is dangerous. Does any person, when pleased with a book, immediately determine to imitate the hero of it in every particular? And has not the Author of our being blended virtue and vice in the great book of nature? Why does Werter interest us? Because he is not a phœnix of romance,[64] but has the feelings and infirmities of man. He is subject to the power of passion – let those who never felt its influence, condemn him; those who *have* felt its influence, too well know that it is absolute, that it is unconquerable. The heart that is bleeding with an incurable wound, needs not the cold counsels of reason, to be informed that such feelings are painful, and ought to be subdued. It is already but too sensible of these truths; but it is also sensible, that its misery is irretrieveable, that it mocks the vain efforts of prudence; and that, if peace depends upon indifference, it is a good which is unattainable, which can never' – 'I must interrupt you,' said Julia, in a faltering voice, 'for I cannot stay any longer.' He did not attempt to detain her, but rose in great agitation to open the door, and she hurried away. She met Mr. Clifford in the hall. 'You have stayed a long time, Sir,' she said, with some difficulty. 'I could not dispatch my business sooner,' he replied: 'but you look very pale, Julia, are you well?' 'Very well,' said she, in a voice scarcely audible, and then hastened to her room. 'How cruel,' thought she, 'is my situation! I make every effort to avoid him, yet am I continually thrown in his way, and have no power to prevent it, without discovering to my uncle that fatal secret, which would for ever rob him of peace. What will become of me? – How shall I act? – Where shall I fly? – Alas, I see no end of my conflicts but in death! Would I were prepared to die! – Oh my dearest, my ever lamented father! if your spirit still hovers over your child, assist and guide her in these perplexities. – Oh never, will she again enjoy those days of sweetness and tranquillity, which were spent under your protecting care! – Yet Heaven, that sees my heart, knows it is guiltless.'

Julia dined that day at Frederick Seymour's, with a large company, Mr. Clifford being engaged with a party of gentlemen. After dinner, Julia found herself so ill, that when the ladies returned to the drawing room, she told Charlotte that she had a bad head-ach, and begged she would allow her to go home. Charlotte no longer felt any wish to detain her; for, though they were still obliged to pass much of their time in each other's society, restraint, perplexity, and uneasiness, had taken place of the tender intercourse of affection. These fair friends were like two roses, which had once grown on the same stalk, but which some rude hand had torn asunder; and though their leaves were still mixed together in *one* nosegay, the tie, that formerly united their stems, was broken for ever.

Julia was anxious to depart before the gentlemen returned to the drawing-room, and sent immediately for a chair; but, at the moment a servant came to tell her a chair was ready, the gentlemen entered the room. Seymour, with a degree of perturbation which he could ill conceal, came up to her, and enquired where she was going: 'I have the head-ach,' she replied, 'and am going home.' 'Let me hand you to your chair,' said Seymour, following her out of the room. A few minutes after, a violent noise and confusion were heard in the hall. Charlotte rang the bell, but it was not answered, and, the noise still increasing, she went to the door, where she heard a number of voices, and a great tumult. She hastened down stairs, accompanied by several gentlemen, and found that one of Julia's chairmen had fallen near Frederick Seymour's door: the chair was broken, and the glasses were shivered. When Charlotte reached the hall, Seymour and the servants were taking Julia out of the chair: her forehead was cut with the broken glass, and bled violently. Charlotte, as she came towards her, cast a glance at Seymour, and, from the despair visible in his countenance, concluded that Julia was dying. She flew eagerly to her assistance, while Seymour, in a voice of horror, uttered words the most incoherent, and seemed deprived of his reason: but, in the general alarm and confusion, the agonies of his mind were unobserved by all but Charlotte; who, though much affected herself by Julia's situation, could not perceive Seymour's violent agitation without an emotion the most painful. A surgeon was sent for, who stopped the bleeding, and found that the wound was but a slight one. Charlotte intreated her cousin to remain all night at her house; but Julia assured her she was well enough to return home. Charlotte's carriage was immediately ordered, and, when it was ready, Frederick Seymour insisted upon attending Julia home: in vain she declared, that she was quite recovered, and that his going was intirely unnecessary. Seymour persisted in his design, which Charlotte felt herself obliged to second; though that look of distraction, and that voice of despair, to which the accident gave rise, were still present to her mind.

Julia, in the way home, remarked to Seymour, 'that it was fortunate his servants saw the accident, and came so immediately to her assistance.' 'The only person who saw the accident,' replied Seymour, 'was myself. I was looking after your chair, and when I saw it fall, flew to the spot, and called to the servants to follow.' Julia, after this information, thought it prudent to say no more on the subject. Seymour was still in too great perturbation of mind to trust himself to speak; and they reached Mr. Clifford's house without uttering another word.

# CHAP. XXXIII.

In the midst of many worldly schemes, which it would have required a length of years to accomplish, Mrs. Melbourne was seized with a dangerous disorder. Mrs. Seymour paid her a visit of half an hour every day; but the remainder of the day was spent in solitude, which afforded no very comfortable reflections to her mind, the opportunities of doing good which she had neglected, being the subjects of her frequent meditation. How different is the opinion which we cherish of ourselves in the days of health, and when we feel the approaches of death! At the appearance of that king of terrors,[65] the delusive mist which self-love throws around our vices and our weaknesses, 'melts into thin air,'[66] and the naked heart shrinks from its own observation.

Mrs. Melbourne now became sensible, that she had not deserved the blessings of friendship, and she found herself left to die without its consolations. Deserted by every body, formal messages to enquire how she did, were all the marks of sympathy she received; for she had no friend to pay her those tender offices, those minute attentions, which smooth the bed of death, and which money cannot purchase of those who are paid for their attendance on the dying. Her servants were more occupied by their own affairs than her sufferings; and, being no longer able to exercise authority, she was left entirely to their mercy. The person to whom she was most obliged was Julia, who, when she found her desolate and unhappy, visited her every day, and administered all the comfort her feeling heart could give.

Mrs. Melbourne left her daughter a considerable addition of fortune; and Mr. Seymour, who had long been weary of those civilities which decency obliged him to pay to the mother of his wife, and who was eager to seize on her property, heartily rejoiced in her death. Besides, it was one of his opinions, that no woman ought to survive the age of fifty; and he had often secretly blamed Mrs. Melbourne for being guilty of so great an impropriety.[67]

Charlotte's apprehensions that the heart of Seymour was wholly devoted to another, had received the most cruel confirmation from his behaviour while he thought Julia's life in danger. Thrown entirely off his guard, by the surprize and horror which the accident occasioned, he had displayed in those moments, to the watchful eyes of Charlotte, the uncontrouled agonies of afflicted tenderness, the distracted solicitude of apprehensive passion. His voice, his look, his frantic movements, being all treasured in Charlotte's remembrance, her coldness and restraint towards Julia daily increased, and gave the finishing stroke to the peace of that unfortunate young lady. To know she was the cause of Charlotte's wretchedness, to see her heart alienated, to read reproach and anguish in her looks, which used to beam with affection and delight, was a species of misery which the sensibility of Julia was unable to sustain. Her frame was naturally delicate; and the uneasiness of her mind at length produced so great an alteration in her, that she grew pale and thin, lost her appetite, and her health sensibly declined.

Charlotte's heart was too honest, and affectionate, to observe these symptoms of decay with unconcern. Julia never made the least complaint, but Charlotte now discerned in her countenance the sadness of her mind. She was conscious she had of late treated Julia with harshness; and revolving in her mind every circumstance of Julia's conduct, she felt that she had not merited this unkindness. She fancied she saw her sinking into the grave without complaint, and struggling to conceal from every eye the anguish that preyed upon her heart. The warm and generous bosom of Charlotte was unable to support these reflections: her jealousy was softened; her suspicions vanished: she thought only of Julia's virtues, and she felt that nothing was dearer to her than Julia's friendship.

Mr. Clifford and Julia coming to dine at Frederick Seymour's Charlotte received her cousin with the tenderness of former days. At dinner Julia sent away her plate when she had scarcely eaten a morsel. Charlotte, who was watchful of her, and observed it, tried to persuade her to eat something more, which Julia declined. When the servants had left the room, 'Indeed,' said Charlotte, with eagerness, 'I can bear this no longer – I am sure Julia is very ill, though she does not complain. Yes, my dearest Julia,' added she, bursting into tears and sobbing, 'my first, my beloved friend, yes, you are ill, and I am miserable!' Julia, equally astonished and affected at this effusion of tenderness, had no power to make any reply. She pressed Charlotte's hand in her's; while Mr. Clifford insisted that a physician might be sent for immediately. Julia made all the opposition she could, from a consciousness of the inability of medicine 'to minister to a mind diseased;'[68] but Mr. Clifford's fears were awakened, and he was not to be moved from his purpose. The physician was sent for; but Julia found, in the returning tenderness of Charlotte, a cordial of more powerful efficacy than any which the art of medicine could administer.

Seymour felt Charlotte endeared to him by the solicitude she displayed for Julia. He saw his wife's excellence – was charmed with her generous affection, and endeavoured, by the most tender and unremitting attention, to convince her how highly he esteemed her virtues. Charlotte's open and ingenuous heart was soothed by this conduct. She perceived that Seymour had the strongest desire to make her happy; and she felt her former tenderness for Julia awakened by the dread of losing her. She could not endure the tormenting idea that her neglect or harshness would perhaps shorten the life of Julia; of the dear companion of her childhood, the beloved friend of her youth, the constant associate of her joys and sorrows. She behaved to her with her former kindness: Seymour carefully restrained his feelings; Julia grew better, and they lived for some weeks in great cordiality and friendship.

Mr. F— called at Mr. Clifford's one evening, and finding Charlotte and Julia sitting at work, he desired their permission to read to them a poem, written by a friend lately arrived from France, and who, for some supposed offence against the state, had been immured several years in the Bastille,[69] but was at length liberated by the interference of a person in power. The horrors of his solitary dungeon were one night cheered by the following prophetic dream.

## The BASTILLE, a VISION.

*I. 1.*

'Drear cell! Along whose lonely bounds,
Unvisited by light,
Chill silence dwells with night,
Save when the clanging fetter sounds!
Abyss, where mercy never came,
Nor hope, the wretch can find;
Where long inaction wastes the frame,
And half annihilates the mind!

*I. 2.*

Stretch'd helpless in this living tomb,
Oh haste, congenial death!
Seize, seize this ling'ring breath,
And shroud me in unconscious gloom –
Britain! Thy exil'd son no more
Thy blissful vales shall see;
Why did I leave thy hallow'd shore,
Distinguish'd land, where all are free?'

*I. 3.*

Bastille! Within thy hideous pile,
Which stains of blood defile. –
Thus rose the captive's sighs,
Till slumber seal'd his weeping eyes –
Terrific visions hover near!
He fees an awful form appear!
Who drags his step to deeper cells,
Where stranger wilder horror dwells.

*II. 1.*

'Oh, tear me from these haunted walls,
Or those fierce shapes controul!

Lest madness seize my soul –
That pond'rous mask of iron* falls,[70]
I see!' – 'Rash mortal, ha! Beware,
Nor breathe that hidden name!
Should those dire accents wound the air,
Know death shall lock thy stiff' ning frame.'

### *II. 2.*

'Hark! that loud bell which sullen tolls!
It wakes a shriek of woe.
From yawning depths below;
Shrill through this hollow vault it rolls!'
'A deed was done in this black cell,
Unfit for mortal ear!
A deed was done, when toll'd that knell,
No human heart could live and hear!

### *II. 3.*

Rouze thee from thy numbing trance,
Near yon thick gloom advance;
The solid cloud has shook;
Arm all thy soul with strength to look, –
Enough thy starting locks have rose,
Thy limbs have fail'd, thy blood has froze:
On scenes so foul, with mad affright,
I fix no more thy fasten'd sight.'

### *III. 1.*

'Those troubled phantoms melt away!
I lose the sense of care –
I feel the vital air –
I see, I *see* the light of day! –
Visions of bliss! Eternal powers!
What force has shook those hated walls?
What arm has rent those threat'ning towers?
It falls – the guilty fabric falls!'

* Alluding to the prisoner who has excited so many conjectures in Europe. (Williams's note)

### *III. 2.*

'Now, favour'd mortal, now behold!
To soothe thy captive state,
I ope the book of fate,
Mark what its registers unfold!
Where this dark pile in chaos lies,
With nature's execrations hurl'd,
Shall Freedom's sacred temple rise,
And charm an emulating world!

### *III. 3.*

'Tis her awak'ning voice commands
Those firm, those patriot bands,
Arm'd to avenge her cause,
And guard her violated laws! –
Did ever earth a scene display
More glorious to the eye of day,
Than millions with according mind,
Who claim the rights of human kind?

### *IV. 1.*

Does the fam'd Roman page sublime,
An hour more bright unroll,
To animate the soul,
Than this, lov'd theme of future time? –
Posterity, with rev'rence meet,
The consecrated act shall hear;
Age shall the glowing tale repeat,
And youth shall drop the burning tear!

### *IV. 2.*

The peasant, while he fondly sees,
His infants round the hearth,
Pursue their simple mirth,
Or emulously climb his knees,
No more bewails their future lot,
By tyranny's stern rod opprest;
While Freedom guards his straw-roof'd cot,

And all his useful toils are blest.

### *IV. 3.*

Philosophy! Oh, share the meed
Of Freedom's noblest deed!
'Tis thine each truth to scan,
Guardian of bliss, and friend of man!
'Tis thine all human wrongs to heal,
'Tis thine to love all nature's weal;
To give each gen'rous purpose birth,
And renovate the gladden'd earth.'

# CHAP.XXXIV.

When Charlotte's hour of danger[71] approached, she intreated Julia to come and stay at her house during her confinement. Julia was gratified by this mark of confidence, but excused herself from staying in the house; promising, at the same time, to spend with Charlotte the greatest part of every day.

Charlotte being delivered of a son, Seymour beheld his child with transport, and Mr. Clifford felt the birth of this infant a renewal of his own existence. A few days after her lying-in, Charlotte was seized with some degree of fever; and Julia, terrified at her danger, no longer hesitated to remain at the house; where she scarcely quitted her bed-side for a moment, and attended her with unremitting care. In a few days the disorder abated; and Julia was sitting in Charlotte's room, soothed with the hope of her recovery, when she received a message, that a person below wished to speak to her. She went into the parlour, where she found Frederick Seymour alone. He told her, that he had had, for some days past, a very oppressive pain in his head, and that he had that morning felt himself so much disordered, that he had made Charlotte's physician feel his pulse. 'He says,' added Seymour, 'that I have a considerable degree of fever, and has ordered me to go to bed immediately. I am terrified at the thoughts of alarming Charlotte; but I find myself so much indisposed, that I must obey the doctor's directions.' Julia promised she would endeavour to conceal his illness from Charlotte, at least for that day, and then, in much anxiety, left the room.

The physician visited Seymour again that evening, and found he was worse. The next day Julia, who could no longer evade Charlotte's enquiries, or find any pretext for his absence, was obliged to inform her of his illness, which she did in the most cautious manner. Charlotte lamented her own confinement, and implored Julia to attend him, and see that no care was neglected. For some days his fever increased. He believed himself in danger, and intreated Julia not to enter his room, telling her that he knew his disorder was infectious, and that he trembled lest she should suffer from her attendance on him.' Julia replied, 'that she was not afraid of the consequences, and that her duty to Charlotte' – her heart grew full, and she paused.

The next morning the physician declared that his patient was better. Julia flew to give this joyful intelligence to Charlotte; who insisted upon being carried into his room, not withstanding Julia's representations of the danger attending it, in her present state of weakness; but Charlotte would not be dissuaded, and was supported into his room by her attendants. She threw her arms round his neck, and wept violently. He was affected by her tenderness, and perhaps not less so from observing that

Julia wept too. 'We shall be happy yet, my dearest husband,' said Charlotte, 'and how shall we ever be grateful enough to Julia, for her care of us both?' 'She has been our guardian angel,' replied Seymour, with emotion. – 'Indeed,' said Julia, 'I must now use my authority as head-nurse, and insist upon Charlotte's returning to her room; for I am convinced, this scene has already been too long for either of my patients.' Charlotte still clung to Seymour in an agony of tenderness, and was with difficulty prevailed on to return to her own apartment; which she at length did, attended by Julia.

As the physician had pronounced Seymour so much better, Julia did not think it necessary to visit him again until the evening. Perhaps, if she had followed the dictates of her heart, she would have gone sooner; but she was too virtuous to do more on this occasion than duty required. When she went to his bed-side in the evening, and enquired how he did, she was shocked by a remarkable change in the tone of his voice. His articulation was thick, and confused, and he spoke with a quickness quite different from his usual manner. He told her that he was much better, but Julia doubted it from the way in which he told her so. She waited anxiously, when the physician came, till he left his patient's room. 'How is Mr. Seymour?' said she, eagerly. 'I am concerned,' answered the physician, 'to tell you, that he is worse.' 'Good God!' said Julia, starting, 'I apprehended this – his voice is changed.' 'It is' said the physician, 'and the fever has increased most rapidly – You look very pale, Miss Clifford, let me lead you to a chair.' She burst into tears – 'Oh, how shall I tell Charlotte?' she exclaimed. 'I intreat you will not tell her, at present,' said the physician: 'he must be kept perfectly quiet: this night will probably determine the issue of his disorder.' 'This night!' said Julia, clasping her hands. 'Do not tell Mrs. Seymour of this change in his disorder, till tomorrow.' – 'But if he should die to-night?' – 'That is not probable,' said the physician. Mr. Clifford entered the room, and the physician, after informing him of the unfavourable change in Seymour's disorder, advised him earnestly to conceal it from Charlotte, at least for some days, since, in her present state of weakness, it might produce the worst consequences to herself.

When Julia returned to Seymour's apartment, she found him delirious. 'Oh, you are come again!' exclaimed he with quickness – 'I thought you were gone for ever – I dreamt you had forsaken me – left me to die alone! – I had a horrible dream! – my head burns while I think of it – Charlotte looked fiercely on me! – Charlotte will never pardon – she was gentle once, but *now*!' – he gave a deep sigh – 'Do not speak, my dear Mr. Seymour;' said Julia, faintly. – 'Dear!' – he repeated, in a low muttering tone – 'Oh Julia! Julia! – If I am dear – I charge you mark the spot where I am buried! – Mark where they lay me – never, never forget it! – And let it be your grave – It will be no crime, Julia! – Tell me if it will be a crime.' – Julia left his bed-side to wipe away her tears. – 'Where is she? Where is she?' said Seymour, in a hurried manner, to the nurse. – 'Do you want Miss Clifford, Sir?' she enquired. – 'Miss Clifford,' he repeated. – 'She will be here, Sir, directly.' – 'Oh bless her! Merciful Heaven, bless her! – If I could pray, my last prayer should – But don't tell Charlotte – poor Charlotte! no, no – I dare not pray for Charlotte!'

Mr. Clifford and Julia sat by his bed-side all night. He continued talking at intervals with the wildest incoherence; sometimes raving of Julia, then fancying he was kneeling to Charlotte for pardon, and calling to his infant to plead for him. Mr. Clifford considered all he said as the inexplicable wanderings of frenzy; but Julia, who well understood their force, listened to them with unutterable agony.

The next morning his pulse grew much weaker, and a few hours before his death the delirium ceased. He called Mr. Clifford to his bed-side, took hold of his hand, which he affectionately pressed, and thanked him fervently for all his past goodness to him – He then enquired if Charlotte was informed of his danger. – Mr. Clifford told him that the physician had declared it would be risquing her life, to acquaint her with his situation. 'Oh, no!' cried Seymour, 'let her be spared a scene of parting – but tell her – since I shall never see my wife and child again! – tell her, that my affection, my esteem for her virtues.' – His voice faltered, and he was unable to proceed. Mr. Clifford, in great emotion, left the room; and Seymour desired the nurse to let Miss Clifford know he wished to speak to her.

When Julia came into the room, he begged she would order the attendants to leave it. He then said, in a faint voice, 'I have solicited this last interview, my dear Miss Clifford, that I may obtain your forgiveness, and may die in peace. Oh, Julia, forgive me all that is past – pardon the uneasiness my conduct has given you – Oh, tell me, while I yet live to hear it, that you forgive me! – The atonement of my errors will soon be made – a few hours.' His voice became choaked by his rising emotion; and her hand, which he held in his, was bathed with his tears. She mixed her tears with his – she assured him, in broken accents, that her heart would ever cherish his memory with esteem and regret. He then directed her where to find the key of his scrutore,[72] telling her it contained some things which he wished to restore to herself, that her feelings might not be wounded by those memorials being exposed to other eyes. Julia unlocked his scrutore, and found her lost glove, together with some verses and notes, in her own hand-writing, which he had preserved on that account. He desired to see those treasures once more. He took them eagerly from her, pressed them to his bosom, his lips, and declared he would only have parted with them in death. Then growing fainter from these exertions, and seeing her violently affected, he said, with much emotion, 'Let not this scene, I conjure you, make too deep an impression on your feeling heart. Oh, if my remembrance will embitter your peace, think of me no more! – Have I desired you to think of me no more? – Alas, Julia, my heart assents not to that request! Oh, no! my heart refuses to be forgotten by you – let me be sometimes recalled to your mind, and when the grave shall hide me for ever from your sight, think not of me with resentment.' 'Alas,' said Julia, in a faltering voice, 'is not the anguish with which I am overwhelmed at this moment, a proof that my resentment is past, and that all that remains is the bitterness of sorrow?' 'I hope,' said Seymour, after a pause of some minutes, 'I hope Charlotte will find comfort in your friendship. Poor Charlotte! I fear she has of late been unhappy; *She*, who is so deserving of felicity – Oh, it is fit I should die, who only lived to embitter the lives of those to whom my soul is most devoted – Comfort my poor Charlotte, dearest Miss Clifford, and assure her that my affection for her was active even in death.' He now became still fainter. 'Oh,' cried he, in a low indistinct voice, 'how often have I wished to die in your presence! – How often have I desired that you might be near me when I yielded my last breath; that your regret might soften my latest moments – that you might be the last object my eyes beheld! – Oh, speak to me, Julia, speak, and let me hear your voice once more!' She tried to speak, but she had lost the power of utterance. She gave him her hand – he pressed it to his lips – she lifted up her eyes, and perceived he had fainted. She rose with some difficulty, and rang the bell for the attendants: he recovered from the fainting, but soon after became speechless. Mr. Clifford and Julia knelt by his bed-side, and he held her hand grasped in his. – Oh, is there any sorrow like that which we feel, when hanging over the bed of our dying friend – when we know there is no hope; when we are certain that a few minutes must tear them from us for ever – when we bathe their stiffening hands with unavailing tears, and see them suffering pains beyond the reach of human aid; and when, at last, we lift our eyes to Heaven, not in the blessed hope of their recovery, but only to implore that the latest struggles may be alleviated, that their pangs may be short?

When Seymour's eyes were closed, he still continued to grasp Julia's hand, and in a short time expired.

Such was the fate of this unfortunate young man, who fell the victim of that fatal passion, which he at first unhappily indulged, and which he was at length unable to subdue. The conflicts of his mind, by insensibly weakening his frame, gave greater power to his disorder, and thus probably shortened the life they had embittered.

Let those who possess the talents, or the virtues, by which he was distinguished, avoid similar wretchedness, by guarding their minds against the influence of passion; since, if it be once suffered to acquire an undue ascendency over reason, we shall in vain attempt to controul its power: we might as soon arrest the winds in their violence, or stop the torrent in its course. It is too late to rear the mounds of defence when the impetuous flood rages in its strength, and overthrows all opposition. With a frame labouring under disease, we may recall, with regret, the blissful hours of health; but have no power to new string the nerves, or shake off the malady that loads the springs of life. Alas! the distempered heart, when it has suffered the disorders of passion to gain strength, can find no balsam in nature to heal their malignancy; no remedy but death. In vain we may lament the loss of our tranquillity; for peace, like the wandering dove, has forsaken its habitation in the bosom, and will return no more.

Julia, so far as she had indulged any sensibility to Seymour's attachment, was proportionably wretched. Women have even greater reason than men to fortify their hearts against those strong affections, which, when not regulated by discretion, plunge in aggravated misery that sex, who, to use the words of an elegant and amiable writer,* 'cannot plunge into business, or dissipate themselves in pleasure and riot, as men too often do, when under the pressure of misfortunes; but must bear their sorrows in silence, unknown and unpitied; must often put on a face of serenity and chearfulness, when their hearts are torn with anguish, or sinking in despair.'[73] Though a woman with rectitude of principle, will resolutely combat those feelings which her reason condemns; yet, if they have been suffered to acquire force, the struggle often proves too severe for the delicacy of the female frame; and, though reason, virtue, and piety, may sustain the conflict with the heart, life is frequently the atonement of its weakness.

* Vide Dr. Gregory's Legacy to his Daughters. (Williams's note)

Julia, when she saw that Seymour was dead, fixed her eyes on his corpse: she shuddered, she groaned deeply, but uttered not a word. From this dreadful stupor she was roused by a message from Charlotte, who suspected, from the anxiety visible in the countenances of her attendants, that Seymour was worse; and Julia's looks confirmed all her apprehensions. She enquired eagerly for her husband: Julia spoke, but her words were incoherent, and only half pronounced. Charlotte, every moment more alarmed, became so positive in her determination to be again carried into his apartment, that Julia was obliged to acknowledge that his fever was increased; and when this only made Charlotte more earnest in her desire to see him, Mr. Clifford was forced to give her the fatal information that Seymour was no more.

Charlotte lamented him with all the violence of unrestrained affliction, and a thousand times reproached her father and Julia for having concealed his danger, and denied her the melancholy consolation of attending him in his last moments. The shock she had sustained long retarded her recovery; but at length she regained her health, and found comfort in her infant, whom she nursed herself, and in whom she centered all her hopes and affections. After some time, she returned to her father's house, where she and Julia lived in the most perfect friendship.

Mrs. Meynell, on the departure of her husband for India, was received into Mr. Clifford's family, where she was treated with every mark of respect and kindness. Captain Meynell, a few years after, died in India; and the fortune he had acquired was transmitted to his wife, who still continued to live in Mr. Clifford's family.

Mr. Seymour, disappointed in his designs on Mrs. Meynell, pursued other objects of pleasure, and formed new schemes of ambition; but neither ambition, nor pleasure, could confer felicity on a mind which was harrassed by impetuous passions, and unsupported by conscious integrity.

Mrs. Seymour perceiving, in a few years, that the bloom of youth was fled, endeavoured to supply the deficiency with an additional quantity of rouge; devoting more hours than formerly to the duties of the toilet, and pathetically lamenting, in secret soliloquies, the inhuman ravages of time.

Mr. Chartres, by his own diligence, and the assistance of powerful friends, was soon enabled to send considerable remittances to his mother; who removed to a house, where the drawing room held her card-tables with more convenience, and discharged Thomas for a fashionable domestic.

Mr. F— spent most of his time at Mr. Clifford's house, remaining unmarried, and preferring Julia's friendship to an union with Miss Tomkins; who also continued single, and suffered the most severe mortification from the failure of her schemes on Mr. F—. Still, however, she continued to impose an artificial character upon the world; uniting, with the miserable triumphs of deceit, the comfortless sensations of selfishness.

Mr. and Mrs. Charles Seymour lived together on the most fashionable terms; too careless to regard decorum, and too indifferent to feel jealousy.

The eldest Miss C— remained single, and, whenever she heard of a splendid marriage, longed to forbid the banns.[74]

The dying image of Seymour was long present to Julia's imagination, and the parting words he had uttered were engraven on her heart. When the all-subduing influence of time had soothed her sorrows into greater tranquillity, she found consolation in the duties of religion, the exercise of benevolence, and the society of persons of understanding and merit. To such people her acquaintance was highly valuable, and she lived admired, respected, and beloved. She refused many honourable offers of marriage, and devoted much of her time to the improvement of Seymour's child, whom she loved with the most partial fondness. But the idea of its father still continued, at times, to embitter the satisfaction of her life; which, but for the one unconquered weakness, would have been, above the common lot, fortunate and happy.[75]

# ENDNOTES

## Volume I

1. *the indulgence which my former poems have met with*: By 1790, Helen Maria Williams had already published her *Edwin and Eltruda* (1782); 'Ode on the Peace' (1783); *Peru: A Poem in Six Cantos* (1784); *Poems in Two Volumes* (1786); and 'Ode on the Bill Lately Passed Regulating the Slave Trade' (1788). Mary Wollstonecraft begins her 1790 review of *Julia* in the *Analytical Review* by stating, 'Miss W. is already known to the literary world as a poet', *Analytical Review*, 7 (May 1790), p. 97. Williams's early success as a poet is also attested to by an anonymous review of *Julia* in the *English Review*'s 'Monthly Catalogue for April 1790', which begins, 'The author of these volumes has already recommended herself to a considerable share of the public favour by specimens of her poetry', *English Review*, 15 (April 1790), p. 304. For early reviews of Williams's poetry see *Monthly Review*, 71 (1784), p. 12–20; *Gentleman's Magasine*, 2(1784), p. 613; *European Magazine* (1786), pp. 89–93, 175–80.
2. *lived upon a captain's half-pay*: Any non-commissioned officer – either permanently, i.e. retired, or temporarily, awaiting a new commission – would be put on half-pay, which was actually slightly more than half of what they earned when commissioned. As a captain in the army, Julia's father is a low-ranking officer who does not have the funds necessary to move up through the ranks. It appears that he has taken a form of early retirement. The creation of a character who feels frustrated by the army's failure to function as a meritocracy suggests Williams's early democratic and revolutionary leanings. The British army is decidedly not a place of liberty, fraternity or equality for Captain Clifford. Helen Maria Williams's own father was a Welsh army officer who died when she was eight years old.
3. *her sensibility was quick*: In Samuel Johnson's *Dictionary* (1786 edition), 'sensibility' is defined as '1. Quickness of sensation; 2. Quickness of perception'. Next, 'sensible' is defined as '1. Having power of perceiving by the senses ... 5. Having moral perception; having the quality of being affected by moral good or ill; 6. Having quick intellectual feeling; being easily or strongly affected'. Williams's poem 'To Sensibility' (1786) conveys a more emotional inflection, opening, 'To Sensibility's lov'd praise / I tune my trembling reed; / And seek to deck her shrine with bays / On which my heart must bleed', ll. 1–4.
4. *'beyond the reach of art'*: A. Pope, *Essay on Criticism* (London: W. Lewis, 1711), i.155.
5. *went in pursuit of fortune to the East Indies*: Julia's uncle has profited from the rapidly growing expansion of trade with the East Indies; the English East India Company was chartered in 1600 and by 1720 had exceeded the Dutch East India Company in size and profit.

6. *benign influence gilds alike the morning and the evening*: A similar contrast between imagery of a suddenly dazzling light and a softly enduring glow appears in 'Ode on the Bill Lately Passed for Regulating the Slave Trade', within which Williams advocates for the complete abolition of slavery by writing: 'Valour is like the meteor's light, / Whose partial flash leaves deeper night; / While Mercy, like the lunar ray, / Gilds the thick shade with softer day' (ll. 51–4).
7. *in search of the golden fleece*: In Greek mythology Jason and the Argonauts set out in quest of the golden fleece of the winged ram Chrysomallos.
8. *The God of Love in the East frames his arrows of massy gold ... bright edge of a diamond*: Williams depicts European matches made in the East Indies as more materially motivated than romantic matches in England. She does so by contrasting imagery of Eastern gold, gaudy plumage, and diamonds, with the soft feathers of the doves that surround Venus and provide her son Cupid with arrows in Greek mythology.
9. *man of parts*: an accomplished gentleman; Samuel Johnson defines 'part' as '7. Particular office or character ... 10. Action; conduct ... 13. [pl.] Qualities; powers; faculties; or accomplishments'.
10. *her nature's plague ... faults that were not*: This description hyperbolically associates the satirical figure of Mrs Melbourne with one of William Shakespeare's villains, Iago. In Shakespeare's tragedy *Othello*, Iago states, 'I perchance am vicious in my guess,– / As, I confess, it is my nature's plague / to spy into abuses, and oft my jealousy / Shapes faults that are not', III.iii.145–8. In Williams's novel, Mrs Melbourne, with her similarly scheming and jealous nature, stands in contrast to Charlotte, who the narrator depicts as completely free from envy.
11. *Hanover-square*: a district of London developed in the early eighteenth century and occupied primarily by Tory aristocrats. The fact that the heavily satirized and unsympathetic character Mrs Melbourne chooses to live a life of luxury in this Tory stronghold further suggests Williams's democratic, republican sympathies.
12. *Shades of Banquo's line*: In Shakespeare's *Macbeth* the witches reveal a line of eight king's descending from Banquo in IV.i.130–46.
13. *Ariel's flight*: an image of freedom. See Ariel's release from bondage in Shakespeare's *The Tempest*, V.i. 320–2.
14. *hags of night ... frighted bosom spare*: see *Macbeth* IV.i. In her *Essay on the Writings and Genius of Shakespeare* (1769), bluestocking Elizabeth Montagu defends Shakespeare against Voltaire's charge of barbarism, writing, 'The incantations of the witches in *Macbeth* are more solemn and terrible than those of the Erichtho of Lucan' (p. 142). Montagu argues that 'Gothic manners, and Gothic superstitions, are more adapted to the uses of poetry than the Grecian' (p. 143), and then calls Shakespeare 'our Gothic bard' (p. 147). She admires his ability to inspire 'that unlimited terror which we feel when Macbeth to his bold address "How now! Ye secret, foul, and midnight hags, / What is't ye do?" is answered, "a deed without a name"' (p. 152–3). The exact phrase 'deed without a name' appears in Shakespeare, IV.i.54. For Montagu, it is the terror evoked by this phrase that proves Shakespeare 'to have had a fertile, a sublime, and original genius' (p. 169). Helen Maria Williams was mentored by Montagu through her contact with the Bluestockings.
15. *Let true Cordelia ... sigh*: See Shakespeare, *King Lear*, I. i.89–107.
16. *Desdemona ... eye*: See Shakespeare, *Othello*, IV.2.25–98.
17. *Opehelia ... despair*: See Shakespeare, *Hamlet*, IV.V.21–67 and 169–202; and also IV.Vii.167–84.

18. *Milton raise the veil... high-tun'd harps creation hail*: See the worship of the angels after the consult in Heaven in John Milton's *Paradise Lost* (1667), III.344–415.
19. *Ere evil's inauspicious birth ... shade on earth*: See Milton's description of the fall in *Paradise Lost,* IX. 378–1189.
20. *Ye southern isles, emerged so late ... all savage life affords, his sure reward*: Williams's mentor Dr. Rev. Andrew Kippis described European discovery of islands in the South Pacific in his *The Life of Captain James Cook* (Dublin: H. Chamberlaine et al., 1788), an account of the exploratory voyages of Cook (1728–79), from which Williams draws the imagery in this stanza and to which she refers in her own footnote.
21. *Spare one small coin, the ballad's price*: Broadsheet ballads sold for a penny.
22. *Wild Poesy, in haunts sublime ... on Nature's face*: this passage contains multiple aspects of the eighteenth-century aesthetic category known as 'the sublime'. The term came into use in Europe with Nicolas Boileau-Despréaux's translation of Longinus's work as *Traité du Sublime ou du Merveilleux dans le Discours* (1674), which was translated into English as *On the Sublime* by William Smith in 1739. The aspect of striking power that Longinus attributed to sublime speech, using Genesis 1:3 as his prime example, were soon transferred to sublime natural landscapes by English aesthetic theorists. In his *Philosophical Enquiry into the Origin of Our Ideas of the Sublime and the Beautiful* (1757, 1759) Edmund Burke defines natural sublimity in terms of the perpendicularity, angularity, suddenness, loudness, and awe-fulness evoked in Julia's poetic mountain scene. Burke, however, genders the sublime as decidedly masculine, which Williams counters with her female figure 'Wild Poesy' who delights in filling sublime settings with her 'lofty'music. This aspect of loftiness comes closest to Samuel Johnson's definition of the sublime in his *Dictionary* as '1. High in place; exalted aloft.'
23. *'Then Thomson ... exalt my soul'*: James Thomson's *The Seasons* (London, printed in 1730).
24. *And Pope ... sylphs shall flutter here*: Alexander Pope's *Rape of the Lock: an heroi-comical poem. In five cantos* (London: Bernard Lintott, 1714).
25. *There Eloise ... too soft a tear*: Alexander Pope's *Eloisa to Abelard* printed first in his *Works* (London, 1717).
26. *melancholy marked her own*: T. Gray, *Elegy Written in a Country Churchyard* (London: R. Dodsley, 1751), l. 120.
27. *ratify thy doom*: T. Gray 'The Bard' in *Odes by Mr. Gray* (Strawberry Hill: R & J Dodsley, 1757), l. 96.
28. *people of ton*: Miss Melbourne does not cultivate a friendship with her country cousin Julia partly because such a connection would not impress fashionable people of town, i.e. Londoners.
29. *Sentimental*: Williams uses the term ironically here.
30. *grew with her growth, and strengthened with her strength*: Williams's use is ironic, but poet and novelist Amelia Opie used this phrase sincerely to describe her commitment to the abolitionist cause (quoted in Roxanne Erberle's 'Tales of Truth?' in *Romanticism and Women Poets: Opening the Doors of Reception*, ed. Linkin and Behrendt (Lexington, KY: University of Kentucky Press, 1999), p. 76.
31. *Minerva's owl ... Jove's eagle*: In Roman mythology an owl accompanies Minerva, the goddess of war, poetry, and wisdom, and an eagle accompanies Jove, the god of sky and thunder. In the 1730s the intellectual Elizabeth Carter was painted in the guise of Minerva by John Fayram. The painting features a small owl peaking out from under the plume of 'Minerva's' helmet and is held by the National Portrait Gallery in London.

Carter would go on to mentor a younger generation of women writers, including Helen Maria Williams.

32. *rigadoon step*: a complex dance step involving plies and hops. In *The Art of Dancing Explained by Reading and Figures* Kellom Tomlinson describes how 'the weight being on both feet ... you sink and give a rise or spring' (London, printed for the author in 1735) p. 42.
33. *Vanity ... vexation of spirit*: Ecclesiastes 1:14. This biblical verse was also referred to by James Boswell in reference to the central message of Samuel Johnson's *Rasselas* (1759), and by Henry MacKenzie in the introduction to *The Man of Feeling* (1771). Mackenzie uses it to describe a state of 'listlessness'.
34. *The nightingale ... dirge*: In Greek mythology Philomela was raped and then later turned into a nightingale by the gods. Her mournful song tells the tale of her suffering. Anne Finch's 'Nocturnal Reverie' (1713) opens with a reference to the song of of 'lonely Philomel'. Johnson defines 'Dirge' as 'a mournful ... song of lamentation'.
35. *pathetic*: 'Affecting the passions; passionate; moving' (Johnson). Also, to evoke pity or pathos, as in Aristotle's definition of tragedy.
36. *Drury-lane*: theatre district in London.
37. *tragedy of Douglas*: performed from 1757 onwards in Edinburgh and from 1758 onwards in Drury Lane and eventually printed as *Douglas: A Tragedy, by John Home, adapted for Theatrical Representation, as Performed at the Theatres-Royal, Drury-Lane, and Covent-Garden. Regulated from the Prompt-Book, by Permission of the Managers* (London: John Bell, British Library, 1791). The 1791 edition claims that the action is 'extracted from an acient Scottish Ballad, entitled CHILD MAURICE', p. viii. Rev. John Home was a Scottish clergyman of whose playwriting activities the kirk disapproved and who found refuge in literary London.
38. *oversteps the modesty of nature*: the original source is unclear. However, Mary Hays also quotes this phrase within her *Appeal to the Men of Great Britain on Behalf of the Women* (1798), printed in Vivien Jones's *Women in the Eighteenth Century: Constructions of Femininity* (London: Routledge, 1988), p. 234.
39. *Mrs. Siddons*: Actress Sarah Siddons (1755–1831) performed the role of Lady Randolph in *Douglas* during the 1783–4 season at Drury Lane (Y. Ffrench, *Mrs. Siddons: Tragic Actress* (London: Derek Verschoyle, 1936), p. 251). She also played Lady Randolph at the Theatre Royal in Edinburgh from 22 May 1784 to 11 June 1784 (R. Manvell, *Sarah Siddons: Portrait of an Actress* (New York: G. P. Putnam's Sons, 1971), pp. 100–4). A painting depicting Sarah Siddons as 'The Tragic Muse' was created while she was playing the role of Lady Randolph in London and is now part of the Huntington Gallery Art Collections.
40. *Lady Randolph*: Lady Matilda Randolph, the elder Douglas's grieving widow, is the actual protagonist of the play. She is mournful and 'pensive', drawn to the sublime in nature, pacifist in her political beliefs, prayerful and contemplative.
41. *sensibility*: The term is here used ironically in regards to Mrs Seymour, whose false sensibility contrasts with Julia and Charlotte's spontaneous flow of tears in response to the tragic action of the play.
42. *Cotillons*: Complex dances.
43. *ragoût*: 'a highly seasoned dish, usually consisting of meat cut into small pieces and stewed with vegetables' (*OED*).

44. *ragoûts, and French wines*: Williams's satirical treatment of the excesses of culinary connoiseurship subtley echoes Jonathan Swift's ironic reference to the delights of a ragoût in his 'Modest Proposal' (1729).
45. *'Defend us, ye kind gods! Tho' sinners, / From many days like these, or dinners!'*: Soames Jenyns, 'An Epistle Written in the Country, to the Right Honourable Lord Lovelace, then in Town, Sepetmber 1735', ll. 107–8, in volume four of *The Works of Soame Jenyns, in Four Volumes* (London: T. Cadell, 1790) pp. 40–9. Helen Maria Williams has slightly misquoted the beginning of this couplet; the original starts 'Afflict us not, ye Gods ...' My thanks go to Dr Deborah Kennedy for identifying this source.
46. *genii*: in Greek mythology, the spirits of a place.
47. *quart and tierce*: technical terms for moves in the sport of fencing.
48. *Julia, however ... auditor*: Julia here parallels Maria in Richard Sheridan's satirical play *School for Scandal* (1777), a virtuous character who flees the room when the scandalmongers begin to gossip.
49. *moving accidents ... flood and field*: *Othello* I.iii.134. This phrase also appears in Laurence Sterne's *A Sentimental Journey through France and Italy* (London: T. Becket and P. A. de Hondt, 1768), p. 87. In Sterne's novel these words are placed in the mouth of Smelfungus as he describes the difficulties of his travel experiences.
50. *stormy cape ... must be hazarded*: Ships had to navigate the Cape of Good Hope on the Southern tip of Africa during their return voyages to England.
51. *made love*: here, flattered and flirted.
52. *whist*: 'A game at cards, requiring close attention and silence' (Johnson).
53. *shewed how fields were won*: Oliver Goldsmith's *The Deserted Village* (London: W. Griffin, 1770), l. 151.
54. *where once ... stranger yet to pain*: lines 14–15 of Thomas Gray's 'Ode on a Distant Prospect of Eton College' (first published anonymously in 1747).
55. *Brown*: Lancelot 'Capability' Brown (1716–83) was a landscape designer and 'improver' of estates. Jane Austen was later to satirize such improvements in novels like *Sense and Sensibility* (1811) and *Mansfield Park* (1814).
56. *long avenues of venerable trees ... give way to new improvements*: Fanny Price voices a similar critique of improvements in chapter six of *Mansfield Park*, quoting William Cowper's poem *The Task* (London: Joseph Johnson,1785): 'Ye fallen avenues! once more I mourn / Your fate unmerited', I.338–9.
57. *thrush or the linnet*: Johnson defines both as 'a small singing bird'.
58. *if I have eaten... not eaten thereof*: The Book of Job 31:17.
59. *have no pleasure in them*: Ecclesiastes 12:1; Jeremiah 22:28.
60. *which cometh from above*: possibly a misquote of James 1:17, 'Every good gift and every perfect gift cometh from above, and cometh down from the father of lights, with whom is no variableness, neither shadow of turning'.
61. *fit for stratagem and spoil*: a proverbial phrase associated with sentimental fiction.
62. *Whitsun' fair:* Whitsun', the seventh Sunday after Easter is also known as Pentecost in the Christian calendar and marks the day that the Holy Spirit descended on the early Christians: 'And when the day of Pentecost was fully come, they were all with one accord in one place. And suddenly there came a sound from Heaven as of a rushing mighty wind, and it filled all the house where they were sitting. And they were filled with the Holy Ghost' (Acts 2:1–4). Whitsun' is an Anglo-Saxon word that contracts 'White Sunday' and refers to the white gowns worn by those baptized on Pentecost each year. On Whitsun' churches were ornately decorated, hymns were sung in the open air, and teas were

held outdoors at the end of the day. It was important to wear one's best clothes, preferably new, to the Whitsun' festivities. Whitsun' lost its status as a bank holiday in England in 1970.

63. *now let me die ... yet alive!*: Genesis 46:30.
64. *patriarch of old*: Jacob.
65. *postilions*: '1. One who guides the first pair of a set of six horses in a coach; 2. One who guides a post-chaise' (Johnson, *Dictionary*).
66. *Vicar of Wakefield*: the title character of Oliver Goldsmith's 1766 novel. Goldsmith's protagonist is generous and benevolent like Julia's grandfather but is less wise and more bumbling and comic.
67. *picturesque variety*: The picturesque was not formally theorized as a category of landscape aesthetics until two years after *Julia*'s publication, with Rev. William Gilpin's *Three Essays: on Picturesque Beauty, On Pictursque Travel, and on Sketching the Landscape* (1792). However, the term was used in English in the early eighteenth century, when Alexander Pope referred, in a letter written in 1712, to poetry being 'what the French call very picturesque' (quoted in M. Brownell, *Alexander Pope and the Arts of Georgian England* (Oxford: Oxford University Press, 1978), p. 104).
68. *hanging wood*: trees planted on a cliff.
69. *Beauty reposing ... horror*: *Julia* appeared before both William Gilpin's work on the picturesque and Uvedale Price's subsequent (1794), yet Williams's narrator describes the Clifford estate in terms both men would later use to formally define the picturesque: boundaries, rudeness, brokenness, rockiness, the rushing water of cataracts, wildness, irregularity, alternating light and darkness, and juxtaposed beauty and horror.
70. *Calypsos's enchanted island ... venerable Mentor*: in François Fénelon's *Les Aventure de Télémaque* (1689, reissued 1717), Minerva disguises herself as Mentor and takes Telemachus onto the enchanted island Ogygia, where the nymph Calypso desires to hear the story of his adventures and offers him immortality. Williams emphasizes Minerva's wise dissaproval by highlighting her frown in the tapestry.
71. *Earl of Essex*: Robert Devereux, second Earl of Essex (1565–1601) captured Cadiz in 1596.
72. *antidivulian*: meaning 'before the deluge', the time period in the Book of Genesis between Creation and the biblical flood.
73. *scymetars*: 'a short, curved, single-edged sword, used among Orientals, esp. Turks and Persians' (*OED*).
74. *aunt Deborah ... Sir Oliver himself*: characters from Sheridan's *School for Scandal*. After living in the East Indies for many years, Sir Oliver Surface returns to England, disguises himself, and bids in an auction for the Surface family portraits. His impoverished nephew Charles Surface sells a pastoral painting of his aunt Deborah, wherein she is pictured as a shepherdess surrounded by sheep (IV.i.59–74). However, he will not sell the portrait of Sir Oliver, which endears him to his uncle (IV.i.123–64).
75. *wild scenery of the north...dream of fancy*: Williams here draws on the standard eighteenth-century contrast between the beautiful, cultivated South and sublime, wild North of England. Helen Maria Williams grew up amidst the Northern landscape of Berwick upon Tweed, but Julia is a child of the South. Julia has written about sublimely rugged northern landscapes in her 'Address to Poetry', but only now sees such scenes firsthand, and they exceed what her imagination had pictured. Through Julia's realization, Williams firmly places the source of the sublime in something outside of the self, in opposition to

the idea that sublimity is generated by the human mind, a concept voiced most notably in Immanuel Kant's *Critique of Judgment*, published the same year as *Julia*, 1790.

76. *enthusiastic*: '1. Persuaded of some communication with the Deity; 2. One of a hot imagination, or violent passions; 3. One of elevated fancy, or exalted ideas' (Johnson).
77. *every other sound ... solemn cadence*: Again, Julia has imagined listening to the 'sweeping torrent roar' through the figure of 'Wild Poesy' in 'An Address to Poetry', but the actual, real sound of a falling torrent strikes her in a way she could not have predicted.
78. *Julia gazed ... raised above the temptations of guilt*: see 'Introduction' to this edition, p. xviii.
79. *and when we ... most gentle emotions*: Here Williams adheres more closely to Edmund Burke's dichotomy between the terrifying sublime and comforting beautiful in her definition of the softer, milder, gentler emotions inspired by beauty in contrast to the more astonishing, bracing, reverential feelings triggered by sublimity. Later in 1790 Williams would continue to draw on Burke's dichotomy by stating in her *Letters Written in France* that Paris was sublime and London beautiful 'according to Mr. Burke's definition of these qualities' (London, 1790), pp. 73–4.
80. *all sadness but despair*: John Milton, *Paradise Lost* IV:156. This phrase also concludes Charlotte Smith's 'Sonnet VIII: To Spring' (*Elegiac Sonnets*, 1786), where Smith documents her own allusion to Milton.
81. *'Can man forbear... every grove is melody'*: Thomson *The Seasons*, ll. 868–71.
82. *Bath*: a city in the West of England where convalescents would go to drink the spa water and soak in the baths. In Jane Austen's *Northanger Abbey* (London: John Murray, 1818), which she began composing in the early 1790s, Mr Allen is 'ordered to Bath for the benefit of a gouty constitution', vol. 1, p. 11.
83. *Nice*: a city on the South East coast of France. The air of the South of France and Italy was believed to have curative effects. Ann Radcliffe represents physicians in Geneva advising the ill La Luc 'to try the air of Nice' in her gothic novel *The Romance of the Forest:Interspersed with Some Pieces of Poetry* (London: T. Hookman and J. Carpenter, 1792), vol. 3, p. 135.
84. *even from the tomb...wonted fires*: Gray, *Elegy Written in a Country Churchyard*, ll. 91–2.
85. *to die the death...end might be like his*: W. Romaine, 'The Knowledge of Salvation Precious in the Hour of Death; Proved in a Sermon Preached January 4, 1759, Upon the Death of the Rev. Mr. James Hervey', in *The Works of the Late Reverend James Hervey, Volume V* (Edinburgh: P. Whyte and J. Roch, 1769), p. 125. The reference is to Hervey's calm composure as he faced death. James Hervey was initially a member of John Wesley's Arminian 'Holy Club' at Oxford, but he ultimately maintained a Calvinist position on salvation. Poet William Blake admired Hervey's devotional texts, as evidenced by Blake's painting 'Epitome of James Hervey's "Meditations amoung the Tombs"' (1820–5), held at the Tate Britain Gallery. Williams moved in Calvinist circles, beginning with her early mentorship by Presbyterian minister Andrew Kippis, and leading to her spiritual guidance of her nephew Athanase Coquerel who went on to lead Calvinist communities in both Paris and Amsterdam. Her interest in Calvinist theology may have led to her admiration of Rev. James Hervey.
86. *Avignon*: a city in Provence in the south-east of France, south of Lyon and north of Marseilles.
87. *the tour of France and Italy*: young British men would complete their education by taking 'the Grand Tour' of continental Europe, visiting as many cultural sites as possible along the way.

88. *fountain of Vaucluse*: a spring in Provence located at the foot of the Vaucluse Mountains, under a 230-metre vertical cliff. The word 'Vaucluse' is derived from the Latin *Vallis Clausa* or 'closed valley'. Charlotte Clifford and Frederick Seymour would have had much to view in the environs of Vaucluse, which include Roman ruins, a medieval village, and the remains of a fourteenth-century castle.
89. *inspiration...sonnets*: The Italian poet Petrarch lived in Vaucluse from 1337 onwards, which explains Williams's reference to the fountain's enduring ability to inspire sonnets.
90. *He then made Julia ... into the locket*: This conjugal joining of locks taken from Julia's mother and father is a virtuous, sentimental version of young men's clipping a lock of their beloved's hair, a fashion satirized by Alexander Pope in *The Rape of the Lock* (1714) and later dramatized by Jane Austen in *Sense and Sensibility*.
91. *'for thoughts, and remembrances'*: In Shakespeare's *Hamlet*, Ophelia, in her madness and grief, says, 'There's rosemary, that's for remembrance; / pray, love, remember: / and there is pansies, that's for thought', IV.v.174–6.
92. *aspect*: '10. The look which one wears; expression of countenance; countenance, face' (*OED*).
93. *Extreme awkwardness ... mode of performance*: Mr Chartres's derivation of his opinions from readings in the wisdom of antiquity paired with his ineptitude in social situations anticipate Mary Bennet in Jane Austen's *Pride and Prejudice* (1813), when paired with his lack of success in discoursing with women, these manners also contain parallels with Mr Collins from the same novel. Mr Chartres's fear of offering a woman a teacup further anticipates Prufrock in T. S. Eliot's 'Love Song of J. Alfred Prufrock' (1918). The character of Mr Chartres provides comic relief throughout *Julia*.
94. *She went out alone...every half-seen object*: Julia enjoys going for long walks alone in wild landscapes, perhaps providing a model for the solitary rambles of Jane Austen heroines such as Marianne Dashwood in *Sense and Sensibility* (1811) and Elizabeth Bennet in *Pride and Prejudice* (1813).
95. *'Are not five sparrows... before God!'*: Luke 12:6.
96. *universal benevolence*: This phrase places Julia's grandfather and Julia herself in the tradition of what Chris Jones has termed 'radical sensibility' in his book *Radical Sensibility: Literature and Ideas in the 1790s* (London: Routledge, 1993), a sensibility that is generously extended in acts of universal benevolence that cross boundaries between family member and stranger, homeland and foreign state, and even human being and animal. For a more detailed examination of sensibility's extension to what Williams's narrator terms 'tenderness to animals' from the 1770s onwards, see David Perkins's splendid study *Romanticism and Animal Rights* (Cambridge: Cambridge University Press, 2003). Perkins considers texts by dissenting women writers such as Joanna Baillie (pp. 21, 48–53, 132) and Anna Barbauld (pp. 8–10, 37–8). Though Perkins makes no mention of Williams, her own emphasis on compassionate behaviour towards animals emerged from her connections to other dissenting women writers, such as Baillie and Barbauld.
97. *Without being announced*: This violates the codes of propriety advised by eighteenth-century conduct books and is a sign that Frederick, as a man of sensibility, follows the impulses of his heart rather than the dictates of social structure.
98. *days of Queen Elizabeth*: Queen Elizabeth I (1533–1603) reigned from 1558 to her death. She was famous for wearing stiff, ruffled collars.
99. *nabob*: 'a British person who acquired a large fortune in India during the period of British rule' (*OED*). In her article 'Rewritten and Reused: Imaging the Nabob through "Upstart Iconography"' Christina Smylitopoulos notes, 'For the first century and a half of the

East India Company's existence, nabob was simply an Anglicization of the Persian term nawab and referred to the Muslim officials of the Mughal Empire of the Indian subcontinent. By the 1760s, however, the term was applied to the servants of the East India Company' in *Eighteenth-Century Life*, 32:2 (Spring 2008), p. 39.

100. *mechanical as those of a watch ... somewhat to fast*: the narrator's critique of Charles Seymour's mechanical and regulated action reflects the late-eighteenth-century critique of mechanistic views of the universe. These views, which compared the workings of nature to the mechanical, regular workings of a wound watch, with God as the watchmaker, were being supplanted by a more organic view of nature in Williams's time and into the Romantic period. Charles Seymour's calculated, mechanical behaviour is anything but spontaneous or organic and strikes Julia as unnatural.
101. *Not like the turbulent torrent ... which it passes*: in her variation on the metaphor of the 'stream of time', Williams's narrator implies that the month was not characterized by the tumultuous passions of the Burkean sublime but rather by the playfulness and vitality of the picturesque.
102. *Procrustus*: Procrustes is a figure from Greek mythology who would torture his victims by stretching them with a smith's hammer to fit the parameters of a bed. The comparison strongly suggests that Mr Chartres is indeed painfully shy.
103. *impropriety*: 'unfitness; unsuitableness; inaccuracy; want of justness' (Johnson).
104. *In the walks...formidable paths*: the sublime landscapes through which Julia and Frederick walk are replete with Burkean danger (see *Enquiry (1759)* Part II, Sec. III 'Obscurity'; Part IV, Sec. XVI 'Why Darkness is Terrible', and Sec. III 'Cause of Pain and Fear'), allegorically symbolizing the potentially destructive danger of Frederick's wild, improper passion.
105. *sublime landscape*: though Williams's narrator has already decribed the sublime landscape surrounding the Clifford estate, this is the first time the actual term is used within the prose of the novel. The dark shade of an old grove of trees and the depth of a prospect view opening suddenly before the viewer are both images in accord with Burkean definitions of sublime landscape (Part II, Sec. VII 'Vastness', Sec. XVIII 'Suddenness', and Part IV, Sec. IX 'Why Visual Objects of Great Dimensions are Sublime').
106. *evening ... tea-table*: Landed gentry would usually have tea at approximately 8:30pm.
107. *erudition*: 'learning; knowledge obtained by study and instruction' (Johnson). The narrator's comic, ironic treatment of Chartres's erudition here again anticipates the social satire directed towards the pedantic behaviour of both Mary Bennet and Mr Collins in *Pride and Prejudice.*
108. *rocky shores ... gloomy meditations*: At this point, Fredrick's indulgence in the overwhelming passion and solitude of the Burkean sublime renders him anti-social.
109. *exquisite sensibility ... influence of reason*: Julia, contrary to Frederick at this point in the narrative, is able to maintain an ethical and socially responsible balance between her faculties of sense and sensibility.
110. *assizes*: '1. an assembly of knights and other substantial men, with the baillif or justice, at a certain place, and at a certain time' (Johnson).
111. *Never been trodden by any human foot-step*: pathlessness is a particular, recurrent marker of the sublime as portrayed within Helen Maria Williams's poetry. See for example, the reference to 'trackless oceans' in line 9 of her 'Sonnet: To the White Bird of the Tropic', printed in her translation *Paul and Virginia* (London: G. G. and J. Robinson, 1795), p. 155.

112. *room for meditation even to madness*: N. Rowe, *The Fair Penitent: A Tragedy* (London: J. Tonson, 1703), V.i.3.
113. *If in the higher ranks ... family groupe displays*: Frederick Seymour voices the opinion of Jean-Jacques Rousseau, voiced in his works *Émile* and *Du Contrat Social* (1762), as well as *Julie, ou La Nouvelle Heloise* (1761), that the higher, more educated, 'ranks' of society are more corrupt and that poorer, less sophisticated, groups, such as the cottagers, are more naturally benevolent and virtuous. Julia's silence in response indicates resistance to an enthusiastic, uncritical embrace of this model of spontaneous, natural, sensibility. In his introduction to a 1995 facsimile printing of *Julia*, Peter Garside states that this resistance contributes to what he terms 'the repressive atmosphere of the novel' ('Introduction', *Julia*, facsimile edn (London: Routledge, 1995), p. xix). However, this resistance also demonstrates Julia's strength of character and may serve as a vehicle for Helen Maria Williams's own critique of Rousseau from her dissenting, Presbyterian, moral and spiritual perspective.
114. *election of the soul*: a theologically Calvinist phrase oddly applied to a Romantic passion.
115. *Described with rapture the falls of the river Clyde*: Williams's narrator uses the term 'rapture' ironically here. Johnson defines 'rapture' as '1. Ecstasy; transport; violence of any pleasing passion; enthusiasm; uncommon heat of imagination'. That the cold-hearted and plotting Mr Seymour could adopt a rapturous response to landscape illustrates how appreciation of sublime landscapes had become a fashionable posture by the late eighteenth century. The falls of Clyde are created when the river drops 250 feet over four miles near New Lanark on its route past Glasgow into the Atlantic Ocean on the Western Coast. In 1802 William Wordsworth depicted Corra Linn, the largest of the falls, in his poem 'Composed at Corra Linn, in Sight of Wallace's Tower' (1802), and J. M. W. Turner painted 'The Falls of Clyde' (currently held by the Lady Lever Art Gallery in Liverpool) in 1841.
116. *Hamilton House*: Dorothy Wordsworth describes the Duke of Hamilton's house, located South East of Glasgow, within her entry for Monday 22 August in *Recollections of a Tour Made in Scotland in 1803*.
117. *gamut*: 'the scale of musical notes' (Johnson).
118. *osier*: 'a tree of the willow kind, growing by the water, of which the twigs are used for basket-work' (Johnson).
119. *the stiff ringlets of our learned counsellors wigs*: The number of rows of ringlets in a wig signified the rank of a counsellor or judge in a court of law. Williams implies that these rows of ringlets signify artificial status rather than real merit.
120. *Thou art a fool ... more bright when she is gone*: Shakespeare, *As You Like It*, III.i.78–9.
121. *edge of a precipice*: Burke asserts, 'we are more struck by looking down from a precipice than, at looking up at an object of equal height', *Philosophical Enquiry*, p. 128. Williams uses the danger of a precipice to explicitly signify the danger of flirting with others when one is already married or engaged, but she by no means labels such coquetry 'sublime'.
122. *emoluments*: 'profit; advantage' (Johnson).
123. *one of those persons whom Sterne describes ... neither to the right hand, nor the left*: Laurence Sterne, *A Sentimental Journey through France and Italy*, p. 88. The full context is a satirical description of how 'Mundungus, with an immense fortune, made the whole tour; going on from Rome to Naples – from Naples to Venice – from Venice to Vienna – to Dresden, to Berlin, without one generous connection or pleasurable anecdote to tell of; but he had travell'd straight on looking neither to his right hand or his left, lest Love or Pity should seduce him out of his road.' Mundungus, in his self-interested single focus,

is the opposite of a man of feeling or sensibility. The phrase is also biblical (see Numbers 20:17, Deuteronomy 2:27 & 5:32.)

124. *steward*: an accountant or financial manager of an estate. The word has biblical roots (see Matthew 20, Luke 12 and Luke 18).

125. *tender and genuine sensibility*: the phrase is used with heavy irony here. For more on Williams's satire of pretenious displays of sensibility in *Julia* see Deborah Kennedy, *Helen Maria Williams in the Age of Revolution* (Lewisberg, PA: Bucknell University Press, 2002), pp. 49–50. Kennedy suggests that Williams's satire demonstrates an increasingly cynical and critical view of established English society.

126. *Miss Tomkins affected to distinguish Julia with particular fondness, in order to conceal the envy and aversion which rankled in her heart*: another strong parallel to the narrative of Austen's *Sense and Sensibility*, within which Lucy Steele pretends to befriend Elinor Dashwood due to their rivalry over Edward Ferrars, though Julia has no romantic designs on Mr F—.

127. *Mr. Seymour's opinion was founded on his observation of Julia's extreme sensibility ... a stronger impulse to virtue*: Williams defends 'pure and ingenuous' religious sensibility against the conservative critique that all sensibility would devolve into sensuousness or sensuality. She suggests that her heroine's integral purity, Christian faith, and moral 'fortitude' in the face of temptation are the result of her sensibility.

128. *'the baseless fabric of a vision'*: Shakespeare, *The Tempest*, IV.i.151.

129. *the ruins of an old abbey*: ruined abbeys were increasingly admired as aesthetic objects through the latter half of the eighteenth century and into the Romantic period. The Bluestocking Elizabeth Carter, for example, on discovering that her friend Henrietta Pultney was travelling 'across the Tweed' to Scotland, wrote on 27 June 1788, 'I hope you will visit every Monument of Antiquity in your Way, & give me a full Description of what you see. – A pretty Comission to a young Lady who is travelling over Hill & Dale to a race Ball, to write descriptions of the old Gothic Abbies & ruined Cathedrals. But indeed I think myself very moderate in not insisting that you should sail to the Hebrides & take an accurate survey of the venerable Remains of Icolmkill' (*Elizabeth Carter, 1717–1806: An Edition of Some Unpublished Letters* (Newark, DE: University of Delaware Press, 2005), p. 165). Jane Austen would satirize the enthusiasm of young women for such ruins in *Northanger Abbey*.

130. *a wild variety of landscape ... rocks, piled rudely together*: with its 'variety' and rudeness the landscape at first sounds picturesque. Gilpin would go on to argue: 'The picturesque traveler is seldom disappointed with *pure nature*, however rude' in *Three Essays: on Picturesque Beauty; on Picturesque Travel; and on Sketching Landscape: to Which is Added a Poem on Landscape Painting*, 2nd edn (London: Blamire, 1794), p. 56.

131. *A ridge of horrid cliffs frowned above...sublime scenery*: the landscape quickly takes on aspects of terror and danger, underlined by Williams's use of the word 'formidable', which are key to the Burkean sublime.

132. *mouldering gothic gate*: a reference to the gothic era of ecclesiological architecture in England (1189–1547). Still intact English gothic structures include Westminster Abbey and York Minster. The term 'gothic' was first applied to architecture in the late Rennaissance, when it was used as a derogatory term of scorn for older styles of building. The term gained new, positive currency in eighteenth-century England with the rise of the gothic novel, which celebrated medieval ruins as aesthetic objects of interest.

133. *solemn emotion so grateful to a contemplative mind*: solemnity is key to the Burkean sublime, as is a 'tranquility tinged with terror', p. 257, but nowhere does Burke himself use

the word 'contemplative'. It was within the writing of the women who followed Burke – such as Williams, as well as Joanna Baillie and Ann Radcliffe – that a gothic, contemplative sublimity was first fully articulated. The work of these women writers enabled aesthetic theorist Mary Anne Schimmelpenninck to draw a firm distinction between the 'terrible [Burkean] sublime' and 'the contemplative sublime' within her *Theory on the Classification of Beauty and Deformity* (London: John and Arthur Arch, 1815). For more detail see my article "Dauntless Faith': Contemplative Sublimity and Social Action in Mary Anne Schimmelpenninck's Aesthetics' (*Christianity and Literature*, Summer 2006) pp. 509–33.

134. *rooks*: 'a bird resembling a crow: it feeds not on carrion, but grain' (Johnson).
135. *martins*: Johnson defines a 'martinet' as 'a kind of swallow'.
136. *Sonnet to Hope*: This sonnet was reproduced in its entirety, as an exemplification of Williams's poetic strengths, in the July 1790 issue of the *Monthly Review* (vol. 2).
137. *like the snake to the cradle of Hercules*: Zeus's wife Hera sent two snakes to the cradle of Hercules in order to kill him as an infant. In the Greek myth, Hercules's strength was already so great that he managed to defend himself with his bare hands.
138. *Damn with faint praise ... teach the rest to sneer*: This heroic couplet is attributed to Alexander Pope, but its original textual source is unknown.
139. *Nathaniel Transfer*: a character who appears at the beginning of chapter 56 in John Moore's *Zeluco, Various Views of Human Nature, Taken from Life and Manners, Foreign and Domestic* (London: T. Cadell, 1789). *Zeluco* is an abolitionist cautionary tale about a title character whose cruel behaviour is the opposite of Julia's benevolent social action. Zeluco murders innocent sparrows as a boy, for example, and becomes a cruel and sadistic slave owner as an adult.
140. *now accustomed to the family ... happiness would be prolonged*: In *Zeluco*, when Nathaniel Transfer is asked why he lives alone, 'Mr. Transfer replied, that he had been put very early to business, and not being accustomed to his relations, he had never cared for any of them, except his sister, who had lived with him several years in Lombard-street; and as he was then *accustomed to her*, he had a good deal of kindness for her, but that she had made an ungrateful return for all his kindness', Moore, *Zeluco*, pp. 75–6. Williams's character Chartres, like Transfer, is a lonely bachelor, but Williams makes him more socially successful, as his affection for the Cliffords is reciprocated by their hospitality.
141. *'double, double, toil and trouble!'*; *Macbeth* V.i.10. Williams narrator here reintroduces the image of Macbeth's witches, which first appeared in Julia's early poem 'Address to Poetry', this time associating their malignancy with the manipulative, wealthy characters, such as Mrs Melbourne and her daughter Mrs Seymour.
142. *visited some of the cottagers*: Julia's time of contemplative solitude in nature is not solipsistic, as it elevates her mind towards God and leads to her to social action on behalf of the poor.
143. *Twilight grey, had in her sober liv'ry all things clad*: John Milton, *Paradise Lost*, 4.598–9.
144. *Pope and Thomson*: Alexander Pope (1688–1744) and James Thomson (1700–48). These were also Williams's favourite poets. In her 'Introductory Discourse' to her *Poems on Various Subjects* (1823), she writes, 'when I seek for consolation from verse I take up Pope, or Thomson' (London: G. and W.B. Whittaker), p. xxxv.
145. *the sublime scenes of Switzerland*: after Thomas Gray crossed the Alps into Italy in 1739, and compared the natural scenes to the paintings of Salvator Rosa, the Swiss Alps came to signify sublimity in the British imagination. In the year of *Julia*'s publication, Ann Radcliffe was also making use of sublime alpine scenes in *A Sicilian Romance* (1790), and

they would figure even more boldly in her *Romance of the Forest* (1792), within which the city of Geneva plays a central role.

146. *Pope's moral epistles*: *Epistle to Burlington* (1731), *Epistle to Bathust* (1733), *Epistle to Cobham* (1734), and *Epistle to a Lady* (1735), gathered together under the heading 'Moral Essays' in volume 3 of William Warburton's *The Works of Alexander Pope Esq. in Nine Volumes Complete* (London: J. and P. Knapton, 1753).
147. *Timon's villa*: Pope, 'Epistle to Burlington', l. 99. Pope's description of Timon's villa is a satire of extravagant artifice, luxury and decadence.
148. *1776*: this date sets Williams novel during the time of the American Revolution (1773–83). Williams also commented on the American Revolution, specifically the Paris Peace Treaty that brought the conflict to an end, in her *Ode on the Peace* (1783). For a more detailed reading of this letter in *Julia* describing the violence and loss incurred during the American Revolution from a personal perspective, see Eleanor Ty's *Unsex'd Revolutionaries: Five Women Novelists of the 1790s* (Toronto, ON: University of Toronto Press, 1993), pp. 81–2.
149. *grenadiers*: specialized assault troops originating in seventeenth-century Europe. They are skilled in throwing small iron spheres packed with gunpowder (grenades).
150. *to be cut off from glory's course*: Home, *Douglas*,V.i.83. The full line is: 'Cut off from nature's and from glory's course'. In the tragic ending of the play the promising young soldier Douglas is killed by his own stepfather.
151. *General Washington*: George Washington (1732–99), leader of the Americans in the revolution and first president of the United States.
152. *Whither thou goest, I will go ... but death part thee and me*: the words of the widowed Ruth to her bereaved mother-in-law Naomi in the Book of Ruth 1:16–17.

## Volume II

1. *palisades*: 'pales set by way of inclosure or defence' (Johnson).
2. *Chelsea-hospital*: The Royal Hospital Chelsea began admitting military pensioners in 1692. King Charles II issued the royal warrant for the building of the hospital in 1681, to be designed and built by Christopher Wren to provide for the soldiers of the English establishment. The hospital still accepts military in-pensioners to this day.
3. 'To press the bashful stranger to his food / And learn the luxury of doing good': Oliver Goldsmith, *The Traveller: A Poem*, 9th edn (London: T. Carnan and F. Newberry, 1774), ll. 21–2.
4. *bumper*: 'a cup filled till the liquor swells over the brim' (Johnson).
5. *Panegyric*: in the *OED* synonymous with 'Encomium: A formal or high-flown expression of praise; a eulogy, panegyric'.
6. *milliner's*: 'one who sells ribbands and dresses for women' (Johnson).
7. *an automaton ... mechanism*: another critique of mechanistic views of the universe. In his *Dictionary* Johnson defines an automaton as 'a machine that hath power of motion within itself, and which stands in need of no foreign assistance'. Williams's narrator satirizes Mrs Chartres for moving in a robotic, unnatural way, without feeling.
8. *visiting tickets*: small cards, with one's name on them, printed from engravings by skilled craftsmen. Jan Fergus notes that they were sold to fashionable gentry in the West End of London, as 'signs of mutual recognition that obviated the need for these clients to actually converse with one another', *Provincial Readers in Eighteenth-Century England* (Oxford: Oxford University Press, 2006), p. 17.

9. *Mingling ... instruction with entertainment*: an ironic reference to Horace's statement 'that poet gets every vote, who unites information with pleasure, delighting at once and instructing the reader', translation by James Lonsdale and Samuel Lee, *The Works of Horace Rendered into English Prose* (London: Macmillan & Co, 1881), p. 214.
10. *coup d'oeil*: 'a view or scene as it strikes the eye at a glance' (*OED*).
11. *loo-table*: Johnson defines loo simply as a 'a game at cards'.
12. *cards of apology*: like visiting tickets, small cards printed from engravings, but this type of card was intended to act as an RSVP, indicating one's inability to attend an event or gathering.
13. *buckram*: '2. A kind of coarse linen or cloth stiffened with gum or paste' (*OED*).
14. *adopt Milton's plan with the evil spirits, and ... suit the dimensions of her company to those of her apartment*: in Milton's *Paradise Lost* the legions in Hell are confined to a very small space, as they shrink themselves down in size to crowd into Pandemonium in Book I. 752–98.
15. *Mr. Parsons, in the entertainment of High Life above Stairs*: a reference to the appearance of actor William Parsons (1736–95) in a comic play by David Garrick, eventually printed as *Bon ton: or, High life above stairs, a farce in two acts, as performed at the Theatre-Royal, Drury-Lane* (London: Longman et al., 1815). My thanks go to theatre historian Dr David Worrall for identifying William Parsons.
16. *Firelock: 'a soldier's gun; a gun discharged by striking steel with flint'* (Johnson).
17. *rubber*: 'In various games of skill or chance, a set of (usually three games, the last of which is played to decide between parties when each has gained one; hence, two games out of three won by the same side' (*OED*).
18. *Foppishly*: vainly, ostentatiously (Johnson).
19. *Cicero*: Roman philosopher, political theorist, and orator (106 BC – 43 BC).
20. *Hume's History of England*: David Hume's *The History of England, from Julius Caesar to the Accession of Henry VII, in 6 volumes* (London: A. Millar, 1762). This book was remarkably popular with women writers. The Huntington Library holds bluestocking Elizabeth Vesey's first edition copy, which contains her original signature and notes in her handwriting. In Jane Austen's *Northanger Abbey*, the erudite Eleanor Tilney also mentions her reading of Hume's *History* during the walk at Beechen Cliff in chapter 14 of volume 1.
21. *Bedlam*: 'corrupted from *Bethelem*, the name of a religious house in London converted afterwards into a hospital for the mad and lunatick' (Johnson).
22. *Macbeth*: given the setting of *Julia* in the year 1776, Mrs Chartres has most likely seen a production of Shakespeare's tragedy starring David Garrick, who revived *Macbeth* during his time as manager of Drury Lane Theatre (1742–76), often playing the title role himself. Mrs Chartres's comments on the play reveal her lack of taste, sympathy, and understanding. The narrator constructs her as a woman of little or no sensibility.
23. *cutting for partners*: at the beginning of the card game Whist, which involves four people, each person cuts or lifts a portion of the cards from the pack, and the two who draw the highest cards play together.
24. *Pangs of Sensibility*: a fictional title that Williams's has constructed to further accentuate Mrs Chartres's bad taste and to satirize excessive displays of false sensibility.
25. *petit-souper*: a term from French culture that actually indicates a feast despite the modesty of its name, 'a little supper'.
26. *Court Calendar*: a periodical publication that listed all the British court officials and their offices.

27. *the frosty Caucasus*: a mountain range that extends along the boundary of Europe and Asia, between the Black Sea and the Caspian Sea.
28. *she said something about the fatherless*: After the reference to God's blessing, this strongly suggests Psalm 68:4, 'A father of the fatherless, and a judge of the widows, is God in his holy habitation'; as well as James 1:27, 'Pure religion and undefiled before God and the Father is this, to visit the fatherless and widows in their affliction'.
29. *jointure*: 'estate settled on a wife to be enjoyed after her husband's decease' (Johnson).
30. *a captain on half-pay*: see endnote 2. This financially straitened circumstance parallels the situation of Julia's own father at the beginning of the novel.
31. *argufy*: 'to prove or be evidence of something; hence, to be of importance, consequence, or use; to signify' (*OED*).
32. *compassion for the oppressed … arm of indignant Heaven tearing the veil by which iniquity was concealed, and making manifest the sufferings of innocence*: strongly suggestive of Psalm 103:6, 'The Lord executeth righteousness and judgment for all that are oppressed'; and also Acts 10:38, 'God anointed Jesus of Nazareth with the Holy Ghost and with power: who went about doing good, and healing all that were oppressed'. Writing out of her dissenting church community, Williams establishes a theological framework for Julia's passionate resistance to gender-based injustice.
33. *agent of Providence*: Johnson defines Providence as '2. The care of God over created beings; divine superintendence'. In the case of Mrs Meynell, Julia acts as a vehicle or agent of divine love, care, and compassion, as she brings about a measure of social justice and equity.
34. *a set of features, or the tincture of a skin*: James Fordyce, 'Sermon VII: On Female Virtue with Intellectual Accomplishments' in *Sermons to Young Women in Two Volumes*, vol. 1 (London: A Millar & T. Cadell, 1766), p. 302. In this chapter, Fordyce cautions young women to not become fixated on physical attractiveness. Williams's construction of Mrs Seymour illustrates how a woman could follow the dictums of these sermons and still be utterly heartless. In her *Vindication of the Rights of Woman* Mary Wollstonecraft objects both to Fordyce's overemphasis on rules of decorum and to his advice that young women should hide their intellectual accomplishments from potential suitors. Jane Austen satirizes these sermons by placing them in the hands of Mr Collins in *Pride and Prejudice*.
35. *Gothic barbarity had placed in a rude and sordid hut, where it lay neglected, by those who were ignorant of its value*: though she earlier points to the aesthetic appeal of a 'mouldering gothic gate', here Williams capitalizes 'Gothic' in reference to the 'Goths', a people group living in Germania from the the second century AD who were viewed as less civilized by the Greco-Roman world to the South. The Goths sacked Rome in 410 AD, and Williams compares Mrs Meynell's situation to that of a graceful Greek statue stolen during the pillaging of Rome and lying unappreciated in a Gothic hut. Williams's narrator's disdain for Gothic dirtiness and rudeness stands in contrast to the earlier sublime descriptions of ruined gothic architecture in *Julia*, but John Ruskin would combine the two uses of the term in *On the Nature of the Gothic* (1853) where he admires the 'savageness' and 'rudeness' still apparent in gothic architecture.
36. *variety of wretchedness*: Thomas Otway (1652–85), *The Orphan, or the Unhappy Marriage: a tragedy as it is acted at his royal highness the duke's theatre* (London: R. Bentley and S. Magnes, 1685), II.i.254. The phrase refers to the clothing of an old woman seen in a prophetic dream. In their critical edition of Helen Maria Williams's *Letters Written in France in the Summer of 1790, to a friend in England* editors Neil Fraistat and Susan

Lanser note Williams's quotation of this exact phrase again in her very next publication (Peterborough: Broadview, 2001), p. 106.

37. *the most sublime and elevating sounds*: Williams's reference to sublime sounds as fine and elevating diverges from Edmund Burke's definition of sublime sounds as booming and overwhelming, such as the striking of a great clock, the beating of a drum, and firing of a cannon (see *Enquiry*, Part II, Sect. XVIII 'Suddenness').
38. *hackney-coach*: a couch let out for hire. See Johnson's fourth definition of 'hackney' as 'any thing let out for hire', within which he quotes Alexander Pope: 'A wit can study in the streets; / Not quite so well, however, as one ought; / A *hackney* coach may chance to spoil a thought'.
39. *Vicar of Wakefield bestowed a guinea upon his daughters; viz. with a strict injunction not to change it*: in Goldsmith's *The Vicar of Wakefield* it is actually the vicar's wife who 'always generously let them have a guinea each, to keep in their pockets; but with strict injunctions never to change it' (Salisbury: B. Collins, 1766), p. 82.
40. *Bijoux*: French, signifying 'jewel'. This lapdog's name suggests that it is one of the fashionable breeds that had been imported from France, such as the papillon, phalene, or French pug. The satire directed towards Mrs Seymour's excessive concern for Bijoux anticipates Austen's satire of Lady Russell's attitude towards her pug in *Mansfield Park*.
41. *potted hare*: a traditional recipe that involves stewing a hare with vegetables, grinding this stew into a fine paste with a mortar and pestle, and then pouring this paste into small pots for serving.
42. *a long Indian shawl*: a detail reflecting the eighteenth-century British orientalist craze for exotic, Eastern clothing, such as turbans and shawls.
43. *stroke of surprise, and horror, which seemed almost to annihilate her mind*: these terms parallel Burke's description of a startling and terrifying sublime experience, wherein 'we shrink into the minuteness of our own nature, and are, in a manner, annihilated' *Enquiry*, p. 119. However, Burke is describing a sense of our own littleness when we are struck by the power of an omnipotent God, whereas Williams's narrator is describing Charlotte's sense of helplessness and horror at the discovery of her husband's transgressive desire for Julia. Notably, Williams does not apply the term 'sublime' here, despite her Burkean language; there is no sense of awe in Charlotte's discovery.
44. *Sicily, when the desolating fires of the volcano*: Mount Etna in Sicily is the world's oldest active volcano with eruptions dating from 425 BC, hence Williams's reference to Greco-Roman temples. Etna had come to symbolize powerful sublimity in the British imagination by 1790. In the same year that *Julia* was published Ann Radcliffe's novel *A Sicilian Romance* eulogized 'Mount Etna, crowned with eternal snows, and shooting from amidst the clouds...grand and sublime' (London: T. Hookham, 1790), vol. 1, p. 12.
45. *'iron had entered into her soul'*: possibly a Scottish proverb; it also appears as a quotation in Mary Brunton's novel *Discipline* (Edinburgh: Manners and Miller, 1814), p. 88.
46. *Philosophical research*: Mr Chartres's project of forwarding philosophical knowledge through his trip to India situates him as a professional 'Orientialist' bent on forming a career out of the study of Eastern culture, science, and religion. Considering his role as a satirized figure of comic relief in *Julia*, the reader is encouraged to adopt a skeptical perspective on Chartres's projected geographical and philosophical explorations. For a more in-depth, critical examination of such Orientalist enterprises see Tim Fulford, Debbie Lee and Peter Kitson's *Literature, Science and Exploration in the Romantic Era: Bodies of Knowledge* (Cambridge: Cambridge University Press, 2004).

47. *mantua-making*: Johnson defines a 'mantua' as 'a lady's gown' and a 'mantuamaker' as 'one who makes gowns for women'. Due to her financial need Mrs Meynell has taken up work as a seamstress, sewing clothes for wealthy women, and she understandably wishes that work to be undisturbed.
48. *parterre*: 'a level division of ground, that, for the most part, faces the front and best part of a house, and is generally furnished with greens, flowers, &c'. (Johnson).
49. *'bides the pelting storm'*: William Shakespeare, *King Lear*, III.iv.29. Lear, while out in the storm on the heath, feels remorse, and sympathizes with the poorest subjects of his Kingdom, wondering, 'Poor naked wretches, whereso'er you are, / That bide the pelting of the storm / How shall your houseless heads and unfed sides/ Your loop'd and window'd raggedness, defend you / From seasons such as these?' in III.iv. 28–33.
50. *'that no man liveth to himself'*: a slight misquote; Romans 14:7 states, 'For none of us liveth to himself, and no man dieth to himself'.
51. *as absurd and monstrous, as that system of philosophy...little speck in creation*: a reference to the pre-Copernican, Ptolemaic idea of a geocentric universe, with all of the planets, and even stars, revolving around the earth. Williams's narrator's strong disdain for this medieval worldview reflects the novel's loyalties to Enlightenment science. As a rational dissenter, Williams, like Anna Barbauld, was fascinated by the interface between theological and astronomical knowledge. Barbauld discerned 'the finger of God' in the scientific wonders of astronomy in her poem 'A Summer Evening's Meditation' (1773), and Williams referenced 'Mr. Herschel's wonderful discoveries' of comets in a footnote to the reprinting of her 'Ode on the Peace' in her *Poems in Two Volumes* (London: T. Cadell, 1786), vol. 1, p. 54.
52. *enigmas and charades*: riddles in prose and verse were recorded on cards and also published in collections, such as *The Masquerade: a Collection of new enigmas, logogriphs, charades, rebuses, queries and transpositions* (London: T. Baker, 1800). By presenting Mrs Seymour as a collector of these riddles Williams suggests that they were a superficial and stilted mode of passing time at social gatherings. Austen also questions the practice by presenting the unclever Harriet Smith as a collector of enigmas and the uncharming Mr Elton as a writer of charades in *Emma* (1815).
53. *Sonnet to the Moon*: this sonnet was reproduced in its entirety at the end of Mary Wollsotnecraft's review of *Julia* for *The Analytical Review*'s vol. 7 (1790), p. 100.
54. *national debt*: The French and Indian, or The Seven Year's War (1756–63) had led the British Government to borrow heavily from Dutch and British bankers, and as a result the national debt doubled in this time period. As a solution, the British Government taxed the colonies more stringently, which was part of the trigger for the American Revolution, and in order to fight the battles in America the British Government had to borrow even more money, creating a cycle of national debt.
55. *Baronet*: 'the lowest degree of honour that is hereditary; it is below a baron and above a knight ... It was first founded by King James I. *A.D.* 1611' (Johnson).
56. *tonish*: a colloquial adjective applied to urbane manners or clothing 'of the town', i.e. originating in London.
57. *They sought for happiness as laboriously as an alchymist for the philosopher's stone*: Johnson defines 'alchymist' as 'one who pursues or professes the science of alchymy'. Usually spelt 'alchemy' today. This was an occult science that sought, among other goals, to transmute base metals into gold, a feat for which it was believed which the legendary philosopher's stone, once discovered, could accomplish.

58. *to exclaim, with Doctor Johnson 'Would it had been impossible!'*: John Hawkins writes of Samuel Johnson, 'I have sometimes thought that music was positive pain to him. Upon his once hearing a celebrated performer go through a hard composition, and hearing it remarked that it was very difficult, Johnson said, "I would that it had been impossible"', (*The Life of Samuel Johnson, L.L.D.* (London: J. Buckland et al, 1787), p. 319).
59. *trifles, light as air, are, to the jealous, confirmation strong as proofs of Holy Writ*: Shakespeare, *Othello*, III.iii.322–4.
60. *'Is all the counsel that we two have shared…is all forgot'*: Shakespeare, *A Midsummer Night's Dream*, III.ii.198–201.
61. *Thomson's Lavinia*: the sentimental heroine of 'Lavinia and Palemon', an episode within the section devoted to autumn in James Thomson's *The Seasons* (ll. 177–310).
62. *'Thomson', said she, 'is, of all poets, to me the most soothing…calm my mind immediately'*: Julia voices Helen Maria Williams's own opinion here (see note 146).
63. *the picture of Charlotte at Werter's tomb*: a 1783 engraving by John Raphael Smith. The scene does not actually occur in Johann Wolfgang von Goethe's sentimental novel *The Sorrows of Young Werther* (1774). Goethe's narrative ends with Werther's body being buried unattended by Charlotte, with whom he had been passionately in love, or her husband Albert. Like Williams's *Julia*, as well as Rousseau's *Julie*, *The Sorrows of Young Werther* tells the tale of destructive, adulterous passion within a tragic love triangle. As in *Julie*, two men are in love with the same woman (Charlotte) in Goethe's narrative, but unlike *Julie*, it is the man swept up in transgressive desire who dies at the end of *Werther*, not the woman. The mention of 'Charlotte at Werter's Tomb' implies that Williams has named her character Charlotte Clifford Seymour after Goethe's heroine and foreshadows the tragic end of her own novel.
64. *phœnix of romance*: the phoenix is a legendary firebird that appears in the tales of Phoenician, Egyptian, and later Greek mythology. These tales describe the phoenix as living up to 1,000 years, after which time it builds itself a nest of twigs, ignites, and burns to ashes, from which a fresh phoenix arises. Early Christian church fathers adopted the phoenix as a symbol of resurrection life, reborn out of death. Frederick Seymour's hermeneutical point in defence of *The Sorrows of Young Werter* is that pathos is created due to the realism and finality of Werter's death; he does not rise from the ashes. Julia, however, holds more orthodox views and is not convinced by Frederick's argument.
65. *king of terrors*: Job 18:14 refers to death as 'the king of terrors'. This phrase was used repeatedly as a reference to death in English sermons from the seventeenth century onwards. Burke uses the phrase without quotation marks in his Part I, 'Section VII. Of the Sublime', p. 60, while explaining the sublimity of anything terrible, especially the threat of imminent death.
66. *melts into thin air*: Shakespeare, *The Tempest*, IV.i.150.
67. *impropriety*: Williams uses the word ironically here.
68. *to minister to a mind diseased*: Shakespeare, *Macbeth*, V.iii.40. This reference furthers foreshadows the novel's approaching tragic conclusion for Frederick.
69. *the Bastille*: this 'bastion', or stronghold, was originally fortified to protect the East side of Paris during the Hundred Years' War in the fourteenth century. By the early seventeenth century it had become a prison. King Louis XIII was the first to regularly send prisoners there, for somewhat arbitrary reasons. As an absolute monarch he imprisoned people through secret edicts, administered by Cardinal Richelieu. The practice of imprisonment through these *lettres de cachét* continued through the reigns of Louis XIV, XV, and XVI, up to the beginning of the French Revolution with the 'Storming of the Bastille' on 14

July 1789, approximately one year before the publication of *Julia*. The setting of *Julia* in 1776 allows Williams's to introduce a character imprisoned in the Bastille for a supposed offense against the state and to grant his poem prophetic status, as it foresees the demise of absolutism in France. Williams would comment more specifically on what she terms the 'dark iniquity of *lettres de cachét*' in her *Letters Written in France in the Summer of 1790*, p. 106.

70. *That pond'rous mask of iron *falls*: The Man in the Iron Mask, or *L'homme au Masque de Fer* was first imprisoned in 1669, spent time in the Bastille, and died on 19 November 1703. Williams may have been aware of Voltaire's speculations regarding this prisoner's identity in his *Questions sur l'Encyclopédie* (1771).
71. *hour of danger*: a reference to Charlotte's approaching labour. Women died much more frequently in childbirth in the eighteenth century, and therefore labour could be a terrifying experience. See Dorothy and Roy Porter's *Patient's Progress: Docters and Doctering in Eighteenth-Century England* (Stanford, CA: Stanford University Press, 1989); and Ludmilla Jordanova's *Nature Displayed: Gender, Science and Medicine, 1760–1820* (New York: Longman, 1999).
72. *scrutore*: 'a case of drawers for writings' (Johnson).
73. *'cannot plunge into business...when their hearts are torn with anguish, or sinking in despair'*: adapted from John Gregory's *A Father's Legacy to His Daughters* (London: T. Cadell, 1774), p. 11. The original is in the second person: 'You cannot plunge into business, or dissipate yourselves in pleasure and riot, as men too often do, when under the pressure of misfortunes. You must bear your sorrows in silence, unknown and unpitied. You must often put on a face of serenity and chearfulness, when your hearts are torn with anguish, or sinking in despair'. In her *Vindication of the Rights of Woman* (1792) Mary Wollstonecraft was actively critical of Gregory's conduct book, and modern critic Peter Garside is disappointed in Williams for not voicing a similar critique, writing, 'Though it would be wrong to assume that Williams's appropriation of Gregory's advice to argue the need for female fortitude is ironical – her belief in religion survived her revolutionary zeal – its applicability is nevertheless contingent on a social structure which confines women to the domestic sphere' (*Julia*, facs edn, p. xix). This is not quite accurate, however, as it is Julia's biblical knowledge and spiritual conviction that have motivated her to travel outside of her particular 'domestic sphere' in aid of the oppressed, suffering Mrs Meynell, creating a form of constructive, even feminist, community between women in the novel.
74. *forbid the banns*: marriage banns are read aloud during church services on three Sundays before a wedding. Within the church community of the groom and bride, their names and intention to marry is announced, along with a request for individuals who have any objections to voice them before the wedding day. Due to the eldest Miss C—'s bitterness and envy in singlehood, she desires to prevent all others from finding marital bliss by discovering a reason to halt the banns before the third and final announcement.
75. *She refused many honourable offers of marriage ... fortunate and happy*: the novel ends with a progressive reimagining of domesticity in terms of the egalitarian, communal household shared by Julia, Charlotte and Mrs Meynell. This ending has prompted diverse responses from critics. Garside considers only Charlotte and Julia, ignoring Mrs Meynell, and laments the repressive, depressing, and 'muted', ending which he argues conveys 'a sense of lost opportunity' (p. xix). Women readers have had a much more positive response to the novel's conclusion. Janet Todd contrasts the end with the conclusion of Rousseau's *Julie*, and notes, 'it is the man rather than the woman who dies under

the strain. The ending leaves the two women comfortably raising a child' (*The Sign of Angellica: Women, Writing, and Fiction, 1600–1800*, (New York: Columbia University Press, 1989), p. 231). Williams would revisit this theme in her translation of Bernardin Saint Pierre's *Paul et Virginie* (1787) as *Paul and Virginia* (1795). In Williams's translation, she emphasizes the situation of the two women in the novel, the widowed Madame de la Tour, mother of Virginia, and the abandoned Margaret, mother of Paul, raising their fatherless children together by including an engraving that depicts de la Tour and Margaret, side-by-side, gazing lovingly at their infants. Encouragingly, Eleanor Ty argues that in *Julia* Williams presents female friendship as central to women's lives and then proposes, 'that Williams refrains from the conventional form of narrative closure has exciting implications for feminist readers' (*Unsex'd Revolutionaries: Five Women Novelists of the 1790s* (Toronto: University of Toronto Press, 1993), p. 84). I would argue that the women's community found at the end of *Julia* has parallels with the utopian, feminist community of a novel like Sarah Scott's *Millenium Hall* (1762). Deborah Kennedy, writes, 'Julia remains an admirable woman, who finds fulfilment in a single life' (*Helen Maria Williams and the Age of Revolution* (Lexington, KY: Bucknell University Press, 2002), p. 50). Kennedy continues by pointing out that what makes Julia admirable are her parallels with Williams: her consolation in the practice of religion and benevolent action in the world. Julia's contentment in singlehood, in contrast to Miss C—, does arise from her sincere spirituality, and the community of affective support painted at the novel's end is as much based in dissenting, Christian ethics as in what Ty terms a 'feminine or maternal ethos' (*Unsex'd Revolutionaries: Five Women Novelists of the 1790s*, p. 77). The protection and refuge extended by Julia to Frederick's fatherless child and to the widowed Mrs Meynell reaffirms the novel's scriptural references to the importance of caring for the fatherless (see Volume II, note 28), the widowed (see Volume I, note 152), and the oppressed (see Volume II, note 32).

For Product Safety Concerns and Information please contact our EU representative GPSR@taylorandfrancis.com
Taylor & Francis Verlag GmbH, Kaufingerstraße 24, 80331 München, Germany

www.ingramcontent.com/pod-product-compliance
Lightning Source LLC
Chambersburg PA
CBHW071408100726
47908CB00004B/1097

* 9 7 8 1 1 3 8 2 3 5 9 1 5 *